YOU SHOULDN'T HAVE DONE THAT

LIZ ALTERMAN

INKUBATOR
BOOKS

Published by Inkubator Books
www.inkubatorbooks.com

Copyright © 2025 by Liz Alterman

Liz Alterman has asserted her right to be identified as the author of this work.

ISBN (eBook): 978-1-83756-532-0
ISBN (Paperback): 978-1-83756-533-7
ISBN (Hardback): 978-1-83756-534-4

YOU SHOULDN'T HAVE DONE THAT is a work of fiction. People, places, events, and situations are the product of the author's imagination. Any resemblance to actual persons, living or dead is entirely coincidental.

No part of this book may be reproduced, stored in any retrieval system, or transmitted by any means without the prior written permission of the publisher.

For Liz Schlossberg, dear friend and secret weapon

"Better an honest enemy than a false friend." — German Proverb

PART 1

1

SATURDAY, DECEMBER 13

JANE

When Jane Whitaker and her husband, Wade, had walked to the Chapmans' for dinner two hours earlier, only a light dusting of snow had swirled. Now sleet pelted the window above the kitchen sink, making Jane anxious to get back home.

It wasn't just that the sidewalks would be slippery and the night air bone-chilling. Jane wanted to go before Ivy asked the question already forming on her lips.

"Any improvement with the Cal situation?" Ivy leaned closer, her whisper almost imperceptible over the dishwasher's hum.

The combination of her expectant stare, the dark fruitwood cabinets, and yellowing floral wallpaper in such a small space heightened Jane's claustrophobia. She poured herself another two inches of cabernet. "Not yet," she said.

Ivy wrinkled her nose and pressed two number five candles into Wade's birthday cake. "Don't worry, he'll call tomorrow." She licked chocolate frosting from her thumb and index finger. "He has to! It's his dad's birthday. They'll work it out. Think good thoughts." Ivy inhaled deeply through her nose and closed her eyes. "I'm manifesting. Do it with me."

Normally, Jane would've teased her and said something like, "Should we assemble vision boards while we're at it?" But by this point she was so desperate for her husband and son to make up and move on, she'd have tried anything.

Following a long sip, she shut her eyes and pretended to join her friend, who swayed slightly, either from the wine or the manifesting. Ivy was a yoga teacher, which Jane felt she proclaimed with an air of confidence better suited to a cardiologist or a US senator.

"If she starts referring to herself as a guru, I may have to end this friendship," Jane had joked to her husband after Ivy began offering random runners stretching advice while the pair took their regular Wednesday morning walks.

Jane knew Ivy was primarily asking about "the Cal situation" out of genuine concern, but if it wasn't resolved soon, it would affect her too, potentially ruining their upcoming trip.

The Whitaker and Chapman families had vacationed together dozens of times over the years. Regardless of flight delays, bad weather, and even a stolen passport, they'd always had a wonderful time.

Back in October when they'd booked this trip to Wyoming to see their sons and celebrate the holidays, Jane believed the bad feelings between her husband, Wade, and their son, Cal, would be long forgotten. Now, they were leaving in a little more than a week and Jane worried it would be a tense and awkward ten days for everyone if things didn't change soon.

Father and son hadn't spoken since Cal left in late August. She assumed he'd call for his father's birthday. *But what if he doesn't?* Jane couldn't bring herself to say it aloud—not even to Ivy, who, despite their differences, was her closest friend.

But she didn't need to utter a syllable. Ivy, who'd finished manifesting and opened her eyes, could read her face. "He'll call!" she insisted.

It was quiet except for the drone of appliances and their husbands' voices drifting in from the living room where they sipped Greg's beloved Macallan 18 and discussed a teardown on Johnson Road that had recently sold for an astronomical figure. While residential property values in their New Jersey suburb skyrocketed, commercial real estate—Wade's specialty—had tanked, causing his mood to follow.

"Cal *will* call." Ivy tried again, sounding like an actor searching for the right inflection. As she reached out, Jane stiffened. Was it Ivy's pitying smile or the fact that she'd just licked her fingers and was about to touch the sleeve of Jane's cashmere turtleneck that made her recoil? Both, probably. Plus, whenever Jane thought about the rift between her husband and son, she couldn't help but blame Ivy. Ivy and *her* son.

Brad and Cal met in preschool. Like their mothers—or perhaps because of them—the boys became friends. Throughout elementary and high school, they'd followed the same trajectory. Then, in the middle of his sophomore year of college, Brad dropped out and moved to Wyoming to work as a ski instructor. Initially it seemed like an impulsive, short-sighted decision made even more surprising when Ivy and Greg didn't try to stop him. Nearly two years had passed since Brad left, and Ivy swore he'd never been happier.

After Cal graduated from college with honors and dual degrees in economics and marketing, he had gone to work for his father. Jane knew Wade expected their brilliant boy to breathe new life into the crumbling real estate business. But two months into the job, Cal interrupted their dinner conversation to announce that he was leaving, heading west to work and "hang with Brad." He'd "probably" return in the spring, he added, tearing into a roll as if he hadn't just knifed his dad in the heart.

Jane had glanced from her smiling son to her startled husband, whose face reddened to the point that she thought he might need the Heimlich maneuver.

"Don't look so shocked," Cal had laughed. "I said I'd give you the summer and, well, it's nearly over, and it's not for me."

Wade choked down the chicken that seemed to have lodged itself in his throat. "What's not for you? Working?"

"Stop, Dad, c'mon. Real estate. It's your thing, not mine."

"Oh really?" Wade scoffed. "And just what is 'your thing?'"

Jane's chest tightened at her husband's use of air quotes.

"I don't know." Cal offered a good-natured grin, dimples flashing. "I'm hoping to figure that out."

"I didn't blow a bundle on your tuition so you could teach toddlers to snowplow!" Wade blustered. "Do you know what I'd have given for a father who'd started his own business? Who wanted to bring me into the fold and basically hand over the keys?"

In the days that followed, Wade assumed Jane would talk some sense into their son, convince him to forget Wyoming and get serious about studying for his real estate license. But when it came down to it, Jane understood Cal's position. He was twenty-three. He had all the time in the world to work. Why shouldn't he travel? One of Jane's deepest regrets was not living on her own after art school. She'd gone straight from her parents' home to the small apartment she and Wade shared after they'd gotten married. She couldn't stop Cal, and she didn't want to try.

But now, after months of being caught in the middle, feeling emotionally distant from her husband and physically removed from her son, Jane wondered if she'd made the right decision.

"Brad texted last night." Ivy smiled.

"Oh?" Jane managed. The subtext—*My son and I are so close!*—felt like a dig even if Ivy hadn't meant it that way.

"He and Cal planned to ski some crazy, off-the-beaten-path trail this afternoon." Ivy pulled four dessert plates, two of them chipped, from a cabinet above the stove. "I just hope Brad's knee holds up. It's bothering him again."

"I'm sure they'll be fine." Jane dismissed Ivy's concerns, her memory searching to recall the last text she'd gotten from her son. She'd sent a message earlier in the day. *Dad's birthday is tomorrow. Please call!* Cal hadn't responded. Because he was skiing maybe?

"How's your mom doing?" Jane changed the subject. Did Ivy perceive this as a "right back at ya!" shot or did her friend think she was merely being considerate?

"She's okay." Ivy leaned forward, avoiding eye contact.

Jane scooted to the side, thinking she was blocking the cutlery drawer. Instead, Ivy grabbed a handful of now-gummy cheese cubes that sat languishing on the appetizer platter and popped two in her mouth.

"Really?" Jane tried to hide her skepticism. "Well, that's a relief."

"Actually—" Ivy winced, thin lines forming parentheses on each side of her mouth "—her new neighbors called the

Board of Health and filed a complaint." She raised her palms. "Not that I blame them. It's spilling into the yard now. How could it not? The house and porch are jam-packed. She's stacking plastic tubs behind a willow tree. The neighbors think they must be filled with food because they're suddenly overrun with squirrels." Ivy paused to swallow. "And mice."

She plucked a few shriveled grapes from the platter. "I'll have to go down there and deal with it when we get back." At five-foot-two Ivy was already petite, but she seemed to shrink as she spoke.

"Let me know how I can help." Jane knew it was an easy offer to make. No matter how many times she said it, her friend would never take her up on it.

"Thank you," Ivy said, her mouth full. "I truly appreciate that." She squeezed Jane's arm, leaving a combination of chocolate frosting, cheddar crumbs, and sticky grape residue on the soft sleeve of Jane's sweater.

IN THE CHAPMANS' dining room, they sang "Happy Birthday" to Wade despite his pleas to skip it. The conversation with Ivy left Jane's stomach unsettled. She barely touched her cake.

"We should probably walk home while we still can," Wade said as if reading her mind. He drained his glass, stood, and feigned a wobble. "Thanks again. This was great."

And it had been—initially. The beginning of the evening was so pleasant. Greg had opened the door, beer bottle in hand, before either of the Whitakers rang the bell.

"Get in here, birthday boy!" He'd smiled and pulled Wade toward him.

"Hey now!" Wade drew back. He wasn't a hugger, but Jane knew he'd tolerate the gesture coming from Greg. After all these years, the Chapmans were more like family than friends. "I've still got a few more hours before the big day," Wade had laughed. "Let's not rush it."

They were all the same age, but, technically, Wade was the oldest of the foursome. Greg had given Jane a quick embrace, his cheek warm from tending the blaze in the fireplace, his breath tinged with the hoppy scent of IPA.

The Chapmans' home was smaller than the Whitakers' but it was uncluttered and cozy thanks to warm wood trim around the windows and door frames and the lush plants and herbs Ivy tended with care. A Chet Baker album Greg had inherited from his dad played softly in the background, lulling them into a state of tranquility.

Ivy hurried out of the kitchen, barefoot in wide-leg velvet pants and a sleeveless silver tunic. Did she want to show off her toned arms or was it the hot flashes again? Jane felt underdressed in black slacks and a mint-green sweater.

On tiptoes, Ivy air-kissed Wade and Jane and squealed, "I've missed you! It's been, what, almost a month? That's insane!"

It had been three weeks. The families had spent Thanksgiving together. But once temperatures dipped below freezing, Jane and Ivy stopped their usual mid-morning walks. They still texted daily, even if it was a quick "Hey!" or a link to a recipe or an article one thought the other might enjoy. Getting together again felt like a reunion, a homecoming. But with the mention of their sons, the mood had shifted, the spell broken.

As Jane and Wade made their way to the door to leave, the Chapmans' French bulldog, Jean-Claude, waddled away from the hearth where he'd been dozing, and began sniffing and snorting.

Wade shot Jane a look. She knew what he was thinking. *The Chapmans needed this dog like a hole in the head.* He said as much after every visit.

They'd gotten the puppy last spring, Ivy filling her empty nest since Brad had settled in Wyoming. Ivy and Greg hadn't anticipated that Max, their oldest, would boomerang back to live with them following the collapse of the tech startup he'd co-founded in Boston.

When they'd first arrived, Jane had wondered if Max would join them for dinner. Now back in suburban Oak Hill living with his parents, the twenty-five-year-old had to be bored out of his mind. But he seemed in no rush to find another job.

"He's keeping his options open!" was Ivy's refrain.

In Jane's opinion, he lacked hustle, but she was in no position to talk. Getting her daughter, Emerson, a high school senior, to finish her college applications proved a constant battle—one she gave herself permission to ignore on weekends.

At the door, Jean-Claude whined and tap-danced, his tags jingling.

"I'll walk him," Greg offered and nodded toward Wade and Jane. "And make sure these two stumble into the right house."

"Oh, we're getting a canine escort, are we?" Wade laughed.

"You're an old man now. Someone has to look out for you!" Greg clipped the leash to Jean-Claude's collar and placed his hand on the small of Jane's back as he ushered them out the door.

. . .

THE HOUSES GREW LARGER, grander as they walked the few blocks that separated the Chapmans' home from the Whitakers'. Beneath the light of the almost-full moon, their breath formed little clouds as Greg noted how bitter it was for mid-December. Jane had tried to stop complaining about the weather because each time she did, Wade said, "If you can't handle this, you should cancel that trip to Wyoming."

The Whitakers' stately brick-faced colonial was dark. Emerson had texted to say she was sleeping at a friend's house. Only footlights along the walkway brightened their property. On the sidewalk, Wade shook Greg's gloved hand, side-stepped Jean-Claude, and crunched his way up the snowy path to the front door.

As Jane went in for a quick hug, she slid on a patch of ice. Greg steadied her, holding her so close their mouths practically touched. Maybe it was the wine or the fact that her marriage had been strained for months, but for a moment she wondered what it would be like to kiss her friend's husband. With her face so near his, she drank in the scent of woodsmoke mixed with scotch, warmed by the combination.

The lamppost flicked on. Jane doubted her husband was watching them. He was probably headed to the bathroom in search of antacids or Advil to preempt his inevitable hangover.

As she started to pull away, Greg's soft breath tickled her ear. "Don't worry, Cal will call, and everything'll go back to normal."

Greg worked as a high school guidance counselor. It suited him. He was prone to assurances and had a gentle confidence that typically put people at ease.

But now his relentless positivity made Jane's jaw tense. Apparently, he and Ivy had been talking about her, discussing her husband and son, their problems. The affection Jane felt toward Greg seconds earlier evaporated as she fought the urge to snipe, "Your family's far from perfect." She didn't want to pick a fight, not with their trip coming up, so she simply nodded and said, "Thanks again for a lovely night."

INSIDE, Jane hung her coat and tugged off her boots. Beneath her feet, the hardwood floor was frosty as a frozen pond. Wade programmed the thermostat to drop to sixty-four degrees overnight. At seven a.m., it rose to a more reasonable sixty-eight. Emerson had removed her AirPods at breakfast earlier that week to say that it was "seriously messed up" that she could almost see her breath in her bedroom.

Wade insisted it was healthier to sleep in a cool environment, but Jane knew it was another cost-cutting measure. Though they lived comfortably, Wade's childhood cast a long shadow. Jane surveyed the grandfather clock standing beside the staircase, a ticking reminder of her husband's past. According to Whitaker family lore, May, Wade's mom, used a hot iron to fight off two men who'd tried to seize the heirloom after his dad lost it in a poker game.

The wine and the gentle swinging of the clock's pendulum momentarily hypnotized Jane. Wade walked out of the kitchen holding a glass of water, snapping her out of her trance.

"It's after midnight." She nodded toward the clock and smiled, wondering if his good mood from dinner would carry over into their bedroom—or even the living room. They had the house to themselves after all. "It's officially your birthday."

She inched closer, brushing her lips against his cool cheek. Maybe it was the freezing house or the fact that she desperately needed to use the bathroom, but a tingling sensation swept through her lower body as she waited for her husband to react. When he didn't, she reached for his belt and began easing the leather strap from the buckle. He hiccuped and listed to the side.

"Room's tilting a bit." He grabbed the corner of the entryway table for support.

A framed photo of the Whitakers and the Chapmans taken in Paris the year they'd turned fifty fell face down.

"We're celebrating our entry into the half-century club," Ivy had told everyone from bartenders to bellhops that week, causing Wade to roll his eyes and mutter, "Does she have to keep saying that?"

In the black-and-white shot, the friends beamed, their champagne flutes raised, bubbles shimmering. As Jane righted the frame, she could hear their toasts. "To fifty!" Wade said. "To France!" she'd added. "To drinking nothing but champagne!" Greg laughed. "To lifelong friends!" Ivy had gushed.

"Greg got me again." Wade stumbled to the staircase. "Guy pours scotch like it's water. I'm going to bed."

After locking the front door and turning off the lights, Jane followed him upstairs. By the time she removed her makeup and brushed her teeth, Wade was already snoring.

. . .

HOURS PASSED as Jane stared at the ceiling, rubbing her feet together to warm them. Wine had a tendency to ruin her sleep. She'd meant to stop at two glasses, but the conversation with Ivy had made her anxious. Her mind drifted back to the August morning Cal had loaded his Jetta bound for Wyoming.

"So this is really happening?" Wade jerked the coffee pot back in place.

"Please, Wade. Cal's got the rest of his life to work."

"Do you ever *not* take his side?" Wade's gray-blue eyes narrowed in a sharp stare.

"Wait, Dad, did you finally realize Cal's her favorite?" Seated at the kitchen table, Emerson snorted without glancing up from her phone. "Cal's always been the golden child."

"Stop, Em." Jane blushed. She'd just snuck a wad of twenties beneath the sandwiches and sliced kiwi she'd packed for her son's road trip. "That's not true. I love you equally."

In her heart she knew her daughter was right. A parent wasn't supposed to have a favorite child but it was unavoidable when one brought you joy and the other's first word was *No!*

As a boy, Cal had been so sweet, not to mention smart. Jane loved recalling the afternoon she sat down to read to him and he'd ended up reading to her. He wasn't even five. His dimples and bright blue eyes stopped strangers in their tracks. "What a beautiful child!" they'd remark, sending ripples of pride through her bloodstream.

Pawing at her nightstand, Jane located her phone and checked to see if Cal had responded to her text about his father's birthday. She had one new message—from Ivy, sent hours earlier.

> Such a fun night! HBD again to Wade!
> Don't worry, Cal will call!

A string of pink heart emojis followed.

Jane knew Ivy thought of herself as an empath, feeling everything fully and deeply, but she wished her friend would back off.

It wasn't like Jane hadn't tried to get them to work it out. But Wade wanted an apology; Cal said he had nothing to be sorry for. Wade wanted him home; Cal said he'd be back in spring. "Maybe." While Cal posted selfies from mountaintops and captioned them, "Living my best life," Wade grew increasingly sullen as deals fell through and stores moved out or went bankrupt. They'd remained at an impasse for months.

Jane pulled the duvet to her chin and thought about her own business. Though she knew it would only lead to disappointment, she peeked at her company's inbox. No new messages. With less than two weeks until Christmas, her sales were abysmal despite spending eighteen hundred dollars on an SEO expert who promised that with the right keywords *Jewels by Jane* would soar to Google's first page and orders would pour in.

She clicked to view her website's traffic. No new visitors. A headache stretched from temple to temple as she flicked between social media platforms. No new followers.

Before they'd sat down to dinner, Jane snapped a photo of Jean-Claude with a sterling silver cuff around his front paw. Emerson swore posts with pets increased engagement. Jane didn't know if her daughter was mocking her, but she had nothing to lose. Plus, she struggled to come up with clever captions. Perhaps the pup's scrunched-up face would absolve her of her clichéd, "Don't spend the holidays in the doghouse!" The post had garnered one lonely like.

Without looking, she knew it was from Danny. He was always the first (sometimes the only) "like." He was so supportive, yet each time it got her hopes up. A potential customer? No, just Danny. Again.

In high school, too, he'd been that way: attentive, always noticing and admiring things like a new sweater or a pair of boots. He'd remember when she had tests and would wait at her locker to find out how she'd fared. Her friends had jokingly called him "the parrot" because of his shock of red hair and the way he seemed to hover just over her shoulder. He'd been kind but shy. Their outings consisted mainly of library study sessions.

Back in June, they'd reconnected in a high school reunion Facebook group when she posted a link to her jewelry business's website. He'd reached out to congratulate her and she'd been flattered, grateful. Wade hadn't taken much interest in her new venture. Cal had tossed out a casual, "That's cool," while Emerson had admonished, "Please don't embarrass me by asking my friends to like your pages or buy your stuff."

Her old classmate said he'd remembered her "sense of style and artistic eye."

When she'd written back "Aw, thanks, Danny!" he'd gently corrected her. "I go by 'Daniel' now."

She supposed it made sense to use a more adult name. She'd studied his profile photo. He'd aged nicely. In high school, he'd been skinny as a pencil. Now he looked fit, athletic. His hair color had softened to a burnished copper with a hint of silver at his sideburns.

Throughout the summer, he checked in regularly, asking about the business, telling her he'd visited her site and loved her latest designs.

Charmed by these small bouquets of flattery, she agreed to meet him to check out an art exhibit and grab lunch. It seemed harmless, nostalgic—friends reuniting after more than three decades. When she spotted him waiting outside the museum, he waved and strode toward her, her heart stutter-stepping.

The weather had been unseasonably warm for September the day they'd met. Perspiration beaded above his thin top lip. Perhaps he was nervous. Could he, somehow, all those years later, still harbor that same high school crush? The thought had struck her as sweet.

It still did. In her bed, she rolled onto her side and another memory surfaced: Daniel walking her to the parking garage, leaning through her car window, whispering, "Let's do this again." Even in her cold room, she could feel the warmth of his fingers when they'd cupped her chin as he'd added, "Soon."

On the drive home, she'd felt disoriented, double-checking the turnpike signs to make sure she was heading north rather than south. She hadn't thought she'd given Daniel any reason to believe it was a date, yet she couldn't shake the feeling that she'd led him on. Maybe Ivy had been right. When Jane mentioned she'd planned to meet an old classmate, Ivy's eyes had bulged. "How does Wade feel about that?"

"I haven't told him. He doesn't care who I eat lunch with."

"Then why not tell him?" Ivy cocked her head as if she were mimicking her dog.

"It's not like that."

"Oh, honey," Ivy had laughed, petting Jane's arm, "it's always like that."

DANIEL WAS NEWLY divorced and saw his daughters Wednesdays and every other weekend. He'd recently moved to a studio apartment outside Philadelphia. When she'd asked how he liked his new place, he'd written, "It's lonely."

His words—their unflinching honesty—had blindsided her. Jane was lonely too; she just hadn't put words to it. Wade rarely spoke about his feelings. He'd barely talked to her at all after Cal left in August for Wyoming. When she'd suggested marriage counseling to help them move past it, he'd shot her down. Was it the expense or was he punishing her for taking Cal's side?

The heart beneath Jean-Claude's post wasn't so much a "like" as it was an "I'm here— thinking of you."

Every few weeks he messaged her through the business website. In his last, he'd mentioned Cal. *Your son's quite the daredevil. Hope he stays safe!*

How had he seen Cal's posts? The app probably suggested her son's account. Wasn't that what people wanted —to expand their network? Hadn't Emerson told her to do the same to grow her business? And Daniel wasn't wrong. Cal *was* a daredevil, which only made his posts and reels that much more exciting. Just picturing his videos, shot from a dizzying elevation, made her stomach drop.

Where was Cal? Why hadn't he responded to her text? She opened the app that tracked her children's locations and watched the searchlight rotate around the screen. Em was at her friend Sasha's house. Or at least that's where her device was. Jane imagined her precocious daughter stashing her phone in the mailbox and then rushing off to a club in Manhattan with a fake ID. To friends, Jane referred to Em as "independent." In truth, she'd lost control of the girl, who'd been more preoccupied and secretive than usual lately. Jane wondered if she was seeing someone but knew she had a better chance of selling out her entire jewelry line than getting Em to confide in her.

It was approaching four a.m. If things were better between them, she would've rolled over and slid her hand inside Wade's boxers. They'd have made love and that might've helped her fall asleep.

Opening the nightstand drawer, she felt around for the brown plastic bottle of sleeping pills. Her doctor said not to take one after two a.m., but what did it matter? She had nowhere to be. No one depended on her anymore. All she had to do later that day was buy a birthday cake, make a nice dinner for Wade, and wait for Cal to call—and if he did, then hope that the conversation went smoothly.

She looked at her phone again. The beam had stopped searching. The dot that represented her son was nowhere on the screen. She tried again. "Location Not Found," the app told her. For all his good points, Cal was notoriously bad at keeping his phone charged.

Not knowing exactly where he was sent a field of butterflies flitting through her insides. Why did even the tiniest fleck of fear mushroom in the middle of the night?

Jane thought about trying one of those calming apps Ivy recommended. Instead, she bit the sleeping pill in half and closed her eyes without bothering to poke Wade to disrupt his snoring.

Outside a bird began to chirp. She took a deep breath and forced her body to relax. Everything would be better in the morning. Cal was probably asleep, worn out from a day on the slopes. Perhaps Em really was at her friend's house. Maybe the "like" on Jean-Claude's post was from a customer instead of Daniel. She forced her thoughts in positive directions. Yet as the pill lowered its black veil of sleep, a single question kept resurfacing: *Where was Cal?*

2

SUNDAY, DECEMBER 14
IVY

Sunday evening's "Sunset Reset" yoga class was usually Ivy's favorite to lead, but tonight she couldn't wait for it to end. On the studio's website, the seventy-five-minute session was described as "the perfect way to ward off the Sunday Scaries."

Ivy disliked that phrase because it clashed with her belief that each week should be greeted with a grateful heart and an open mind. She tried her best to impart these sentiments to her students, but she could tell they'd tuned her out.

Ivy couldn't deny she was fidgety and unfocused herself, unintentionally telling them to do back-to-back warrior poses on the left instead of switching sides.

She'd barely adjusted the lights when attendees began rolling up their mats, checking their phones, and elbowing to be first out the door, shedding any peace she'd tried to instill.

Ivy waited before following them into the front room where she'd left her Birkenstocks and jacket. Piper, the studio's owner, sat at the front desk, her tattooed arms moving in a steady rhythm, a ball of orange yarn in her lap.

"Another shitty turnout." She pantomimed stabbing herself in the heart with a knitting needle.

Ivy smiled in sympathy. The rent for the space in Oak Hill's upscale downtown cost a fortune and attendance had plummeted over the past two months. Ivy shared posts on social media to boost interest. It didn't help. Amid the rush of the holiday season, they were lucky a dozen people showed up for that evening's class.

Ivy wanted to ask Piper for a favor but considering the young woman's mood, she simply blew her a kiss and stepped into the twilight.

At six p.m., the sky was already an inky, middle-of-the-night blue. Despite the chill, the streets bustled with people ducking into boutiques and restaurants, everywhere trimmed with white fairy lights woven through ropes of green garland.

Ivy picked her way toward her Fiat carefully. Rock salt crusted the sidewalks where ice glistened beneath a thin layer of snow.

As she opened the trunk to toss in her yoga mat, her phone buzzed in the pocket of her leggings. She smiled, frigid air hitting her teeth. Without looking, she knew it was Brad. He called every Sunday. Ivy fought the urge to check in with him more frequently. She didn't want to smother him or hover—not like Jane who was still tracking her kids' locations even though they were twenty-three and eighteen. Instead, Ivy texted or forwarded a funny meme or animal video and Brad would respond with a thumbs-up or a *Haha!* It wasn't real communication, but she didn't want to push.

"Hey, honey!" Her voice sounded overly loud after whispering inside the dimly lit yoga studio. She was competing with blaring horns as drivers lost patience with parallel parkers. "How are you?" She waited. She could usually gauge her son's emotional state within his first few words. He'd seemed better since moving to Wyoming. Still, she worried about him.

"Okay." He yawned. "You?"

Ivy's maternal senses tingled at the bottom of her sacrum. He sounded strange. Her hand formed a fist around her keys. "I'm good. Class just ended. What's new? How's your week been?" She didn't want to rush to judgment. Her son put in long hours. Most weekends during the busy season he taught adaptive lessons to children with special needs. Maybe he was simply tired. She closed the trunk and hurried inside the quiet cocoon of her car so she could listen more closely. When he didn't answer right away, she tried again. "How's work? Getting busy?"

"Yeah, pretty much." His voice was flat, spacey.

Ivy's body, warm inside her hoodie, tensed against the cold leather seat. "Did you ski yesterday? Knee hold up all right?"

"I twisted it pretty bad actually."

"Oh Brad, no, not again." Ivy's mind traveled back to the September evening the high school football coach had called to tell her Brad needed to get to the hospital ASAP. Dizziness had swept through her as she imagined another concussion—or worse, a neck or spine injury. Only when she'd heard the word "knee" had she been able to breathe again, emitting an embarrassing sheeplike bleat in relief.

But a torn ACL was no picnic. The surgery and its aftermath—physical therapy, pain management—had been brutal. Here they were, five years out and it still caused trouble.

"Do you think you need an X-ray? An MRI? I can search up places." Ivy reached in her pocket for her phone, forgetting she was using it. "You're covered by our insurance so don't worry about the cost."

At the end of November, Brad mentioned he'd loaned Cal some cash and had to cover his share of the rent. She remembered when Cal had gotten mixed up in sports betting during high school. Jane had bailed him out and somehow kept it from Wade. Ivy couldn't imagine hiding anything so important from her husband. She hoped Cal hadn't fallen back into bad habits, but more importantly, she didn't want her son skipping medical care because he'd given all his money to his roommate.

"How did this happen?" The twitch behind her eye—the one she usually got when speaking to her mother—began pulsing. "Were you wearing your brace?" She hated speaking to her son as if he were a child but couldn't stop herself. She needed him to say more.

"I *was* wearing the brace." His voice was an odd combination of defensive and groggy. "Just, you know, took a turn too fast. It was icy. Cal was way ahead. I had to call for help."

Okay, so this is serious. Maybe he sounded off because he was embarrassed. After working there for two years, Brad knew nearly everyone on staff. Getting rescued as a twenty-three-year-old ski instructor had to be pretty humiliating. She took a deep, centering breath. "Are you in a lot of pain?"

"I was," he mumbled.

She paused, afraid to ask the next, most important question. "What are you taking for it?"

"Cal had stuff. It's not a big deal."

Ivy pressed her lips together to stop from saying something she'd regret. "Is Cal there? Can I talk to him?"

"He's not here."

Ivy stayed silent. One thing she'd learned in a quarter-century of parenting was that if you didn't fill the gaps in conversation, your child might. When Brad volunteered nothing, she forged ahead. "When will he be back?"

"I dunno."

"Well, like later tonight? Is he working?"

"I haven't seen him since yesterday."

"He left you there? Injured?" Ivy knew Cal could be self-centered, but even for him, that would be pretty low.

"I couldn't drive back so I got a ride with the ski patrol guys."

"How did Cal get home?"

"I don't know."

Ivy shivered as her sweat turned cold, her shirt sticking to her torso. She turned on the car before she caught a chill and reached for the emergency box of Teddy Grahams she kept under the passenger seat. It wasn't there. Had Greg found it?

On the nearest street corner, costumed carolers burst into a spirited "Joy to the World." Ivy plugged her ear with her finger. "You haven't seen Cal since when exactly?" She pictured Jane checking her phone. Wherever Cal was, she hoped he'd called Wade by now.

"Yesterday."

Leaning into the headrest, Ivy pinched the area between her eyes. "Do you think maybe he went to a bar and met someone?"

She usually spoke openly with her sons about sex, but it seemed weird and inappropriate to speculate about Cal's hook-ups or whatever kids called it.

Brad grunted.

Was that a yes or a no? Some conversations with her sons forced Ivy to morph into an interrogator. She needed to lob question after question to get anywhere. Was it easier with daughters? It had to be, though according to Jane, Emerson would rather gargle glass than have an in-depth conversation with her.

"Did you take a nap today? Maybe Cal came back and went out again?"

"Maybe," Brad said.

Ivy's thoughts splintered: Should she be worried about her son, his knee, and all that could possibly set in motion, or the fact that Cal might be missing?

Pressing the defrost button, she waited for the windshield and her mind to clear. Cal was a strong skier. Jane routinely shared videos of his latest runs—as if Ivy didn't have a son doing the exact same thing. Still, shouldn't Brad be more concerned, even through the haze of whatever pain medication he'd stupidly taken?

Ivy felt a hot flash building. Someone needed to conduct a study on how parenting-related stress triggered menopause symptoms.

"Are you and Cal getting along?" She tried again. Working and living together had to be a lot. Maybe Cal had gone to stay with a friend? "Any problems?"

"Problems?" Brad repeated.

Memories from late August surfaced in Ivy's mind. When Brad had called to tell her Cal was coming out to live with him, he hadn't sounded as happy as she would've expected. To Ivy, Brad had seemed so terribly alone out there, so far away. The idea of Cal moving in with him had been a comfort.

"Have you called or texted him?" she asked.

"His phone was dead so he left it here."

"And is it still there?"

"I haven't looked."

Ivy unzipped her hoodie, her breath coming in short, shallow puffs. "Have you checked in with friends?"

"No. Not yet."

"Well," Ivy ran a hand through her blond pixie cut and tried to keep her voice steady, "maybe you should."

"Yeah, maybe."

Ivy waited for her son to assure her this behavior wasn't unusual for Cal, who, for years, had reminded her of a puppy. He left a mess nearly everywhere he went and people found him irresistible anyway.

"I was going to call Jane tonight. I'll ask if she's heard from him."

"Okay." Brad yawned again.

"Call around too. If he's out there or got lost or hurt—" Ivy couldn't allow herself to finish that sentence.

"I'll try. I'm kinda out of it."

Ivy gripped the cold steering wheel. "Brad, listen to me. Don't take any more of those pills. I sent you extra-strength Tylenol. Stick with that. Promise me."

"Hmm-mmm."

A horn wailed, muting their goodbye. Someone wanted Ivy's parking spot. Her zen and her middle finger went straight out the window.

"Asshole," she hissed before turning the wheel hard to the left and tapping the gas. The Fiat skidded into the street, narrowly missing a jaywalker. "Asshole!" she repeated, voice high and tight.

She had to call Jane. What would she say? She didn't know, but she was certain of one thing: her son wasn't telling her everything.

3

SUNDAY, DECEMBER 14

BRAD

Brad didn't know how long he'd been staring at the TV after the call with his mother ended. Maybe he shouldn't have told her about Cal. His mom might've prided herself on being super chill but when it came down to it, Brad considered her just as anxious and neurotic as any other suburban mother he'd ever met. He closed his eyes, *Sunday Night Football* droning softly in the background.

Had Cal bet on the game? A better question was how *many* games had Cal bet on? And how long before some goons came knocking if he lost? Correction—*when* he lost. Being forced to hand over the keys to your car might've been enough to stop most people, but Callaway Whitaker wasn't most people.

Without him, the apartment was quiet. How often had Cal ruined a game by ranting at the players, the coaches, the refs, and pacing the small living room like a zoo animal too big for its cage?

Not for the first time, Brad took a second to imagine life without Cal. What would that be like? Peaceful. Or maybe that was the Oxy talking. Earlier in the afternoon, Brad had hobbled into Cal's room and found the stash of pills he kept inside Altoids tins beneath his boxers.

Cal supplemented his income with small-time drug deals. He'd charmed a pharmacist's daughter who worked in the lodge's gift shop. Melinda was a sweet girl with a lazy eye and easy access to her father's supply. Cal gave her a small cut of his profits and hung out with her after the staff happy hour a few times. Initially, Brad had been disgusted by his friend. Now it was paying off. He could barely feel his knee yet there it was, stretched out in front of him on the coffee table. His whole body felt as if it were floating.

Yes, it was peaceful without Cal.

Brad tossed another Cheeto toward his mouth and missed. Digging between couch cushions, his hand touched something cold, hard. Cal's phone. He stared at it. The screen was dark. With his index finger, he traced the pitchfork-shaped crack in the upper left corner. *What a dumbass. Who couldn't remember to keep their phone charged?*

Without thinking, Brad stood, head swimming like he'd stepped off a Tilt-A-Whirl. The pain in his knee flared as he put weight on it. *He* was the dumbass. He'd wanted to stay in Saturday but Cal insisted they ski, and, like always, he'd done whatever Cal said.

Those days are over. Brad closed his eyes and waited for the dizziness to pass. Groping the wall to steady himself, he knocked off the circular clock that still told the wrong time. He and Cal were locked in an odd, silent stand-off, neither willing to change it after Daylight Saving time ended in November.

Cal could be a dick. Brad pictured his friend on the trail the day before, snow whipping around them, the setting sun shining a spotlight on Cal as he snickered, "Let's hustle, Nana, storm's coming. Think you can make it?"

Brad had been limping earlier in the day and Cal had mocked him.

Inside Brad's head, his roommate's laughter bled into the voice of one of the ski patrol guys who'd rescued him just before he thought he'd black out from the pain and the brutal cold.

"Fucking idiot. Ever hear of a weather app?" he'd asked. Another rescuer had added, "Hey, don't you work here? You should know better."

Brad winced, more from embarrassment at that memory than from the throbbing in his knee. He pushed off the wall toward his bedroom. It must've been later than he realized. His room was dark. He fumbled through the mess on his bedside table until he found the charger he hid from Cal inside a sock. Whenever Cal borrowed something, he either broke it or lost it.

As Brad switched on his lamp, he looked directly at the bulb. Little gold and black circles floated in front of him. It took three attempts before he successfully plugged in Cal's phone.

After staggering back to the living room, Brad sank into the sofa, its softness enveloping him like a marshmallow. He propped up his leg with throw pillows. Along with a twinge of discomfort came a flicker of worry even the Oxy couldn't keep at bay.

Above the chatter of the football announcers and the cheering fans, Cal's phone emitted a medley of chimes and pings. People were looking for Cal. Popular Cal, who'd never known a lonely Saturday night, who broke the high school record for single-season pass completions and most promposals received. Cal, who always came out on top.

Minutes later, Brad heard distant ringing. Cal's mom, his boss, and all the people he owed were probably calling.

Brad's thoughts roamed to the day before, to the drive to the mountain. Cal was convinced a black SUV was following them.

"Tap the brakes," Cal had ordered.

When Brad ignored him, Cal jerked forward, arm stretching to the floor like he was going to reach down and punch the brake pedal with his fist.

"Dude, what the fuck?" Brad yelled. "Get off me!"

"Hit the brakes!" Cal thrust his hand between Brad's boots.

"This is messed up. You know that, right?" Pumping the brakes, Brad watched as the SUV swerved before accelerating and blowing past them. He kept his eyes on the road, certain the SUV's driver—or passenger, if there was one—would flip him off.

"Now speed up again!" Cal commanded. "Help me remember the plate. Just in case."

"Why? Are you gonna tell the police, 'I owe some bad guys money and they're following me?'" Brad almost laughed. Would Cal ever be accountable? Could he even envision a scenario in which he wasn't ultimately a winner?

Then Brad spied Cal's anxious face as he twisted in his seat.

"Anyone else back there?"

Brad glanced in the rearview mirror at the soaring spruces, their branches heavy with fresh snow. "You're losing it, man."

"Sorry." Cal put his head in his hands. "I'm just... you

know... I've got a lot..." His voice trailed off. He shifted toward the window, blew on the glass, and used his index and middle fingers to make a smiley face. "I'm glad we're doing this. Finally, right? How long we been talking about it? Skiing the backcountry, and with a storm coming? That's some next-level shit. We're mavericks!"

Brad had gripped the wheel tighter. "Yeah, man, total mavericks," he'd echoed, turning into the parking lot, wishing he were home on the couch.

Exactly where he was now.

He decided he'd shut his eyes and let the image of the mountain's unspoiled white powder replace the face of his oldest friend. He began drifting off but was awakened by the faint sound of incoming texts and notifications. He jacked up the TV's volume, unprepared to deal with any of it.

4

SUNDAY, DECEMBER 14

JANE

Jane cleared the dinner plates and rinsed them before loading the dishwasher. She preferred to do it herself rather than ask Emerson to help and endure her daughter's exaggerated groans and sighs. Plus, Jane needed a distraction. She'd spent the day waiting for the phone to ring—Wade's phone, the house phone, her phone, any phone. Wade usually left his cell in his home office on weekends, especially since business had been slow. But she'd noticed him checking it during commercial breaks while watching football, grinning or chuckling as birthday texts and greetings arrived from friends and family. If he'd heard from Cal, he hadn't mentioned it.

Em slid up behind her, opened the fridge, and, as if she could read her mother's mind, whisper-taunted, "Has the golden child not called yet?" She grabbed a seltzer, drummed her blue nails against the can, and raised her sculpted eyebrows.

Even when Em was snarky, Jane was still struck by her daughter's beauty. She'd gone ice skating with friends earlier and her cheekbones were flushed pink as peonies. With her gold-green eyes and long dark hair, she was radiant. Jane, who'd been staring at her image reflected in the kitchen window, looked haggard by comparison, her face as saggy and lined as a "before" photo on a cosmetic surgery website.

"I'm sure your brother will call." Despite her confident tone, Jane wasn't sure her son would call. She wasn't even sure where he was. The same three words appeared each time she opened the tracking app: "Location Not Found". "And he is not the golden child," she added, handing her daughter dessert plates and forks.

"Right, sorry." Em smirked. "He's the prodigal son."

Jane ignored her and removed the plastic lid from the mini cheesecake she'd picked up at the supermarket. By the time she'd gotten out of bed and showered, the bakery had closed. After days of winter storm warnings, grocery store aisles looked as if they'd been ransacked. She'd picked up the pale cheesecake topped with a mound of glazed strawberries that reminded her of a festering rash. It was that or a trio of soggy eclairs.

As she lit the birthday candles, her phone buzzed against the windowsill above the sink. *Cal, finally!*

When she turned it over, her stomach lurched. Ivy.

> Hope Wade's enjoying his b.day! Cal call yet?

As Jane read the message, melting wax dripped into the strawberries. She blew out the candles and wondered if that was bad luck.

> Nothing yet.

She wrote back. Then, because she didn't want Ivy making a whole big thing about it, she added:

> Thanks again for dinner. I need your squash recipe!

She didn't want the squash recipe. In fact, it had the texture of baby food. Jane set the phone on the counter, relit the candles, and watched text dots appear then vanish.

"Are we doing this or what?" Emerson tapped her fork against her plate.

"Yes, we're doing this!" Jane lifted the cake and walked toward the table. Her phone buzzed against the counter, ringing this time. She glanced over her shoulder, hoping to see Cal's name and the graduation day photo that flashed whenever he called, but it was Ivy. She probably wanted to talk about how she came up with the squash recipe or provide a post-yoga-class update. She'd promised to ask Piper if Jane could set up a little jewelry display in the studio.

"Just a few pieces—bracelets, earrings—things to pair with gift cards. They're the perfect last-minute add-ons!" Jane had rehearsed those words a dozen times throughout the week, but as she'd said them aloud in Ivy's kitchen she'd cringed at how desperate she sounded. It was such a small, dumb ask, but what if Piper had said no? She couldn't handle one more disappointment.

"Mom!" Emerson snapped. "Let's go! Dad'll be eighty by the time you put the cake down."

Jane forced a smile and moved toward Wade slowly so the candles wouldn't blow out. Em rolled her eyes before launching into a monotone rendition of "Happy Birthday."

. . .

AFTER DESSERT, Wade retreated to the basement. Earlier in the year, he'd begun assembling a home gym down there. It was mostly weights and a couple of stationary bikes he'd found on Facebook marketplace. Jane knew Wade expected Cal to be impressed and join him. Instead, he'd clapped his father on the back and said, "That's cool, Dad. Don't get too buff now!" without ever touching a single kettlebell.

During the summers when Cal was in high school and staying in shape for football, he and Wade would wake at dawn and run a few miles together, sprinting the last block. Through the living room window as she sipped her coffee, Jane had watched them laughing and panting in the driveway.

"Maybe it's a bit much—working together, working out together?" she'd reasoned. The fact that she'd been right seemed to offend Wade just as much as Cal's decision to join the local gym with his former teammates who'd also returned home after college.

Beneath the living room's hardwood floor, Jane heard the clank of weights mixed with Wade's grunts.

Who exercises after eating lasagna and cheesecake? Jane knew her husband was stressed about Cal, too. Wade tried to play it off like it didn't matter, but the fact that his only son had left the family business and then not wished him a happy birthday was a double blow.

Jane sat on the sofa and stared at her cell. She'd called her son twice, once in the morning, and again in the afternoon. The calls had gone straight to voicemail. She'd waited through his upbeat, "Hey, it's Cal. Leave a message," only to be told the mailbox was full. It still caught her off-guard that her child sounded more like a man than a boy.

> Please call Dad. It's his birthday!!!

She'd texted. The messages remained green rather than blue. Did that mean Cal's phone was dead? Broken? She wanted to ask Em but every time she brought up Cal or needed tech help, her daughter groaned.

Anyway, Em wasn't home. After mashing the cheesecake with her fork and pushing her plate away, she'd announced she was going out.

"Out where?" Jane had asked. Beyond the kitchen windows, snowplows scraped the streets. "The roads are—"

"Relax!" Em huffed. "I'm taking a walk. I gotta get out of here. Not that your party wasn't rockin', Dad." She attempted to fist-bump her father, but he didn't understand the gesture and ended up giving her a limp wave. "Seriously, have you seen the icicles? They're like dangling crystals. They're art."

Like most teens, Em was obsessed with curating the perfect life online. Nothing could just be. A cup of coffee, a piece of fruit, a raindrop on a leaf—everything was a prop. Take a picture, paste a quote from a sad poet beside it, and rack up the likes.

Jane was convinced the only reason Em hadn't begged to skip their upcoming Wyoming trip was the photo ops. New scenery meant new reels, which led to new followers.

As she thought about Em, Jane's mind turned to Cal's social media. She could check an app to see how recently Cal had been online. He often posted photos and videos from work: a hawk in flight, white powdery snow cascading like foam on ocean waves, a cluster of small children forming a prism of primary-colored parkas as they clutched the tow rope.

Why hadn't she thought of it earlier? She opened the app, feeling as if she'd been underwater and could only now breach the surface and breathe again. She scanned her son's last activity, the word "Yesterday" sending a chill up her spine.

It was after eight p.m. The temperature was dropping both inside and out. The draft sweeping through the front window made her tense, her shoulders involuntarily rising toward her ears. The phone pulsed in her hand and she startled. This had to be Cal. She turned the device over. Ivy again. If she didn't answer, her friend would only keep trying.

"Hey!" Jane mustered fake cheer and pulled a throw blanket onto her lap. "Sorry for not calling you back. We were doing the cake thing."

"No worries!" Ivy's voice was high-pitched, anxious, the way it sounded when she talked about her mother. "You got my message?"

"I didn't listen to it," Jane confessed, braiding the blanket's fringes. She didn't feel like talking—texts were so much easier—but maybe this would kill time while she waited for Cal's call. "Hey, how's your head today? I don't know if it was the wine last night or the weather, but I've been out of it all day. Got any herbal remedies to share? Is there a special kombucha for hangovers?"

"Of course! I'll send you that recipe too." Ivy's laugh came out like a whinny. She cleared her throat. "So, Brad called a couple hours ago..." Her tone turned serious.

Another chill zipped up Jane's back, making her neck tingle. Maybe she was coming down with something?

"... and, well, did Cal call?"

Jane stiffened. "Yes!" The lie slipped out quickly and unexpected as a hiccup. "He and Wade had a great conversation." She'd been freezing moments earlier. Now she felt feverish, flushed with deceit. Why had she said that? Why not just tell her closest friend the truth? Because she didn't want Ivy making some big unnecessary drama out of her family's personal business.

"Oh, that's fantastic!" Ivy exhaled. "I'd been so worried. They skied together yesterday and Brad hurt his knee again. He had to be rescued and—"

"Oh no!" Jane rubbed her knee in sympathy then tucked her legs beneath the blanket. "Is he okay? That's awful—I mean, an instructor having to be rescued. I hope Cal was able to help."

"That's the thing," Ivy paused, "Brad said Cal had gone ahead..."

Jane heard the *whiz* of the coffee grinder in the background, muffling the rest of the sentence. She held the phone away from her ear, annoyed by her friend's penchant for multi-tasking and the implication that Cal abandoned her son.

The grinding stopped.

"... and then there's some big storm out there, I guess..."

Jane wondered if that was why she couldn't get through to Cal. Perhaps the lines were down, the cables out, or whatever made cell phones work. But if Ivy had talked to Brad, that didn't make sense.

"And maybe it's this thriller Betsy picked for book club, but when Brad said he hadn't seen Cal since yesterday, my mind went to this totally dark place."

Jane stopped fiddling with the blanket's fringes. Her

pulse thrummed faster. "He hasn't seen Cal since yesterday?" She untucked her legs. Her first thought was to end the call, try Cal again, or hurry to the basement to tell Wade something was wrong. Very wrong.

Instead, she froze.

"I told Brad I'd call you—"

In the background, Jane heard the hiss of water. Had Ivy turned on a faucet? She strained to hear. Why couldn't Ivy just pay attention to their conversation?

"—to see if you'd heard from him. And you have, so *phew*! But I have to say, I'm semi-freaking out about Brad and his knee..."

Jane stopped listening. For a moment, she debated telling Ivy she'd lied. Was it too late to walk it back and say something like, "Well, I think it was Cal who called. Let me double-check with Wade to make sure it wasn't his sister."

No, that would make her look like a crazy person. And just because Brad hadn't seen Cal, that didn't mean anything was wrong. They were grown men leading independent lives. They didn't need to constantly check in with each other.

Jane's mind spun in slow motion, trying to slough off the lingering hangover and assemble Ivy's sentences in an order that led to a different outcome. Ivy was always dropping little jibes like, "Land your helicopter, Janie! Our kids are going to be just fine." Why had she been so quick to worry now?

"Well, I'll let you get back to celebrating Wade's birthday. Maybe he'll be in the mood for a little..." Ivy's half-meow-half-growl was punctuated by her dishwasher's beeping.

Oh Christ! Had she mentioned their nonexistent sex life

last night? A sudden heat spread across Jane's cheeks. Sometimes when she drank, she revealed more than she intended.

"Maybe!" The few bites of cheesecake she'd consumed crawled up into her mouth. She swallowed hard and forced a chuckle. "Talk soon!"

PACING THE FRONT HALLWAY, Jane frowned at the grandfather clock, its tick loud and irritating. It was nearly nine p.m. Seven in Wyoming, but still. She considered going to the basement to tell Wade what Ivy had said but that would ruin what was left of his birthday. He'd also point out that Cal would be home right now if only she'd supported him back in August.

"He had four years of college to do whatever the hell he wanted," Wade had argued the morning Cal backed out of the driveway bound for Wyoming. "I worked nights and weekends to put myself through school. He probably didn't even take out the recycling at that frat house!"

She tried Cal again. This time it rang instead of going straight to voicemail. Heart racing, she waited through four, five rings, rolling her neck and attempting to lower her shoulders, which had crept up to her ears.

"C'mon, Cal," she pleaded. "Answer your damn phone." Then she heard his voice, "Hey, it's Cal. Leave a message." Her head throbbed. *It rang! He charged it.* She sent another text.

> Call Dad! Please!

It turned blue. Delivered. He was there, just ignoring her —them.

Jane couldn't understand her son's behavior. Aside from a couple of little blips, Cal had always made good choices, done the right thing. That ugly business his sophomore year of high school wasn't even his fault. It was just what happened when you were smarter than your peers and a gifted athlete. You moved into advanced placement courses, onto varsity teams, and that meant you fell in with a group of older boys—boys who knew where the parties were, boys whose parents or older siblings were willing to supply alcohol, boys who took sports betting well beyond fantasy football leagues with a fifty-dollar buy-in.

Cal won a few times before his luck ran out. Jane knew nothing about it until he'd gotten in over his head placing bets for friends—friends who denied it later when Jane called their mothers.

She'd withdrawn two thousand dollars from the savings account she'd opened to buy extras for the children on their birthdays or holidays. She wanted to avoid telling Wade, whose father had gambled away nearly everything his family had.

For months after, Jane had worried that Cal would take after his grandfather, who'd died just before he was born. But the incident was a one-off. Her son had learned his lesson. She remembered the note he'd written thanking her for bailing him out. He'd drawn a smiley face at the bottom and written "xo" above his name. He was supposed to do chores all summer to pay her back, but by July Fourth Jane let him off the hook.

IN BED, Jane tried to focus on a novel but found herself rereading the same paragraphs without absorbing their meaning. She set it down, its cover a swirl of purple and indigo vines. Why did their book club always choose the darkest tales? Orphans, widows, women always drunk and beaten down, or written off as crazy. Why didn't they ever choose something upbeat? Wasn't reading supposed to provide an escape?

Wade came in, a ring of sweat around his neckline, damp half-moons under his armpits. Despite knowing the answer, she gathered the nerve to ask the question that weighed on her all day. "Did you hear from Cal?"

"Nope." Wade unfastened his watch and dropped it on his dresser. "Not a call. Not a text."

She'd braced for anger but his voice was flat, making the situation somehow worse. "I'm sorry." Jane removed her reading glasses and rubbed her eyes. "I'm sure he just—"

"Met a woman and followed her to Bali?" Wade snorted.

"No. He probably just—"

Wade whirled around, his face turning from pink to fuchsia. "Jesus Christ, do you even hear yourself?"

Jane shrank into the mountain of pillows.

"Stop making excuses for him." Wade pulled his shirt over his head. "He's let us—*me!*—down again and again." His pale flesh jiggled as he flung his gray tee toward the hamper. "And you basically sit there applauding his every move. He doesn't respect me."

"That's not true." Jane's eyes flicked up, searching for his. "Cal loves you."

Wade let out a belch. Though he was lactose intolerant, he'd requested lasagna for his birthday dinner. The faint smell of garlic wafted between them as he knocked on his chest with his fist, burping himself before continuing.

"He doesn't respect you either. He plays you with his

smiles and his innocent act." Wade made an exaggerated jazz hands gesture that would've cracked Jane up under different circumstances "He has no impulse control. He does whatever the hell he wants, whenever he wants, without regard for anyone else's feelings or even his own future."

Jane wanted to tell him to keep it down, but she hadn't heard Emerson's footsteps on the staircase. Where had her daughter gone exactly? Should she be concerned about her too? How many people could she worry about simultaneously?

Her husband scowled, waiting. For what?

"Wade, it's your birthday," she managed. "Please don't get yourself so upset."

"I'm not five, Jane. I'm not disappointed that a clown didn't show up for my party. I'm angry that our son is turning out exactly like my father!"

Jane had learned that when Wade brought up his dad it was best to remain quiet or risk a "You have no idea what it was like!" speech. She wanted to remind her husband that Cal was only twenty-three. Didn't he deserve some time to figure things out? But because of his father's problems, Wade had never gotten a chance to be carefree and irresponsible. As long as she'd known him, he'd helped his mother pay her mortgage. He regularly added money to her account for groceries.

On some level, was Wade jealous of their son? Her husband's business was suffering as interest rates climbed and retail stores died a slow death thanks to online shopping. Wade had been counting on Cal to bring in fresh ideas and keep their social media accounts and website updated.

Her husband had stripped down to his boxers. He looked exposed, vulnerable. For a moment, she felt as if she'd betrayed him by taking Cal's side. She remembered Ivy's half-meow-half-growl and thought about asking Wade to lie beside her. With her hands and maybe even her mouth, she could try to salvage what was left of his birthday. But before she could suggest it, Wade stalked off toward the shower. The bald circle at the back of his head expanded more each day.

"I'll speak to Cal tomorrow," she called after him.

"Don't bother. We'll hear from him when he runs out of money or his car dies." He let out another belch. "Did you buy more Tums?"

"Try the hall closet."

Jane picked up her phone and opened the tracking app. Em was on Ivy's street. Did Ivy's block have better icicles? Ivy, whose sons checked in regularly. Jane knew she was being ridiculous; lack of sleep and the wine from the night before were making her irritable. She watched the screen and waited, expecting to see Cal's condo address, but the searchlight swept the screen, struggling to locate him. A notification popped up: a new message through her business's website. *Finally, an order.* She swiped to read it.

> *Happy birthday to your husband. Did he get everything he wished for? Do any of us?*

Daniel. Her spirits lifted. He'd recently ordered two bracelets for his daughters as Christmas gifts. She appreciated his support. He assured her they'd share pics and links on social media.

Any chance I can get in-person delivery? he'd asked, adding a winking emoji.

Would love to, but so busy this time of year! she'd written back.

He'd been asking about getting together again, but she'd stalled, trying to resist temptation.

She'd met Daniel once more for dinner in mid-October at an oceanfront spot in a beach town that was a midpoint between them. Wade had been golfing with potential investors. Em was at a football game with friends. Ivy and Greg had rented a place in upstate New York for the weekend to celebrate their anniversary. Ivy sent selfies of the two of them hiking and admiring the foliage. Jane, who'd been alone, was grateful for Daniel's last-minute invitation.

As they'd watched the sun slip below the horizon, Daniel had covered her hand with his. "I'm so glad we're back in touch," he'd said, his eyes searching hers as he interlaced their fingers. She hadn't pulled away.

Even before Daniel had begun messaging her, in quieter moments, Jane allowed herself to envision another life. What if, after Em left for college, she left too? She didn't necessarily crave a new relationship, it was more a desire to live with ease, no longer subject to Wade's ever-changing moods, to step away from the tension between her husband and son that started when Wade insisted Cal work for him. And, of course, the ever-present stress about money. Both her children would soon be off on their own paths. Maybe she needed to create a new one for herself?

Jane hadn't shared these thoughts with anyone—not even Ivy, who, for all her free-spiritedness, was very old-fashioned when it came to marriage and family.

Daniel had been pushing to see Jane again, but with the holidays, Wade's birthday, and their family vacation coming up, it hadn't felt right. She'd see how things went in

Wyoming and then, in the new year, with clear eyes, she'd take a hard look at her life.

She read the next few lines.

Did he get everything he wished for? Do any of us?

A laughing-crying emoji followed.

Had she mentioned Wade's birthday? She flicked to Emerson's account. Jane told her daughter repeatedly to keep it private, but stubbornly Em insisted it stay public so she could grow her following. What following? Seventeen hundred people?

The top post was a split-screen photo. On the left, Wade held Em as a toddler. With his full head of dark, wavy hair, he looked handsome. He was smiling at Em, whose tiny nose was pressed to his cheek. Her shiny, chestnut curls peeked out from under a furry white hat with cat ears. The other picture, taken just hours earlier, showed Wade at the kitchen table, blowing out his birthday candles. Jane saw Wade's father in her husband's face, in the hollows beneath his eyes. His work stress took a visible toll. She had no idea Em had snapped the photo. The caption—*HBD to the BDE (Best Dad Ever)!!*—made her sigh. Another show for the followers.

She heard a blast as Wade turned on the shower. It would take a while for the water to heat up.

She looked at Daniel's message again. He was so attentive. It was a comfort to know someone was out there, thinking of her.

She texted back.

Lovely day, thanks! Hope yours was too!

But it hadn't been a great day—or even a good one. Not hearing from Cal cast a shadow over the celebration. Where was he? She clicked over to the tracker. The familiar words "Location Not Found" stared back. There had to be a glitch with Cal's phone. She'd try Brad or even the ski resort in the morning if she still hadn't heard from him. He usually worked Mondays. Someone would find her son. It might embarrass him, but maybe that would teach him to not ignore her calls.

In the hallway, Wade rummaged through the closet, shaking the bottle of antacids. Opening her bedside table drawer, she reached for the brown plastic bottle of sleeping pills. She knew she should stop but she couldn't, not when things were so stressful.

She spilled the pills into her hand. She needed a whole one tonight—and maybe the other half of last night's too.

5

MONDAY, DECEMBER 15
BRAD

The knocking made its way into Brad's dream. In his subconscious it was spring, not a trace of snow in sight, only budding leaves, blue sky, and a woodpecker tapping the trunk of the maple tree outside his childhood bedroom window.

The thumping, light at first, got louder, more insistent, until it woke him. Blinking and disoriented, Brad used the sleeve of his sweatshirt to wipe a puddle of drool from his cheek. Sunlight bounced off the TV screen where a talk show aired, volume muted. The knock came again. Which day was it? Why was he fully dressed and sleeping on the couch? He sat up, pain ricocheting up his right leg. An empty Cheetos bag crinkled beneath him. The knocking escalated.

"Coming," Brad called, his voice hoarse from lack of use. He limped to the door, lightheaded, and licked the salt from his fingers.

The blast of cold air startled him but not as much as the

sight of his unexpected visitors: two uniformed police officers standing shoulder to shoulder.

The taller cop had his knuckles raised, ready to knock again. He stared at Brad, his eyebrows bushy as squirrels' tails. Beside him, his sidekick stomped his boots, dropping clumps of snow onto the *Hope you brought beer!* welcome mat—Cal's sole contribution to the condo's decor.

"Afternoon," the knocker said. "Bradley Chapman?"

Brad winced. He hated his full name. Growing up, his older brother, Max, told him their parents had hoped he'd be a girl. They'd planned to name him Shirley, Max said, after their grandmother. To taunt him when their mom and dad weren't listening, Max would sing-song, "Bradley Shirley, Shirley Bradley," until Brad lost it and flailed his fists at his always-taller, always-stronger brother. The story wasn't even true, but it stuck just the same.

"I'm Lieutenant Lynch," said Eyebrows. "This is Officer Hanlon." He jabbed a thumb toward the younger man, who was blowing into his hands for warmth, puffing out his pink cheeks.

"Afternoon." Hanlon nodded.

As Brad's cloudiness faded, anxiety settled in his chest and his arms began to tingle. He had a pretty good idea of what or who brought them to his doorstep. His mother. Why had he told her about Cal? Bits of their conversation came back to him, making him slightly nauseous—or maybe that was the pills. He tried to remember what he'd said exactly, but he couldn't focus with these men staring at him.

"What's up?" Brad attempted to sound casual but, much like spotting the flashing lights of a squad car in the rearview mirror, the sight of their uniforms was enough to get his pulse pumping. If the painkillers hadn't plunged him into a semi-trance, he imagined his heart might've jackhammered through his ribcage.

"We received a call this morning from—" the baby-faced cop began.

"Seems there are some concerns about your roommate." The older officer peered past Brad's shoulder into the condo.

"Oh." Brad kept his voice neutral. He hadn't invited them in, yet he found himself backing up as they advanced.

"Freezing out there." Hanlon closed the door behind them. "Mr. Callaway home?"

Brad swung his head left to right, the living room swaying with him. "No, not right now."

"When's the last time you saw him?" Hanlon asked, not in a hard-ass kind of way, more with an eagerness. Maybe he was new. He looked only a couple years older than Brad. If they'd met under different circumstances, they might've been friends. Brad pictured them sharing a pitcher of beer, shooting pool.

What was his question—something about time? Out of habit, Brad's eyes drifted to the spot where the clock had hung. The wall's beige paint was scuffed in a couple of places.

"What happened here?" The older cop jutted his chin toward the clock lying face up on the brown carpet. "You fellas get into a tussle?"

"Who? Me and Cal?" The officers exchanged a look. Brad continued. "Nope. I—I knocked it off by accident yesterday." Was it yesterday? Time had begun to blur. The clock read three thirty, which meant it was really two thirty, since they'd never adjusted it.

"When did you last see Mr. Callaway?" the younger cop asked again.

"Callaway's his first name." Brad glanced from one man to the next. If they didn't even have the name right, they probably didn't know much else. "He goes by Cal." He paused, expecting one of them to take out a short pencil and a tiny notebook like a TV detective would. Neither officer moved.

Brad thought maybe he was still dreaming until the lieutenant—what did he say his name was? Lewis? Lunch? When was the last time he'd eaten? Not Cheetos, but real food. His mouth was so dry. *Lynch!*—Lynch leaned forward and spoke loudly and slowly, the way people did with toddlers and the elderly. "You haven't answered my partner's question. When was the last time you saw your roommate?"

Brad rubbed his face. His cheek hurt. "Saturday."

"You remember what time?" Lynch asked.

"And where you were?" Hanlon added.

"We were skiing over at Wyndmere."

"Saturday's the last time you saw him?" Lynch spread his feet, hands on his hips.

Brad thought of his mother in Mountain Pose. No, he never should've called her. He should've texted, told her he was beat, and promised to call later in the week.

"What time was this around?" Lynch continued.

"I don't know. It was getting dark. Four-thirty? Maybe five?"

"And you haven't seen him since?" Hanlon's voice rose, carrying a hint of excitement, like maybe this would turn out to be more than a routine wellness check, more than the usual "spoiled rich kid who spent the weekend partying and forgot to check in with his parents" situation.

"Nope." Brad shifted, gripped by a sudden and powerful need to use the toilet.

"So, you went skiing, but you didn't come back here together. Is that correct?" Hanlon's smooth forehead contracted into a grid of horizontal and vertical lines.

"You feeling all right, son?" Lynch's eyes narrowed. "You're sweating quite a bit."

Brad hadn't felt the beads of perspiration that dotted his hairline until he wiped them with the back of his hand. He pointed at his leg. "My knee. I twisted the hell out of it Saturday. Cal was way ahead of me. I had to get a ride back from ski patrol. So, yeah... no, I mean, I'm not feeling great." He looked from one cop to the other hoping for a bit of sympathy.

"Is this unusual behavior for Mr.—"

"Whitaker," Lynch bailed out Hanlon before he screwed up the name again.

"Not coming home, you mean?" Brad shrugged. "We're friends—roommates, obviously—but we're not inseparable. Cal does his thing; I do mine."

Lynch's heavy eyebrows stitched together and arched like bat wings. "Again, that doesn't answer the question."

"Have you tried calling or texting him?" Hanlon asked.

"No." Brad shook his head and the dizziness returned. "I haven't been feeling—"

"So, you're not concerned then?" Lynch frowned.

"'Cause his mom sure is." Coming from Hanlon, it sounded like a schoolyard "your mama" gibe.

Of course, Mrs. Whitaker had called them. In his mind's eye, Brad saw the dominos fall: his mother contacting Cal's mom, Mrs. Whitaker calling Cal, getting no answer, freaking out. He remembered his own phone ringing hours earlier. He'd shoved it under the couch. She'd probably tried to reach him too. When he didn't answer, she must've called the police.

It didn't surprise Brad. Since he and Cal were kids, Mrs. Whitaker had made worrying a competitive sport. Cal was the only child who'd been trained to check expiration dates on cartons of chocolate milk in the school cafeteria. He never would've been allowed to play football if Mr. Whitaker hadn't overruled his wife.

"He hasn't reported to work the past couple days." Lynch's eyes searched Brad's face for a reaction.

Work. *Shit!* Brad was due there hours ago—not that he'd been in any condition to go.

"Good-looking guy," Hanlon said.

Brad almost laughed. How many times had he heard that? He'd been getting compliments on Cal's behalf as far back as he could remember.

The young cop must've realized how it sounded because he added, "His mom sent us photos, you know, in case we need 'em." He looked to Lynch for approval before continuing, "You know if he's seeing anyone?"

This line wasn't new to Brad either. How many girls had smiled at him, making the blood rush to his head and other places, only to ask, "Is Cal seeing anyone?"

Melinda—the gift shop girl, the pharmacist's daughter—flashed through his mind. Cal had told him that up close she smelled like wet wool and pancake syrup.

"No one serious." The longer Brad stood, the more his leg throbbed. Sweat trickled down the side of his face, but he didn't want to call attention to it by wiping it with his sleeve. He took an awkward step toward the door, hoping they'd get the hint. "If I think of anything or if I hear from him, I'll call you."

Lynch ignored him and moved deeper into the condo. "Mind if I take a look around?" His hooded eyes scanned the surroundings.

Insides twisting, Brad swept his arm toward the living room and kitchen area as if he were a real estate agent showing the place. "Be my guest." He wanted to ask them to leave, not give them a fucking tour. But if he'd said, "No," wouldn't that seem suspicious?

Long and lean, Lynch was already loping past the couch like a uniformed cartoon giraffe.

"Entertaining?" The lieutenant tipped his hat toward two tall boys on the coffee table.

Brad didn't remember drinking them but that explained why his bladder was on the verge of exploding. He shook his head.

"Football Sunday. I get it." Hanlon chuckled. "Did you catch the end of that Denver game? Real nail-biter."

Brad ignored him. His eyes were trained on Lynch's giant black boot, practically the length of a snowshoe. He'd kicked something and stooped to pick it up.

"This yours?" He waved a phone, home screen bright with a flood of notifications.

"Yeah, thanks." Brad took it and slipped it into the front pocket of his sweatshirt.

"Anything?" Lynch's eyebrows crept toward his hat.

"Huh?" Brad asked.

"Call? Text?" Lynch stood straighter, thumbs pressed into his silver belt buckle. "From your roommate?" His eyes shot to his partner and then back to Brad. "Didn't seem like you even looked."

Brad slid out the phone and scrolled, squeezing the device hard to steady his trembling fingers. "Just my mom."

"Moms." Hanlon laughed, then coughed when no one joined in. "Who else does your roommate hang out with?" he asked. "If you can help us put a list together, that'd be..."

Brad didn't answer. He followed Lynch as he stalked toward Cal's bedroom and flicked the light switch. The ceiling fan spun, recycling stale air. Cal's dresser drawers were open, boxers and tees poking out. Brad had a fleeting memory of digging around in the dark for more pills. Lynch squatted to study a framed photo of the Whitaker family at Cal's graduation, his black cap and gown stark as a crow against the rolling green hills of campus. His mom had sent the pic with a tin of chocolate chip cookies Cal had shared with Brad right before asking for an extension on October's rent.

Lynch stood and moved to the foot of Cal's unmade bed. He did a slow three-sixty before ducking beneath the doorway and heading to the kitchen. Over the hum in his ears, Brad heard Hanlon still rambling about names and contact info.

Lynch sniffed at the air like he was part bloodhound and pointed to the sink where the faucet had been dripping steadily for days.

How high was the water? Brad was almost afraid to look. Cal never scraped his plate, just let shreds of chicken, rice, and corn slide down the drain. When it eventually clogged, he'd offer a lame, "Sorry, man, I keep forgetting you don't have one of those disposal thingies."

Brad hobbled closer. The sink was half-filled with murky water. Another problem courtesy of Cal.

"I'd deal with that sooner rather than later." Lynch headed toward the hall but turned back. "What happened to your knee?"

"I wrecked it skiing. I already told you." As soon as the words left his mouth, Brad heard how defensive he sounded. He attempted to walk it back. "I tore my ACL in high school. Football injury. I had surgery but it's never been the same. With that storm, it got icy real quick. I wanted to stay home, but Cal—"

Lynch walked into the bathroom. Did he expect to find Cal in the shower? Brad leaned against the doorframe. Standing that close to the toilet and not being able to use it made his skin prickle with impatience. He told himself to chill. They'd be gone soon enough. It was a small place. The grand tour was nearly over.

Lynch headed toward Brad's room at the back of the condo, Hanlon on his heels like a puppy not wanting to miss anything. Brad should've been embarrassed by the balled-up socks and underwear scattered across the floor, but he was too distracted by the object on his nightstand. He flicked his eyes away to avoid drawing Lynch's attention to it.

"Cal's mom said he didn't call his dad for his birthday yesterday, and that's not like him," Hanlon babbled.

Should Brad mention that Cal and his dad weren't speaking because they were both too stubborn to think of anyone but themselves? He turned to see Hanlon rubbing his smooth chin.

"Naturally, she's very concerned," he went on. "She said he's been acting different these past couple months since he's been out here—with you."

Brad had had enough. First they showed up unannounced and went on some stupid scavenger hunt, like they were going to find Cal under a bed or crouching in the closet. Then this glorified mall cop implied that *he'd* been a bad influence on Cal.

Between the pain in his leg and his urgent need to pee, he wanted to tell these two to get out but he knew that would only make it worse. He took a deep breath like his mom would've suggested.

"Sounds like you and Mrs. Whitaker had quite the conversation. She's usually not a big talker, prefers to keep things pretty private." Brad suddenly remembered how hurt his mother had been when she found out Emerson had to take a summer class to pass ninth grade Algebra and Mrs. Whitaker had never mentioned it.

"I tell Jane everything and yet she's secretive." His mother had frowned. "I don't get it."

"People tend to ramble when they're nervous." Lynch offered a crooked smile before running his large hand over a snowboarding poster. "Getting back to Saturday, you tell anybody your buddy might still be out there? When you called ski patrol, did you say your roommate could've been on the mountain?"

Brad shrugged, immediately regretting the weak gesture. "I expected him to be at the base or back at the car. Cal's a strong skier. Believe me, if he were here he'd tell you that himself."

"Well, Bradley, if Cal were here, we wouldn't be asking these questions, now, would we?" Lynch clucked his tongue. "What happened to your face there?"

Brad touched his cheek. He'd noticed it stung when he woke up but that discomfort was nothing compared to his knee.

"I walked into a cabinet door. Edge caught me."

"Hate when that happens." Lynch moved to the nightstand and switched on the lamp.

Inside his sweatshirt, Brad's phone pinged but he didn't

reach for it. He couldn't take his eyes off the lieutenant. His hairy knuckles and skinny fingers reminded Brad of a tarantula as they crept toward the device that sat beside the lamp.

Lynch wheeled around. "Didn't I just hand you a phone?"

Brad nodded. *Keep it together. This is almost over.*

"So then whose is this?" Lynch's creepy hand hovered like he was itching to pick it up.

Brad knew how it looked. Who went anywhere without their phone?

"It's Cal's," he said and felt a trickle of urine slide, warm and startling, down his thigh.

Hanlon's sharp inhale let Brad know this wasn't almost over. In fact, it was just beginning.

6

MONDAY, DECEMBER 15

EMERSON

Emerson walked into the house and let her backpack slide to the floor. She'd never admit it, but her legs were cold as popsicles in her short skirt. When she'd gotten dressed that morning she'd forgotten she'd signed up to volunteer after school. She wasn't a do-gooder, but posting a few short videos of helping out was great for her brand. Plus, according to her mother, colleges loved community service and that part of her application was embarrassingly spare—not that Em cared.

She'd nearly frozen her ass off standing in the gym stuffing canned food into drawstring sacks for kids who'd otherwise go without over the holidays. Some idiot insisted on keeping the doors open the whole time, letting in gusts of air that made her bare thighs pimple with goosebumps. From the second her shift started, Emerson had been fantasizing about putting on her fleece-lined leggings. She'd been so impatient to get home, she rolled through a stop sign and had to flirt her way out of a ticket. When the cop peeked in her

Jeep window, she'd inched her skirt higher with her pinky and he'd let her off with a warning.

It wasn't exactly toasty in her house but it was better than the gym. In the entryway, she dropped her keys into the blue and white bowl that sat on a table between picture frames. The clinking sound was softer than usual because her mother's keys were there also. *Shit.* Emerson had hoped her mom would be out buying more stuff for their ski trip. She didn't want to answer the "How was your day? What's new with your friends?" questions her mom asked each afternoon now. She'd been weird and clingy since Cal left in August.

As Em unwound her scarf, her stomach growled. She sniffed at the air but didn't smell dinner cooking. Maybe they were having leftover lasagna.

"Wade?" her mother called from the living room.

There was no way Emerson could sneak upstairs, pretending she hadn't heard. She'd give her mom a minute, maybe two, then, as she'd done for the past few months, she'd lie and say she was going to work on her college essays. A day rarely passed without her mom reminding her that Cal had all his applications submitted well before Thanksgiving. If that was supposed to motivate Emerson, it backfired. Each time she read the prompts for supplemental essays that required her to explain why she wanted to attend a certain university, or describe a time she'd witnessed an injustice and did or didn't make a difference, it only reinforced her gut feeling that college was not for her. Yes, it would be fantastic to ditch her parents and, sure, the parties would be epic, but college wasn't the only path. She was waiting until after their ski vacation to tell her mom and dad she had no intention of spending another four years studying.

"Wade? Is that you?"

Emerson walked the few steps to the living room. Her mother looked small, almost childlike, sitting in the center of the sofa bent forward. Did she have a stomachache? She wasn't in one of her usual sweater twinsets. Instead, she was wearing Cal's college sweatshirt, its cuffs stretched over her hands.

"Hey," Em said.

Her mother lifted her head as if it were a boulder resting on her slim neck. "Oh, Emerson, it's you."

Em crossed her arms. "Thrilled to see you, too," she muttered, unmoving.

"Come. Sit." Her mother wasn't wearing makeup. Without it, she appeared paler, plainer.

Emerson crossed the room. Peering down, she was stunned by the amount of gray in her mother's hair. She'd mention it to her later.

"What's up?" Em lowered herself onto the couch cushion, bracing for its coolness against the back of her bare thighs, and wondered what her mom's problem was this time. If she was freaking out about that stupid jewelry business or had questions about how to use an app, Emerson swore she'd get right back in the Jeep and drive to her friend Sasha's house.

"It's Cal." She wiped her nose with a wad of crumpled tissues.

Em stared at the back of her mother's hand where the skin was thin and loose. Aging was gross and unfair—the way your body turned on you. She made a mental note to drown herself in moisturizer when she finally got to her room. "What about Cal?" she asked.

"Have you heard from him?"

"No. Why would I?" Em watched her mother's forehead wrinkle. This shouldn't have come as a shock. They were hardly close. That's what happened when there was a five-year age gap between a brother and sister and one child was treated like a constant source of delight and the other like a disappointment.

Emerson only needed to look around the living room to know her place in the family. As much as she hated anything math-related, she'd counted the number of times she and Cal appeared in the framed photos topping the side tables, piano, and mantle. Her brother beamed at them in nine different shots, she in only four—and Cal was in two of those. When Em brought it up to her mother, Jane justified it by saying that because Cal had been born first, there would always be more pictures of him. Emerson studied photos in her friends' homes to check this logic and found it flawed. Did her mother think she was ugly? The two-point-two thousand people who followed her didn't think so. In fact, they repeatedly told her she was "beautiful," "gorgeous," "flawless." Reading their comments made her feel alive, like stepping into the sunshine after a rainstorm.

"He didn't call yesterday." A sob clogged her mother's throat.

So that's what this was about? Cal forgot their father's birthday and their mother turned into a puddle? Emerson felt a sudden smugness. Was the golden boy's shine starting to tarnish?

"I'm sure he's just busy," she said.

Her mother shook her head, tears springing to her bloodshot eyes. "No one has seen him."

Emerson snorted. "God, Mom, he's twenty-three. Seriously. He doesn't have to check in every day." Maybe there was something to be said for not being their mother's favorite. Once she moved out, Em imagined Jane wouldn't notice if they went weeks without talking—especially if Cal was back home by then.

"It's been forty-eight hours." Her mother's voice had a strange, distracted quality to it, the way it did in the morning before she'd had coffee.

"Okay. Sorry, he doesn't need to check in every *two* days." Emerson stood. "I'm going to work on my essays now."

Her mother's cold hand clutched the back of her knee. Emerson shivered.

"He didn't show up for work yesterday or today."

Em sat again, mainly so her mother would release her grip. She was dying to escape to her bedroom, put on those fleecy leggings, post the volunteering video, and await the praise of her followers, but her mother was obviously having some kind of breakdown.

"That's hardly a shocker." Em tried to not lose what was left of her patience. "Cal hasn't had the best track record work-wise. Hello? Look how he ditched Dad! And remember when he had that internship selling copiers and almost got fired for napping in his car?" She expected her mother to laugh or at least smile.

"He went skiing with Brad on Saturday."

Jane's hands flipped and flopped in her lap. They reminded Emerson of the goldfish she and Cal won at the town carnival when they were little. The poor things flailed against the net each time their father removed them to clean their bowl. Most hadn't lasted a week.

"Cal didn't go home with Brad. No one has seen him." Jane made a strange noise, half-hiccup, half-cry. "It's like he's disappeared."

People don't just disappear, Emerson wanted to say. Someone had seen him. A woman, most likely.

Em remembered the summer before Cal went to college. Back when she still worshipped him. He'd taken her to Six Flags. They were supposed to have a special day, just the two of them. As they waited in a long line for El Toro, she noticed her brother and a girl with a butterfly tattoo on her shoulder smiling at each other. Just before they passed through the turnstile to board the roller coaster, she saw their fingers touch on a metal railing. Cal had said they'd get lunch after the ride, but next thing Em knew, they were crossing the park, following the girl to the Sky Screamer. Cal sat with her while Em was forced to ride beside the girl's friend, who was tall as a WNBA player with muscle-y thighs that took up most of the seat, leaving Em squished and miserable.

When they returned to the ground, Cal gave Emerson two ten-dollar bills and told her to meet him by the fountain at closing time. She went on a few rides by herself. It wasn't the same as when she and her brother had sat together arms raised, screaming and laughing. And twenty bucks didn't go as far as Cal thought it would. For hours, Em roamed the park alone, scanning the crowd for him, eager to leave before it got dark.

On the drive home, Cal took her to McDonald's—a bribe so she wouldn't tell their parents. There'd been a rock in her stomach from the moment he left her standing near the Ferris wheel's entrance, but she shoveled down large fries and a McFlurry because eating made not speaking to him easier.

She hadn't thought about that day in ages, but she was pretty sure it marked the moment she started hating butterflies and stopped buying into the myth of the almighty Cal.

If Em were a gambler like her brother, she'd have bet Cal found an option that was more appealing than going home with Brad. She was about to tell her mother that when Jane reached for her cell phone and tapped the home screen. She had a notification she quickly swiped away.

"The police officer I talked to said—"

"Wait—you called the police?" Emerson wanted to point out how crazy that was but knew it would be a waste of time. All her mother's passwords were combinations of Cal's name and birthdate. Em was surprised the woman wasn't in her Lexus, halfway to Wyoming by now.

"I had no choice!" her mom said. "I couldn't reach him and Ivy said Brad hasn't seen him, so I asked them to do a wellness check." She put the phone face down on the ottoman and dropped her head into her palms.

"And?" Emerson's patience was cratering.

"They found your brother's cell phone in Brad's room."

Okay, that was odd, Em had to admit. Who went anywhere without a phone? A weird tingle filled her stomach. She wanted to blame the veggie burrito she had for lunch.

"Did Brad say why he had it?" she asked.

"The police said Brad wasn't very 'forthcoming.'" Jane made air quotes, her used tissues waving like a white flag. "But they're putting a list together: friends, coworkers. They'll start calling around."

"Well, Brad's Cal's roommate, not his bodyguard." Emerson felt protective of Brad. She'd known him her entire life. She remembered how sad and out of it he seemed when he came home from college and said he wasn't going back.

As much as her mother had tried to get Mrs. Chapman to tell her what had happened, she never did. Em wondered if Max knew the full story.

"There was a snowstorm Saturday afternoon." Her mother's shoulders floated up. She was going to cry again. "I asked them to send people out to search the mountain, but they said they need to eliminate the most obvious possibilities first. If we don't hear from him soon, I'm going to insist..."

Emerson stared past her mother's shoulder through the large window behind the couch. It wasn't even six o'clock and the sky was already so velvety black it could've passed for two a.m. Could her brother really be out there? Lost? The thought made her shiver.

The front door groaned and Jane sprang up like a Jack-in-the-box. "Wade?" she called.

Another set of keys clanked in the bowl and then Em's father appeared. "What's going on? Why are you in the dark?"

"Did you get my message?" her mother asked.

"I had a meeting at the bank. My phone was off." He looked at Jane then Emerson, who shrugged, uncertain if this was a real crisis or one of her mother's self-created dramas, like the time she was convinced she'd been left off the Fashion Show fundraiser email chain and later found the messages in her spam folder.

"Cal's missing." Jane dropped to the couch, fish hands flopping again.

"What?" Wade switched on a lamp.

Jane repeated what she'd told Emerson as Wade frowned and peeled off his coat. Beneath it he wore one of his signature Patagonia vests, collar turned up like he thought he was a catalog model.

"There have to be surveillance cameras—are they checking those?" To Em, her father sounded more irritated than worried. "I'm sure they'll find him out there 'living his best life.'"

Em had shown her dad one of Cal's recent posts and together they'd rolled their eyes at his ridiculous, over-the-top hashtag.

"Wade! This is serious." Jane grabbed her cell. "I don't know if they're checking cameras. I just—I'll call back and ask—"

Emerson was grateful when her phone pulsed. As she pulled it from her pocket, her mother jumped again as if the sofa had become electrified. "Is it Cal?"

"No." Emerson kept the phone close to her body as she peeked at the caller ID. *Man of My Dreams* flashed on the screen. She hadn't entered it that way. He—the self-proclaimed "man of her dreams"—had done it when he'd taken her phone, his fingers brushing hers, and added his contact info. The boldness of it had made her laugh, her cheeks already sore from smiling.

"*Man of My Dreams?* You wish," she'd said, trying to play it cool when he handed her phone back.

They'd been in his basement. Thanksgiving. She'd gone down there to avoid all the usual questions about college and to play with the dog, who'd been banished after devouring a platter of pigs-in-a-blanket. In between scrolling through her phone and tossing a tennis ball to Jean-Claude, Emerson guzzled a super-sized serving of mulled wine because it was a holiday and no one was paying attention to her anyway.

Max, too, had been seeking refuge from her parents, who seemed a lot more interested in his job search than he did. Emerson had overheard him say things were tough in the tech sector at the moment and he was thinking of taking some low-key gigs, then spending the summer traveling around Europe. When Max said it, Emerson had watched her father's nose wrinkle as if Jean-Claude had taken a shit on his loafers.

"It's just an idea, nothing set in stone," Mr. Chapman had said. "Max's applying for some really exciting opportunities!"

"He's keeping his options open!" Mrs. Chapman had rubbed Max's back and Em tried not to smirk as he wriggled away from her.

"I think it's really cool that you're going to do some traveling," Em told him to fill the awkward silence when it was just the two of them and the dog in the basement. *Do some traveling? Really, Em?* She sounded like a grandmother—a really boring one. Em usually wasn't intimidated by anyone, but Max had a certain way of looking at her that made her stomach flip. She typically thought in captions—short, clever statements—but around him, her mind went blank. He was so tall, he had to duck to not hit his head on the low basement ceiling. He had broad shoulders and a narrow waist, ginger hair and dark brown eyes. Em thought he was the perfect mix of hot and cool, smart but not a dick about it. When he picked an acoustic guitar off a stand in the corner and strummed a few chords, her self-consciousness disappeared.

"Teach me!" She clapped, desperate to put her hands where his had been.

She'd leaned in to kiss him first. Later, she'd blamed the wine for making her brave or crazy, but, really, she'd wanted to do that for the last two years—since that summer when their families had rented a beach house together and Max had snuck her and her friend Sasha Grey Goose and cranberry cocktails as fireworks exploded overhead.

On the basement futon that smelled faintly of dog, surrounded by yoga blocks and belts, she and Max kissed, losing all track of time until the door at the top of the stairs opened and Mrs. Chapman yelled, "Pie!"

It had only been a couple of weeks, but things were moving fast, and their plans made Em's head float like a helium balloon. She could see it all: adventures in Montmartre, Brugge, Costa del Sol. The pics alone would be magical. She was sure the Chapmans would be cool with them hanging out and Em joining Max on his travels. Her own parents? No fucking way. She'd deal with that after the trip to Wyoming.

"Who is it?" Her mother asked as Em turned toward the staircase.

"Sasha," she lied, a secret thrill spiraling inside her as *Man of My Dreams* looped around the top of her screen.

She swiped left and whispered, "Hey," as she jogged up the steps to her room.

Max said something she couldn't hear over the grandfather clock's chimes and her dad's sharp tone. She didn't need to stick around to know that he was about to embark on one of his "I told you so" tours. Her mom would respond with a mix of tears and "I'm sorry!"s.

"Sorry," Em said into the phone. "What did you say?"

"I heard about Cal."

She waited for him to continue. When he didn't, she checked the screen to see if the call had dropped. Then a thought hit her: *So this is real then, not just Mom creating unnecessary drama?*

"What—what did you hear?" For a second, she couldn't

catch her breath. Was it from hurrying upstairs or fearing Max had new info?

"Just that I... I don't know... he's missing?" He made a sound like he was sucking in air. "Want me to come over? I know we're trying to keep this—us—quiet but I can be there—"

"No," she said quickly. Explaining that she and Max were a thing would only make her parents more nuts. "But that's cool of you to offer. Wade and Jane are kind of losing it right now so it's probably not a great idea."

"I'm so sorry, Em." Max's deep voice, the kindness in it, was so spectacularly attractive it made her forget what they were talking about for a second. Then she passed Cal's room. She stopped to look at her brother's Blackwatch plaid down comforter and matching curtains, the framed poster of a red Lamborghini, his collection of golf tees in shot glasses on his dresser. Same as it always was.

Em stood straighter and moved down the hall. "I'm sure he's fine. He'll turn up, all dimples and apologies, and my dad will lecture him and my mom will send him money."

"Yeah, you're probably right," Max said unconvincingly.

"Maybe we could hang out later?" Em flopped down on her bed, stretching her legs over her footboard. Cal being gone for a little while could be a good thing. Her mother would be distracted, which meant Em could come and go without all the "Who are you meeting?"s and "When will you be back?"s—unless she went the other way and became even more smothering.

Max said something but his voice cut out again. "Hey, this is Brad on the other line. Let me call you back."

"'K." She set the phone down on her nightstand, slid off her skirt, and pulled on the leggings. They were every bit as warm and plush as she'd remembered. She really had to post something about them. Her followers would appreciate this solid rec. Maybe the brand would reach out to offer her a sponsorship deal?

At her vanity table, she dusted her cheekbones with pale pink powder, considering the most flattering poses. She reached for her phone. Her last post—the birthday split screen of her with her dad—had gotten tons of engagement. She was quickly realizing that people loved sneaking a peek inside her life: a glimpse at her home, her family. Beyond the products, the promotion, and stunning pics swirling through cyberspace, everyone craved authenticity. Her real, vulnerable posts always got the most likes and comments.

Whenever she talked about how the college application process made her skin break out, they lapped it up. *Show us your mess, your sadness. We're here for you!* they seemed to say.

Her mind shifted to Cal. Where was he? She thought of all those viral news stories about young women who'd gone missing. The ones that got the most coverage had one thing in common: they were attractive. So was Cal.

That wasn't Em being weird, creepy, or even boastful about her good genes, it was just something people had been telling her as far back as she could remember. As early as seventh grade, friends who came for sleepovers would go all tongue-tied when Cal entered the room. "Your brother is so hot," they'd moan as soon as he left. Sometimes she wondered if certain girls were there to hang with her or to catch a glimpse of Cal.

The more she thought about it, the more she wondered how much attention this could get. A great-looking guy from a nice town—it was the kind of story the media loved. All-American boy, everything going for him until one night...

Em swept her wavy hair over one shoulder and held the camera so it captured her best angle. She'd begin by talking about Cal, her happiest memories: him teaching her to ride a two-wheeler, taking her and her friends for smoothies the afternoon he got his driver's license. Then she'd cut to photos of him. She already knew which ones she'd use. Her followers would "like" and share the post. It would become a movement with hashtags like FindCal! or Where'sCal? that went viral. Her brother would be found and she'd be a hero.

And when that happened maybe she could finally step out of Cal's shadow and into the light.

7

MONDAY, DECEMBER 15
IVY

Ivy hated liars. Discovering that someone had willfully deceived her took her straight back to her childhood home, to her mother standing amid the chaos, swearing she'd "tidy up."

Because it was all she'd known, Ivy hadn't realized her mother had a sickness. Until she was nine, Ivy thought of their house as a museum of sorts—not unlike the ones her class visited on field trips, a place where otherwise-useless items could be saved, treasured.

That ended the day Ivy invited the new girl, Sally Hobbs, to come home with her. Sally's blue eyes bugged as she took it all in: the shoebox towers, the stacked-up lawn furniture, the laundry baskets holding everything from duck sauce to bowling balls.

"Did you just move here too?" she asked. When Ivy said no, Sally frowned. "Then what is all this stuff?"

The sudden realization—*This isn't normal. We aren't normal*—hit Ivy hard and made her stomach hurt the way it had the previous spring when she'd lost the second-grade spelling bee to a boy.

"Just doing a little redecorating!" Ivy's mother called from the doorway, holding a lamp with a torn shade in one hand and a snow shovel in the other.

Ivy wanted to crawl under the mini-billiards table her mom had hauled home from the dump the previous weekend.

In the months that followed, whenever Ivy cried and asked her mother why they were living that way, her mom placed her palms on Ivy's wet cheeks and whispered soft, empty promises. "I'll tidy up tomorrow while you're at school. I will! You'll see. Then you can have a friend over. Maybe even a sleepover party? How does that sound?"

Ivy fell for it every time. Off she went, envisioning her Girl Scout troop tucked inside sleeping bags on their freshly vacuumed living room rug, watching a movie, passing bowls of popcorn back and forth. She allowed herself to believe her mother would—could—change. And then when her mom did, her father wouldn't be so angry, and they would be a regular family in a regular house.

But each afternoon, Ivy returned home and nothing had changed. That's not true. Often it was worse. Like the day she found a plastic birdbath in the living room teetering atop the turntable where she played *Revolver*, *Rubber Soul,* and other albums she kept hidden beneath her bed so they wouldn't disappear in the sea of debris.

That day, Ivy waded past garden gnomes and broken TV sets to get to the kitchen. She ate a pint of Rocky Road while standing because there was nowhere to sit. That was when it began: the insatiable hunger. Once she'd satisfied it, the full feeling in her belly offered an odd sense of calm and control… until it turned on her just as quickly, leaving shame and nausea in its place.

As Ivy stood beside the kitchen sink in her grown-up home, she felt consumed by that familiar craving for comfort amid chaos. Instead of packing away the leftover roasted chicken and vegetables from dinner, she reached for the Chick-Fil-A sauce Max adored. The bottle made that embarrassing farting sound as she squirted a fat dollop onto her plate and began swiping Brussels sprouts through the orange puddle. She popped them into her mouth until the skin on her cheeks strained, exhaling through her nose, surrendering to what her body needed in that moment.

Jane had lied to her.

Ivy fiddled with the necklace her friend had given her for her most recent birthday. Two interlocking circles on a thin gold chain.

"It's a symbol of our connectedness," Jane had said.

Typically, Ivy wore a brown leather cord with a silver pendant embossed with the words "Just Breathe" that she'd picked up at a yoga retreat.

"You have one and I have one." Jane had proudly plucked a matching circle necklace from beneath her light summer sweater and let it fall between her breasts. "If anyone asks where you got it, send them to my website."

So, was it a gift or was Ivy a walking advertisement?

Leaning against her kitchen counter, she twisted the delicate chain and then released it before she broke it in frustration. She'd spent much of the day trying to get in touch with Brad to make sure he'd called the doctor about his knee. She knew her son. He'd put off getting it checked out and try to push through, re-aggravating his injury with every step. Brad's history with pain meds was her larger worry.

He hadn't answered her texts or responded to her voicemails. She couldn't imagine he'd gone to work in that condition. But her big-hearted boy never wanted to let anyone down. Still, he'd sounded so out of it on the phone the night before, if he lived within a reasonable driving distance, Ivy would've gone straight there and taken him to urgent care.

When Brad finally got back to her around six p.m., he told her two cops had just left his condo. They'd been sent by Jane, he said. Jane, who told the police she hadn't heard from Cal in days—the same Jane who'd assured her not even twenty-four hours earlier that Cal had called for Wade's birthday.

Liar.

Ivy squeezed more sauce onto her plate and swiped a roasted carrot through it. With each crunch, her heart beat faster, a rising mix of anger and indigestion. None of it made sense.

The back door opened and a rush of cold air blasted the exposed part of her shins where her stretch pants didn't meet her ankle socks. Jean-Claude pranced in, nails clicking against the tile floor. Ivy dropped into a kitchen chair and watched the little dog shake off snowflakes while Greg hung the leash on its usual hook. She glanced at the clock. It was after eight p.m.

"You were gone a while." Ivy licked her lips. The grease and salt tasted gritty and delicious but a familiar heaviness was already settling in her stomach. "I was afraid you'd slipped on ice. I was just about to look for you."

Greg removed his old brown barn jacket. It was much too light for the weather. He needed to get a good parka before the trip. *God, the trip—was it still on?* It was all they'd talked about since October when she and Jane had booked it, thrilled by the idea of seeing their sons and savoring the landscape's wild beauty.

Ivy wiped her mouth with a napkin. Why would Jane pretend Cal had called when he hadn't? How many other lies had Jane told over the course of their friendship? Ivy shook her head, scolding herself. If something was going on with Cal, couldn't she find the grace to extend her longtime friend a pass? Wasn't Cal's safety the most important thing?

"I walked over to Wade and Jane's," Greg said.

Ivy's insides churned. She was stuffed and yet she wished she had a few more Brussels sprouts. Jean-Claude danced around her feet, whimpering like a little bulging-eyed beggar.

"I had to ring the bell three times." Greg opened the canister where they kept the quinoa dog treats Ivy baked every Sunday. He waited until Jean-Claude sat nicely before rewarding him. They watched the dog run off to devour the biscuit in private. *He'll be back for more*, Ivy thought, *just like me.*

"Wade finally answered the door," Greg continued.

He'd always been a painfully slow storyteller. Ivy wanted to leap from her chair and shake him, but she was too full to move.

"And what did you say?" She bit her thumb, her tongue searching for any sauce trapped beneath her nail. "And what did he say?"

Greg leaned against the counter, arms crossed. "He said, 'Now's not a good time,'" Greg scoffed, "as if I were there to ask him for a favor."

Ivy winced. "How did he look?"

"He looked vaguely pissed—same as he always does. I

told him we're worried about Cal and to let us know if there's anything we can do to help."

Ivy nodded. Their friendship with the Whitaker family spanned nearly two decades. Ivy knew fundamentally she and Jane were very different. Jane had been raised in some fancy-pants town in Connecticut while Ivy had grown up inside a veritable yard sale with a roof in South Jersey. Yet as their boys grew closer, they had too. In time, they introduced their husbands. Wade was more reserved, but Greg was like an Irish setter in tan chinos. Even-tempered and friendly, he brought out the best in Wade—Jane always said so.

During elementary and high school, Cal had dinner with them a few nights a week. He complimented Ivy on her cooking and asked if she could recommend any yoga poses to help him stretch his shoulders during football season. Even after everything happened with Brad's torn ACL, Ivy never stopped thinking of Cal as her third son.

He'd always been free-spirited, someone who followed whatever moved him in that moment. Plus, he was smart and handsome. The combination made him seem almost invincible. That's what made it hard to believe he could be in any real danger. Still, if something was wrong, she and Greg would be there to support the Whitakers every step of the way.

"And then what did Wade say?" Ivy studied her husband, his forehead creasing in an uncharacteristic frown, lips clamped in a thin line. He hadn't moved since tossing Jean-Claude the treat.

"He said Jane was on the phone with the police, trying to find out what they've learned so far, what their next steps might be. She wants them to send crews to search the mountain."

"Oh my God." Ivy swallowed the barely digested vegetables that backed up into her mouth.

Jane has to be losing her mind. Her friend could be so private, so careful about safeguarding information about her family. Would Jane even turn to her for comfort or would she attempt to struggle through this potential nightmare alone?

Ivy never would've known about Emerson's shoplifting incident a few summers back if their mutual friend Betsy hadn't been in that boutique when Em got caught.

It was only after a few glasses of wine that Jane let her mask drop. They'd been stumbling home from their book club when Jane confided about Cal's high school gambling trouble. Even then, Ivy figured Jane only shared it because she assumed Brad already told her and Greg. It wasn't Jane leaning on a friend so much as it was Jane attempting to establish the narrative: her poor, naive Cal had been lured by the promise of easy money, duped by older boys, unable to stop himself because of the same competitive spirit that enabled him to lead the football team to the state championship.

For a moment, Ivy wondered if Cal's gambling had anything to do with his sudden disappearance. She remembered Brad complaining about Cal missing a rent payment, having to sell his car, borrow money.

Ivy looked at her husband and thought about floating that theory past him. Greg had a calming effect on people. He'd assure her she was just jumping to conclusions out of concern. He'd say something like, "When I was twenty-three, I followed Phish for an entire summer—probably called my parents once the whole time. Cal'll turn up. Give him a few days." But her husband's posture, arms crossed, unmoving, made her realize he had more to tell her.

Was she ready to hear it? She wanted to wait. She'd offer to make them a pot of tea— maybe ginger-peach to calm her nerves and soothe her stomach. She had a box of Nilla Wafers stashed in the cabinet above the fridge. She'd open those. But before she could stand, Greg spoke again.

"I told Wade they know where to find us if they need anything. I wanted to say something like, 'Hey, I'm sure it's all going to be fine. Remember what we were like at that age?' but he had that look, the one he'd make when he disagreed with a ref." Greg clenched his teeth, furrowed his brow, imitating Wade. "I half-expected him to shut the door in my face so I said goodnight and started to walk away. All of a sudden, he calls my name." Greg stopped and rubbed his chin.

Ivy brought her hands together in prayer pose and softened her gaze, focusing on the dishwasher's red indicator light.

"He said, 'Look, Greg. There is one thing you could do. Have your son tell the police why the fuck he's got Cal's phone.' Then he stepped inside and slammed the door."

Ivy's stomach lurched and she covered her mouth with her hands.

They'd seen Wade argue with coaches and snap at waiters, but his rudeness had never been directed at them. Ivy knew he and Jane had to be sick with worry. There was nothing worse than believing that your child was in trouble.

She thought back to the brief conversation she'd had with her son. Brad had sounded winded, almost like he'd gone for a run, but she knew that wasn't possible—not on that knee. She'd asked him what the police said and if he'd talked to anyone who'd seen Cal. It had been hard to get him to focus enough to answer her questions. At one point, he changed the subject to ask the best way to unclog a sink. When she said he sounded strange and brought up the pain meds, he'd sworn he hadn't taken anything stronger than Tylenol.

As Ivy looked down at her plate, bare but for a smudge of orange sauce, her subconscious served up an unpleasant thought: Jane wasn't the only person lying to her.

8

TUESDAY, DECEMBER 16
BRAD

Brad sat in the empty waiting area, leg outstretched. The place had a smell, a funk that made him think of withered skin after a cast came off. Or maybe that's just where his mind went after so many visits to orthopedists.

The sheer effort of getting there had worn him out. He hadn't realized how bad the storm had been, how much snow had fallen. He had to take an Uber to get back to the parking lot where he'd left his car Saturday afternoon. Then he spent fifteen minutes cleaning off the front and back windshields. Folding his leg enough to get it inside his Highlander sent sparks of pain shooting up his leg. He was glad he'd taken another couple pills before leaving the condo. But that, combined with the car's warmth and steady motion, made it nearly impossible to stay awake.

Through the haze of pain meds, the world looked kind of cool: the starkness of it, the contrast of shining black roads and the blinding white of the landscape. It reminded him of a Christmas card or the puzzles of wintry scenes he and his mom used to do together on snow days.

His mom. That's why he'd made the appointment. It seemed like the only way to get her to stop text-bombing him. He was glad he'd called the doctor's office when he did. Someone had just canceled. "Otherwise you'd be looking at a couple weeks' wait," the receptionist had said.

For a second after she'd said it, Brad felt like maybe his luck was changing. Then his mind returned to Cal.

Hanlon had called a few hours after he showed up at the condo Monday afternoon. He asked if Brad had heard from his roommate or remembered anything that might be helpful. He hadn't.

"How are the calls going?" The young cop's tone was upbeat. "Friends, neighbors, anyone got any leads? Tell you something we can use?"

"Not yet." Dazed as he was, Brad hadn't made any calls.

That conversation coupled with his throbbing leg made it difficult to sleep. He didn't want to keep dipping into Cal's stash, but what choice did he have?

As he waited to be taken to an exam room, he closed his eyes, trying to block the sound of Kenny G piped in overhead mixing with Rachael Ray on the TV in the corner. He was drifting off when his phone rang. He swiped to answer without looking at the caller ID.

"Hello?" His voice was a growly whisper from not talking to anyone other than Donna, the receptionist, all day.

"Hey, Brad! Officer Hanlon here."

Fuck!

"Hey," Brad parroted.

"So Lieutenant Lynch and I are hoping you can come down to the station for a bit and help us sort out a couple things."

Brad sat straighter and cleared his throat, suddenly

aware of the sweat pooling in his armpits. "I'm at the doctor's right now."

"Excuse me!" Donna whined. "Read the sign, please."

Brad's eyes followed her finger to a poster of a cell phone with a big black X over it.

Brad gestured toward his leg.

"Sorry." She didn't look sorry as she scowled at him. "Either take it outside or hang up."

Brad struggled to his feet, muttering, "Are you fucking serious?"

"What was that?" Hanlon asked.

"Hang on a sec." Brad hobbled to the door.

The air outside was arctic. He'd left his hat and gloves under the chair in the waiting room so he shoved his free hand into his coat pocket and tried to hear the cop over the whipping wind.

"...so by four then?" Hanlon was saying.

"What? Can you repeat that?"

"You can be here by four?"

"Like I have a choice?" Brad wanted to quip. "Yeah, I guess," he said and turned toward the rapping on the glass door behind him. A woman in pale blue scrubs with a light-up candy cane necklace was waving him inside. "I have to go."

"See you soon," Hanlon chirped. "Drive safe."

"Bradley Chapman?" the woman asked.

"You know it's me. I'm the only one here," he nearly snapped. The mellow high from the pills seemed to wear off faster with each dose. He thought of what his mother would suggest and took a deep inhalation followed by a long exhalation. "Yup, that's me," he said, offering a half-smile, suddenly aware of how chapped and crusty his lips were.

"Got a bum wheel there, I see." She nodded at his leg. "I'm Linda, a nurse. Follow me, and don't forget your stuff." She pointed to his hat and gloves beneath the chair.

Couldn't she just pick them up? Every extra movement made Brad grit his teeth. He put all his weight on his left leg and bent to collect his things before trailing her down a narrow hallway to a rectangular room.

"Gown open in the back. Have a seat. Dr. Brown will be in shortly."

Brad slid off his sweatpants. His bare thighs were goose-bumped from his brief time outdoors. Beneath the exam room's bright light, his knee looked grotesque, like the monstrous head of an alien. The swelling exaggerated the scar, a line that divided his leg and his life into "before" and "after" as his football career moved from the field to the sidelines.

Brad shimmied out the ledge at the end of the table that would support his legs and hoisted himself up. He lay flat, staring at the ceiling tiles, their squiggly little lines almost moving as Hanlon's voice floated through his mind. "Help us sort a couple things out." He'd made it sound like they'd be cleaning out an attic together.

Brad closed his eyes and only opened them when he heard a knock.

A man with thinning hair styled in a desperate combover peered down at Brad's busted knee. "Whoo-wee. You really did a number on it, didn't you, son?"

No shit.

"Dr. Brown." The man held out a pink hand. "Let's take a look."

The doctor's cold fingers grazed Brad's knee and he winced at the touch.

Shouldn't he be wearing latex gloves?

The doctor stepped away from the exam table to skim the endless forms Donna forced Brad to complete when he'd arrived.

"And this happened skiing?" Behind dandruff-flecked glasses, the doctor squinted. Did he think Brad made that up?

"Uh-huh." Brad nodded, wishing the guy would get on with it, but then he remembered his next stop: the police station.

"Re-injury isn't uncommon, but this looks... whoo-wee!" Dr. Brown said again, adding a low whistle. "What've you been taking for the pain, son?" He stared into Brad's eyes. Were his pupils dilated? Or were they small as pinpoints? What did the doctor already know?

"Just some Tylenol," Brad lied. "Actually, about that—any chance I can get something stronger?"

Cal's Altoids tins weren't nearly as full as they had been. In two days, Brad must've gone through a dozen or more pills and he didn't have the same relationship with Melinda—or any relationship with Melinda. In fact, he was pretty sure she had no idea who he was.

"You're better off staying away from that stuff," the doctor said. "People start and they can't stop. I'm sure you've seen the news. It's a crisis. A whatchamacallit—" he snapped his fingers "—an epidemic! Plus, they cause nasty side effects."

Now that he thought about it, Brad couldn't remember the last time he'd taken a shit. His appetite was off too, but that could've been nerves.

The doctor looked at Brad's paperwork again. "How's your insurance? Good? Decent? I'd like to send you for an

MRI. Get a better look at what's going on in there. Maybe start you on some PT. In the meantime, rest. Ice it every couple hours. Keep weight off it. You know the drill." He nodded as he stepped halfway out the door. "Donna at the front desk will get you squared away."

Brad tugged on his sweatpants, pissed that he was leaving without a prescription. At least he'd ask for a doctor's note to give his supervisor. He'd called out for the rest of the week.

Back in the waiting area, he wobbled toward Donna. Dr. Brown stood behind her, poking through rows of files. Brad was about to make another push for pain meds when Donna pointed at something over his shoulder. Brad turned to see Cal's face on the flat screen in the corner and the words: *Local Man Missing: Have You Seen Cal Whitaker?*

The shot was a close-up, a good one. Hell, Cal never took a bad picture. In this photo, he looked tan, his blue eyes practically neon. With his perfect smile, he could've been an actor in an ad for toothpaste.

"Oh my Lord, that poor baby. Would you look at that," Donna murmured, pressing a hand to her heart.

Dr. Brown picked up the remote and raised the volume. Brad held his breath.

"The family of a twenty-three-year-old man from New Jersey is asking for your help," an attractive, dark-haired newscaster said. "Callaway Whitaker went skiing Saturday afternoon and hasn't been seen since. The young man, who moved here in September, works at Wyndmere Crest ski resort. His mother reported him missing after days of being unable to reach him. Whitaker failed to show up for work Sunday and Monday."

"I hope they find him soon." Donna scratched her head with the eraser end of a pencil.

Nurse Linda appeared beside Brad. "I saw it this morning while I was drinking my coffee. Shame." She *tsk*-ed. "I've been praying for him ever since."

This is the same woman who couldn't bend over and pick up my hat and gloves.

"Good-looking kid," Donna said.

"Handsome as they come," Linda agreed.

"I looked a bit like that in my youth," Dr. Brown added.

Linda chuckled while Donna swatted the doctor's arm with a file folder.

"With temperatures expected to drop to near-record lows, anyone with information about the missing man is being urged to please come forward," the newscaster said before moving on to a story about Santa's visit to a local nursing home.

Donna opened the folder and shot an accusatory look at Brad, eyes narrowing. "Says here you work at Wyndmere. Do you know him?"

"Yup," Brad managed. He thought about Lynch saying people ramble when they're anxious and closed his mouth.

"Well, you ought to be out there looking for him!" Linda chastised.

"I can barely walk," Brad said.

"That's why you never ski alone." Dr. Brown shook his index finger. "Always go in pairs is what I tell my grandkids..."

"Oh please," Linda snorted. "This generation doesn't listen. Kids today only think of themselves."

. . .

THE SUN WAS SINKING, making it hard to spot patches of black ice on the winding road. Each time the car swerved, Brad thought about Cal reaching between his feet to slam the brakes Saturday on their way to the mountain.

Then he remembered Hanlon saying, "Drive safe," like he knew Brad was far from town. Had he told the cop where he was? The name of the doctor? Had he been followed?

Jesus, I'm becoming as paranoid as Cal. He switched on the radio, hoping the noise would quiet his mind.

THE POLICE STATION WAS A SQUAT, single-story, stone-front building. Since Brad moved to Wyoming, he'd passed it a bunch of times but never had any reason to go inside. It figured that within months of Cal showing up, he'd be summoned there.

Brad made an awkward hop from his car to the door, his leg screaming as the pain meds wore off.

Over the squawk of radios and ringing phones, he told a woman at the front desk, "Brad Chapman, here to see Officer Hanlon."

She sized him up, then scowled like she'd been expecting someone better. "Have a seat." She waved her hand toward a bench.

"I'll stand." Getting in and out of the car and on and off the doctor's exam table had left Brad weak and shaky.

"Roommate's here," the woman said into a phone.

Roommate. Is that how they referred to him? Was this their only case? Or suddenly their biggest?

Hanlon strode down the hall. Brad envied his easy gait. The young cop seemed more official, less boyish in this, his natural habitat.

"Brad! Thanks for coming down." Hanlon shook his hand as casually as if Brad had shown up in his backyard for a Fourth of July barbecue. "If you'll follow me." Noticing Brad's leg, he added, "Take your time now."

Hanlon led him down a hall, making a series of quick lefts and rights until they came to a small room with a single window. Brad had lost his bearings on the way and couldn't tell if the window looked out on the parking lot or if it was like the ones on TV where a bunch of cops were standing on the other side watching him. His stomach churned as he slumped into a chair, sweaty and drained from the effort of moving.

"I'm gonna grab Lieutenant Lynch," Hanlon said. "Want anything? Coffee? Tea? Water?"

"Nah, I'm good, thanks." Brad wasn't good. In fact, that shit he hadn't taken in days felt like it was suddenly locked and loaded. Was it nerves? He'd never so much as had a parking ticket. Now he was here. Because of Cal.

The ticking of the clock on the far wall seemed to grow louder the longer he waited. It felt like forever since Hanlon went in search of Lynch. Was it a test? They were watching him, weren't they? His bowels clenched as he scanned the room for a camera and found one suspended from the ceiling in the corner. It was pointed right at him. Had Hanlon guided him to that chair or had he chosen it himself? Brad couldn't recall, and that happened seconds ago. Would he be able to remember how he'd answered the questions they asked when they were at his condo? He'd watched enough *Dateline* episodes to know that if you screw up even the slightest detail you're fucked.

Hanlon had left the door open and the smell of hazelnut coffee wafting in added to Brad's nausea.

"Sorry to keep you waiting." Lynch appeared, seeming taller, more intimidating in the narrow room. "So," he pulled up a seat across from Brad, "we haven't found your roommate. Not that you asked."

Brad kept his face neutral and reminded himself that they were trying to rattle him.

"It struck me as odd that both times Officer Hanlon called you—last night and earlier today—you didn't ask about Cal." Lynch raised his bird-nest eyebrows. "Enjoying the suspense? Wanted to wait for a big reveal?"

"If you had any news you'd tell me, right?" Brad refused to let the cop bait him. "I was at the doctor's office."

"We won't take up much of your time. We've just got a couple questions we're hoping you can answer that may help us find Mr. Whitaker." Hanlon smiled like this would be easy-peasy.

Were they doing the good cop/bad cop routine? "Happy to help." Brad shifted in his seat. His back already hurt from the metal chair.

"So you and Mr. Whitaker went skiing together and you hurt your knee," Hanlon established.

Every time he said "Mr. Whitaker," Brad pictured Cal's dickhead dad in his pretentious Patagonia vest, his meaty hand clapping Brad's back, saying, "Couldn't hack it, huh? College isn't for everyone."

Brad had wanted to punch Wade's smug face. He'd been standing in Brad's living room at the Super Bowl party the Chapmans hosted every year, insulting him while shoving one of his mother's sweet potato skins in his mouth.

Brad tensed at the memory and fought to keep his hands from curling into fists.

"You called for help, but you didn't call Cal," Hanlon continued.

Brad nodded. "He didn't have his phone."

"And you knew this how?" Lynch asked.

"I saw him toss it on the couch before we left."

"Why didn't he bring it with him?" Hanlon frowned.

"It was dead. Cal could never remember to charge it."

Lynch turned to Hanlon, who looked up from his legal pad.

"When you called for help, you didn't mention that Cal was with you," Lynch continued. "Why was that?"

"I'd just blown out my knee," Brad said. "I was freezing my ass off. I told them on the way to my place. They asked why I was alone and I said I wasn't, my roommate was there but he was way ahead of me."

"If we ask the fellas who rescued you, think they'll remember that?"

"I don't see why they wouldn't." Brad's skin turned hot and prickly. Had he used deodorant that morning? He couldn't remember but it definitely didn't smell like he had.

"When you got home Saturday night, did you check to make sure Cal was there?" Hanlon asked.

"His door was closed. I figured he was asleep."

"How'd you think he got home?" Hanlon continued.

"I didn't know," Brad said.

"Didn't know or didn't care?" Lynch leaned forward. His coffee breath made Brad's nose twitch.

"Was that typical?" Hanlon asked. "Cal finding his own way back?"

"What we're getting at here is you knew your friend didn't have a phone, didn't have a car," Lynch ticked these off on his skinny fingers, "but you didn't think to look for him. Something about that doesn't sit right."

"I figured he bumped into someone. Went to a bar, a party."

Lynch shot another glance at Hanlon.

"Look," Brad's head began to pound from trying to anticipate their questions, "I didn't even want to go in the first place. My knee was in bad shape before that run. By the time I got home, I was wrecked."

"If your knee was bothering you so bad, why go skiing? Especially with that forecast?" Hanlon asked.

"Cal and I had been talking about it for weeks. He really wanted to—"

"Cal boss you around a lot? Make you do things you didn't want to do?" Lynch sat back and stretched his long legs. His eyelid twitched. Was that a wink? Was Lynch implying there was something sexual between him and Cal?

"It wasn't like that!" Brad's voice filled the small space. Lynch and Hanlon exchanged another look he couldn't decipher.

Stay cool, he told himself, his belly gurgling. He folded his arms, eyes flicking to the wall clock. 5:20 p.m. He'd been there forty minutes; it had to end soon.

"Getting back to your knee." Lynch pointed. "How'd you say you injured it—originally?"

Brad took a deep breath. Football was the short answer; Cal was the long one. He recalled the pain shooting in every direction after Cal blasted him sideways during what was supposed to be an easy practice. He could still hear the *pop* before an ocean-like roar filled his head. He'd tried to stand, his body in shock, moving purely from memory, only to crumple beneath the purply-blue September sky. Looking back, it always struck Brad as fitting, like he'd watched the sun literally set on his football career.

As he laid there writhing, artificial turf tickling the back of his head, Cal stood above him, laughing, reaching out a hand, saying, "C'mon, man, get up. You're wasting daylight."

What a dick.

Brad glanced from Lynch to Hanlon and let out a long exhale. "High school football. Running plays. Long time ago. I barely remember it."

Lynch stared at his giant boots. Was it possible he knew Cal had caused the injury that ultimately killed Brad's dream of playing college ball? Brad's parents had always considered it an unfortunate accident. Were the Whitakers aware of what happened? If so, Brad imagined Wade saying something douchey like, "You don't want to get injured, take up basketweaving, not football."

Would the cops and Cal's family think Brad had been holding a grudge?

"You and Cal argue much?" Lynch asked.

"Nope," Brad said.

"Really?" Hanlon questioned. "Me and my roommates—"

"Neighbors said they heard yelling a few nights back," Lynch interrupted.

"Must've been the TV." Brad's cheeks burned. He knew which night they were talking about. Cal had asked him for a hundred bucks.

"No way. You already owe me over a grand," Brad had told him.

"Listen, shit is about to get bad if you don't give it to me," Cal had shouted.

"You should've thought about that before you placed another bet," Brad yelled back.

They'd been in the kitchen, Brad attempting to fix the drain Cal had clogged, Cal slamming cabinets before storming out.

"So, no arguments, no disagreements at all then?" Hanlon asked.

"I mean, not outside the usual—who drank all the beer and didn't buy more or who was supposed to take out the trash."

Lynch unwrapped a cough drop and pushed it between his lips. "Know anybody who might have a problem with your roommate?"

How much time have you got, Brad thought but instead said, "Not that I can think of."

Should he mention Cal's gambling? The black SUV that Cal suspected had trailed them to the mountain? Was it weird to bring it up now? Was it even a thing? *Fuck!* He never should've come here without a lawyer. But wasn't hiring one the first sign of guilt?

It went on like that for another thirty minutes, same questions posed a million different ways like one of those personality tests that claim to know which career you should pursue.

This is a game to them, Brad thought. *They're testing me, trying to get me to lose my cool so they can paint me as a guy with anger issues, a guy who left his best friend for dead. They have nothing except Cal's mom's foot up their asses.*

The ache in his leg and back stole what was left of his patience. He'd had enough. As soon as there was a lull between questions, Brad stood, hoping they wouldn't notice the trembling in his good leg.

"Look," he said. "I've given you all I got. Cal's a grown man. I'm his roommate, not his nanny. If I hear from him, I'll call you."

Lynch rose to his full height. He was maybe six foot five, a good four inches taller than Brad, maybe eight more than Hanlon. He flicked the cough drop from one side of his mouth to the other. It clicked against his teeth.

"You told the folks over at Wyndmere you won't be in for the rest of the week." Lynch frowned. "Not planning on leaving town, are you?"

Brad shook his head. "Gonna take it easy. Doctor's orders."

"Good, 'cause if Cal doesn't turn up soon, we're probably going to be seeing a lot more of each other." One side of Lynch's mouth turned up in a crooked smile, revealing his silver fillings.

What evidence did they have? None. Still, if they hooked him up to a polygraph and asked those same questions—*You and Cal argue much? Know anybody who might have a problem with your roommate?*—he'd be fucked.

He put his head down and concentrated on taking one step, then another. He needed to reach the door, then the hallway, and finally his car so he could get the hell out of there. He was twisting the doorknob when Lynch cleared his throat.

"If we could circle back a second, Brad, I've got a riddle for you."

Brad turned and placed his hand on the table for support.

"You know who doesn't ask if their roommate's been found?" Lynch raised those ratty eyebrows.

Brad shrugged. "Who?"

The cop smiled with both sides of his mouth this time and raised his hands in finger-guns. "Someone who already knows the answer."

9

WEDNESDAY, DECEMBER 17
JANE

Cal was alive, Jane knew it. If something catastrophic had happened to her child, she would've sensed it. He was somewhere; they just needed to find him. She'd hold that positive thought and picture his safe return. That's what Ivy would do.

Ivy. Jane hadn't responded to her calls or texts. At first, she ignored the messages because she didn't know how to explain her lie. She couldn't say, "I wanted you to stop asking about 'the Cal situation' so I told you he called." That would only make it more awkward.

She could've doubled down and said Wade lied to her so she'd stop asking if he'd heard from Cal, but digging in deeper felt wrong too. So she'd left Ivy's messages unanswered. It was so strange. Unnatural.

Since the day Ivy invited Jane and Cal to come to their home after preschool so the boys could play, the women had been practically inseparable. Jane usually smiled when she recalled that afternoon. Ivy's mom had recently brought her a fondue set. On the Chapmans' deck, beneath a canopy of autumn leaves, Jane, Ivy, and their sons had speared and plunged berries and banana slices into a pot of silky semi-sweet chocolate. Hours later, Jane and Cal floated home, giddy from the double high of sugar and new friends.

Ivy had a way of making light moments more fun and dark ones bearable.

Jane had wanted to set things right between them, then her husband slammed the door in Greg's face.

When she and Wade spoke with police, they were advised not to interact with the Chapmans until the officers knew more—in particular, why Brad had Cal's cell phone and why he'd waited an entire day before telling anyone Cal hadn't come home Saturday night.

Up until Monday when police described her son's oldest friend as "less-than-forthcoming," Jane had had a soft spot for Brad. It couldn't have been easy growing up alongside her son—the inevitable comparisons, Cal always coming out on top: better-looking, smarter, the stronger athlete. It must've been especially difficult in high school, watching Cal excel at football while Brad limped along the sidelines. Then he dropped out of college. Ivy always swore Brad was "in a good place" now, that he was "following his bliss," but of course she'd say that. What parent wanted to admit their child was floundering? And Max wasn't exactly thriving either, living back at home—jobless.

Jane had tried Brad's phone a half-dozen times Monday morning before calling the police. He was obviously avoiding her—that alone was suspicious. How many nights had he slept at their home, sat at their table for dinners, breakfasts? How many hours had she spent driving him and Cal to and from games and practices? Thousands. She'd practically raised him.

Sitting at her kitchen island, she stared at her cell phone, scrolling through Ivy's old messages. Typically, not a day went by without them texting. Now it had been two. She wanted to press her friend, get her to force Brad to tell them everything he knew, but Wade told her not to interfere. "Let the police do their job," he'd said.

Jane held her landline phone to her ear while the airline rep checked to see about exchanging their existing tickets. Originally, they planned to fly to Wyoming Monday, but there was no way Jane could wait through the weekend at home feeling frantic and helpless if Cal were still missing. She'd have gladly purchased new flights. Who cared about money at a time like this? Wade cared. He insisted she at least try to make the switch, but with holiday travel underway and snowstorms pounding the Northeast and Midwest, options were limited.

The night before, Jane had begged a different airline rep for help. "We don't need to sit together," she'd offered even though she was a nervous flyer and liked to hold a family member's hand on take-off and landing.

"Our system is down right now," the agent said. "You'll have to call back tomorrow."

"But I need—" Jane began before she realized the rep had hung up.

She'd barely slept. Black coffee and a steadily rising panic were the only things keeping her upright.

"It shouldn't be this hard to find three seats," she'd raged that morning.

Emerson, looking bright-eyed, her makeup flawless, said, "Don't change my flight. I can't go now."

"Why not?" Jane demanded. She knew Em and Cal had grown apart but she wanted to believe the teary video Em posted asking her followers to send "good vibes" that her "big brother Cal is found safe ASAP!" was genuine rather than another ploy to get more likes and shares.

"I have finals." Em pierced a grape with her fork. "Colleges are going to see my transcript. I can't just bail."

Jane's first thought was, *This is a family emergency! Your teachers will understand!* but then she wondered if maybe finding two seats would be easier than three. She didn't like the idea of leaving her daughter home alone, but what would Em do in Wyoming other than stare at her phone and complain about the cold?

"Ma'am?" the airline customer service agent said. "Hello? Are you there?"

"Yes!" Jane jumped off the stool and clutched the corner of the cool marble island to steady herself. "Yes? Did you find something?"

"No, I'm still checking, but I see here you're not a member of our Skyways program. For every dollar you spend, you'll get triple the miles. Are you interested in learning more?"

"No." Jane's grip tightened around the phone. "My son is missing."

She hadn't said the words aloud to anyone other than the police, and the shock of hearing the sentence caused her to sink back onto the stool.

During Cal's college years, she'd read dozens of heartbreaking posts in Facebook groups. Parents shared warnings about accidental drug overdoses, hazing incidents, even mold in a dorm that had sent a student to the hospital. It seemed like a steady stream of horror stories. Safe behind her screen, Jane always said a silent prayer for these strangers and another for her family. There were moments when she couldn't wait for Cal to graduate, to return home, safe. Would he ever walk through the front door again, showering them with smiles and tales of his adventures?

In the silence, Jane feared the call had dropped and she'd need to start over but then she heard the agent stumble. "I'm —I'm so sorry. How old is he?"

"Twenty-three." Jane blinked back tears. Would this woman think she was ridiculous? He was an adult after all. "He went skiing with a friend," she rambled, "but then that friend came home without him." She hated how it sounded, like Cal was some loser another guy ditched.

More silence. "Well, I certainly hope he's okay," the customer service agent cooed.

Jane waited and wondered if the woman might empathize and add, "I'm a mother myself. I can't imagine what you're going through." Instead, she said, "I'm sorry, ma'am. I'm going to place you on another brief hold while I speak with my supervisor."

Jane bit her lower lip to keep from screaming. Over the sound of Tchaikovsky's "Waltz of the Flowers," the floorboards creaked. Wade paced upstairs as he spoke with police, demanding they escalate search efforts.

Against the countertop, Jane's cell phone vibrated. With each ping, she felt her heart leap, certain it was Cal. She clung to the hope that this was all a misunderstanding. Cal had so many friends. A young woman with a sweet southern accent had called in November to ask for his new address to send him a Christmas gift. Jane had provided it, beaming. So many people adored her son. Maybe he'd bumped into a high school or college classmate who was out west on vacation and he'd gone off with them to catch up. As much as she wanted to believe that, Jane wasn't stupid. People lost track of time for minutes, hours, not days.

When she'd bailed Cal out of his high school gambling debt, Jane had done it on the condition that he add her to his bank and credit card accounts. She'd logged in and studied them. There'd been no activity since Friday when Cal withdrew three hundred dollars, bringing his balance to six dollars and eighteen cents.

Her cell phone vibrated again. Over the past twenty-four hours, texts and calls had poured in from Emerson's friends' mothers who'd seen Em's video and were offering their help. They meant well, but Jane knew these women. Without even listening to their messages, she could hear their voices, some low and conspiratorial, others high-pitched, frantic. All would say some variation of, "Oh my God, Jane! Is it true? What happened?" They'd want details, a peek behind the curtain. If she obliged, they'd sit back and, regardless of what else was going on in their lives, they'd exhale and say, "At least I'm not dealing with *that!*"

She hadn't responded to any of them.

But this new message came through her business's website. It figured that now, at the worst moment of her life, she'd start getting orders. She opened the app. Daniel.

She set the phone against the counter and pressed her fingertips to the spot between her eyes. It didn't feel right keeping up a regular, ongoing correspondence, especially not now, with Cal missing.

Daniel's messages had become more frequent after the dinner they'd shared in October.

Great time! Let's do it again soon! He'd written the next morning.

She agreed it had been nice. Unsure of what she wanted,

she tried to keep things vague. *Yes! What a treat to take one last look at the ocean before winter!* and *So glad you chose that apple crisp for dessert. Yum!*

His response was immediate.

When can I see you?

Jane hadn't known what to do. Normally, she would've consulted Ivy, but her friend had basically warned her that "lunch" probably meant more than a meal in Daniel's eyes. And she hadn't told her about dinner, about how, at the end of the evening, Daniel had gone in for a hug, kissing her first on the cheek, then turning his head to place his lips on hers.

Gently, she'd pushed him back, "I'm sorry, I—"

He cut her off. "It's fine, Janie. Old high school Danny would be ecstatic he'd gotten this far. And, hey, I've waited this long..."

Daniel's interest was so genuine, his compliments so welcome, yet Jane didn't see a future with him—not really—and cheating wasn't in her DNA. She worried that by not cutting it off, she'd given him false hope, and now, she didn't have the energy to address it the way she needed to—not with everything else going on.

In her cold kitchen, Jane shook her head. Nothing else mattered. Finding Cal was her sole focus.

She stared straight at the fridge, at the picture of her family held in place by a magnet they'd picked up while vacationing on Martha's Vineyard. In the photo, Cal beamed in his cap and gown, his arm over her shoulder, Wade and Emerson on his other side.

Jane shivered as her phone pinged once more. She picked it up and opened the app. Daniel again.

She wished she could talk to Ivy. Younger women opened up to her friend, shared their problems, their secrets, inside the sanctuary of the yoga studio. Ivy was a great listener. But they weren't speaking and while Ivy wasn't one to say "I told you so," she'd do that smug thing where she wrinkled her nose and pursed her lips, and that was just as bad. Plus, she'd go home and tell Greg, and over one of her weird vegan casseroles they'd feel superior in their rock-solid marriage. The Chapmans did everything together, even the grocery shopping. Sometimes Jane spotted them holding hands like lovestruck teens while walking Jean-Claude.

The last time Daniel asked about getting together, Jane had tried a gentle brush-off. *Would love that! Maybe in the spring?*

What about next week? he'd countered.

She attempted a different strategy. *I'm so busy with my new business!*

Really? That's wonderful. I was afraid things were slow. Your posts get so little engagement.

His words had stung because they were true. She'd forgotten he had a tendency to be cutting when he felt ignored.

Sitting at the kitchen island, she read his latest:

I'm so sorry to see this about your son.
I'm here for you, Janie, whenever you need me.

Did he know about Cal from the news or from watching Emerson's videos? He was only being kind, supportive, yet the messages made her feel worse, her family's vulnerability, her failure as a mother, on full display.

"Ma'am?" The airline rep's sharp voice sliced through her thoughts. "Thanks again for your patience. We can get you on our last flight out Friday night. There's a layover in

Nashville, then another in Chicago. I'm afraid it's the best we can do."

"That's fine." Jane exhaled, relieved but shivering. Snow fell outside the kitchen window. Her hands and feet felt like blocks of ice.

"There's an additional charge of two hundred and fifty dollars."

"That's fine," she said again. It would be on the next credit card cycle. By then, they'd have found Cal and Wade would be forced to admit there were things more important than money.

"Per ticket," the agent added. "Will you have any oversized bags? Sporting gear? If so, that's a separate fee."

"Um, I—I don't know." How long would they be there? Jane couldn't imagine coming home without Cal. It wouldn't *be* home. She was about to say yes, put them down for one oversized bag, when Wade appeared in the kitchen doorway, his face slack, ashen.

He held up his cell phone. "The police think they found something."

10

WEDNESDAY, DECEMBER 17

IVY

Ivy and Greg had sex on Wednesdays and Saturdays, maybe one other time during the week if it were a birthday, anniversary, or they had the energy.

When the boys were little, Ivy'd read a self-help book that suggested this was the key to safeguarding intimacy while raising a family, and they'd stuck to this schedule ever since.

Ivy loved her husband but having him on top of her was the last thing she wanted. She'd felt sick all day and the night before too—pretty much from the moment she'd heard Brad's voice late Tuesday.

She'd started with, "Hey, honey, how'd your doctor's appointment go?" but he'd cut her off, blurting, "I need a lawyer."

Each time that sentence echoed inside her head, Ivy experienced a disorienting sensation as if she'd slipped into an alternate universe where madness replaced the peaceful life she'd tried so hard to cultivate.

A lawyer? How would they pay for that? And why

should they have to? There was no way Brad had done anything wrong. As a child, he'd fished ladybugs out of pool filters and placed them gently on the grass. Even in middle school, he never jumped off the bus without calling "Bye!" and "Thank you!" to the driver.

Cal was still missing, yes, but why were the police hounding her son? They had no right to bring him in for questioning—and why, why had he answered without a lawyer present? Ivy had grown up watching *Charlie's Angels*, *L.A. Law*, even *Matlock* when her house had gotten too crowded and she'd gone to stay with her grandmother. She knew those things. Her son spent his childhood watching *Impractical Jokers* and sharing memes. He had no clue how the real world worked.

"I need a lawyer," Brad had repeated when Ivy fell silent. "So far I'm the last person to see him and I've got his phone!"

While that might be true, that didn't mean Brad was guilty of anything. Cal could be anywhere. Ivy thought back to the summer the boys were seventeen. They'd just gotten their licenses and planned to drive to Maine to hike and camp for the long July Fourth weekend. Brad had been looking forward to it for weeks. Hours before they were due to leave, while Brad packed the tent and folding chairs and cleaned the coolers, Cal got invited to their classmate Quinn Huntley's beach house.

"I'm sorry," Jane had said when she called to do Cal's dirty work. "It's just that—he'd kill me if I told you—but he's had a crush on Quinn all year. The Huntleys' place is in Montauk, right on the water. I heard there's even a hot tub on the roof. Can you imagine? I told Cal to send me pics. I'll forward them."

"But Brad's been so excited—"

"Maybe Max can take him?" Jane had interrupted.

Take him, like Brad was some sad little tag-along.

Cal was an opportunist. It wouldn't have surprised Ivy if he'd found himself a sugar mama at the resort and jetted off to Cabo to ring in the new year while her son had his life and reputation destroyed.

Ivy told Brad she'd do her best to find him an attorney. She'd spent the day reviewing websites, making calls.

Now she sat on her bedroom floor in lotus pose, attempting to send all her positive energy to her son, but her mind wandered and the heaviness in her belly was a constant distraction. While Greg walked the dog, she'd scarfed down a canister of Pringles and a tub of onion dip. Her breath could've toppled a rhino but that didn't stop Jean-Claude from climbing into her lap and licking her face.

"Stop, JC," she whispered, not meaning it, tears stinging her eyes. Hadn't she struggled enough in her childhood? Shouldn't these be the easy years? Each day things seemed to get harder, stranger. Earlier that afternoon she'd received a call from her mother's neighbor, Florence Reilly, who'd phoned to say she'd seen Ivy's mom lugging a tricycle into her home that morning.

Apparently, the news of Cal and Brad hadn't traveled to South Jersey yet. In Ivy's town of Oak Hill, it was quickly gaining traction thanks to Emerson's videos, the story shifting from "Where's Cal Whitaker?" to "Who Is Brad Chapman: The Roommate Who Failed to Report Cal Whitaker Missing?"

Perhaps Florence had seen the headlines and was, in her own weird way, trying to offer Ivy a distraction.

"You should come by, check in," Florence had said. "When was the last time you were here, dear?"

"I'm already dealing with my own pile of shit right now," Ivy wanted to shout, but instead said, "Mom and I meet at diners these days." She stopped short of adding "on the advice of my therapist." It was all about establishing boundaries, Dr. Llewelyn insisted.

In the comfort of a clean, vinyl booth, Ivy and her mother stuck to neutral topics: the boys, the weather, Ivy's yoga practice, her mom's favorite game shows. After she'd watch her mother drive away, her wave barely visible above the newspapers and puzzles piled to her hatchback's roof, Ivy would gobble the emergency box of Teddy Grahams she kept under the driver's seat and weep before getting back on the parkway.

"I understand," Florence had said, reasonably, "but not everyone is as sympathetic. I saw Kathleen Garvin today. She said your mother hasn't moved a thing—not even after the Board of Health citation. She's very—"

"Let me see what I can do. Talk soon!" Ivy had hung up before Florence could point out other issues like missing roof shingles and snow-covered sidewalks.

Thinking about the one-two punch of Brad and her mother made Ivy's stomach churn. She tried to call out sick but when she phoned the yoga studio, Piper answered immediately, her voice giddy, "Your classes are packed, my friend. Namaste!"

And so Ivy went, her spirits lifting. Maybe word was spreading that she was a good teacher, a calming presence in an increasingly chaotic world. When she arrived to find a mix of neighbors and women she'd never seen there before, it slowly hit her. *They're here to gawk at me.* Was she paranoid or were they scrutinizing her every asana?

She thought of Emerson's latest video. She had to hand it to the girl, she was a social media whiz, narrating over a montage of photos of Cal looking clean-cut, handsome. The few she'd included of Brad—a.k.a. "Cal's roommate"—weren't the best. Ivy had no idea where Emerson had found these images. With his gaze never directly at the camera, his mop of unruly hair and ruddy cheeks, her son looked sloppy, shifty. Emerson wasn't necessarily accusing Brad of anything, but there was a definite undertone. She was stoking a slow-burning fire, feeding it. Her questions—"Why does my brother's roommate have his phone?" and "Why didn't Cal's roommate alert someone Saturday night when he didn't come home?"—acted as kindling.

At the end of each class, Ivy typically went around the room and dabbed peppermint oil on students' temples or the base of their neck with their consent. Today, she'd hung back, afraid to get too close for fear of them popping up from corpse pose like gophers on a golf course to ask, "What's the latest with Cal?" "Is it true Jane isn't speaking to you?" "What's really going on with your son?"

No one said or did anything unusual but as they left, she felt their side-glances, their judgments. Their thoughts were as clear as if they appeared in cartoon bubbles above their heads: *Brad should've said something sooner. How could you have raised such a thoughtless young man?*

In the privacy of her bedroom, the tears Ivy had held in all day slid down her cheeks. Jean-Claude licked them too. She ached to carry him to the bed, melt between the sheets, and sleep for a decade. *Wake me when it's over,* she wanted to whisper to Greg, who appeared now in the doorway.

They'd barely spoken at dinner, just sat there picking at the cauliflower stroganoff and lentil salad, the weight of their new reality ruining their appetites.

Ivy wiped her face with the sleeve of her sweatshirt. "Do you think I should go out there early? Like ASAP?" After nearly three decades together, she and her husband could toss out sentences without context or explanation, knowing the other would understand.

Greg walked to the bed, unbuttoned his plaid shirt, and removed his pants while Ivy kissed the top of Jean-Claude's bristly head.

"I don't know." Greg slid off his socks. "Let me think about it." He headed toward the bathroom.

Ivy and Greg had almost always been on the same page when it came to parenting. They agreed it was best to let their sons work things out on their own. But look where that had gotten them. Brad had gone from needing an MRI to needing an attorney. He was on sick leave indefinitely. Would Wyndmere hold his position if he needed another surgery? By the time he recovered, the season would be over.

And Max—where did he keep running off to each night? And shouldn't he have found a new job by now? Ivy's stomach roiled.

Jane still hadn't reached out, and the more Ivy thought about it, the angrier she got at Wade for how he'd spoken to Greg: *Have your son tell the police why the fuck he's got Cal's phone.* She'd held out a foolish hope that Wade would call or text Greg to apologize when he got more answers, once he realized how ridiculous it was to think Brad had anything to do with this. But they hadn't heard from either of the Whitakers.

Ivy was certain they were on their way to Wyoming, if

they weren't there already. Her eyes burned. Maybe it was better for her to fly out next week as planned—unless Brad asked her to come sooner.

Greg returned, smelling minty from brushing his teeth. "It's Wednesday," he said, not in a playful, sexy tone, more with the way he'd state, "It's recycling day."

He snapped his boxers' elastic waistband and offered a half-smile. Maybe this was the comfort she needed. Maybe not even comfort, but a way to release the restless energy that made her want to eat an entire sleeve of Fig Newtons.

If she sat on top of him, rode him like a mechanical bull until she was sweaty and panting, would she finally be able to sleep?

"What about JC?" With her index finger, she stroked the dog's soft jowls.

"I thought the idea of an audience might turn you on." Greg winked.

Ivy knew he was trying to lighten the mood, but she frowned.

"I'll take him downstairs for a t-r-e-a-t," said Greg. As he pulled on a T-shirt, the dog scampered out of the room, bounding down the steps to the kitchen. "See that? I taught him how to spell. You're welcome."

Ivy returned his half-smile. Greg was worried too, she knew, both of them clinging to the hope that there was a simple explanation for Cal's disappearance, that it was only a matter of time before he was back, their lives restored to normal.

Ivy stood, stretched, and removed her bra. A chocolate morsel fell to the floor. She picked it up and popped it in her mouth before shutting off the overhead light. She folded down the comforter and switched on the lamp. Opening the nightstand drawer, she found the tube of jelly she now needed. She'd joked with Jane that menopause had left her vagina drier than two-day-old cornbread.

Jane hadn't laughed. "I wouldn't know anything about that," she'd said and changed the subject.

Ivy shouldn't have been surprised. Jane never talked about sex.

Between cool sheets, Ivy slid off her cotton underpants, their elastic shot. Then she unfastened the circle necklace Jane had given her and dropped it in the nightstand drawer.

As she waited for Greg, she stared at the ceiling and wondered if their friendship with the Whitakers would return to the way it had been. Probably not. But maybe that wasn't a bad thing.

11

FRIDAY, DECEMBER 19
BRAD

Brad sat on his couch, holed up like a fucking fugitive. He hadn't left the condo since he got back from the police station Tuesday night. He'd closed the vertical blinds to block the view beyond the sliding doors, convinced every flash of light was the high beams of a cop car.

Since the local media began covering Cal's disappearance, people had gathered out there. Despite the insane cold, they stood in the parking lot holding battery-powered lanterns and white posterboards that screamed "Where's Cal??" "Find Cal!" "We Love You, Cal!"

Just after dusk Wednesday, a young woman from Wyndmere's rental shop sang "Bring Him Home." Brad recognized it from the Les Misérables soundtrack his mother played when he and Max were little. Brad had jacked up the TV volume and attempted to space out to a home renovation show. Even with the demolition and the overly loud commercials, he heard the crowd growing, buzzing like a bee hive.

He needed to leave the condo in twenty minutes and dreaded limping past the mob. More than anything, he wanted to swallow a couple pills and feel his body become loose, liquidy.

But he had to get up, shower, or at least brush his teeth. His mother had found a lawyer and gotten him an appointment. Brad didn't think he needed some hot-shot attorney like Saul Goodman or Johnnie Cochran—not at this point—but he feared his options were limited in a resort town. He imagined firms with ridiculous names like Cowboy Justice or Giddyup Legal. Also, his parents weren't exactly loaded. He worried he'd end up with a clueless rookie or an old bird coasting toward retirement.

When Ivy called Thursday morning, she'd said the guy was a sole practitioner.

"He's primarily a real estate attorney."

"What?" Brad spat out his Gatorade.

"Take a deep breath," Ivy exaggerated inhaling and exhaling, "and let me finish. He's seen the news and he's willing to talk to you. He sounds like a nice man."

"A nice man?"

"Eager to help, I mean. He can see you tomorrow afternoon. He said—hold on, I wrote it down here—he said, 'Time is of the essence.'"

"No shit!" Brad wanted to bark, but instead grumbled, "Whatever. Okay. Thanks, Mom."

Brad had heard rustling and pictured his mother opening a bag of rice cakes or carrots. The last thing he'd eaten was a can of corn he'd found at the back of the cabinet beside what looked like a fresh pile of mouse turds.

"Did you schedule that MRI?"

"I called. It's a six-week wait. They said they've got the machines but not the staff. I'm on a cancellation waitlist."

"Call every morning," Ivy crunched, then spoke with her

mouth full, "There's bound to be an opening, and maybe try other places, too, even if you have to drive a little farther."

"I will," Brad promised, wanting to add, "if I'm not in jail," but that was just self-pity talking. Lynch and Hanlon had nothing—nothing, in his opinion, except bad breath and big dreams of cracking a case that was getting more attention because Cal was an attractive white male and his hot sister had chosen this moment to try to become an internet star. But Brad had a lawyer now. His good leg bounced involuntarily as he wondered what the guy would ask, how he should answer. The thought was interrupted by his phone pulsing. A text from Max.

> Don't freak out. I'll talk to her.

Brad assumed he was referring to their mother, but in case he wasn't, he sent back:

> ??

> Emerson. Don't worry. I'm handling it.

> ??

Brad tapped again before opening Instagram.

On Tuesday night, a news station included a clip from one of Emerson's videos in their segment about Cal's disappearance. Brad hadn't seen her in a while and the first thing he noticed was that she looked a hell of a lot older than eighteen. Maybe it was the dark lipstick. To Brad, she'd always just been Cal's kid sister, the girl he'd taught to dive at the town pool. His mother had told him Em got caught shoplifting a few years ago. At first, he'd had a hard time believing it, but then he remembered how once she'd started filling out her bikini top, she'd flirt with guys at the snack bar and skip away with free ice cream or fries, pocketing her mom's cash.

He clicked on the video at the top of her page and chewed his bottom lip as he waited for it to load.

"Hey, everyone. I just wanted to say thank you. Your support means everything to me and my family." Emerson paused and fanned her face like she was trying to keep her tears at bay. "We still don't know where my brother Cal is."

It was nearly winter yet she was wearing a low-cut, white tank top. As she bowed her head, her hair spilled across her face. When she looked up to sweep it over her bare shoulder, her eyes were wet and wide.

"I know everyone is looking for Cal and we're so, so grateful, but there's one person who could, who really *should* be helping our family, and, well, he isn't." Her lips puffed out in a pout, her gaze so intense, it was like she was speaking directly to him.

Shut it off! Brad told himself but he couldn't look away. She was mesmerizing even as she was about to destroy him.

"Cal's roommate." Her voice was breathy, soft. "I wasn't going to say his name because that feels... I don't know... Icky. But I've seen some of you linking to news stories in the comments so I'll just say it: Bradley Chapman."

A burning filled Brad's belly—canned corn mixing with stomach acid. He'd be lucky if he didn't shit the couch.

"Brad," Em's voice cracked, "was Cal's friend, the guy he went skiing with, the last person to see him. We just found out..." Her shoulders rose then fell. "I... I don't know if I'm supposed to say this..." her eyes drifted toward the ceiling before looking straight into the phone again, "but whatever.

We just found out Brad did something super messed-up." Her nostrils quivered. "Sorry, I have to take a sec." She covered the camera with her hand.

The video stopped. Brad's heart flipped like it was on a trampoline. Pins and needles tingled up and down his arm as he stared in disbelief. The video had barely been up for an hour and already it had more than twenty thousand likes and hundreds of comments. Most of them were the same emoji—the one that some people said meant prayer hands while others insisted was a high-five. Like it mattered.

Brad dropped the phone in his lap. "Fuck!" he shouted, his voice ricocheting off the walls of the quiet condo. He picked up the phone and went back to her feed. A new video popped up.

"Hi, everyone!" She'd placed a dark green cardigan over the tank top, her makeup freshly retouched. "Sorry to go like that, but this is still super raw and so, so hard to process. What we found out was that Brad, the guy Cal's been living with—" she pressed her lips together like it was going to take real effort to push out the words "—placed an ad for a new roommate."

Holy shit! Brad paused it. How did she know that? Someone at the *Teton Tribune* must've told the Whitakers—and the cops, too, probably. The ad wasn't even live yet. He'd submitted the classified form online in early December when he'd had to cover Cal's portion of the rent—again. The ad wasn't due to run until mid-January. Brad was sure Cal could get that month's rent money from his mom during her visit. But by February Brad would have to spot him again and that's when he'd ask him to go. He might be offended, but Callaway Whitaker always landed on his feet. He'd couch-surf, or if worst came to worst, he'd go home and work for his dad.

How had Brad forgotten about the ad? His fucking knee and all this other bullshit had distracted him. Why weren't Lynch and Hanlon banging down his door? They were probably putting together an arrest warrant while he sat there with his thumb up his ass watching Emerson's videos.

He needed to see the lawyer. Now.

Pain ripped through his right leg as he stood and grabbed his jacket. The knock came as he pulled a hat over his mess of knotty hair. If the assholes from the parking lot had the nerve to get this close, he was going to lose it.

Brad opened the door to find another person he didn't want to see: the skinny guy in the leather jacket who'd driven away in Cal's Jetta after his big parlay didn't hit.

"I said get lost." The bookie's lackey sneered at a young woman who'd followed him up the steps carrying a "One of Cal's Crusaders!" poster. She glared at Brad before heading back to ground level.

Outside the condo door, the guy took a long drag of his cigarette and blew a plume of smoke straight into Brad's nostrils. "Where's your boy?"

"Not here, obviously." Brad waved toward the lot below where someone had set up a fire pit, the vigil expanding to more than a dozen people.

"How do I know this isn't staged—that he's not paying these dipshits twelve bucks an hour to stand there like they're waiting to see Harry fucking Styles?"

Brad almost smiled. Here was someone who also saw through his roommate's shiny exterior. "We both know Cal doesn't have twelve dollars."

"If he skipped town, we'll find him." The guy ashed on

the faded *Hope you brought beer!* welcome mat. "And when we do, it's not gonna go great for him. You hear from him, let him know Jason said that." He wore a cap like an old-time paperboy and tugged it down in front.

"Whatever." Brad stepped forward, snapping the condo door closed behind him. He took a halting step toward the short flight of stairs, but Jason grabbed his arm and pressed the cigarette into the sleeve of his jacket, leaving a black mark and a bad smell.

Brad smacked his arm away. "What the—?"

"No, not *whatever*. Give him that message or I'm coming back and leaving with whatever's in that little shitbox apartment of yours."

Take it, Brad wanted to say. All he cared about were the pills, and that supply was dwindling by the day.

As he limped toward the Highlander, Brad tried to keep his head down. Even beneath the darkening sky, he could see the crowd in the parking lot had doubled since he'd last looked outside. There were new signs too—ones with his name on them.

"Where's Cal, Brad?" A girl approached. He hobbled faster to the car, icy wind making his eyes tear.

"Back off," Brad grunted through clenched teeth as he dropped into the driver's seat and locked the doors. The rear defrost wasn't working. He could barely see through the back window but he could make out the silhouettes of people blocking him. The pain in his leg made him rabid. "Get out of my way," he shouted out the window and threw it into reverse, forcing the group to scatter.

Who were these people who'd freeze their asses off for a guy they barely knew? Some were Wyndmere employees, others were locals who must've recognized Cal from around town. Were they customers who wondered where they'd get their Oxy and Adderall if Cal didn't return?

The whole thing was bizarre yet so familiar. Brad had lived there for two years; Cal had been there three months, and still everyone had already taken Cal's side. Brad would've laughed at the absurdity of it if a sense of unease hadn't been spreading fast and itchy as poison ivy inside him. Or maybe that was the narcotics on an empty stomach.

As he barreled out of the parking lot, he couldn't avoid reading the posters: "Confess, Brad!" "What did you do, Brad??"

The sun was already dipping low, the roads icing over. Ivy had texted the lawyer's name and address. "Don Carmichael & Associates." It sounded like an alias. Brad made a mental note to look for a framed diploma in the office if he ever found it. Six miles and three U-turns later, he pulled into a short driveway in front of a two-story house. Beside the doorbell, Brad read a label, Carmichael & Assoc: 2, and pressed the buzzer. Through the crackle of the speaker, a voice warbled, "Yeah, come on up."

The old wooden door creaked as Brad opened it. It took a few seconds for his eyes to adjust to the dark, paneled entryway. Newspapers and junk mail sat on top of a hissing radiator, reminding him of his Grandma Shirley's house. The only bit of light came from a slim, rectangular window beside the steep staircase. It might as well have been Mt. Everest. There was no way he'd make the climb to Carmichael's office.

Fuck this. Brad stepped back into the cold and hit the buzzer again.

"Yeah, I said come on up."

"Can you come down? I hurt my knee." Brad was embarrassed. He sounded like a baby.

After a delay, Carmichael's voice came again, "Give me a sec."

Did Brad detect a huff of annoyance or was that the wind?

A man stepped out of the house, zipping a tan parka with one hand, holding an iPad and file folder in the other. Wearing khaki pants and a cream-colored button-down, he was tall, maybe six foot three but stooped a bit, giving off "tired uncle" vibes. A lock of his sandy gray hair hung limp across his forehead. Brad could hear his mother assessing Don's aura and declaring it beige.

"Don Carmichael." He stuck out a hand.

Brad shook it without removing his glove. "Mind if we talk in my car?" he asked.

"Whatever works." Don folded into the passenger seat and angled himself toward Brad, who tried to picture him in a courtroom shouting "Objection!" but couldn't.

Don sniffed. "You hunt?"

Brad shook his head. He couldn't recall the last time he'd showered. It was difficult on one leg. He cracked a window and waited for Don to take the lead.

"So your mom gave me her credit card to retain my services but before we get into the nitty-gritty, sign this." He handed Brad an iPad.

"What is it?"

"Standard contract. Whatever you tell me now, that stays between us."

It took Brad three tries to submit the form.

"Usually take my meetings indoors." Don grinned. "Wi-Fi's stronger in there."

"Yeah, sorry, my knee..." Brad started then closed his

mouth, wishing he'd brushed his teeth now that they were sitting so close.

"So." Don stuck the device between his maroon loafers. One was missing a tassel. "I've seen the news coverage." He whistled, pulled a pencil from behind his ear then scribbled the date on a legal pad. "You and your roommate have been friends since you were kids. Now he's disappeared and you're the last person to see him."

Was he going to list everything he knew? Probably. His mother said Don was charging in ten-minute increments. If he talked about how handsome Cal was, Brad was going to punch the windshield.

"Because you were the last one to see him you're considered a person of interest." Don paused, tapping his pencil against the pad. "But *were* you the last person? Have police pulled surveillance footage from the resort? The parking area? Are they talking to your colleagues? Your neighbors? Have they gone to local bars? Who knows, maybe your pal popped in for a nightcap or a booty call?"

Brad winced. Was his future in the hands of someone who used the phrase "booty call?"

"What I'm getting at is, how hard are they looking? Right now they've got nothing. No evidence of foul play. No body. Just the concerned parents of an adult who very well may have decided to take himself off the grid for a while, right?"

"Right." Buoyed by that logic, Brad felt himself coming around to Don.

"Holiday season's rough. I'll tell ya, my mom and dad are in their eighties, both of 'em speeding down the fast lane to Dementia City." He waved his hand as if this were a real destination waiting in the distance. "I can't tell you the number of times I've thought about faking my disappearance." He shook his head and laughed. When Brad failed to join in, Don cleared his throat. "I understand you talked to the police without a lawyer. Big mistake, but, look, you weren't arrested and you haven't been charged with anything."

Brad nodded.

"And if you've watched even a single episode of *Law & Order*, you know the good news is, should worst come to worst and your buddy's found—not alive, I mean—it's on them." He jabbed a finger at the dashboard as if a team of tiny prosecutors were trapped inside the glovebox. "They have to prove beyond a reasonable doubt that you did it. So let's start there."

"Okay." Brad squirmed, trying and failing to get comfortable.

"Now Cal's a good-looking guy..."

There it is! Brad fought the urge to snicker.

"...and they're talking him up like he's the greatest thing since Nutella, but there've got to be people out there who aren't big fans." He poked Brad's shoulder. "Those are our people."

Brad stared out the driver's side window. Why did it always feel like his unspoken duty to cover for Cal? Maybe it was because his earliest memories featured Cal sharing his graham crackers during preschool snack time or Cal fighting off bullies before that speech therapist helped Brad correct his lisp. Most likely it was that a pattern had been established and until that moment it hadn't been broken.

Brad took a hard swallow and told Don about the gambling, Cal losing his car, Jason, the bookie, showing up at their door, making threats.

"This is great stuff." Don flipped to a fresh sheet of legal paper. "I mean, c'mon, debt? Huge motivator to skip town. What else you got?"

Brad explained how Cal used the pharmacist's daughter to start his drug dealing side hustle. He debated mentioning Melinda's lazy eye, wondering if that would make him seem like just as big an asshole as Cal.

"Maybe this gal, Melanie—"

"Melinda," Brad corrected.

"Maybe she wants him gone? Or, maybe her dad finds out and *he* takes action—better than getting the cops involved and incriminating his own daughter, right?"

"Maybe." Brad wished he could believe it.

"Or—" Don tapped his stubbly chin with his pencil "—maybe Cal's attacked by some junkie? Left for dead in the woods."

"Maybe," Brad repeated.

"I knew it!" Don's head bobbed like a pigeon's. "I saw him on TV and I thought, 'This guy is gonna turn out like my Aunt Peg's lasagna—looks great but dig in and, whoa, Nelly, what the fuck is going on here? It's all fake.'" Don leaned closer to Brad. "Aunt Peg was a vegan. Ahead of her time, but still, who wants tofu and plant-based cheeses?" Jutting a thumb toward his chest, Don confirmed, "Not this guy." He placed his right ankle over his left knee. Brad wished he could move so effortlessly. "You tell the police any of this?"

"No, I—"

"Okay, look, it's time to stop thinking about Cal," Don interrupted. "It's time to start thinking about *you*. It's Brad time."

Brad time. He liked that.

"So what about you?"

"Me?"

"You got any beef with your pal? If I end up defending you, I'd prefer not to get blindsided."

How much did Brad want to share? There was the knee injury that hadn't felt like an accident, and then there was the other accident—the one Brad never talked about. He stared out the windshield. Snow had begun to fall.

"There was this thing that happened when we were in college." Brad got that weird fluttering in his stomach, almost like he'd swallowed a bird, every time he thought about it—her. "There was this girl—"

Don clucked his tongue and shook his head. "There's always a girl."

"Her name was Chloe. We had a couple classes together freshman year. I liked her. A lot."

Whenever Brad pictured her, the scent came rushing back: warm and powdery, courtesy of a dryer vent located below her dorm room window.

"She had a high school boyfriend she was still seeing. Fast forward to sophomore year, she came back from Thanksgiving and they'd broken up. I wanted to make a move but it never felt like the right time."

Don stopped writing and waited.

"Then it's mid-December, a Thursday. I'm in Connecticut, Cal's in New Hampshire. He's done with finals. On his way home he decides he'll swing by, hang out, and give me a ride after my last test Friday. He wants to party. I tell him I have to study. He says if I'm not prepared by ten o'clock the night before an exam, I never will be, and, like I'd done my entire life, I listened to him."

"And?" Don motioned like Brad should hurry it up.

"Freshman year, I'd told Cal about Chloe. First mistake."

He wants to meet her. We go to her dorm. She says she needs to stay in and study, but Cal convinces her to come out with us. It's snowing. She's from Georgia, so snow's a big deal. She's giddy. The semester's almost over. It's starting to feel like the holidays. We're pumped, bouncing from one party to the next, knowing it's getting late, not caring.

"Cal's feeding her shots, tugging at her scarf, this long, pink thing her grandma knit for her. She wore it everywhere. She was on a swimming scholarship and she had this weird thing where she thought her neck was thick or something. It wasn't."

Brad banged his knuckles against the steering wheel trying to make the memory of her face dissolve. He exhaled and could see his breath. He wanted to stop there but Don's face made him keep going.

"Cal's all over her. She's drunk, laughing, but still shrugging him off. It's killing me. I was pissed at him, but more pissed at myself for not knowing that's exactly how it would go.

"Around midnight I'm like, 'Fuck this,' and head back to my dorm. Second mistake. They stay out. I get in bed but can't sleep. I hear sirens. Don't think much of it. There's a hospital near campus. Cal comes in after two, says my name a bunch of times, tries to shake me awake. I act like I'm asleep 'cause I don't want to deal with him. Third mistake.

"He starts shuffling around. I figure he's looking for condoms or packing up to stay with her. I hear him slip out. I never hated anyone more."

A light came on outside Don's building. Was someone watching or was it on a timer? Dusk had settled but when Brad looked at Don he could make out the deep lines creasing the man's face as he waited for the rest.

"Chloe had stepped into the street and gotten hit by a snowplow, head slammed into the curb. It happened near these food trucks on a main street where people hung out after the bars closed." Brad stopped. The fluttery feeling in his stomach stilled and hardened into a stone that sat heavily, unmoving.

"Two days before Christmas, her family took her off life support, donated her organs."

Don's eyes narrowed. "And you blame Cal? Why? You think he pushed her?"

Brad shook his head. "She didn't usually drink that much. He let her stumble into the street. The worst part is, he left her there. Maybe she wasn't as charmed by him as the rest of the world. Either way, he freaked out, came back to the dorm, then drove home. The plow driver said one second she wasn't there, the next she was. People thought they saw her jump into the street, but no one could say for sure. By that time of night everybody's wasted. I wasn't there but I could see it all—Cal grabbing at her, Chloe darting away."

"What happened to the driver?"

"The guy was a wreck but he wasn't charged because of her blood alcohol level and witness accounts."

"And Cal?"

"Cal went back to school in January. I dropped out after that." Brad remembered the way his mother's face contorted when he told her he wasn't going back, how she'd tried to coax him to talk, bringing him smoothies, sitting beside him while he watched snowboarding videos on YouTube. "I kept thinking if I'd never introduced her to Cal, she'd still be alive. The university, the media, they painted her as just some girl who had too much to drink. Others said it was the pressure of finals that got her. Her family was devastated. I heard her sister was on campus that spring asking a lot of questions, trying to get answers. I followed them on social media for a while. Really sad."

"You ever confront Cal?" Don asked.

"Before he left to go back to school that winter, he came by and told me to 'get over it,' stop blaming myself. I told him, 'I do blame myself, but I blame you more, you selfish prick.'"

"How did he respond to that?"

"He was like, 'You didn't see her. She got crazy after the last bar. If you can't handle yourself, don't hang out.' I didn't talk to him for a long time after that."

Don shifted in the passenger seat. "So, just to play a little devil's advocate here, why stay in touch? Why ask him to room with you?"

"I didn't." The question made Brad equal parts desperate and defensive. "He called and told me he was coming." Brad took off his hat and scratched his head. The quick flash of anger at Cal, combined with the pain in his knee, made him hot with rage. "It's complicated."

Don leaned forward. "How so?"

"Our parents have been friends forever. There's no way to avoid him. Running from all that is what brought me here in the first place."

Don settled back and flipped through his notes. "Anything else?"

Brad shook his head.

"One more thing," Don said. "Cal's sister and her videos? I've known girls like that. Give 'em a little attention, they're gonna take a whole lot more. They're dangerous. Somebody needs to shut her up."

"My brother's going to talk to her."

"Good." Don opened the car door. A rush of air blew in, cold but welcome. "I know it's not easy, but sit tight. Get some rest. You look like shit. No offense."

ON THE DRIVE BACK, Brad felt worn out but better, the way he used to after a good football practice. Still, his mind kept spinning back to Don. The lawyer'd never asked if Brad had done something to Cal.

How could you represent a person—defend them—not knowing if they were innocent or guilty? Brad didn't understand it, but he was grateful there were people capable of such a thing.

12

FRIDAY, DECEMBER 19
EMERSON

Emerson stood by the front door, waiting for her parents to leave. Over the past fifteen minutes, her mother had trudged up and down the steps a dozen times, returning with more sweaters to stuff into her bulging suitcase. Was she planning to move to Wyoming?

"We'll call you as soon as we get there." Jane fumbled with her jacket's zipper. Her face looked ravaged, cheeks pale and drooping. Em felt as if she were watching her mother lose collagen in real time. "Won't that be like four in the morning? Just text me."

"Please—" Jane begged with her red-rimmed eyes "—don't get into trouble."

Em wanted to say something snarky, but between her lackluster grades and the weed pen her mom had found in her Jeep, she didn't have room to argue. Under normal circumstances, her mother would've asked Max's mom to check in on her, but now they weren't speaking.

"And please don't have people over," Jane added.

Of course she was having people over. Cal always had parties when their parents went out of town. It wasn't like she was going to host a rave. She'd invited her friends Sasha and Libby—and Max. If he showed, she hoped he'd be chill.

He'd called her Thursday night, freaking out. Apparently people were harassing Brad, lurking outside his condo, throwing snowballs at his sliding doors.

"Oh no, not snowballs!" Em had mocked.

"It's not funny," Max snapped. "It's messed up. You and I both know Brad would never do anything to hurt Cal."

Do we know that? Cal could be a dick. Didn't everyone have a limit to how much bullshit they could stand?

"Look, Cal's my brother—obviously, duh—I just mean, if my posts are bringing attention to the fact that he's missing and that gets people looking for him, that's a good thing."

"You can do that without implicating *my brother* in his disappearance." There was an awkward pause before Max added, "For real, Em, stop."

She didn't like his tone and she definitely didn't like being told what to do. Her mother was controlling enough. It was then that she decided she'd double down—have some friends over and record them in Cal's bedroom sharing what her brother meant to them. Of course, they barely knew Cal, but she'd fill them in. No one was going to fact-check the sister of a missing man.

"Fine, I'll stop," she'd told Max—adding "for now" silently to herself.

AS SOON AS HER PARENTS' car backed out of the driveway, Em pulled out her phone and texted Max.

> When will you be here? R U gonna stick around or do you still feel "too old" to hang with my friends?

The phone pulsed in her hand. Instead of texting, Max was FaceTiming. She bit her lip hoping he'd missed the story she posted earlier that afternoon. She hadn't said anything specifically about Brad, just that her parents were on their way to try to get answers. After tearing up a little, she ended with a vague line about how sometimes even people you've known your whole life can surprise you. "And not in a good way." She hadn't planned to say that last part, but she'd been struck by the urge to keep things interesting.

"Hey!" She smiled and moved into the kitchen where the lighting was more flattering.

"Hey." Max was wearing a brown henley. It worked with his rust-colored hair and made his shoulders appear spectacularly broad.

Em's stomach flipped a little, thinking about him possibly spending the night at her house, but his expression was mega-harsh.

"What happened to not shit-talking my brother?" he asked.

Em swept her hair behind her ear and opened the freezer. Sasha and Libby would be there soon. She needed to pregame so she pulled the bottle of Grey Goose from the lowest shelf. Her friends had been super-sweet about Cal, checking in, bringing her chai lattes, trying to make sure she was never alone at school. But it was becoming a bit smothering. She poured the vodka into a tall glass over ice and splashed in some cranberry juice. She'd asked Max to bring beer and hard seltzers, but if he was going to be a drag, she'd just serve whatever was on the bar cart in the dining room.

"Hello?" Max said.

"Sorry, I think we've got a bad connection." She sipped to hide her smirk. Her cocktail was weak from all the water she'd added to the vodka bottle over the past month to fool her mother.

"Your parents are going out there, Em. Let them and the police take it from here." Max's jaw was tense, his voice low. "You're creating this false narrative and I don't think you get how dangerous that is."

It was kind of hot to see him so fired up.

"If Cal's out there and he's hurt—or worse—" he paused "—and people are focused on Brad instead of looking at other possibilities, you're not helping."

She considered this for a sec. Maybe he was right, but she didn't want to stop, not when she was getting DMs from brands with sponsorship offers, not when her follower count was exploding. Plus, now people were on this journey with her. They cared about Cal, sending all those "thoughts and prayers." Sure, a lot of it was bullshit, but didn't they deserve updates? Of course, there were plenty of assholes who wrote things like, "Here's an idea: Put down your phone and go look for your brother!" Others made rude sexual references or said her eyes were "buggy" and her nose "looked fake." It took everything for her to not reply, "It's called contouring, dumbass."

Maybe she had pushed it too far, pointing the finger at Brad, but why did he have Cal's phone? And why had he ignored her mother's calls?

For a few moments, Em considered toning it down,

calling off her plans to record her friends—until Max said, "Go back to posting about lip gloss and leggings."

Her body went rigid. "When I'm in a relationship, I expect to grow, not shrink." She'd never been in a relationship before this one. She was paraphrasing a quote she'd read in her guidance counselor's office, where she'd landed after routinely cutting gym.

Max's shoulders sagged as he sighed. "Look, I know you're just trying to do your thing but don't do it at my brother's expense. That's all I'm saying."

Em made a pouty face and waited for him to apologize. She knew he was into her. Most of his life he'd been a nerdy comp-sci guy, only reaching his full potential after college once he started working out and dressing better. He'd never gotten the "hot girl" before.

"Sorry," he said.

She smiled. They were at the stage where it was all so new she could count on him wanting to please her. Plus, the sex was great—not that she had a lot to compare it to but still, it was intense. Though they mainly did it in his basement, and once very uncomfortably in Ivy's Fiat, their chemistry was undeniable. She wondered how much of it was because they were sneaking around, or maybe it was the fact that she'd known him her whole life yet they were only exploring this connection now.

She wanted him in her bed that night, to have him on top of her between clean sheets instead of scrunched up on a lumpy old futon. It would be nice to inhale his scent without getting a whiff of Jean-Claude's doggy breath mixed in.

She heard a woman's voice.

"My mom's calling me," Max said.

Em thought it was both sweet and cringey that he ate dinner most nights with his parents.

"How is Ivy holding up?" she asked.

"Not great. I think I saw her eating one of Jean-Claude's biscuits."

"Gross." Em took a sip of her drink and got an instant brain freeze. "So what time can you drop off supplies?"

"Gimme an hour."

"Get enough for the weekend, okay?" she said but Max had already ended the call.

IN HER BEDROOM, Em reapplied her makeup and put on her favorite jeans and a black sweater.

On her way downstairs, she stopped in Cal's room. The space seemed so empty, dead, even after she flicked the light switch and the ceiling fan took a slow spin.

She thought about her brother out there without a phone. On one hand it was completely deranged, on the other, it sounded kind of amazing—free, unreachable. She'd wanted to get to the place where she now was—lots of people following her, connecting with her. A high-end handbag designer had asked if she'd carry one of their vegan leather satchels on her trip to Wyoming. A company that made sustainably sourced water bottles wanted her to place a couple in the background of her next videos. Both offered her thousands of dollars to collab. Her influencer fantasy was coming true; it sucked that it took Cal's disappearance to make it happen.

Regardless, the attention was completely addictive. Her mother always thought she lacked Cal's competitive fire, but watching the likes and comments add up made her crave more. Maintaining it, however, was a lot. Planning what she'd wear. Finding the right angles, cool backgrounds. Figuring out what to say and how to say it. It had become all-consuming in just a few days. That said, Cal could be back at any moment. She needed to capitalize on it while she could.

Even with some of the awful things people wrote beneath her posts, like "RIP Cal," and "Dude's buried in an avalanche. Wait 'til spring, then you'll find him!" Em continued to believe her brother was out there living his best life—his favorite hashtag—and he'd resurface when he got bored or ran out of money.

She was staring at Cal's bed, his desk, picturing how she'd position her friends, when she heard the front door open.

"Em! Emerson!" Libby and Sasha's voices echoed through the foyer.

"Hey." Em floated downstairs, holding her empty glass. Either the drink was stronger than she thought or it was the lack of food in her system; something was making her head swim.

Though they'd seen each other at school only hours earlier, her friends embraced her like she'd returned from battle. As they released her, she looked them up and down: Libby in steel-colored corduroy overalls with a white cropped top beneath, Sasha in a short silver and white plaid skirt and sleeveless black sweater. She'd told them about her idea to film in Cal's room and, clearly, they'd coordinated their color scheme to complement one another. They'd taken their time with hair and makeup, too, Em could tell. It was cool they'd made an effort, but she didn't want them looking too good. This was about her, her family.

Libby held out a canvas tote bag filled with snacks. "My mom sent these."

"Lib!" Sasha snorted. "What the fuck? *Sorry your bro is MIA. Have some Terra chips!*"

"Stop! It's the thought that counts, right?" Em hated how much she sounded like her mom.

"Hope it's cool," Sasha headed into the dining room to ransack the bar cart. "I tossed out some invites. People are super-concerned about you."

The thought made Em tired. She wasn't in the mood to play hostess anymore. Max's words and the way he ended their FaceTime without a goodbye left her wondering where they stood. He was the person she'd been most looking forward to seeing. Plus, throwing a party while her brother was missing was a bad look. But maybe it would be a good distraction.

"Yeah, sure, that's fine," she said as the doorbell rang. A bunch of girls Em vaguely recognized as Sasha's volleyball teammates poured in, trailed by a couple of random guys, their loud voices punctuated by laughter.

She waited to receive their "So sorry,"s and "Any news?" but they filed past her in search of booze or anything they could eat, drink, or smoke. Someone synched a playlist to the speakers suspended in various corners of the kitchen and living room, and suddenly the house throbbed with rap music.

Em fixed another drink and sat on the kitchen island. Sasha passed her a shot and went to work mixing vile cocktails with whatever she found in the fridge. Em eyed the clock on the microwave. Max would be there soon. She needed to start filming before her friends were hammered and slurring. Standing on the island, she clapped. "Hey!"

Sasha shouted for someone to kill the tunes.

"Thanks." Em paused and waited for the room to quiet. "Tomorrow it'll be a week since anyone's seen my brother Cal." She let her guests absorb the weight of her words. "We still have no clue what happened to him. It's so messed up, you guys."

More people crammed into her kitchen, crowding the dining room doorway. Some were eating chips, others stopped crunching out of respect.

"As you know, I'm trying to raise awareness, so if anyone wants to talk about Cal, what he means to all of us, come upstairs."

A guy wearing a Titleist hat muttered, "Who the fuck is Cal?" but Em ignored him.

"Thanks for being here for me!" She raised her glass to a few cheers and started to sit down but popped back up. "And please like and share my posts! I'd love to get the hashtag "Where's Cal?" trending. Oh, and don't trash my house—our cleaning lady doesn't come until Monday!"

Emerson led Sasha, Libby, and a handful of others to Cal's room. Most entered in hushed whispers, as if attending a wake.

A guy Em didn't know opened the closet and slid his arms into her brother's varsity football jacket. Libby and Sasha flounced down on Cal's bed. Em took their red Solo cups, placed them out of sight, then held up her phone.

"I can't believe Cal isn't here," Sasha said, punching one of his pillows. "It sucks."

"He was like a brother to me," Libby added, wiping an imaginary tear.

They kept their heads bowed for a few moments before Sasha popped up. "How was that, Em? Too emo?"

"It's a start," Em groaned. "A little cliché, right?" She looked around for confirmation and saw kids picking over items on Cal's dresser, opening drawers. A girl sat at his desk twirling a cigar cutter. The vibe had gotten weird.

"All right, let's try that again," Em said.

Sasha and Libby had a small "You go! No, you go!" battle before Em shouted, "Guys, c'mon!" The call with Max had thrown her off. She hated feeling out of control.

"Cal was my first crush." Sasha's cheeks flushed, probably more from whatever she'd poured into that party cup than any true feeling. Still, it worked. "I remember when he'd drive us home from the pool and he'd keep all the windows down and the radio loud. He's literally the coolest guy I ever met."

Em gave them a thumbs-up and panned to the random dude in Cal's jacket.

"Cal's the best," he said. "I'm not taking this off until he's better."

"What?" Em spat, lowering the phone.

"You know, 'til he beats this."

"He's not sick, asshole," Libby jumped in. "He's missing."

"Whoa, shit, no way," the kid said. "That blows."

"I'll edit this later." Em spun back toward her friends on the bed and lifted her phone. "C'mon. What else?"

Sasha tapped her chin with her finger. "What I—and I think everyone—wants to know is: what's the deal with Brad Chapman?" Her dark eyebrows united, transforming her into a young Frida Kahlo. "I mean, why's Cal friends with him in the first place? Remember that time we were at the beach and he got clobbered by a wave and Cal had to rescue him? Then he whined about his knee for the rest of the weekend. What a tool—they're like total opposites."

"Total," Libby echoed.

The question made Em's nerve endings tingle. On one hand, it was so mean. Brad on his worst day was probably still nicer than Cal, but Sasha had provided Em with a chance to paint her brother in a better, brighter light—one that would make viewers like him even more. He wasn't just handsome and athletic, he was kind, compassionate.

Em flipped the camera and smiled at her own image. "Great question, Sash. I think the answer is that's who my brother is—a good guy, generous with his time, his friendship. He has a soft spot for people who haven't had things come as easily as they do for him." Em cocked her head to the side, hoping it came off as genuinely sympathetic. "Brad was bullied a lot as a kid because he had this speech thing—a stutter, I think? Cal was totally there for him. Always has been." She paused. "With everything that's happened, I can't help wondering if maybe Brad's jealous of my brother." She lowered her voice. "And maybe those feelings caused him to snap? Maybe—"

Something in her background shifted. Em stopped staring at herself and saw Max behind her wearing an olive green puffy coat and an epic scowl.

"What the hell are you doing?" he demanded.

Before Em could react, he grabbed her phone. The fingers of his other hand circled her wrist like a handcuff, pulling her toward the hall, then into the bathroom. He locked the door and blocked it with his body.

"Look," she said, "before you say anything, that wasn't live."

"What the hell are you thinking?"

His anger scared and excited her; goosebumps rose on her arms.

"What?" she asked, the alcohol making her bold, curious about how far she could push him.

"The videos! I asked you to stop and you promised me you would."

Promised? What was this—first grade? No one was exchanging pinky swears. In the silence, she heard a thunderous crash, followed by breaking glass and kids screaming then laughing. She reached for the doorknob to go check it out, but Max didn't move.

"We're not done here," he snarled. "The things you're saying about Brad," he held up her phone and she flinched, imagining him tossing it into the toilet, "your videos are making his life an absolute shitshow. People are camped out in the parking lot outside his condo. He can't even leave. You have no idea how big this has gotten out there."

"It's kind of a-mazing, right?" Emerson hiccuped. "I mean, did you see? I'm up to eighty thousand followers. That's insane."

"No, Em. You're insane. This isn't Netflix. This is real life. *My* brother's life. *Your* brother's life. Do you not get that? Your brother could be dead and you care about followers?"

"Nobody knows what happened. Cal could be in Ibiza—"

"And Brad could be in jail. My parents had to hire a lawyer. I heard them arguing about it."

"My parents fight all the time."

"That's not the point. It's a huge expense."

"I can loan them the money!" Em offered. "There's this watch brand willing to pay me—"

He dropped her wrist. "Who are you?" His eyes searched hers. "Seriously, it's like I don't even know you anymore, Emerson. This has to stop. *You* have to stop."

Em rubbed her wrist. "Okay, fine. I'll stop." She inched closer, drawn by the heat coming off him. He smelled like snow and flannel. "But this could fund our trip. Screw the youth hostels and shared bathrooms, we could five-star it all the way, baby!" When his expression didn't change, she stuck out her lower lip. "I thought you supported my dreams."

"Is it your dream to build a brand on tragedy?"

"Of course not." She tucked a lock of his auburn hair behind his ear. She needed to reset the energy between them, remind him of who she was, what they had. "You're so tense."

"Because of *you*!" He knocked his head against the back of the bathroom door.

Did this count as their first real fight? She ran her hand down the front of his jeans. He was semi-hard. At first she was a little offended, but then saw it as a challenge. She'd unzip his fly, take him in her mouth, do that thing with her tongue that made him buck his hips and moan, and he'd forget all about her videos.

"I didn't come here to fool around, Em." He pushed her hand away, gave her back her phone, and opened the door. "You've fucked up enough things already."

She watched in disbelief as he headed for the stairs. "That's not how the man of my dreams is supposed to act!" she called after him.

He stopped on the top step. "Since you've got all this cash coming in, the booze was seventy-two dollars. Venmo me."

Em stood in the hall, certain he was joking. *He'll be back.* She was gorgeous and practically famous.

When he continued down the steps, she went in search of Sasha or Libby. Cal's door was closed. She nudged it open. The light spilling from his closet was enough for her to see a couple going at it in her brother's bed. It was the guy who was still wearing Cal's varsity jacket, jeans bunched around his ankles, and a girl from the volleyball team, Em guessed, based on her clownishly large sneakers.

Em shuddered, grateful for the alcohol's numbing effect, and drifted downstairs. Sasha and Libby waited at the bottom. Shiny chunks that looked like diamonds or crystals glittered at their feet.

"What is this?" As she rounded the final step, she saw the grandfather clock face down on the floor, glass everywhere. Above the pulsing music, she thought she could make out faint chiming.

"Holy shit! You guys!" Em's hands flew to her face as she sank to the bottom step. "How the hell—?"

"Evan bet Zander fifty bucks he couldn't climb it and swing from the light thingy." Sasha pointed to the chandelier.

"He almost had it," Libby said.

"I am so dead." A terrible, vomity taste filled Em's mouth and she swallowed it.

"Tell your parents there was a home invasion," Sasha said.

"We'll totally back you up." Libby nodded like a bobblehead.

The doorbell rang. Em's spirits lifted. She was certain it was Max. He'd apologize for storming off and help her clean up this mess. She'd promise not to post about Brad again, and she'd mean it this time.

She sprang forward, hopping over shards of glass, and opened the door. "I knew you'd be back!" she chirped.

Two guys she didn't recognize stood on the reindeer welcome mat her mother had put out before Cal went missing. They were too old to be in high school or college. Shit, one was bald and the other had a full mustache. The cold night air sobered her up fast.

"Think you guys got the wrong house." She started to shut the door but the bald guy blocked it with his foot.

"Cal Whitaker here?"

Em shivered.

"Is this the pizza?" Sasha poked her head over Em's shoulder and then mumbled, "Who the—"

"Cal's not here," Em said. *Who the fuck were these two?* "Don't you watch the news? He's missing." Em tried her best to act unbothered by these unwanted guests. During middle school, she'd attended summer theater camp. Instructors said she had "natural talent and real potential," but she found memorizing lines mind-numbingly dull so she didn't pursue it. Now she called upon her acting skills to appear braver than she felt as they glared at her beneath the light of the full moon.

"He owes an associate of ours some money," the bald one said.

"Not a small amount," Mustache added.

"Jesus," Sasha whispered in Em's ear.

For once, Em was silent.

"He's got 'til Sunday."

"Then we come back and start breaking and taking. I don't think you want that."

Em's mouth had gone impossibly dry. The men took a few steps backward toward an old sedan idling at the curb, its muffler providing a menacing drumroll.

Em shut the door and slid to the floor. Maybe it was the alcohol, the fight with Max, the goons outside, the slivers of glass piercing the soft denim of her jeans, or the fact that her brother may very well have gotten into some deep, dark shit, but for the first time in ages, her eyes filled with tears. Real ones.

13

SATURDAY, DECEMBER 20

JANE

Each leg of the trip was worse than the one that preceded it.

Jane wanted to take an Uber to the airport to avoid any additional stress, but it was a Friday during the holiday season and prices were surging. Wade found a Groupon for an off-site, long-term parking lot then proceeded to ignore the GPS and Jane's directions, plunging them deeper down the dark, icy streets of Newark.

By the time they reached the TSA line, Jane and Wade were no longer speaking. In the terminal, surrounded by fake trees, inflatable menorahs, and flight attendants in Santa hats, Jane was forced to face the very real possibility that Cal might not be with them for Christmas. The thought made it difficult to breathe.

In a daze, she watched excited travelers pile last-minute presents purchased at duty-free shops onto the conveyor belt. The ski trip to Wyoming was supposed to be everyone's big gift, but she'd planned to surprise each family member with a little something extra: a spa day for Emerson, new gloves for Wade, cash for Cal. His paychecks were meager and she'd noticed his bank account balance steadily disappearing. But once he'd gone missing, none of that mattered.

On the flight to Nashville, Jane and Wade weren't seated together. Neither asked a fellow passenger to switch. They waited on the runway for an hour as crews de-iced the plane's wings, Jane's anxiety spiking. Trapped in the middle seat, she fought the urge to turn to the strangers beside her and say, "My son is missing," desperate to relieve herself of shouldering this burden alone in row thirty-four. She was certain they'd assure her it was all a misunderstanding.

"You'll find him," they'd insist, as if Cal were an earring or a set of keys she'd misplaced.

But she couldn't say the words and her fellow passengers wouldn't have heard her anyway. They were on their phones, AirPods planted firmly in their ears, reminding her of Emerson. She wished she hadn't left her daughter home alone. Em promised to use the time to work on her college applications. Jane didn't believe her. The girl had been distracted lately, and it had nothing to do with composing the personal statement required by the common app. Em was more secretive, smirking and giggling behind her phone. It was probably a crush. Despite her pretty face and popularity, Emerson hadn't had a real boyfriend yet. Apparently, teenagers didn't date anymore. Whatever Em was up to, it would have to wait. Finding Cal trumped everything else.

The leg from Nashville to Chicago was turbulent, with the fasten seatbelt sign illuminated for the duration. Each time she closed her eyes, she saw her son buried beneath an avalanche, his strong limbs trapped and twisted. The images made her eyes fly open, screams stuck in her throat.

Though it had been years since Jane entered a church outside of attending weddings and funerals, she began to pray: for Cal, for her marriage, even for Brad. She pictured the boy who'd hidden behind Ivy's hippie skirts sucking his thumb during those first days of preschool before Cal befriended him. Was he capable of violence? She would've said no but she was sure he knew more than he was telling, and though she rarely admitted it, Cal wasn't always perfect.

On the way from Chicago to Wyoming, Wade snored, head back, mouth open, waking only once when the beverage cart ran over his foot. Across the aisle, Jane wept softly when the combination of Ambien and merlot failed to knock her out.

At one point a flight attendant tapped her shoulder.

"Ma'am?" The woman's pinched face made Jane's pulse race. Was it Cal? Did she know something? Had word traveled to thirty thousand feet? Jane gripped the armrest as if the plane were nosediving. She'd been existing in a heightened state of alert for almost a week, bracing for the worst possible news. Was she about to receive it?

"Yes?" She couldn't hear her voice over the roar in her ears.

"We need your seat-back in the upright position for landing," the attendant said sternly before striding away.

IT WAS STILL dark beyond the windows of the baggage claim area shortly after six a.m. As they waited at the carousel, a bone-deep tiredness made Jane yearn to stretch out on the floor, not caring about germs or her appearance.

"Mom!" a male voice boomed behind her, sending her heart skittering. She spun around to see a gangly teen loping toward a dark-haired woman in a sweatsuit, MILF emblazoned on her backside. Even Ivy, with her collection of

Lululemon knockoffs, would never wear something so tacky. The boy handed his mother a crumpled fast-food bag, grease stains polka-dotting its sides.

"What am I supposed to do with this?" the mother asked as Jane staggered back, disappointment nearly toppling her.

"I don't know. Recycle it?" the boy said.

Eyes burning from lack of sleep, Jane hated these two for their easy banter. Would she and her son ever have the chance to do that again? She turned away and watched snowboards, skis, and suitcases begin their slow rotation. She pictured Cal as a child on the merry-go-round at the town fair near her parents' home in Connecticut. His round cheeks rosy, his tiny voice calling, "Faster! Faster!" to the ride operator. Even then, Jane had loved and feared her son's constant desire for more.

That felt like a lifetime ago. How had they gotten here—to a place where that little boy had grown into a man? A man who was missing. Her parents dead, their home gone too, thanks to her brother's bad financial advice.

And how was it that she and the person she usually turned to for comfort weren't speaking? Though the term "best friend" called to mind middle-schoolers and sleepovers, secrets about bras and boys, that's how Jane had thought of Ivy for at least the past decade. Even back when Ivy would go to South Jersey for days at a time to help her mother get a handle on her "house of horrors," they'd made time for calls or texts. Of course, there'd been a few periods in the past when they'd drifted apart over some silly disagreements, but they always found their way back to one another.

When they'd planned this ski vacation together, Jane imagined the six of them—her, Wade, Emerson, Ivy, Greg, and Max—arriving at their rustic but spacious Airbnb. The men would build a fire while she and Ivy opened some wine and relaxed before meeting Cal and Brad for dinner.

Jane had envisioned this trip, in its original form, as a reset for her marriage. Once Wade stepped away from the stress of his work, inhaled that crisp mountain air, and basked in the unparalleled beauty of the mountains, he'd understand why their son had taken this career detour. He'd forgive Jane for supporting Cal. Maybe he'd even apologize for his coldness over the past few months.

Wade was always softer, more affectionate, on vacation. As she shifted from foot to foot, waiting to see their suitcases emerge from the gray mouth of the tunnel, Jane's mind traveled back to the cruise she and her husband had taken for their second anniversary after he'd closed a lucrative deal.

On the last night, they'd made love on a lounge chair on the top deck beneath a blanket of stars, the gentle rocking of the ship matching their own steady rhythm. She couldn't say for sure because they'd had more sex than college students on spring break that week, but she'd always believed that was the night Cal was conceived. Perhaps that was when the seeds of her son's impulsive nature took root.

She and Wade had never done anything like that before or since. Of course, that was before there were cameras everywhere and people with cell phones waiting to catch you embarrassing yourself. Now their lovemaking would be a viral joke and they'd be mocked mercilessly, if not arrested for public lewdness. That was also before online shopping began bankrupting businesses and shuttering storefronts, leaving Wade's properties vacant, a permanent scowl etched on his face.

She looked at her husband, frowning as he scrolled through his phone. Of course, sex couldn't be further from her mind, but when was the last time they'd even held hands? Other couples in crisis leaned on one another. Wade stood several feet away, anger radiating off him like a dark forcefield. He hadn't said it yet, but she knew what he was thinking: If she'd backed him instead of Cal, they wouldn't be standing inside this freezing airport, blinded by harsh overhead lighting at the crack of dawn, having no clue what had happened to their son.

Her eyes darted back to the carousel. She'd tied a sky-blue ribbon around the handle of her black suitcase so it would stand out. She still hadn't seen it pass. It wouldn't surprise her if their luggage was back in Nashville—or Newark. She was about to turn to Wade to say as much when she heard him grumble, "Jesus Christ!" He held out his phone. "I set a Google alert for Cal. Read this!"

Jane squinted. Her glasses were in her purse. She was too tired to search for them. She turned the phone sideways and zoomed in to enlarge the headline. The words "Missing Man May Have Battled Multiple Addictions" appeared in bold above a photo of her son. The photo she'd sent police.

Weakness flooded her joints as she scanned the story, catching only phrases—"gambling problem," "owes a considerable amount," "selling pills to keep cash coming in," "a source close to Whitaker confirmed."

Jane couldn't process the words. The article ended with the police department's phone number and a hotline readers could call if they were struggling with addiction.

Wade snatched the phone out of her hand. "What time is it in New York? I'm calling Victor. This is libel, defamation of character. We'll sue."

Jane knew the word "gambling" was a trigger for Wade, dredging up memories of his father, of ketchup sandwiches for dinner, toes poking through holes in sneakers, long winter nights without heat.

That's why Jane had never mentioned Cal's high school issue to Wade. Plus, she'd wanted to believe it was an isolated incident. Cal promised her it was.

Wade stabbed his way through his contacts muttering, "ludicrous" and "disgusting." Fellow travelers, bored with waiting for their bags, turned to stare as his deep voice rose. "We'll sue this podunk paper into bankruptcy."

"Wade, no, wait. It's—" She touched his wrist and was jolted by a sharp, electric shock. "I have to— There's something I never told you."

"What?" He looked up, eyes already hard and accusing. "What is it?"

She fumbled through how she'd handed over cash to a stranger outside a sub shop when Cal was sixteen. She lowballed the figure, changing it from thousands to hundreds, and downplayed how the seediness of the exchange had made her want to race home, shower, and lock Cal in his room indefinitely.

The blue-green vein that always reminded Jane of a lowercase "y" pulsed in the center of Wade's forehead.

"How the hell could you not tell me that?" His arms went slack. "Jesus Christ, Jane!"

"It wasn't a good time." Her nose tingled and she wiped it with the back of her hand. "That health food chain had gone bankrupt. I wanted to spare you." Jane bit her lower lip. "He swore he'd never—"

"And you believed him?" he scoffed.

Wade had a tendency to make a bad situation worse, especially if it involved money. The first time Jane had realized this was their third date. He'd gotten a parking ticket outside a movie theater and stomped his foot like an overgrown toddler. Initially, she thought he was joking. When she understood he wasn't, she considered not seeing him again. The fine was twelve dollars—more than a movie ticket, he pointed out, complaining the entire ride back to her parents' house. Money had never been an issue for her family—at least not until her brother took over their parents' investments and lost it all.

If she'd told Wade about Cal's gambling, he'd have blown it completely out of proportion, lecturing and punishing their son. She'd viewed it more as a blip, a teachable moment. Now she couldn't help questioning her judgment.

"So, how do *they* know this?" Wade jabbed at the screen. "Who's the source? Who else knew?"

"Ivy," she whispered.

How could Ivy do this to her? Betray her, her son? Destroying Cal's reputation while he was missing—for what? To deflect attention from her own son, obviously.

"You didn't tell *me,* but Ivy knew?" Wade spat. "And the drug dealing? You're aware of that too?"

"No! Wade, stop. Of course not!" Out of the corner of her eye, Jane noticed a security officer step closer. She lowered her voice. "I don't know anything about that." Her cheeks burned. Rage or a hot flash, she couldn't tell, but she knew one thing: if anyone was mixed up with drugs, it was Brad. Ivy had nearly sent him to rehab after he'd gotten hooked on pain meds following his ACL surgery.

Before she could say more, their bags appeared. Wade yanked them from the carousel and dropped Jane's suitcase at her feet, his gaze as frosty as the air that smacked her face as she hurried after him to catch the shuttle to the rental car area.

As Wade completed the paperwork, handing over his credit card and their licenses, a sweaty sheen crawled across Jane's body. She wanted to believe her son was out there, alive, but the headline, "May Have Battled," written in past tense, made her feel delusional, like she'd been clinging to false hope that he was still alive. It had been almost a week since Brad had seen him—and that was *if* Brad was telling the truth. She clutched the counter, exhaustion and dizziness making it hard to stand. How would this story impact search efforts? What if people believed those things about her son? Would they stop looking? Stop caring?

Listening to the rental car agent attempt to convince Wade to purchase extra insurance, Jane felt trapped in a horrible nightmare that worsened by the second. She pulled out her phone and scrolled to Ivy's last messages, sent late Monday.

> Call me. Please.

Three heart emojis followed. The fakeness of it caused a sour taste to spring into Jane's mouth.

> Whatever's going on, we want to help.

Ivy had written. How quickly that had changed.

Where was the woman who'd been there for Jane when her parents passed within three months of each other, the friend who'd brought over meals during their never-ending kitchen renovation, who'd driven her to doctors' appointments when her pap test had revealed the presence of precancerous cells and distracted her with silly dog videos in the waiting room? Who was this other Ivy? A person who'd taken something Jane had told her in confidence and weaponized it. A mother willing to do anything to protect her child.

After all we've been through together, Ivy, how could you do this to me? To us? Cal loved your family like his own. Jane typed furiously then stopped. There it was, the past tense again. She backspaced.

At the rental counter, Wade raised his voice. She needed to harness her husband's fury. If Ivy had done this, didn't she deserve Jane's wrath? She started again. *How could you say these things about Cal? Look at your own family!* She stared at the phone, a twitch forming behind her left eye. She deleted the words, outrage making her chest tight.

> Hurt my family again and I will destroy you.

She read it twice, hit the send arrow, then blocked Ivy's number.

WADE BASHED his head against the roof of the toy-sized Mazda as he lowered himself into the driver's seat.

"Goddamn clown car," he hissed.

They'd been lucky to get it. The Airbnb wouldn't be available until Monday so they were forced to stay at some no-name motel. They probably couldn't get into their room until three p.m. but maybe someone at the front desk would take pity on them given their situation and they could shower before heading to the police station.

Jane opened her email to find the motel's address. When

had she booked it? The days bled into one another. She scrolled, her inbox jammed with a mix of messages from concerned friends, curious reporters, and retailers announcing holiday deals.

A new message had come through her company's website. Em told her to mark everything "sold out" or note that "due to increased demand" items were backordered, but in her daze she'd forgotten. She needn't have worried. It wasn't an order. It was Daniel.

Headed to Wyoming? I was there recently.

She frowned and reread it. What would bring Daniel to Wyoming? Did he ski? Had he taken a vacation with his daughters? Traveled for work?

"So?" Wade's voice made Jane jump and inch closer to the passenger's side window. "Are you going to tell me or are we going to sit here?"

Her hands trembled, a combination of nerves and the bone-chilling cold. She angled her phone away from him, her eyes landing on Daniel's next sentence.

That's some dangerous terrain.

She looked through the windshield at the unfamiliar landscape. Everything was white. Wade had pulled out of the parking lot. They were moving. She hadn't noticed. In the distance, the mountains loomed, sinister and imposing, their rocky peaks poking at the sky like jagged teeth.

"Tell you what?" Her voice was weak. Daniel's words had left her disoriented.

"The directions to the motel!" Wade hissed.

"I'm looking." She fumbled with the phone, found the confirmation email, copied the address to the map app, and listened as the robotic voice told them to turn left.

Her stomach churned as her eyes drifted back to the message. Maybe she was hallucinating. Exhaustion and anxiety could do that, couldn't they? But no. She read the words again.

Headed to Wyoming? I was there recently.

He must've been watching Em's videos. It felt invasive, too much, his interest, his disregard for boundaries.

She read the next line again.

That's some dangerous terrain.

Then the one beneath it.

I hope you find your son in one piece.

Kidney beans from the minestrone soup she ate at the airport mixed with the merlot she'd consumed. The combination swam into her mouth. She gagged, covering her face with her freezing fingers.

"Goddamnit," Wade roared. "If you're going to be sick, I'll pull over. The last thing I need is a fine from that rental car asshole."

She pawed at the door to lower the window but couldn't find the button. It was too late. She vomited all over the floor mat.

"What the—?" Wade pulled the car to the shoulder with a sharp jerk.

"Just keep driving," Jane managed. "It's over. I'm okay," she added, not that he'd asked.

She wiped her mouth, pieces of tissue clinging to her lips, and felt around inside her handbag for a tin of mints.

Leaning into the headrest, she closed her watery eyes to block the winding roads. As she tried to still her racing thoughts, Daniel's words flashed like a neon sign: *I hope you find your son in one piece.*

14

SATURDAY, DECEMBER 20

IVY

Ivy stood beneath a ball of mistletoe on Betsy Gallagher's doorstep, fingers curled tight around the edges of her serving platter. Before leaving her home, she sat on her bedroom floor, stroked Jean-Claude's coarse fur, and attempted breathing exercises to ease her anxiety. But somewhere along the two-block walk to Betsy's, any sense of calm she'd cultivated disappeared.

As she raised her hand to ring the doorbell, Greg's voice traveled back to her, causing her to hesitate.

"You really think you should go?" he'd asked while she dressed.

"Won't it look worse if I don't?" she'd countered, poking her head through a roll-neck sweater featuring Rudolph, complete with a red pom-pom nose on the front and a white tail on the back.

Betsy's holiday cookie exchange was a tradition, a bit of grown-up fun for the neighborhood moms amid the frenzy of the season. Jane always pretended to "forget" the ugly sweater component. Each year, Ivy asked if she wanted to accompany her to TJ Maxx to hunt for something festive. Jane consistently declined.

"C'mon, I'll treat you to soup and a sandwich at Panera after," Ivy would offer.

Jane, who preferred restaurants with wine lists and linen napkins, would laugh and say, "Believe me, that doesn't make the prospect any more appealing!"

Jane. Thinking about her made Ivy's muscles tense. What she'd written was so vile, Ivy had to read the text twice and triple-check the sender to fully process the words:

> Hurt my family again and I will destroy you.

A week ago, Ivy had been preparing dinner for the Whitakers, stuffing an organic chicken with lemon and rosemary, preparing side dishes, and even baking a birthday cake. Now Jane was threatening her. How had it come to this?

That morning, as Ivy stood in her kitchen whipping up three dozen oatmeal fig cookies for Betsy's party, her phone pinged. After rereading the text, she sank to the floor, nearly landing in Jean-Claude's water bowl. She hadn't known how to respond to Jane's message so she simply wrote ?? and watched as "undelivered" appeared beneath the question marks.

When Greg came in to refill his coffee, he found her on the floor, the dog licking dough from her sticky fingers.

"Hired a new taste-tester, eh?" he asked.

She handed her husband the phone.

"What?"

Ivy shook her head, muted by shock. The lines creasing the corners of Greg's eyes deepened as he squinted and scrolled upward, reading the messages Ivy had sent Jane earlier in the week asking how they could help. Jane hadn't written back. Until then.

"Something must've happened." Greg typed a combination of words that brought up the story about Cal, his gambling, his drug dealing. He read the article aloud, then extended a hand to pull Ivy to her feet. "So... what?" he asked. "She thinks you're the anonymous source?"

"I would never..." Ivy's voice trailed off as she turned her back to Greg, pinched a wad of cookie dough from the bowl and popped it in her mouth. Yes, she knew Cal still gambled because Brad had told her, but how deep was his debt? She had no clue about the drugs, yet it made sense. When had Brad's voice started sounding strange, spacey? Recently? Right after he hurt his knee. What if it had been like that for months but because she was helping Max find a job and fielding calls about her mother from Florence she'd been too distracted to notice?

When Brad was in high school, how many hours had she spent on the phone with insurance companies and outpatient treatment facilities trying to get her son help before things got worse? At the time, Cal had been in their home, at their dinner table. He knew how they'd battled to pull Brad back from the brink of a serious problem. But if Cal were strapped for cash, she could imagine him selling drugs to Brad. It wasn't a nice thought, but Callaway Whitaker typically put himself first.

Ivy stabbed Betsy's doorbell as if she were poking Cal in the eye. The Whitakers were in Wyoming. Wade had a temper. She remembered once she'd stopped by to bring Jane a basket of apple-bran muffins and noticed a hole in the entryway wall. Emerson, who'd answered the door, caught her staring.

"My dad's top agent quit. He's super-pissed," Em had whispered. "My mom's upstairs. Want me to get her?"

Jane's text, *I will destroy you,* shot to the forefront of her mind. What if Wade had written it? *Was Brad in danger?* Ivy had called and texted her son all morning but he hadn't responded. Was that because the Whitakers were there with him? Ivy's wrists went limp and she nearly dropped the platter. What was she thinking? She couldn't go to some stupid cookie party. She was about to turn and rush home when Betsy opened the door.

"Ivy!" Betsy's eyes widened.

If she hadn't been wearing a red sweater with a fluffy, cotton-ball Santa beard, Ivy might've thought she'd shown up on the wrong day.

"Come in!" Betsy stepped back then called over her shoulder, "Ivy's here."

Was she warning the other guests? The fine hairs on the back of Ivy's neck prickled. Had they been talking about her? Wondering if she'd show?

"I'll put these in the kitchen." Betsy accepted the platter and abandoned Ivy in the foyer.

She took her time removing her snowy boots. From the corner of the dining room, Lindsay Jordan and Kelli Moore watched her. When she said, "Happy holidays!" they returned to their conversation without so much as a wave.

The raw cookie dough Ivy had eaten sat heavy as a boulder in her stomach. *Stupid! Stupid! You're so stupid to come here,* she berated herself. These women had sons who'd played football, who'd worshipped the almighty Callaway Whitaker. If their neighbors were taking sides, they weren't on Brad's—or hers.

She was still bundled in her coat. Could she leave

without anyone noticing? As she took a step back, a hand closed around her shoulder.

"Ivy!" Bethany Cleary. Max had briefly dated her daughter, Willow. "How are you doing? I thought you'd be in Wyoming!"

"We leave Monday." Ivy didn't know what to do with her hands so she shoved them in her coat pockets and twisted the wrappers of the peppermint candies she stashed there.

Bethany cocked her head the way Jean-Claude did when he waited for food scraps to fall. "How's Brad?" Her eyes searched Ivy's face.

"He's being really brave, you know, under the circumstances." She paused. In her head she heard her husband's voice from earlier, not stern but cautioning, "I wouldn't talk about the boys while you're there. You say anything and it'll spread like a bad game of telephone."

But wasn't this a chance to establish her son's narrative publicly? His alibi? *Christ*. Was that how she'd come to think of it? She wouldn't have needed to say anything if Emerson hadn't started a viral smear campaign against Brad.

Before she could stop herself, Ivy added, "He and Cal went skiing and he re-tore his ACL." She didn't know that for sure, but it sounded terrible and had the desired effect. Bethany cringed while Ivy continued. "He was in so much pain, he didn't realize that Cal hadn't come home."

Bethany nodded while swiping a mini-quiche from a passing tray.

Ivy babbled to fill the silence. "He needs an MRI, but he's in this resort town so it's not like he has the same treatment options as here. It's awful."

"No, right, of course." Bethany leaned closer, curiosity, pungent as a strong cheese, wafting off her. "Well, I hope everything works out. It's always something when you're a parent, isn't it?" She rubbed Ivy's arm in sympathy.

The gesture made Ivy want to bite her. What parental hardships had Bethany endured other than Willow not receiving that Fulbright she'd hoped for?

"Excuse me," Ivy said and headed into the living room where women clustered on the couch, chairs, and piano bench. She'd known most of them since her sons were little, but others had only moved to town over the last few years. The heat of their stares as she entered sent her temperature soaring. Greg was right; she never should've come. Taking a seat on the edge of a sofa cushion, she hoped Betsy's dog or children might appear to shift the focus away from her.

Reluctantly, she shrugged her arms out of her coat. How soon could she slip into it again and leave? Each time she glanced at the clock on the mantle, the hands had barely moved. Occasionally, she'd toss out a "Right!" or an "Absolutely!" so it seemed like she was paying attention. She had nothing to add on the topics of nice but affordable gifts for teachers and solutions for crepey skin.

Before long, talk turned to the Whitakers.

"Cheryl and I are thinking of starting a fundraiser for the family," Lucy Baker said, her voice low.

Ivy's head snapped to attention. "For what?" she blurted. If anyone deserved an influx of cash, didn't she and Greg? They were the ones who'd had to hire a lawyer when she was certain their son had nothing to do with Cal's disappearance.

"To offer a reward for information," Cheryl said.

"Or to hire a team of private investigators." Lucy leaned forward. "From what I've heard, the police aren't doing much. It's been, what? A week, and still nothing?"

"And there may be other costs down the line as well." Cheryl shivered.

Had they seen the article about Cal's gambling debt? Or did she mean medical? Or worse—burial? Jane wouldn't like this, any of it, Ivy knew. Deemed a charity case was not the Whitaker way. She mulled how to tactfully shut down the discussion.

"I'm sure Jane and Wade would be touched, but I don't think they need any additional funds."

Cheryl snorted. "Oh, no, they definitely do." She looked around the room, taking care to make eye contact with each woman. "It doesn't leave this room, but Wade couldn't get a mortgage for the last property he wanted to buy." She cast a glance toward the front door as if Wade might suddenly appear. "He's missed some payments. A few of his buildings are in foreclosure actually."

"How do you—?" before Ivy could finish her sentence she remembered Cheryl bragging that her husband had been promoted to senior vice president at some big bank.

"Jack would kill me if he knew I was sharing this, but Wade went to him for help, like, personally, but everything's so strict now, even though Jack's a senior VP, his hands were tied. They'd golfed together a few times so apparently Wade, with this mountain of debt, thought Jack could wave a magic wand and approve a million-dollar loan."

Ivy clutched the sofa cushion, thoughts spinning. *The Whitakers had money trouble?* Jane always played off Wade's financial concerns as if he were just cheap. How had she not known?

"That's why Jane started that jewelry business!" Lindsay Jordan snapped her fingers as if she'd solved a riddle.

"And my girls told me Emerson is selling leggings online," added Jillian Reed, eyebrows arched. "Is that right?"

A few women nodded. Others stared into their wine glasses, pretending not to savor the gossip, though Ivy was sure they found it more delicious than Betsy's wheel of baked brie in puff pastry.

"You didn't know?" It took Ivy a moment to realize Cheryl's question was directed at her. "I'm so surprised Jane didn't confide in you."

Ivy and Cheryl had been on good terms until the day Ivy offered gentle guidance on Cheryl's upward facing dog. After that, Cheryl stopped coming to the studio. At last year's cookie exchange, Ivy overheard her telling the group she'd switched to Pilates.

"I'm enjoying it so much more. I found this amazing instructor. I'll text you ladies the info," she'd crowed, eyes locked on Ivy's.

Betsy appeared in the doorway, ringing a bell like a Salvation Army Santa. "It's time, ladies! Grab your tins and join me in the kitchen!"

Ivy followed the herd toward Betsy's marble island where Miles, Betsy's eighth grader, passed out disposable plastic gloves and tissue paper to ensure proper cookie handling.

"Ivy!" Betsy gasped. "Where's your tin?"

Ivy had forgotten to bring one.

"Don't worry, I bought extras in case we had a few absentminded Abigails!" Betsy, who'd recently returned to teaching Kindergarten, disappeared into the dining room.

As they walked in circles around the island, women—even ones Ivy had known for years—seemed to step away from her. Did they all think Brad was somehow responsible for whatever had happened to Cal? She wanted to ask but couldn't bear the answer.

Ivy's oatmeal fig cookies were the last to go. When all the platters were empty, Betsy announced that her son Miles would perform a few pieces from his recent recital. The women refilled their glasses and took their places in the living room.

Miles's fingers flew over the keys, filling the room with Vince Guaraldi's "Skating," and Ivy found herself tearing up.

"Excuse me," she whispered to no one and headed to the powder room located at the far end of the kitchen right beside the breakfast nook.

"Tragic placement," Jane had said when Betsy invited them to show off her latest renovation. "We must get the name of her architect so we make sure we never use him."

Ivy closed the toilet's lid. Throughout her childhood, the bathroom had been a sanctuary, the only common space not overrun by her mother's debris. While the vanity had been covered with more eyeliner pencils and tubes of lipstick than her mother could've worn in her lifetime, the toilet and shower were always clear and usable.

Ivy wiped her eyes and plucked a raspberry thumbprint from the bottom of the tin. The buttery sweetness worked like a balm on her fraying nerves. She chose a sprinkle cookie next, then a macaroon. As she gobbled her way through the box, she wondered if she could slip out the backdoor without anyone seeing her. She'd send Betsy a *Thanks for a lovely afternoon!* text later. No one would miss her.

Her coat was in the living room but she didn't care. She stood, crumbs falling to the floor in a pale yellow pile. On the other side of the door she heard voices, followed by chairs scraping the hardwood. Women sitting. *Who?* She held her breath and waited.

"I mean, holy shit, your best friend's son is missing, your son may be involved—is now the time to show up at a cookie exchange?"

"I cannot believe she came."

"I hate to talk about someone else's child, but remember when Brad dropped out of college and he'd be out there walking the streets at all hours? That was some dark-night-of-the-soul shit."

"Yes!" came another voice, looser, louder from the wine, no doubt, "and that was before they got that ugly little dog. It was so weird to see him, no phone or earbuds. He looked lost, disturbed even. Not gonna lie, Jack and I were pretty relieved when we heard he was moving." *Cheryl.*

"Same." *Lucy.*

A cork popped. They were dissecting her son over prosecco. Ivy wanted to open the door and ask if they'd read the article about Cal and *his* demons?

"Of course, I hope Cal's okay, but let's be honest, he—"

"What?"

"Well, when he turned down Kaci's promposal, I thought Dan was going to murder him with his bare hands." *Jillian Reed.*

"Aw, poor Kaci," was followed by moans of commiseration, then, "Are you watching Emerson's videos?"

"Fucking crazy, right?"

"What's crazy is that Jane is off basically hoping to reclaim her son's body and Ivy's here stuffing her face dressed like Rudolph. I'm sorry, that's just not right."

"I think it's fair to say that friendship is over."

"Seriously."

. . .

IVY DROPPED to the toilet again, her breathing ragged. A bell rang, its tinkle dulled by the bathroom door.

"Ladies!" Betsy sing-songed. "It's time for the grab bag!"

Ivy hadn't remembered the grab bag gift either, not that it mattered; she had no intention of staying. As soon as the women left the kitchen, she'd drop her empty tin on the counter and race home.

Beyond the door, chairs scratched the floor again. Voices grew distant. Ivy stood and looked in the mirror. Her face was the splotchy pink and white of a canned ham. She ran a napkin under cool water and pressed it to the back of her neck then practiced a fake smile in case anyone had lingered in the kitchen. A red sprinkle was wedged between her front teeth.

She was beginning to look as out of control as she felt.

15

SATURDAY, DECEMBER 20

BRAD

The chanting woke Brad from a deep sleep. They were back. In the parking lot. Shouting, "Where is Cal? Where is Cal?"

What did they call themselves? Cal's Crusaders? Cal's Crew? He'd seen it online last night before he silenced his notifications and passed out. He'd gone a little overboard with the pills. He knew he should cut back, ration what was left, but he'd wanted to treat himself. He'd done something difficult and it was over. For now.

The meeting with Don had been less terrible than expected. Still, thinking about Chloe, talking about her death, was like pressing on a bruise that had never healed.

On the drive from Don's office to the condo, he thought about Chloe's family. Her high school swim coach had started a GoFundMe to cover medical and burial expenses. Her mom was still on the hook for the private loans they'd taken to pay for stuff her swim scholarship hadn't covered. What a fucked-up system it was that even in death, debt followed you. Brad hadn't had much money, but he'd donated one hundred and eighteen dollars—all that was left in his bank account at the time. The total amount raised blew way past the fifty-thousand-dollar goal.

At the top of the page was a collage: pictures of Chloe as a kid in goggles and her swim cap perched on an orange diving block. In others she was surrounded by family, her head thrown back laughing or pitched forward blowing out birthday candles. Brad had stared at the photos endlessly, trying to imagine her voice in the moments before and after each was taken. When he couldn't sleep, which was just about every night for months after it happened, he read the messages people left on the site, things he'd never have known about her. Weird but cool stuff like she was afraid of clowns and her favorite flower was a daisy. She was studying to become a teacher, but he'd had no clue it was because her cousin was dyslexic and she'd spent a summer helping him learn to read. She loved to paint but was shy about showing anyone her work.

He thought about writing something too, but his words seemed small and ridiculous. He always ended up deleting them.

After about six weeks, new messages stopped coming. He read the old ones so many times he could've recited them as if they were a beautiful and heartbreaking poetry collection.

By the time Brad had pulled into the condo parking lot after talking to Don, his cheeks were wet. At least Cal's Crusaders had taken their posters and gone home. Single-digit temperatures were good for something. He'd half-expected to find his door kicked in or the lock broken if Jason, the bookie's bitch boy, had decided to come back. But everything was just as Brad had left it.

His head felt lighter after unloading on Don, but his

knee had tightened up from sitting in the cold car for an hour. He went straight to Cal's drawer and popped three pills, desperate to feel like nothing could touch him, like he was preserved in bubble wrap, the world and all his problems trapped on the other side of an impenetrable barrier.

He'd slept better than he had in days until the noise coming from the parking lot cut into his dream. When he awoke, for the first time in ages he wished Cal were there because every once in a while he made excellent coffee. Cal had spent about eight days as a barista before he quit, declaring he'd rather be "broke than bored."

Brad glanced toward the kitchen as if someone would magically appear with a steaming pot of French roast. What he saw instead was a thin river of water trickling out of the kitchen onto the brown carpet.

Fuck! The sink must've overflowed. When he'd pulled the last beer from the fridge the night before to wash down the pills, he'd kept his eyes averted, not wanting to deal with the leaking faucet and the clog. He'd have to call a plumber. Would anyone come out on a Saturday? If they did, would they recognize him? Emerson's videos were fucking everywhere. Would they say something like, "Hey, aren't you the guy who didn't report his friend missing, the one who placed an ad for a new roommate right before his current one disappeared?"

He sat up and rubbed his eyes. The hum of the TV had kept him company overnight but now the false cheer of it irritated him. The news was on. A weatherman pointed at a map dotted with cartoon snowflakes. His family was due to arrive late Monday. It would be a comfort to have his parents and brother there with him, by his side, *on his side*, protecting him. He just had to hang on until then.

"Looks like we're in for an extra-white Christmas!" The weatherman laughed before the camera panned back to the anchors.

Brad was about to shut off the TV, get up and take a shower, when a photo of Cal appeared on the screen. He dropped the remote. It was already battered and scuffed from Cal hurling it at the wall each time bad calls and bungled plays cost him more money.

The newscaster's mouth seemed to move in slow motion as she said, "We turn now to a story we've been following all week. New information is coming to light this morning in the case of Cal Whitaker, the ski instructor who's been missing since last Saturday. A source close to the twenty-three-year-old told the *Teton Tribune* that this young man's hobbies weren't limited to skiing."

Brad felt his heart beat in his throat. It was as if the woman weren't reading a teleprompter but staring directly at him. Was he hallucinating? No. Searing pain gripped his knee. He was awake. This was real.

"That source alleges that Whitaker may have gotten in over his head with sports betting and amassed a significant debt. Additionally, the paper is reporting that Whitaker turned to selling ill-gotten prescription drugs to keep creditors at bay.

"Once again," she continued, "police are asking for the public's help. Anyone with information about Whitaker's whereabouts should contact the number on the screen."

The fellow anchor shook his head. "Your heart goes out to this young man's family. Definitely not what anyone was hoping to hear." He took a beat and changed his inflection. "Still struggling to find the perfect gift for your partner? After the break, we'll chat with…"

How did they know all that?

Don. Feeling around the floor, Brad found his phone and searched for the lawyer's contact info. Everything ached from so many nights of crashing on the couch. As he waited for the attorney to pick up, he twisted his neck, hoping to crack a few vertebrae.

"Don Carmich—"

"Don!" Brad cleared his throat, trying to make his voice louder, more intimidating. He hadn't considered what he'd say when Don answered, so he simply blurted, "What the fuck?"

"Who's this?"

"Cut the shit, Don. It's me. Brad. What happened to 'Whatever you tell me stays between us?' You called the paper? What the hell were you thinking?" He ran his hand through his greasy hair as he waited for Don to explain himself. When was the last time he showered? Maybe he should shave his head. Then he'd be less recognizable.

The sound of Don's breathing filled the silence. Why wasn't he saying anything?

Focus! Brad struggled to find words. "How? I mean, how did you even get that in the paper without naming a source?"

"Got a friend at the *Tribune*," Don said finally. "His sister had an issue with a squatter at one of her rental properties. I did my thing, got the guy out. This fella owed me one." Don chuckled. "Plus, the days of real journalism are long gone, kid. They'd write that Cal's half-Yeti if it'd get clicks and sell papers."

Brad's head throbbed like it might explode. He wished he had coffee, something to make him more alert and kill the awful taste in his mouth. Even a glass of water. Water. Out of the corner of his eye, he watched the murky puddle expanding, the carpet darkening. He had to stop it before it leaked into the condo below. How had this become his life? A week ago, he had a twinge in his knee and minor issues with his roommate. Now that roommate was gone, his knee hurt like a motherfucker when he wasn't high on Oxy, he had a shady lawyer, and he was about to incur the wrath of Wade and Jane Whitaker.

"I called in a favor for you, Brad, though, geez, you certainly don't sound very appreciative."

Brad was silent.

"Hello?" Don said.

"Yeah, I'm still here." Brad rested his heavy head in his palm. "I—"

"Look, you know what they say: the best defense is a good offense! Thought you played football, son."

"It's the other way around," Brad wanted to shout, but checked himself. The last thing he needed was to lose Don, to have to share his whole story all over again with a new attorney.

"I told you that stuff in confidence, in case you ended up defending me, in case we needed it, not to lob a grenade at the Whitakers."

"First, I gotta ask: Why keep protecting this guy? Ever consider you may have Stockholm Syndrome? After everything you told me last night, if I were in your shoes, I'd want to nail this son-of-a-bitch to a wall."

Brad scratched his itchy head. Don was right. *Fuck Cal.* Why, after all the shit he'd put him through, was he still treating Cal like a brother? It was more than that clichéd business about old habits dying hard. According to Emerson's latest video, Wade and Jane were in Wyoming. He didn't need a showdown with those two. He wanted to tell

Don, "You have no idea what the Whitakers are capable of," but he knew how over-the-top it sounded, like they headed up a crime family. Still, he remembered Cal bragging about his mother getting a new Language Arts teacher fired during their junior year.

"She was going to torpedo my GPA," Cal had laughed. "Bitch had to go."

Brad could picture Wade pacing behind the fence at every football game, screaming at the coaches, throwing water bottles, stomping his feet, giving refs the finger behind their backs.

"Second, Brad," Don continued, "turns out we needed it."

"Needed it how?" Brad asked.

"They found something." A kettle whistled in the background. "I tried to call you this morning. Would've left you a message but your mailbox is full."

"What? What did they find?" Brad's insides spun like a bald tire in the snow.

"A ski glove." Don waited.

Brad rubbed his eyes. "So what? This is a resort town. You can't go ten feet without finding a hat, a pole, a glove—"

"This one's... different." Don paused. "Had a little doggie snack inside."

"What does that mean?" Sweat pooled in Brad's armpits.

"A finger—part of one, I guess, from the knuckle up—was stuffed inside. A search-and-rescue dog found it."

Brad's stomach was empty. Still, he thought he'd dry heave.

"They're testing it. Looking to see if it's Cal's. Checking for your DNA too, of course."

"How?" Brad couldn't form whole sentences. "Where?"

"In a field along Route 89. Isn't that on the way to your place?" Don asked.

"Yeah." Brad swallowed. *Fuck!*

"Look, son, at some point, the family's probably going to offer a reward. That's what usually happens, and once it does, people are going to start coming out of the woodwork."

It was a lot to take in—too much. Brad pictured the pills in Cal's drawer, perfect white circles that made everything else almost bearable. His skin crawled and itched for more.

"So what... what happens next?" The chants from the parking lot grew louder. Brad closed his eyes. "What am I supposed to do now?"

"They're expediting the testing, but it could take up to seventy-two hours. Sit tight. Try not to worry."

That was like saying try not to breathe.

"I've got friends down at the station," Don said. "Soon as the results are in, I'll give you the heads-up. They're trying to keep it out of the papers."

Brad's tongue was so dry it might as well have been Velcroed to the roof of his mouth. He couldn't speak.

If it turned out to be the glove Cal was wearing Saturday, he didn't need to wait for them to test it. He knew his DNA was all over it.

16

SUNDAY, DECEMBER 21
JANE

Jane paced the narrow space between the double bed and dresser in the small motel room.

"Sit!" Wade commanded as if she were a dog. "You're gonna wear a hole in the carpet and they're going to charge us to replace it."

She couldn't sit—not on the bed. Its mustard duvet cover reminded her of a *Dateline* episode in which investigators had shone a blue light on a hotel bedspread and found it polka-dotted with semen stains. She couldn't sit at the desk, not on the vinyl chair, its torn seat held together by duct tape.

She would've walked circles around the parking lot if the bitter cold didn't cause her to lose feeling in her toes and fingers.

Fingers. Jane's mind was reeling from the news. After they'd checked in Saturday, she and Wade had gone to the police station. On the short drive, her husband had warned her, "These are the same guys we've talked to on the phone, remember?"

"What does that mean?" The stench of vomit still lingered in the rental car. Jane thought she might be sick again.

"It means manage your expectations."

The police station was more modern than Jane had envisioned it. She'd pictured a wooden, shed-like structure with metal desks, rotary phones, and a snoring basset hound in the corner. When she saw the stone building and its clean, shiny interior, she experienced a momentary surge of hope.

Lynch came out first to shake their hands and lead them to a back room. When Hanlon appeared, looking not much older than her son, her optimism shriveled, a flower bud that never had the chance to blossom.

The young cop fetched stale coffee while Lynch showed them a map dotted with pushpins that marked the areas where teams had searched for Cal.

She'd stared blankly as the officer pointed out "avalanche country" and "treacherous terrain." That last word smacked her with full force. Daniel's message: *That's some dangerous terrain* came back to her.

Lynch told them to take a seat as he went over transcripts of interviews with Cal's neighbors and his co-workers. He'd already covered most of it over the phone. Someone from a local bar, The Chill Factor, thought they'd seen Cal the night he didn't return, but he wasn't on camera and there was no record of payment. Jane already knew that from checking his bank and credit card accounts.

"No one else remembers seeing him." Lynch sighed.

Cal's face wasn't one anyone forgot, Jane wanted to shout. With his perfect bone structure and twinkling blue eyes, he was hands-down the most attractive person in any room.

"We've got one new lead." Lynch made a "gimme" gesture and the boyish cop slid a tan folder toward him. "Dog found a glove with a partial finger inside it just before dawn."

The room seemed to tilt. Jane clutched the table and stared at her own fingers, a cold sweat creeping across her skin.

"We didn't want to tell you while you were in transit." Hanlon smiled like he'd done them a favor and was expecting a "thank you."

"Got photos," Lynch said, "if you'd like to see them."

"Of the glove?" Jane asked at the same time Wade said, "Of the finger?"

"Both." Lynch opened the folder.

Jane wanted to appear brave but her limbs betrayed her, growing heavy and weak the way they did when she came down with the flu.

"I'm not—" she began.

"Yes," Wade said.

Lynch pulled out the photo of the glove first. It was black, basic. Jane wasn't in the habit of cataloguing her son's ski gear. It could've been anyone's. She tried to picture Cal's gloved hands in social media posts but with the shock of this news, her memories slipped into a black hole.

Wade cleared his throat. "And the other?"

"Mrs. Whitaker, you may not want to—"

"It's fine," she said, irritated that he would treat her differently from her husband.

Lynch removed the photo of the finger. Blood had pooled and crusted around the nail bed and in the horizontal creases of the knuckle.

Jane slid lower in her seat, black dots floating in the corners of her vision.

"We know it's a lot to take in," Hanlon finally said. "Do you think this could be your son's?"

Was this Cal's finger? She couldn't tell. Shouldn't she know? She forced herself to picture her son's hands—toddler hands, chubby, dimpled, reaching up to touch her cheek; teen hands throwing a perfect spiral; a young man's hand strumming a guitar in a hammock on a summer night.

Her eyes traveled between the bloodied nail and the gruesome end where the bone had been severed and back again. Could she say with absolute certainty that this was her son's finger? No.

Tears dripped down her cheeks. Lynch unwrapped a cough drop while Hanlon shuffled his feet beneath the table. Both avoided eye contact.

Wade emitted a *pfft*, filling the air with his coffee breath. "I— I can't say. Not for sure." He rolled his neck and rubbed his brow.

"Is this—could this have something to do with..." Jane could barely get the words out, "...Cal's gambling? If it's his, I mean? Is someone sending a message?" She didn't know what to hope for. If this wasn't Cal's finger, then they had no new leads. If it was, what then? She couldn't fathom someone mutilating her beautiful son.

"We're not ruling anything out at this point," Lynch said.

"When will you—?" Wade waved his hand above the photos.

"We should know something Monday. Tuesday at the latest." Lynch slipped the pictures into the folder.

If they were lucky enough to find DNA, it might only lead to a suspect, not directly to Cal. And what if that person was long gone? Or, what if that person was Cal's roommate and the police had been ignoring the obvious?

"Why isn't Brad Chapman being questioned again?" Jane asked. She pictured him sitting in the condo watching television or ordering take-out and wanted to shake him until he revealed every last thing he wasn't telling. "This isn't enough. There has to be more you—we—can do," Jane ranted. "What about that ad he placed for a new roommate?"

"Your son couldn't cover the rent," Lynch said. "Chapman's lawyer forwarded emails, texts, and bank statements."

"What if we offered a reward?" she volunteered.

Wade had protested each time she'd brought it up. She waited for him to shoot down the idea but he stayed silent as the officers glanced at one another.

"That can help, but—" Hanlon said.

"Tends to bring out a lot of crazies, wastes our time, creates a lot of false hope..." Lynch concluded.

"There has to be—"

"Ma'am, we can assure you, we're—"

"You can't assure us of anything, not really." Wade's tone, so resigned, confirmed what Jane had feared. Her husband didn't think their son would be found. At different points as the torturous week had dragged on, she'd seen her husband staring into the distance, squaring his shoulders as if bracing for something. Once she'd caught him wiping the corner of his eye with a knuckle. After that, she'd tried not to look at him.

"We'll be in touch," Lynch said as he walked them to the exit.

Beneath the officer's bushy eyebrows, Jane saw pity, possibly even disgust. To them, Cal was probably another young, spoiled asshole who blew into their town to party and put off real life.

These cops likely assumed her son was dead from the

moment she called them. They'd no doubt speculated that he'd gotten lost and disoriented as darkness descended and temperatures plummeted, snow swallowing him. His body would surface in spring, his death confirmed as the earth came back to life.

They walked to the rental car, icy wind stinging Jane's tear-streaked face. She couldn't remember a time she'd felt so hopeless, not even after the deaths of her mother and father. When they'd passed, she'd had Wade, Cal, Em, even Ivy, for support. Now each of them seemed so distant, they might as well have been living on separate continents.

On the way to the motel, Wade picked up a pizza and two bottles of a no-name, screw-top red. They ate in the room, the brown drapes and olive carpet reminding Jane of the backdrop of a bad 1970s sitcom.

She'd barely slept. Each time she started to drift, doors slammed and startled her back to consciousness. She'd bolted upright in the bed, unsure of where she was, only to have the horror of her situation wash over her again.

At five a.m., she reached for her phone and began scrolling. That's when she saw them— photos from Betsy's cookie party. These women in their gaudy sweaters, grinning like extras in a Hallmark movie. These women were supposed to be her friends. Yet there they were, their lives continuing on unaffected. In the background of a candid shot, she spotted Ivy, her dark roots visible beneath blonde highlights.

It hit her like a sucker-punch. *How could she?* Jane swiped left. There were fourteen images—cookies, Miles perched at the piano, Betsy's well-appointed tree and Nutcracker collection on the mantle. Jane let out the whimper-whine of a wounded animal and twisted her pillow until her hand cramped. Then she pictured the finger, possibly Cal's, somewhere in a lab. She imagined her son's hand without it. Was it a ring finger, a middle finger? How had she not even asked?

By nine a.m. her eyes burned from crying and lack of sleep. She didn't know how to be useful here. She'd convinced herself that once she was in Wyoming, she'd get answers, be that much closer to finding her son. But she was every bit as helpless here as she'd been in New Jersey. Another day with nothing to do but wait.

The organizers of Cal's Crusaders invited her and Wade to a vigil set to take place in the condo parking lot that afternoon. Jane thanked them but declined. If they went, it would be impossible not to confront Brad. He had a lawyer now. That told her everything she needed to know.

With Wade in the shower, Jane continued to pace. Outside the bathroom door, she was about to turn for her hundredth lap when Wade's phone vibrated against the desk. She froze. Each call offered equal doses of hope and fear. Cal could've been found. In what condition?

In two strides, she crossed the room. She didn't know the number but recognized the New Jersey area code. With trembling fingers, she swiped and whispered, "Hello?"

"Mrs. Whitaker? This is Robert Willis with Garden State Life Insurance. I'm returning your husband's call."

Disappointment and relief rushed through her. "Yes?"

"Wade had a question. I'm getting back to him."

It must've been work-related—important, too, if this guy... what was his name? Richard? Robert?—was calling back on a Sunday morning.

"Wade's in the shower. I can take a message."

Silence. The heat kicked on, filling the room with the faint scent of mold.

"Hello?" She moved toward the window in case cell service was stronger.

"I can call back."

"It's fine." Jane returned to the desk, annoyed. What was so urgent that Wade had called while they were searching for their son? "I have a pen. Go ahead."

"You sure?"

"Yes." She tried to keep the irritation out of her voice. Did he think she wasn't capable of relaying a message? Because she was a woman in her fifties? She thought of Lynch's reluctance to show her the severed finger.

"Tell him it's complicated. Death in absentia is a complex thing to navigate. Getting a death certificate without a body isn't easy, but it's necessary in order to file a claim."

"What?" Jane sank to the bed, her head spinning. She thought this call was about property insurance. *Getting a death certificate without a body isn't easy.* Was this about Cal?

He was speaking again but she couldn't hear him above her pulse echoing in her ears.

"...if he has any additional questions, he can call me back. I'll be in and out all day."

Jane couldn't form words.

"And, Mrs. Whitaker?"

She didn't want to hear more.

"I'm sorry about—"

She ended the call before he could finish his sentence.

Seething, she waited for her husband, who always took longer showers when he didn't have to pay for the water.

When Wade finally opened the bathroom door, a cloud of steam preceded him as if he were a magician. His pale skin was mottled, a thin, off-white towel wrapped around his middle. He rubbed a facecloth over his wet head, only stopping when he noticed her watching him.

"What?" When she didn't speak, he looked at the phone in her hand and asked again, more urgently, "What?"

She wanted to stand, to get up from that filthy, disgusting duvet, but her legs had turned to jelly. It was all she could do to hold the phone aloft. "Your insurance agent called."

"Oh?" Wade's face flushed as pink as his chest.

"You took out life insurance on Cal? Why? When?" With each word, Jane's voice rose. The motel's walls were paper-thin but she didn't care who heard her. "You think our son is dead and you're trying to cash in?"

Wade sighed as if he'd been tasked with explaining long division to a child. "It's part of our standard benefits package. I never canceled it because I assumed he'd get bored being a ski bum and come back to work for me. And now..." His voice was a low monotone. "I'm being realistic, Jane. It's been over a week. I'm not giving up hope, I'm... I'm—"

"You're what? Wondering how much and how soon you can collect?" She threw the phone at his head. He caught it. The towel dropped to the floor, revealing his flaccid penis nesting in his salt-and-pepper pubic hair. "Everything comes down to money. You let me pay for that parking ticket on our third date. Twelve dollars!"

"That's what you're thinking about! At a time like this!" He strode toward her, his low-hanging, wrinkled ballsack swinging. "You offered!"

"And you took it! I knew then you would always put money before me, but ahead of our son? Your own child?"

Bare-assed, he sat beside her, forcing her to inch toward the edge of the bed.

"We're in trouble, Jane." He rubbed his face. His hair—what was left of it—stuck up at wild angles. "My business. The vacancies. It's basically over. As soon as Em graduates, we can sell the house. Even then it won't be enough. I've—"

Sell the house? Jane loved that house. A hum filled her head. *Trouble?* How did she not know any of this? She felt as if she were watching her life from a distance, a bad movie she couldn't shut off.

"I'm sorry. I should've told you sooner. I thought things would turn around. I thought I—"

She'd stopped listening. Wade couldn't see it, but he was exactly like his father. A gambler. He didn't bet on horses or athletes but on property. A grown man playing Monopoly with real money. *Their money.*

"How much?" she asked. She couldn't look at him.

"How much what?"

"If Cal is—" a sob clogged her throat "—gone, how much is that worth to you?"

"Stop, Jane. It's not... We have to be honest with each other." He reached for her hand and she recoiled. "It doesn't look good. That finger? I think we have to prepare ourselves for the worst."

No. She wouldn't. With or without a finger, whatever had happened, wherever he was, Jane needed to believe that her son would survive.

In that moment, though, she couldn't say the same for her marriage.

17

MONDAY, DECEMBER 22
EMERSON

Emerson's eyes were closed as Sasha made the turn onto her street.

"Holy shit!" Sasha gasped.

"Holy shit," Emerson echoed, blinking.

News vans lined the curbs. Reporters and camera crews stood on the sidewalk in front of the Whitakers' home. It wasn't even seven a.m.

Sasha slowed her Jeep to a crawl. "Want me to turn around?" She had a poppy seed in her teeth. Em didn't tell her.

"No, it's fine." Em flipped down the visor and cringed at her reflection in the mirror. She looked like crap. The skin beneath her eyes was a puffy, purply-blue while a monster zit bloomed on her forehead. Her period was due any sec. It was making her ugly, hungry, murderous.

"Okay, here we go." Sasha wailed on the horn.

People blocking the driveway scattered and reassembled in little anxious clusters.

Sasha pulled up to the three-car garage. "You don't have to get out yet. We can chill."

"Cool. Yeah. Let's." Emerson's stomach cratered.

Another day, another time, seeing the media waiting there for her would've been as welcome as wildflowers poking through sidewalk cracks in early spring. Now it terrified her, and not just because she looked worse than one of those pathetic celebrities-without-makeup photos, but because maybe they had news for her. Had something happened overnight? Had Cal been found? Were they there to ask her for information or to capture her reaction when they dropped a bomb about her brother?

She hadn't really been worried about Cal—not at first. Even when he'd gotten in trouble and lost all that money in high school, their mom had bailed him out. Her brother was like an Olympic gymnast, always landing on his feet with a bow and a satisfied smirk.

Cal got bored easily. Their mother believed it was because he was so intelligent, so naturally curious. But Emerson knew better. Once he discovered he was the smartest, best-looking person in the room, he went to find another room. She assumed wherever he'd gone, he'd be back in time for their arrival in Wyoming.

It was only after those creepy assholes showed up at the door Friday night that things started to shift in her mind. What was Cal involved in? How serious was it? She didn't know if the bald man's threat to return Sunday and start "breaking and taking" was real, but she hadn't wanted to sit around and find out. That night Sasha said Em could stay at her place. Her parents were divorced, and her mom was busy with a new boyfriend.

Emerson's mother, on the other hand, seemed to check in constantly, texting then calling, voice shaky and weird.

"What now?" Em had screeched at her. "Stop calling! You're freaking me out!"

"It's like she has no consideration for my feelings," Em complained to Sasha. "I keep thinking she's gonna tell me Cal's dead, but she's just calling to remind me to get to the airport early for my flight, to lock the house, to make sure the oven's off—like I'm five fucking years old!"

A thousand miles could separate them and still her mother annoyed the shit out of her.

No longer able to stand her reflection, Em flipped up the visor. It was more than exhaustion and the hideous pimple that seemed to be growing like an erect nipple between her eyes. It was Max. *He* was killing her confidence.

After he'd stormed out of her bathroom Friday night, she'd sent him a dozen texts, Venmo'd him the money for the alcohol, and even called twice.

He was ghosting her.

"Em, for real, you're crossing into stalker territory." Sasha had grabbed her phone so she'd stop making a fool of herself. She'd taken it back in a middle-of-the-night panic and written:

> What about what we had? What about Amsterdam? What about Nice?

The next morning he'd responded:

> It's over. You're not worth it.

Now she wanted to hang out in Sasha's Jeep forever.

The heated seat wasn't enough to stop her teeth from chattering. Maybe they could drive through Starbucks and grab a latte or a hot chocolate like they used to when they'd first gotten their licenses. But she couldn't hide much longer. She needed to pack and get to the airport where she was bound to see Max and his stupid family.

Em reached for the door handle and turned to Sasha. "Thanks. For everything."

"Hey, come here." Sasha hugged her. She smelled like French toast, strawberry lip balm, and a thousand sleepovers. Em inhaled deeply and tried to ignore the noise of the growing crowd.

"You're gonna find him." Sasha squeezed her arm.

Em felt tears swim in her eyes so she bit the inside of her cheek and nodded. "I'll text you."

She stepped out to a chorus of voices blending, certain words—her name, her brother's, and Wyoming—rising above the rest.

The pack swelled toward her.

"Any information?"

"How are you holding up, Emerson?"

It was that last question that got her. No one had really considered how she was doing, not since Max asked on the phone the night she found out Cal was missing.

Fuck it. She looked awful but maybe that made her appear vulnerable, real, more likable. She'd posted a video over the weekend, a montage of Cal, a mix of baby pictures and more recent shots set to instrumental parts of Sufjan Stevens's "Should Have Known Better." It had done so-so. Not terrible but not phenomenal. She didn't want to lose her audience, not after all she'd put into building it. If she spoke to the media, she needed to get it right. For herself, but also for Cal.

Instead of ducking into the garage, she moved toward the walkway. The shiny black front door would work as a decent backdrop. She took a quick mental inventory of things she wanted to say. She'd thank people for looking for Cal, ask them to keep searching, insist that she and her parents would never give up—all the stuff families said in the true crime documentaries she'd watched with Sasha on Friday nights when they were in middle school.

She opened her mouth, prepared to give a short but emotional speech when she heard, "Emerson! What do you know about the finger?"

"Is it Cal's?"

Finger? What were they talking about? She frowned and felt the pinch of that monstrous pimple blooming on her forehead.

Is it Cal's? There was no way to mask her confusion.

Hushed murmurs rippled through the crowd.

"She doesn't know."

"No clue."

"Oh shit!"

A few chuckles followed with a wry, "This is about to get interesting."

A bouquet of microphones were thrust in her face.

"Emerson!" a raven-haired woman shouted. Her out-of-style herringbone coat caught Em's attention. "A finger was found in a glove. Is it your brother's?"

Her stomach hurt like she'd had the wind knocked out of her. It was the same sensation she'd experienced when she'd collided with a senior during freshman field hockey practice. *Cal could be missing a finger? What the fuck?*

"I—I," she stammered. "I hope it's not." She sounded young, dumb. There wasn't time to recover, regroup. The questions were rapid-fire.

"Did you know your brother had a gambling problem?"

"How long has he been selling drugs?"

She should've gone through the garage. What was she thinking?

"Do you still believe his roommate may be responsible?"

She hadn't slept, barely eaten. Her parents had left her. Max had abandoned her when she needed him most. She pictured his text: *You're not worth it.*

Fuck him. She took a deep breath. "Cal's roommate, Brad, has stopped communicating with my family. He's got a lawyer now. He thinks he's untouchable." Her voice, weak at first, steadied, her confidence building. "But he's not. Not with all of you, all of us, out there, searching for Cal and relentlessly pursuing the truth." Her spirits lifted. This was going fine. Well, even. She was poised, powerful, under pressure. "If you're seeing this and you're in the area where Cal went missing, please help us. We're desperate for answers. We won't stop, and I'm begging you not to stop either—not until my brother is found."

She bowed her head and then looked up, staring into as many cameras as possible.

"Thank you."

She took a step back then moved forward again.

"And please, let's keep the pressure on Brad Chapman. He knows more than he's telling."

Dramatically, she spun around but then fumbled to slide her key into the lock. Finally, it turned. She stepped inside, glass crunching beneath her boots. The grandfather clock still lay face down.

"Em!"

"Emerson!"

The rush and roar of follow-up questions filtered through the door. Despite their shouts, the voice she heard clearest was her own, whispering, "You messed with the wrong girl, Max."

18

MONDAY, DECEMBER 22
BRAD

Brad made it through the weekend without leaving the condo, eating only a can of refried beans and a couple of scrambled eggs. The pills killed his appetite anyway.

When he'd felt up to it, he bailed water out of the overflowing kitchen sink and poured it into the toilet. Then he'd limped downstairs to apologize to Neal, his neighbor, in the apartment below.

"It's cool, man, no worries." Neal hadn't removed the chain or made eye contact, only added, "Just call a plumber, okay?" before shutting the door in Brad's face. Neal had been friendly when Brad first moved in. They'd once split a six-pack and a pizza while watching a hockey game. Now he acted like Brad was a serial killer.

Despite everything, for the first time in more than a week, Brad felt optimistic. Yes, he'd taken more pills, but it wasn't just that. His family was coming. Soon. He'd pick them up in a couple of hours. It was three thirty and they'd land close to six. He was practically counting the minutes. Maybe he'd even stay with them at their hotel. The

Whitakers had claimed the Airbnb. Wade had texted Brad's father to say that, given the circumstances, the Chapmans should be the ones to find other accommodations. *Fucking Wade.*

It didn't matter. Any place would be better than the condo as long as it was away from the growing pack of assholes in the parking lot. Don had hoped the story about Cal's gambling and drug dealing would paint him in a negative light, but it had the opposite effect. Cal's troubles made him more relatable and the number of his supporters multiplied.

Brad ran his tongue over his teeth where a slick layer of film had collected during the week. His breath was so foul, it was as if an animal had died in his mouth. Lynch and Hanlon had bagged his and Cal's toothbrushes. He hadn't thought to object and he hadn't remembered to buy a new one. He needed a shower, a shave, a haircut. He could practically hear his mother's concerned, "Oh honey!" If she saw him like this, she'd try to send him to rehab again. He needed to get his shit together. Fast.

He stood and the room swiveled. He'd swallowed the last of Cal's pills an hour earlier. As excited as he was to see his family, he couldn't shake a mounting sense of dread. He had this awful feeling Don would call any second with news about the glove, the finger, and his life would implode. Thinking about it made it hard to breathe, like invisible hands were squeezing his lungs.

As he wobbled toward the bathroom, his phone vibrated against the coffee table.

"Here it comes!" he said aloud to no one. But where he expected to find Don's number, he saw one he didn't recognize.

"Hello?"

"Bradley Chapman?"

"Yes?"

"This is Cherise from Elevated Imaging. We've had a cancellation this afternoon and I wanted to see if you're free."

"Free?"

"To get the MRI? Of your knee?"

Shit! Now?

"What time?" Brad asked.

"Five fifteen, but we need you here by five to complete some paperwork."

"Can I check with my mom?" He sounded like a six-year-old. "I'm supposed to pick her up from—"

"Let's schedule it and you call me right back if it doesn't work," she said. "Cancellations are rare, especially this time of year. You're lucky to get this."

He didn't feel lucky. At all. "Okay," he said.

He'd text his mother, but he was pretty sure she'd have her phone in airplane mode, and, anyway, he knew what she'd say. "Take the appointment! We'll get a car!"

After the MRI, he'd meet them at their hotel, have a real meal together, and maybe that awful, uneasy feeling in his stomach would go away, at least temporarily.

IN THE SHOWER, he used the wall for support and avoided looking at his knee. The warm water felt tingly and amazing but he was so tired, weak. Cal had used all the shampoo and hadn't replaced it, so he took the bar of soap and rubbed it over his head. He shaved, nicking himself only twice. The toilet paper was all but gone.

In his room, he pulled on a clean pair of sweatpants, so loose he needed to double-knot the drawstring. He sniffed a gray, long-sleeved thermal, found it acceptable, and buttoned a flannel shirt over it. In the cloudy bathroom mirror, he stared at his reflection—better than earlier. Yes, he was making a comeback. He found his wallet and car keys on his nightstand and put them in his pocket.

In the living room, he looked at the wall where the clock had been. It still lay on the floor telling the wrong time. He grabbed his phone from the coffee table—4:36 p.m. The notifications caught his eye—three missed calls from Don. *Shit!* He hadn't cleared his voicemail box so the lawyer couldn't leave a message. Brad didn't want to call back. He needed to get through the MRI. Maybe his mom could talk to Don for him later. She'd deal with it. Fix it. The way she always did.

As he stuffed the phone into his pocket, it rang. *Fuck!* He swept a hand through his hair, fingers catching in the gluey spots where he hadn't washed out the soap. He stared at the number. *Don.* Could he ignore it? No. Better to just deal with it. He swiped left.

"Hey," he said. "Can I call you back? I got an appoint—"

"Brad," Don skipped a greeting, "we got a problem."

Brad exhaled and shifted all his weight to his good leg.

"The results are back. It's your buddy's finger. Your DNA's all over the glove."

Brad's head filled with a *whoosh*ing sound as if a giant fan switched on inside his mind, blowing his thoughts around. *Cal's finger. My DNA. Fuck. Fuck. Fuck.* He knew it would come back like this. Of course. How could it not?

"Listen, kid, I—"

"They're my gloves, Don. Cal was always losing his own shit. He borrowed them. They're mine." Brad's speech was slow, slurry, undermining what he was trying to say. "I get that that sounds like some bullshit excuse, but you gotta believe me. They're—"

"Look," Don interrupted, "I'm going to refer you to a colleague of mine. She specializes in this type of thing."

"But you told my mom you'd—"

"Your mom sounded like a nice lady. I didn't want to let her down and, honestly? I didn't expect it to go like this. I'm out of my depth here."

Brad thought he heard a kettle whistle. It was the worst moment of his life and this motherfucker was sitting down to Earl Grey?

"The glove's mine but I— I didn't do anything to Cal," Brad stammered. "You gotta believe me. Last time I saw him, he was at the top of the mountain, yelling, 'See you at the car, Nana.'"

"That might all be true," Don blew a long exhale, "but it also may not be enough. As I said, you'll be better off with my colleague. Let me give you that info. You got a pen or you prefer I text it? Up to you."

Snowballs pelted Brad's sliding doors. The crowd outside chanted something he couldn't understand. He was going to have to face them to get to his car.

"Hey? You still there?" Don asked.

Brad hung his head. "Yeah. Whatever. Text it."

"Another thing," Don said. "The results came back a while ago. Unfortunately, my buddy at the station was out most of the day on a call. There's no telling if it's been leaked."

"Meaning?"

"Meaning you'll want to be extra careful now."

"Am I going to be arrested?" Through the haze of painkillers, Brad's heart hammered.

"I'd imagine so. Getting a warrant could happen fast or it could take a couple hours."

Hours?

Brad had to get out of there.

"Listen, good luck."

"Don, I didn't—"

Don was gone. The phone beeped. The dark screen glowed again as a text appeared.

Lauren Sinclair, Esq.

Phone number and email.

Don hadn't wasted any time dumping him. Brad let out a sound that was half-laugh, half-whimper. Cal's finger. His glove. His DNA. Even when he wasn't there, Cal was screwing him over.

Brad tugged on his coat and checked his phone: 4:52 p.m. He was supposed to be at the imaging center in eight minutes. It would take him that long to get through the mob in the parking lot.

He opened his door and kept his head low. The wind had picked up. As he lurched toward the Highlander, it was either sleeting or people were spitting at him. He wiped his face on his sleeve. Snow and ice crackled beneath his boots. He just had to make it to the car. He'd get the MRI, see his family. They'd know what to do next. They'd help him. Finally, he'd have people on his side. A warm sensation spread between his ribs at the same time someone in the crowd shouted, "Where is he, Brad?" "You're a fucking monster!"

He tried to ignore the voices but it was impossible to pretend he didn't see the figures coming at him from all sides.

A woman stood in front of his car, blocking the door. Melinda, the pharmacist's daughter. Between the dusky sky and the dim parking lot lights, he couldn't read her expression. Was she smiling at him? Brad had been kind to her when she'd come to the condo looking for Cal. He'd invited her in, offered her a drink, never mentioned that his roommate was out with someone he referred to as "that hot waitress." Maybe Melinda was there to support him?

But as he got closer, her mouth twisted.

"How could you? His finger?" Her voice cracked. "This was going to be our first Christmas together. Where is he? What did you do?"

Behind him, a large man in a puffy jacket grabbed his shoulder and spun him around.

"Going somewhere? I don't think so." He shoved Brad hard in the chest, sending him stumbling backward into the sea of onlookers.

"Where's the rest of him, asshole?" The man sprang forward shouting, his saliva landing in Brad's open mouth.

Another guy pushed Brad hard. Someone else thrust him back again. He was light now from a week of barely eating, and they tossed him around the circle as if he were a sock puppet. It was like Kindergarten again, bullies taunting him, mocking his lisp. This time Cal wouldn't be there to step in and save him.

"Give his family closure. Tell the police where he is," a woman pleaded.

"I don't know where he is!" Brad roared, windmilling his arms in anticipation of the next hit.

"The hell you don't!" Someone punched him in the stomach.

Brad was doubled over groaning when he saw the headlights. A news van turned into the parking lot—to film his arrest, no doubt.

The men who'd been shoving him stepped back to watch as the crowd shifted toward the van.

Seeing an opening, Brad lunged for his car, hopped in, and started it. The front and rear windows were crusted with snow. The wiper blades only scraped the surface. He couldn't see but he had to get out of there. He threw it into reverse and hit the gas.

Someone smacked the side of the Highlander and screamed "Asshole!" He slammed it into drive, barreling toward the exit, the back of the SUV fishtailing as he pushed the pedal down and skidded onto the main road. His chest heaved, his breath forming white clouds that fogged the inside of the windows. Even with the defrost cranked, there was only a tiny half-moon of visibility through the windshield. He leaned forward, the mix of adrenaline and drugs making him feel suddenly invincible as he sped along the icy roads, navigating their bends and curves from memory.

He made it a mile, maybe two before someone caught up to him. The car was close. High-beams bouncing off his rearview mirror blinded him. He thought about jamming on the brakes, but as he squinted and swerved he saw it wasn't just one car but a line of them. One sped up and pulled alongside him, horn blaring.

"Jesus Christ," Brad shouted.

He couldn't think as the horn's wail mixed with sirens in the distance and Willie Nelson's cover of "White Christmas" whined through his shitty car stereo. The swirling snow, the endless darkness ahead, the intense light behind him—it all made him dizzy as he sweated through his thermal and flannel.

Grunting, he punched the rearview mirror to block the high beams. It fell to the floor. The car beside him was closing in, edging him out. It was a single lane in each direction. They were going to run him off the road.

"Motherfucker!" Brad pushed the accelerator to the floor and pulled the wheel hard to the right.

Suddenly, he was flying, sailing over a sea of white. The windshield had cleared enough that he could see trees—a forest of pine looming in the field, growing nearer. There was no point in pumping the brakes, tugging the steering wheel.

The SUV slammed into the tree and the airbag exploded, bursting like a balloon in Brad's face, whipping his neck back then forward. The stink of gasoline mixing with burning metal flooded his nostrils. He had to get out of the car, but he was tired. So tired. He couldn't feel anything. Not his legs. Not his arms. Not his fingers as they groped in vain for the door handle.

Closing his eyes, he surrendered to all of it and listened as the wind and sirens formed a terrible lullaby that sang him to sleep.

19

MONDAY, DECEMBER 22
JANE

Jane and Wade had just set their bags inside the Airbnb when the call came.

"Mrs. Whitaker?" Lynch's voice, usually void of emotion, hitched upward, revealing his news before he spoke again. "No easy way to say this, it's your son's finger."

Jane dropped to the couch—a futon covered in a faux suede cow pattern—and took a sharp inhale. In the kitchen, Wade opened cabinets. The squeak of their hinges mixed with the rising roar in her ears. Jane had stopped speaking to her husband the night before after that call from his insurance agent, but when she gasped, Wade appeared in the doorway, mouth open.

"It's his," she said. "It's Cal's finger."

"Mr. Chapman's—Brad's—DNA was found too," Lynch continued, "inside the glove."

His words hit her like a second blow. She pictured Brad as a child, his mess of curly hair, those chubby cheeks strangers loved to pinch, which invariably made him cry. Cal was usually so kind but there were moments when he'd lost patience with Brad and muttered, "Quit being a baby," which caused Brad to blubber harder.

"There's also some trace DNA—small amounts of genetic material that may belong to other people," Lynch went on. "We have no idea how long the glove's been out there—who else may have touched it."

Jane's chest tightened like a rubber band stretched to the point of snapping. She twisted a clump of hair around her index finger and stopped when she pictured her son's finger.

"What—what happens next?"

"We'll bring Mr. Chapman in again—obviously. Tonight."

Each time Lynch said "Mr. Chapman," she pictured Greg. Greg with his perma-grin, as if his life and family were perfect. What a fraud—a guidance counselor who offered his own children no direction, letting his sons do whatever felt right in the moment. If Greg and Ivy had forced Brad to return to college instead of allowing him to "follow his bliss," none of this would be happening.

Her free hand curled into a fist as her mind replayed the same gruesome image over and over again. The finger. *Cal's finger*. Bloody. Detached.

She struggled to focus on Lynch, who was still talking. "... not the news we wanted, but we hope to have more answers soon."

Before she could ask any other questions, he added a somber, "We'll be in touch."

JANE HADN'T PLANNED to go to the airport with Wade to pick up Emerson. Her daughter had been increasingly rude and dismissive on their last few calls, and the thought of being trapped beside her husband in that tiny car made her jaw clench. But she couldn't be alone, not with the news she'd just received.

She pressed her back into the rental car's cold, hard vinyl upholstery and fought to empty her mind. She didn't want to think about it, but what if this was the beginning? What if more parts of her son's body were found?

As they slipped along winding roads, the sunless sky bore down, growing darker. She closed her eyes to block the landscape. In Cal's photos, it appeared so picturesque and peaceful, but in person the mountains were oppressive, making her feel small and hopeless.

Had they arrested Brad? How was this the same person who'd needed a nightlight for every sleepover until he was twelve? What had he done? Why? When he'd dodged her calls, when they'd learned he had Cal's phone, she hoped he'd offer some explanation. But he hadn't. Instead, he'd gotten a lawyer. Now his DNA was all over Cal's glove. Proof. Her hope that her son's oldest friend wasn't involved evaporated faster than snowflakes on the windshield.

Her phone pinged. Was it Lynch? Already? No. Emerson.

> Meet me at baggage claim. FYI phone at 1%

"I'm not paying to park." Wade talked over the GPS as it guided them toward the airport. "I'll loop around. Look for me."

JANE STEPPED into the icy wind and jerked her way through the revolving door. She kept her hood up as she scanned the crowd for her daughter. Announcements screeched through the overhead speakers, interrupting Christmas music. The air stank like fast food, feet, and people who'd spent too long in the same clothing. It was hard to believe just two days earlier she and Wade had stood there, back when she'd believed her son was still whole, before she knew Wade's business was crumbling and they were about to lose their home. Her knees nearly buckled from the weight of it, but she pressed forward, determined to find her daughter and get out as quickly as possible.

Unless they'd changed it, Ivy, Greg, and Max were on Em's flight. Were they nearby? Did they know that the police were coming for their son? Jane's body tensed. If she spotted them, could she control her anger?

Her eyes scanned to the overhead monitors that told travelers where to expect their luggage. She spotted Em in her light wool coat and hurried over. When she placed a hand on her daughter's shoulder, Em spun around and shrugged it off.

"Hey," she said, as casual as if they'd bumped into each other at the mall, as if they hadn't just been separated for days at the worst time in their lives.

Jane leaned in for a kiss, eyes landing on a pimple, red as a bullseye, sprouting from Em's forehead. Her daughter recoiled.

"Stop!" Em's hand flew to cover her face. "I can see you staring."

"I'm sorry." Jane took a step back. "Your father is circling. Let's go."

"My bag's not here yet."

"Right. Okay." Jane gave an odd wave toward the carousel, unsure what to do with her hands. "Why aren't you wearing your ski jacket? This isn't nearly warm enough."

"I assumed skiing was canceled," Em huffed. "If I'm cold, I'll borrow yours."

"What if we want to go out together?" Jane asked.

"I seriously doubt that'll happen." Em turned back to the carousel.

They stood, waiting like strangers, jostled by people eager to begin their holiday. Without thinking, Jane allowed her tired eyes to drift. That's when she saw them: Ivy, Greg, Max. She knew she shouldn't, but she couldn't stop herself. Leaving Emerson's side, Jane lunged toward the Chapmans.

Ivy's face looked bloated and pale as her eyes widened in surprise. Or was it fear?

"Your son cut off my son's finger!" The words burned like hot stones on Jane's tongue. She couldn't spit them out fast enough. Saliva shot from her lips. Inches separated them. Jane's arms extended toward her former friend. What would she do if she got her hands on her? She didn't know. Rage short-circuited her brain. She couldn't think clearly.

"Jane, please." Greg stepped between them, palms up as if protecting his family from an attacker.

"Mom!" Em was behind her, pulling her away.

"You know Brad would never do anything to Cal." Ivy moved in front of Greg and pointed a trembling finger at Emerson. "What about what your daughter has done? Starting a social media crusade to destroy Brad without a shred of evidence! He can't leave his condo!"

"There is evidence! Brad's DNA! It's all over the glove where Cal's..." Jane's throat closed around the word "finger." Out of the corner of her eye, she saw a half-circle of people gathering, cell phones aloft.

A security guard cut through the crowd. "Is there a problem here?"

"C'mon." Em tugged her mother's arm, her cold eyes laser-focused on Max. "They're not worth it."

THE ADRENALINE RUSH made it impossible for Jane to remember the make and model of the rental car. When a horn blared, she saw Wade through a lowered window.

Em wrestled her suitcase into the backseat. "Mom just went apeshit on the Chapmans," she said as she slammed the door.

"What?" Wade turned to Jane.

"Just drive, Wade." Jane commanded. "Go!"

As they left the airport, Wade glanced in the rearview mirror to look at Em in the backseat. "How was your flight?"

"Flights. Plural," Em corrected. "They sucked." She sniffed. "Did someone barf in here? It smells gross."

No one answered. They drove in silence, the only sound the car's heater cranked to full-blast. Wade turned on the radio, and finding only static, switched it off again.

"Is someone going to tell me what the hell is going on?" Em's luggage toppled onto her lap and she shoved it toward the far window. "Reporters were at our house. They said there's a finger. Is it Cal's?"

"They think so." Wade nodded.

Jane let out a muffled cry followed by a shrill, "Slow down!"

In the distance, flashing lights turned the dark sky cherry red. Police cars, a firetruck, and an ambulance clogged the shoulder. Two cops arranged blockades while a third redirected traffic. Smoke rose from the woods on the far edge of the field.

"Whoa," Emerson murmured.

As Wade made a U-turn, Jane had a terrible, fleeting thought: *I'm glad someone else's night is as awful as mine.*

"THIS PLACE LOOKED WAY NICER ONLINE," Emerson said as she dragged herself through the Airbnb, leaving a trail of slushy boot prints on the blond wood floor. When she reached the end of the hall, she groaned. "Mom! Why is your stuff in here? I want this room."

Jane ignored her. In between checking out of the motel and into the Airbnb, she and Wade had killed time at a grocery store and picked up prepared salads and sandwiches. She pulled them from the fridge and placed them on the oval wooden table that sat in the corner of the living room.

Em appeared, holding her stomach. "Got any Advil? I have cramps."

"Look in my purse," Jane said. "If you're hungry..." She could barely finish the sentence; she couldn't imagine eating.

Wade and Em slumped into cheap wooden chairs with spindly backs that made Jane's spine ache just looking at them. While they picked through the offerings, Jane collapsed on the couch, spent from shouting at Ivy, and too tired to care about the filthy strangers who may have rested their heads there just hours earlier.

Em was right. The place had looked much nicer online. Ivy was the one who'd found it and convinced her it was "perfect" for the six of them. But Ivy and Greg were used to their small house.

"We don't need much room," Ivy had said, smiling and sitting in her husband's lap. Sometimes it was too much for Jane—all that affection between the two of them. When they traveled and strolled unfamiliar streets, Greg always took the outside, closest to the curb, his arm around Ivy's shoulder, while Wade charged two feet ahead of the group.

They held hands while window-shopping, fingers interlaced.

And just like that, Lynch's voice came back to her. *It's Cal's finger. It's Cal's finger.* She clicked on the TV to block her awful thoughts. Flicking past weather forecasts, Jimmy Stewart, and cartoon reindeer, she settled on a shopping channel before turning to her phone. Would Lynch call again tonight? Would he get anything useful from Brad? Should they be there at the station? It was all too much. She rubbed her temples and closed her eyes.

Drool was trickling from the corner of her mouth when she awoke to Em shouting, "Holy shit!"

Her daughter stood and moved toward the couch, phone in hand, charger dangling like a long, white mouse tail.

"What is it?" Wade asked.

"Find the local news!" Em loomed above Jane and grabbed the remote, changing channels until she landed on a station.

Jane sat up and blinked to clear her blurry vision. On the screen, a road appeared. It looked like the one where they'd been forced to backtrack on their way home from the airport.

"We turn now to a developing story," the anchor said. "Bradley Chapman, the young man who's lived under a cloud of scrutiny this past week after his roommate Cal Whitaker went missing, has been in a car accident."

Wade lurched from the table to the middle of the room, blocking half the screen. "Turn it up!"

"I'm trying!" Em shouted. "Move out of the way!"

The image changed to a reporter at the scene.

"That's right, Darla. Thank you. In what could only be

described as yet another horrifying twist in this case, witnesses say Chapman's SUV was traveling at a high speed when it left the road and collided with that tree."

The camera swung to the field, to the Highlander, its front end crushed, before returning to the reporter, her expression grim.

"Some are speculating that the young man may have attempted to end his life after police confirmed earlier today that his DNA was found on a glove that contained Whitaker's finger.

"Others believe Chapman may have been chased by so-called internet sleuths who've been relentless in trying to understand his involvement in his roommate's disappearance." The reporter shivered. "Whitaker's sister sparked nationwide interest when she began posting videos that galvanized the community against Chapman, who, according to a source, declared his innocence before getting behind the wheel just hours ago."

Jane sat straighter. "Emerson?"

"Shh!" her daughter hissed.

"We're told Chapman was taken to an area hospital where he remains in critical condition." The reporter fiddled with her earpiece. "We'll update this story throughout the night. Stay with us."

Emerson muted the TV. A heavy silence settled over the room. Jane found it hard to swallow. A picture flashed through her mind. The boys together, five, maybe six years old, racing across the lawn in the late summer evening. Brad holding a Mason jar while Cal caught fireflies. Their smiles, gapped from missing baby teeth, radiated joy, bright as the rising moon, their giggles colliding until they sounded like a singular song.

Up until ten days ago, that boy had been like Jane's second son. Now he was fighting for his life. And what about her son's life?

"Holy shit," Em whispered at the same time Jane said, "My God." Her mind spun to Ivy in the airport. She hadn't known. "This can't be happening. If he doesn't—" She couldn't finish that sentence. "Brad may be the only one who knows where Cal is—what really happened."

"You don't know that." Wade paced. "You have no clue what kind of people Cal got involved with—how much money he owes them. The men my father dealt with—" Wade pressed his palms to his forehead as if to stop whatever memories he'd conjured at the mention of his father.

"You shouldn't have done that." Jane turned to her daughter. "Any of it."

"Done what?"

"Accused Brad publicly. Said the things you did. Started all this!"

"You cannot be serious!" Em wheeled around to face her. "You and Dad both think he did something. You basically attacked Mrs. Chapman at the airport. Brad's the last person who saw Cal. He's got his phone." She ticked off items on her fingers. "He placed an ad for a new roommate—"

"That's enough!" Jane raised her voice to stop Em from continuing to build her case. "Still, you shouldn't have broadcasted it to the world! You wanted the attention. For yourself. Not your brother."

Em sat uncharacteristically still on a black leather ottoman, eyes narrowed.

"The police, the search teams, they're trying... everyone's trying..." Jane's voice wavered. "And now this... If Brad wasn't involved, this is another tragedy and a terrible waste of resources... The focus should've been on finding your brother, not condemning Brad."

Em leveled her gaze at her mother. "I'm the one who put a spotlight on this, who got your precious Cal national attention. Me! I did that. And if Brad isn't responsible—I mean, the glove, the DNA? C'mon, that's a coincidence?"

"We don't know anything for sure. They're roommates. Brad could've touched the glove." Jane was attempting to convince herself as much as her daughter. "There could be another explanation."

Em bit her lip. "You ever think Daniel might've done something?"

Jane sucked in her breath and shook her head. "What?"

"Did you forget you added me to your website?" Emerson cocked her head, the hint of a smirk forming on her rosy lips. "I've read all your messages."

Wade hurled a "Merry Everything!" throw pillow to the ground and sank into a rocking chair. "Who the hell is Daniel?"

"This creep Mom flirts with online."

Jane's stomach dropped like she'd been riding in an elevator and its cable snapped. She played with the interlocking rings on her fingers, rings she'd designed for the business that brought Daniel into her life. "He's— he's—he was an old friend from high school."

"Mom met him for lunch—or was it drinks and dinner?" Em eyed her mother, then looked at her father. "He sends her these cringey messages. She writes back. It's been going on for months."

"Emerson, it's nothing..." Jane managed.

"'I miss you.'" Emerson whined in a male voice. "'When can I see you again?'"

"Jane?" Wade removed his glasses and rubbed his face. "You're having an affair?"

"She's sleeping in the guest room," Em snarfed. "What do you think?"

"Emerson! This is between your father and me. Go to your room!"

"No way!" Em snorted and looked at her dad. "You never noticed how she giggles and touches her hair around Mr. Chapman? She even laughs at his dad jokes."

"Emerson! That's enough!" Jane stood.

"You're so embarrassing," Em picked at her angry red pimple. "You should look at this guy's messages, Dad. They're messed up." She turned to Jane. "Can you seriously be this clueless? He asks when he can see you again and you string him along. And how about his last message?"

"Let me see them." Wade held out his hand.

Jane had no intention of giving him her phone. She'd done nothing—nothing but crave a bit of attention. Wasn't Wade's attitude, his obsession with his company, which he'd destroyed anyway, part of the reason she'd let the Daniel thing drag on? He'd hidden plenty from her. There was no way she was allowing him to look through her private messages.

But there was Emerson, pulling them up on her phone, showing them to her father, who read aloud:

"'Happy birthday to your husband. Did he get everything he wished for? Do any of us?'" Wade stared at Jane, his frown deepening. She felt like a child trapped at a terrible story time as he continued. "'How's your week going?

Thinking of you. Your son's quite the daredevil. Hope he stays safe!'"

Her heart began to race as his thumb jabbed at the screen, scrolling, toggling.

"'Would love to catch up again, but I'm swamped with orders,'" Em read Jane's words followed by Daniel's. "'Sort of feels like you're blowing me off.' Ugh." She pointed at the phone. "He used a winking emoji."

"'Headed to Wyoming? I was there recently.'" Wade's voice sharpened. "Jesus, Jane! How could you—how could you not mention this? This guy's been watching our family—for months!"

Jane thought about Daniel as she'd known him in high school: thin and awkward, always on the periphery. Her mind flashed back to what he'd said at lunch the day she'd met him. He'd been talking about his divorce, how his ex had turned his daughters against him.

"Girls can be challenging," Jane had commiserated over a bottle of Pinot Grigio. "My daughter and I butt heads most days."

Daniel had raised his eyebrows. "Really? Why?"

"Just the usual mother-daughter drama. We don't seem to agree on anything."

"I've noticed she dresses quite provocatively."

At first, the comment and the way he'd licked his lips after he said it made Jane bristle, but then he added, "She reminds me of you at that age. A real knock-out." Daniel had lifted his glass as if to toast to her long-ago loveliness. "Still are." He'd winked and polished off at least four ounces in one swallow.

Jane glanced from Emerson to Wade, her cheeks burning. What had she been willing to overlook because *she'd* felt overlooked?

"'That's some dangerous terrain,'" Em chimed in, reading over her father's shoulder. "'I hope you find your son in one piece.'"

"Do you not hear how these sound?" Wade shouted.

Could Daniel have done something? No! But then she thought of the bloody hunk of finger. Her son was no longer in one piece.

Wade stood, hand curled around their daughter's phone, and yanked his coat from the back of the chair.

"Where are you going?" Jane asked, her voice wavering.

"To the police station." Wade was patting his pockets, scanning the room for the rental car's key fob.

"I'll go with you!" Em jumped to her feet.

Jane didn't want to be near either of them, but she needed to know what would happen next.

"I'm coming too." Lightheaded, she struggled to her feet. Was it possible she'd brought this on their family and, if so, how would she ever live with it?

20

TUESDAY, DECEMBER 23

IVY

Resting her head on the hospital bed's guardrail, Ivy stretched her arms through the openings to clutch her son's hand, careful not to knock the port and tube.

She wouldn't have said she believed in God—more in a divine force, a benevolent entity—but as she closed her eyes tight against the milk-white glow of the overhead lights, she found herself whispering prayers she'd learned as a little girl in Sunday school. Lyrics from that Regina Spektor song floated back to her, something about people not laughing at God when they're in a hospital or a war.

A war. That's what this felt like: an ongoing war with the Whitakers. She understood they were coming from a place of fear and extreme distress, but they had to know Brad would never hurt Cal. Didn't they remember how upset he'd gotten as a child when Cal refused to release the fireflies they'd collected on summer evenings in the Whitakers' backyard? Brad sobbed as the golden flickers dimmed.

"Let them go! Please!" he'd begged while Cal laughed, only relenting after Brad ran to ask a grown-up to intervene.

Jane had threatened to destroy Ivy, and this—what had happened to her son—very easily could. The Whitakers were to blame. Emerson in particular. So desperate for attention, attention Jane gave exclusively to Cal.

Part of Ivy couldn't believe any of it was real. She hoped maybe she was still on that last leg of the trip, having a nightmare as she soared over mountains and rivers, their wildness somehow leaching into her subconscious.

But no, she remembered the landing clearly. As soon as they'd touched down, she'd switched her phone out of airplane mode and read Brad's text telling her he was going for the MRI.

> Finally! See you at the hotel! XOXO.

Greg had ordered an Uber. They'd been piling into it when Don Carmichael called. Exhausted from traveling and reeling from her confrontation with Jane, it took Ivy a full ten seconds to place the name.

Don Carmichael?

The attorney!

"Are you sitting down?" Don had asked in a steady tone that made the hairs on her arms rise.

She was, not that it mattered. The fact that he was calling meant something was wrong. Very wrong. Her face turned hot, tingly. She reached forward to the front passenger's seat to rest a hand on Greg's shoulder as if it might ground her, help her absorb the shock.

"There's been an accident..." The world took on that faraway, floaty feeling as Don's words seeped into her ear and traveled through her system, settling in her connective tissue.

They'd gone straight to the hospital where a physician's assistant, who looked barely old enough to babysit, met them in the ER. Brad had been rushed into surgery, something about a brain bleed and the next seventy-two hours being "critical."

After a long wait with no news, Max had gone to the hotel while Greg and Ivy remained in a small area with a broken vending machine. Ivy's hunger was insatiable. She chewed her fingernails, then gnawed at her cuticles until Brad was moved to the ICU and they could finally see him. Her son was barely recognizable beneath all the wires, tubes, and bandages.

Beyond the pale blue curtain that separated their tragedy from someone else's, a police officer stood. Was he there to protect Brad or take him into custody when *or if* he regained consciousness?

Ivy tried not to picture the car, its front end compressed like an accordion. Max told her someone who'd been following Brad had posted a video of the Highlander slamming into the tree. The world had lost its humanity. She thought about what the surgeon had said. Brad was lucky. "Lucky to have survived the accident," she'd told them.

But this wasn't an accident. Brad had been chased—nearly to his death. She wanted someone to pay for this. Fury spiked inside her and she startled upright.

Mistaking her sudden movement for jolting awake, Greg repeated his offer. "Go to the hotel, take a hot shower, try to rest. I'll call you the second anything changes."

She shook her head. Ivy typically appreciated her husband's evenness, his calming presence, but now she wanted him to be as furious as she was. She had a sudden urge to scream at him to do something. But what? And the last thing they needed now was to turn on one another.

She took a deep breath to the count of four, held it seven seconds, and blew it out for eight. It didn't help.

Beside him in his hospital bed, Ivy squeezed Brad's cold fingers and waited. When he was a small boy, they'd done this. Each time they encountered something that scared him —a barking dog, a sewer grate, the grumpy crossing guard near the elementary school—she'd taken his hand in hers and squeezed. It became an unspoken code. *I'm here. I won't let anything hurt you.* He'd squeeze back. *Thanks, Mom.*

She remembered those moments when he was brave and willed him to tap into that energy now. She focused on his fingers—thin, pale, unmoving. *Squeeze.*

What had Jane said at the airport? "Your son cut off my son's finger!" The brutality of it—the image and the accusation—made her shudder.

What had she said about Brad's DNA? Ivy tried to remember but she'd been focused on Jane's body language. She'd stopped inches from Ivy's face, poised to attack.

Brad's DNA! It's all over the glove! Was that what she'd said?

The phone in Ivy's lap buzzed and she jumped, swiping to answer without reading the caller's name or number.

"Ivy? It's Florence."

"Florence?" Ivy's body stiffened with irritation. "This isn't a good time. I'm in the—"

"Ivy, dear," her mother's neighbor interrupted. "I'm at your house."

"My mom's house?" Ivy bit her lip and widened her eyes at Greg, who looked suddenly very old and tired.

For decades, Ivy had tried to help her mother. She was

done. It was time for her to clean up her own mess. Her son needed her now. Tears blurred her vision. She released her son's hand and wiped them away, her sadness shifting back to rage.

"No, dear," Florence said. "I'm in your home. In Oak Hill."

Ivy experienced a fleeting sense of vertigo, the same feeling she got when she did her sun salutations too quickly. She shook her head. "I don't under—"

"It was supposed to be a surprise," Florence continued. "I made you a fruitcake. I know how much you like it. And I have a few little things for the boys. Since you haven't been to see your mother in such a long time—" Ivy gripped the guardrail, guilt worming its way under her skin— "I thought I'd come to you."

"Florence, this isn't a good time. I'm in—"

"I wanted to speak to you about your mother, too, of course."

Florence was talking right over her. Ivy wondered if the woman had left her hearing aids in South Jersey.

"When I got here, dear, your door was open."

Shit! Ivy had hired Betsy Gallagher's son Miles to take care of Jean-Claude because she'd forgotten to reserve a spot at the In the Doghouse kennel and they'd been fully booked.

"You mean unlocked?" Ivy asked.

"No, dear," Florence corrected. "Wide open."

Ivy's pulse thrummed. "Florence, do you see Jean-Claude?"

"Who?"

"Our dog." Ivy ran her fingers through her hair, tugging at her fringe-y bangs. "His name is Jean-Claude. Can you call him? Please. He's small—" Could Miles have forgotten to lock the door? Could the wind have blown it open? What was she thinking, trusting an eighth grader?

Greg shifted in his seat and leaned forward, visibly confused from only catching one side of the conversation.

"Well, now, I don't see—"

"Go in the kitchen. Shake the canister marked 'treats.' Please." Ivy waited for the familiar rattle that was usually followed by the soft click of Jean-Claude's nails as the little dog hurried across the tile. She heard nothing.

"Ivy," Florence sounded out of breath, "there's something else."

"What?" Tears swam back to Ivy's eyes. *What now?*

"I don't know how to say this but someone spray-painted the word 'butcher' in your dining room."

"What?" Ivy looked at Brad.

"It's all over your lovely wallpaper. It looks like spray-paint... maybe?"

The slow, rhythmic beeping of Brad's monitor changed to a long, high-pitched alarm.

"Get a nurse!" Ivy commanded. Greg was already moving toward the hall.

"Will you be home soon, dear?" Florence asked. "Because I'm happy to wait."

Ivy couldn't speak as she watched a nurse enter the room and press the monitor.

"Time to hang a new bag. That's all." She offered Ivy a pitying smile. "Be right back."

Ivy nodded and sagged in the small chair, limbs shaky from the scare.

Whom could she call to look for Jean-Claude? Everyone in Oak Hill hated her family—apparently so much so that someone had broken in and defiled their home. Did they take her dog or had he wandered off?

She felt nauseous and starving at the same time.

"Florence, I have to call you—"

"The neighbors—the Garvins, Kathleen and Bill—they're considering a civil suit against your mother, Ivy. They're relocating to California and they're having trouble selling because of, well, the situation. Will you be home soon, dear? I can wait. I'll make some tea and we'll..."

The weight of it all pressed down on Ivy as she stared at her unmoving son. As long as he made it through this, nothing else mattered.

21

WEDNESDAY, DECEMBER 24
EMERSON

With her parents not speaking, Em hung out in a back bedroom surrounded by antler lamps and framed paintings of elk grazing in fields.

She'd taken a photo of bigmouth bass bookends to send to Sasha with the caption "kill me now" then deleted it and simply wrote *Found the perfect gift for you!* with a laughing emoji. That didn't feel right either. She didn't know how to act. How to be. She shoved her phone under the nubby chenille bedspread that smelled like an old lady's bathrobe and picked at her fingernails.

It was Christmas Eve. Her friends were busy with their families. Her socials were filled with pics of presents, twinkling lights, dogs dressed like Santa. PR people were gone until after the new year. Not that it mattered. No one was offering her deals or sponsorships now. Cal's finger. Brad's accident. It was too much. She'd gone from an interesting and sympathetic young woman—a hero, maybe—on a mission to save her brother, to someone connected with ugliness, tragedy. She was over-exposed and now the situation, particularly the finger, gave off gross horror-movie vibes.

Days ago, she'd been in touch with an artist who designed rings using healing gemstones. Celebrities wore them on red carpets. The company was going to overnight some stackable and interlocking samples to Em. She'd wear them and post pics with snow-covered mountains in the background. "If you can get a hawk or an owl in the shot, that would be phenomenal and totally on-brand," the rep had said.

She and Sasha had given each other manicures in preparation.

While waiting at the gate on her way to Wyoming, she'd gotten an email from the artist's publicist.

"We won't be moving forward, obvi," she'd written and signed it:

All the best for a warm and wonderful holiday season,
Aimee.

"Asshole," Em had grunted and kicked her carry-on. This bitch couldn't even take the time to change her cheery email signature while delivering bad news.

Internet trolls blamed Em for Brad's accident. *Fuck. Them.* Couldn't they see that clearly he was running from something? It wasn't her fault he'd crashed into a tree. Accidents happened all the time, especially in the snow. Still, she wondered how serious it was. The news cycle had turned to holiday recipes and Santa trackers. Her brother's story and Brad's were too grim for Christmas Eve.

Her mind drifted to Max. She'd seen him on the flights. He'd avoided eye contact except once. On his way to the bathroom, he'd glared at her like she was a hunk of dogshit stuck to the bottom of his Tevas, which he'd been wearing with socks, giving her the ick. She'd cringed as she remembered joking about joining the mile-high club with him on the longest of the three flights.

What would she do now? The thought of seeing London, Barcelona, and the south of France with him while she promoted clothing, watches, handbags, and grew her brand had filled her with a joy she'd never experienced. The idea of freedom, of being with someone who was both familiar but also kind of new to her had seemed romantic yet reassuring.

Screw him. She could still go to Europe. She'd meet people. Make new friends. Her parents were so distracted by Cal, Daniel, and the mess they'd made of their marriage, it bought her time to figure things out. Plus, her mother was the one who'd hung that framed "Paris is always a good idea" poster in her bedroom when she was in middle school. She'd practically put the idea in Em's head.

Her mother. What a joke. As if things weren't already a shitshow, someone was one-star bombing her mom's business. Out of boredom, Em had checked the account, even the email, knowing her mother was probably too distracted to change her password. As disgusted as she was by her mom's behavior, her hands shook as she read the brutal reviews.

Doesn't respond to emails.

Owner makes promises she can't keep.

Disappointing experience with this "artist."

Em knew they were from Daniel. Her mother hadn't sold enough for them to be real.

Then the email came.

What a piece of work you are, Jane. Sending the police to interrogate me on Christmas Eve when you knew my daughters would be here. I was in Wyoming for work—on a flight home the day your troubled son disappeared. You'd know that if you'd read my messages—if you cared about anyone other than yourself. I was merely taking an interest in your life. You seemed so unhappy, so lonely. I can see where your daughter gets it. Stay away from me and my children. You have enough to worry about.

It was easy to dismiss Daniel as some asshole loser, but as Em spent more time in the room alone, she started to wonder if she'd gotten everything wrong.

She could hear Ivy's voice at the airport, "You know Brad would never do something like this. He isn't capable of it!"

Em remembered a beach vacation her family had taken with the Chapmans. Midweek, they woke to a gray, drizzly day. Ivy made banana pancakes and sent them fishing. Max must've been seventeen, making Cal and Brad fifteen and her ten. Cal and Max cast their lines while she collected seashells and picked at her nail polish. Brad sat on the dock, reading a book. He hadn't wanted to catch a fish. He couldn't even look when Cal and Max pierced the wiggling worms with their hooks.

"What you got there, Oprah?" Cal had teased. "Starting a book club?

Brad showed them the cover. "*The Captain*. It's about Derek Jeter."

"Figures," Cal said.

"What's that mean?" Brad asked.

"Just, I know you." Cal smirked. "I didn't think it was about Captain Ahab."

Brad looked confused.

"You know, like in *Moby Dick*?" Cal said. "Hey, at least you've moved up from picture books."

"Let's keep the dick talk to a minimum," Max had said, tilting his head in Em's direction.

She remembered thinking her brother was the real dick, but Brad had let the insult go, like he always did. Had she ever seen him be anything other than chill? No.

The memory made Em's stomach hurt.

If Brad hadn't done something to Cal and Daniel had an alibi, where was her brother?

PART 2

22

SATURDAY, DECEMBER 13
CAL

Cal waited beside Brad's car in the near-empty parking lot. Ten minutes passed, then twenty, goosebumps creeping across his skin as his body lost its heat. How long would it take Brad to finish the run? Fucking forever with that knee. Such a baby.

Cal would've left if he'd had a car or his phone.

A woman in a hot pink ski jacket walked toward him. "Hey!" Her blond hair spilled from under a navy hat, her blue eyes bright. "Think you could help me? Got a flat." She poked her thumb over her shoulder. "Never changed one myself." Her Southern accent was warm and sweet as hot cocoa.

He couldn't understand people like his dad who were too cheap to pay for on-call roadside assistance. Life was full of accidents, bad breaks. Never knew when one might come your way. He felt for her. Still, it wasn't his problem. He considered saying, "Sorry, my friend'll be here any sec," but there was something about her. Pretty girls—women, whatever—were his kryptonite.

"Please?" she asked again, snowflakes landing in her lashes. She bit her bottom lip, eyes flicking around the lot. "*Brrr!* It's freezing."

She looked familiar, like someone he knew—like if you aged *that* person just a little you'd get *this* person. She raised her eyebrows. A plea. If he refused, she'd be screwed, stuck there indefinitely.

Shit, why me? He'd never changed a tire in his life, but he'd watched a frat brother do it once. Couldn't be that hard.

"Okay, lead the way," he agreed. What else did he have to do?

"Yay!" She rocked up on the toes of her boots, clapping her gloved hands. "Thank you! Thank you!" She turned and pointed. "It's just over there."

They walked the length of a football field, farther away from the lighted area.

"Sure you didn't park in Idaho?" he joked.

She giggled. "Almost there."

When he spotted a black SUV, he stopped. Was it the one that had been following them on the way to the mountain?

No.

Couldn't be.

Could it?

Those gas-guzzlers were everywhere, as common as decorative antlers, hauling tourists and their gear from the airport to resorts and back again. But he couldn't be too careful. What if someone hired this woman to trick him? Eleven thousand dollars—probably more like twelve, depending on how that last game ended—wasn't chump change. People would be looking for him. People were *already* looking for him.

When he hesitated, the woman laughed. "You don't think I drive that big, old thing, do you? My ride's just on the other side."

Something about her eyes, her smile, tugged at his memory. Whom did she remind him of, and why did it make him nervous? And her voice, too. It was like hearing a popular song but being unable to remember who sang it. Could he have hooked up with her once maybe when he first got to town? A one-hit wonder?

He followed her to the far side of the SUV. There was no smaller car in the space—just two guys. One with a chain, the other a tire iron.

He stepped back, full picture coming into focus, slow and then all at once, the way an optical illusion suddenly pops out. *How did I miss it?* Panic buckled his knees.

"My—my buddy's on his way. I—I better..." He turned to look behind him. *Where the hell was Brad?*

The woman's hands were on her hips.

"Told you I'd get him," she said, her voice cold, taunting.

It was the last thing Cal heard before the metal bar smashed the back of his skull.

23

SUNDAY, DECEMBER 14
CAL

Everything ached. Worse than any football pounding. His mouth was a desert, his tongue shriveled and leathery as a strip of beef jerky. Was he hung over? His head throbbed. What the hell did he drink?

He looked around the small room with its dark wood walls. Where was he? It hurt to move his eyes, but he shifted them anyway, slowly, side to side as he studied the space. Nothing looked familiar. Not the plywood nailed over what he guessed was a window. Not the footboard where his ankles were shackled. Not the guy sitting inches to his left, watching him, working a knife back and forth over a small log. He'd seen him before—standing, waiting by the SUV.

Cal tried to move, but his arms were restrained, too.

"He's awake," the guy called.

The woman stood in the doorway. Any trace of the smile that had made Cal follow her to her car was long gone.

"He looks too comfortable, babe." She stepped into the room. "Get him up."

The guy slipped the knife into his pocket, unchained Cal's legs, then his arms, and pulled him upright. Cal's head felt heavy as an anchor. *What was happening?*

"Put him here," the woman ordered.

Cal limped the few feet from the bed to a high back chair in the middle of an area rug, his arms and legs turning from numb to pins-and-needly. How long had he been there? What day was it?

He knew nothing good was about to happen in that room; still, he was grateful to sit again.

"Chain him back up," the woman ordered.

"Look at him." The guy stepped back. "I don't think we need—"

"Do it!"

"What—?" Cal's voice was hoarse, shaky. "If this is about the money, I—I can pay, I swear. My mom'll be here in a couple days. Give me 'til then. I can get it." He looked from the man to the woman, fear flooding his veins.

"This isn't about money—or your mom," the woman snorted. "You'd know what it was about if you'd answered my texts, Cal. Remember those?"

They knew his name. How? What texts?

The woman circled him, her eyes never leaving his face. Who were these people? If it wasn't about money, what did they want from him? And where the hell was Brad?

"I was nice in the beginning," the woman continued. "But you didn't write back. I left a couple voicemails, too. I just wanted to talk." She wore black leggings and kept her arms folded tight to her chest. When she got close, the fibers of her wool sweater tickled his ears. He couldn't scratch with his wrists bound.

"You got those, didn't you, Cal? Before you let your mailbox fill up so you 'can't accept any new messages at this time.'" She did a nasally imitation of the phone's computerized voice.

"I—I don't know what—"

"He's up?" The second guy—the one who'd bashed him with the tire iron—stood in the doorway and flicked a switch. A bright overhead light bounced off something silver. An axe. The guy stepped closer, stroking a scraggly goatee, the smell of winter and wood smoke wafting off his jacket.

"Yup," the woman said. "I was just saying if he'd called me back, we might not be here."

"I—I..." Cal's mind spun like a tornado, touching down on one thought only to spiral off again. What was she talking about? Lots of girls messaged and called him—girls from high school, college, part-time jobs, the gym. Yeah, he was bad about calling back, but everyone was busy. Grow up. Was this some woman he'd ignored?

"I—I..." he started again.

"Nervous?" The woman moved closer and leaned down. Their noses nearly touched. Cal tried to wriggle back. "You should be." She stood.

Cal looked up. The room spun and dipped each time he moved his head. "What?" He cleared his throat. "What—what's this about?"

"What do you think it's about, asshole?" She kicked him hard in the shin with the tip of her steel-toed work boot.

Cal yelped and gripped the arms of the chair. Her boots reminded him of his dad, of all the construction sites he'd taken him to visit on Saturday mornings when he was a kid, when business was good. *Shit!* His father's birthday. Had he missed it?

"Chloe. It's about Chloe. You don't remember her?" She kicked his other leg, harder, and he pressed his lips together to keep from wailing again.

"Scotty," she turned to the guy with the axe, "he can't seem to remember our sister."

Sister? Chloe and these psychopaths were siblings? He wanted to scan Scotty's face, look for the family resemblance, but his eyes kept darting back to the axe, his heart ticking like a bomb.

Of course, he remembered the girl. What a fucking mess that was. Could he have handled it better? Yes, but nothing prepares you for that, for what to do, how to act. He'd panicked, run. If he'd stuck around, he'd forever be the guy who didn't save a drunk girl from getting hit by a truck. That was a bad look—not to mention all the legal bullshit. He'd need to answer a million questions, and behind every accident was a family ready to sue. Plus, his parents had wanted him home right after finals. His dad needed help with spreadsheets and marketing he planned to intro in the new year. His mom insisted he get back in time to pick out a Christmas tree. *Family tradition!* she'd texted.

If they found out he'd bailed on them to hang with Brad, they'd be pissed. He needed one last night to party before he was trapped in Oak Hill with his family for a month. Wasn't he entitled to that? Hadn't he earned it?

Brad hated him for a while after the Chloe stuff went down. Then he dropped out of college like he was some young widower when he and that girl hadn't even hooked up. It was pretty ridiculous actually. Thankfully, they'd put that behind them.

Cal shook his head to clear the memory, the ache at the base of his skull spreading.

But what did *these* people want from him? And why now? And where the hell was Brad? What had his roommate done when he'd gotten to the parking lot Saturday night and Cal wasn't there? Probably nothing. How many times had he ditched Brad for a girl, a party, or any better offer? But Cal had done plenty for Brad, too, over the years. Their friendship alone made Brad's personal stock rise. He owed it to Cal to find him.

"Yeah. No. I remember. My—my head—" Cal stammered. "You, you got anything I could take for it? I'm not thinking—"

"You'd better *start* thinking. Real fast." Scotty tapped his open palm with the blunt side of the axe.

"You got her drunk and left her there to die. In the street," the woman said.

Cal flinched as Scotty stepped closer, floorboards groaning beneath his boots. The guy who'd chained him to the chair stood by the window, slouching against the wall like he'd been dragged to a concert and didn't know the band. He was the woman's boyfriend, but what was his part in this?

"Two years we've been searching for answers," the woman said. "It was easier for the college to say Chloe was a dumb sorority girl who drank too much. She went from an athlete and honor student to a bad example: 'Don't be like Chloe.' Un-fucking-believable." She grunted. "And her classmates? Her supposed friends? Some claimed they weren't there, and the ones who were couldn't remember, bombed out of their minds. But you, you know exactly what happened, what you did." She continued to pace around his chair.

It made him dizzy. The dark walls drew closer with each lap she took.

"The plow driver? He didn't see her until it was too late—the snow and all, he said. He wasn't charged."

"His life's turned to shit, though," Scotty said. "Works part-time at a sub shop, medicated to zombie levels, right, Shelby?" He stared at Cal. "Not that you give a shit."

The woman stopped circling him and nodded at her brother, her eyes narrowing.

Alarm bells rang inside Cal's battered skull. *When would this end? How? What did these people want?*

Shelby wheeled around fast and smiled. "We'd almost given up, and then someone, someone with a conscience, told us about you. A student. It haunted her too, she said, how you gave Chloe shot after shot, flirting with her, chasing her into the street. Why? Because she wasn't interested in you?" Shelby's smile disappeared as her lips curled back, teeth bared like a mad dog. "You might as well have driven the plow yourself."

Sweat soaked Cal's shirt. "It wasn't like that."

"Really? What was it like? Back in the summer, back when I was patient, I wanted to hear—" she waved a hand toward her brother "*we* wanted to hear you explain it. Your silence said it all. Now you're out here 'living your best life!'" Her nails, sharp as cat claws, curled into quotation marks. "And that's when I thought, I'm done waiting. *We're* done, Cal."

He remembered her calls, calm at first, then each one a little crazier than the last. In the final message—one she left in mid-August before he let his mailbox fill up—she said she was coming for him. He'd been thinking about moving, getting out of Oak Hill anyway. He needed some place like Manhattan where he could disappear, not that he could afford it on the shitty paycheck from his dad. His debts were piling up again after a couple of sure-things hadn't panned out. Just as he'd begun to panic, Ivy had texted his mom, and with that *ping!* came the idea. *Brad. Brad in Wyoming.* Who'd look for him there? And even if they did, what could they do? It was two years ago. If anyone could've tied him to that girl's death they'd have come forward by now.

"We wanted to see the piece of shit who left her there," the woman said.

"Look," Cal began, "Your sister had too much—"

"She has a name!" Scotty roared.

The guy by the window shifted his skinny frame from foot to foot. Cal looked at him. He'd kept his brown eyes on the floor mostly, like he couldn't watch. *Like maybe he wanted no part of this?* Would he step in, stop whatever might happen next?

"Chloe... she... drank too much." Cal tried to keep his voice even, reasonable, the tone he used when he explained turning techniques to kids at ski school, but it came out condescending, as if he didn't care.

He needed to start again, sound sad, remorseful, but his mouth was so dry and his head, already aching, started to pound remembering that night—the way the air had smelled like snow and stale beer outside the bar, the way Chloe's warm mouth had tasted like cinnamon from the Fireball shots. She might not have wanted them at first, but she'd come around.

"She—she had a lot to drink." His fingers were splayed, gripping the arms of the chair, nails digging into wood. He was getting impatient. What could he say that would change the outcome? Nothing. She was gone. They needed to accept it and move on. It had been two years. "She was wasted, actually. How was I supposed to know she'd stumble into the street? I'd been drinking too."

"Oh, what? So you're the victim now? Poor little Callaway Whitaker," the woman mocked.

He didn't like it, his full name in her mouth.

"What kind of stupid name is that anyway? Callaway!" Scotty snickered and scratched his mangy goatee. "Did your mom name you after the golf club she stuck up her twat?"

Shelby snickered.

Cal remembered his mother telling neighbors and acquaintances that Callaway and Emerson were family names. When he'd asked which family members, she'd grinned and placed a manicured finger to her lips. "I'm fibbing. But look at you." She'd booped the tip of his nose. "You deserve a name as unique and special as you are."

Who were these assholes to mock his mother, his name? The chain securing his left wrist to the arm of the chair had just enough slack. Cal twisted his hand around and gave them both the finger, his eyes lingering on the woman.

For a second, Chloe was there in her face. They had the same nose, same smile. It was like seeing a ghost.

He'd been so distracted, he hadn't registered what was happening, not until it was too late: Scotty's hand grabbing his and pressing it down. The flash of silver. The almost imperceptible *whoosh* of air that passed his face as the axe fell fast and hard, severing his finger. The pain was immediate, excruciating, a blinding white heat that sent his body into shock.

The woman jumped back. "Jesus Christ, Scotty! What the—"

"We didn't come here to fuck around, remember?" he growled. "This asshole is the reason Chloe's dead. He doesn't get to flip us off. Ever."

A buzz, then a high-pitched scream filled Cal's head. Otherworldly. Like an animal caught in a trap. It was coming from him. He was its source.

The man beside the window turned white as cotton as he watched blood leak from what was left of Cal's finger. Then he shot forward.

"Scotty, what the hell?" He turned to the woman. "This is not what we agreed to, Shelby! This is not what you said!" He rubbed his hand over his face and dragged it through his dark hair. "You wanted information, a confession! Nobody said anything about smashing his skull with a tire iron, taking him hostage, or chopping off his finger!"

The woman's chest puffed in and out. "Stop, Lincoln, Jesus. It's enough we've got this asshole screaming." She looked at her brother. "Scotty didn't mean it."

"It was an accident. Right, Cal?" Scotty's eyes bulged, wild as those of a spooked horse.

"Doesn't change the fact that his finger's missing!" Lincoln spun around, palms raised. "Where is it? The finger! We gotta pack it in ice or something."

No one moved.

"Where's his fucking finger?" Lincoln shouted.

Shelby looked sideways and down. Blood crisscrossed the top of her boots. "I must've kicked it under the bed."

"Get it!" Lincoln yelled. "Motherfucker!" He raked his hands through his shaggy hair again and glared at Scotty. "You shouldn't have done that! I told you we shouldn't do any of this! We gotta get him to a hospital."

"Like he took Chloe to the hospital?" Shelby snorted. "Nah-ah. He's not going anywhere."

Scotty knelt, dropping the axe on the area rug. He patted his hand under the bed and fished out the nub of skin and bone. A ball of lint stuck to the severed end.

His half-finger, dangling from another man's hand, was the last thing Cal saw before he passed out.

24

MONDAY, DECEMBER 16
LINCOLN

Lincoln needed fresh air. The coppery scent of Cal's blood had been lodged in his nostrils since the night before when he'd cleaned up Scotty's mess. He volunteered to go buy supplies. It would be a relief to get out of the cabin. He wanted time alone in his truck to think. For a while there, he was afraid Scotty was going to insist on tagging along to keep an eye on him.

"Can we trust him?" Scotty had said, petting his goatee like it was a lab rat and he was a mad scientist.

"Of course we can trust him," Shelby said. "He's in this, too."

"Don't forget that, Linc." Scotty nodded.

How could he forget? It was all he'd thought about since the second Scotty drove the axe through Cal's finger like a goddamn maniac. Even in the stillness of his truck's cab, Cal's screams, high and terrified like those of a pig on its way to the slaughterhouse, played inside his head.

He wanted to gather his thoughts but one kept repeating: *It wasn't supposed to go like this.*

He passed a gas station and considered filling the Ford F-150's tank and driving straight back to Georgia. But he'd promised Shelby he'd help her get answers. Still, *it wasn't supposed to go like this.*

Stepping into the store, Lincoln dipped his head to avoid the camera above the automatic door. He disliked shopping in general—his mom always sent him to grab butter, eggs, sweet potatoes—but he really hated it in new places.

He moved up and down the small market's narrow aisles in a daze. He didn't know where anything was and he sure as shit wasn't going to ask for help. Lincoln considered himself fairly generic-looking—brown hair, brown eyes, six feet tall, slim build. People always thought they knew him. They'd tap him on the shoulder and ask, "Hey, didn't we go to high school together?" or "Didn't you use to tend bar at Pete's?" Ninety-nine percent of the time they were mistaken.

He was counting on his unremarkable appearance to help him fly under the radar. Shelby drew attention everywhere. Her golden hair and bright eyes turned heads. Back in the day, she'd had the pep of a cheerleading squad. Men and women alike seemed to fall under her spell. Hell, he'd spent the better part of his twenty-seven years chasing that girl. Since the summer before high school when he'd first spotted her sipping a blueberry ICE-E on the hood of Scotty's Chevy Nova, Lincoln was a goner.

He'd waited around, watched while she dated half the football team, then older guys with money, fast cars. He wasn't proud of the fact that he'd only won her over because of what happened to Chloe. Grief made people vulnerable, unable to think straight. It was never his intention to capitalize on that.

Days after the funeral, he'd gone to her place to drop off his mom's chicken and waffles and a cherry pie.

"Nobody feels like eating, but you gotta keep up your strength," Doris, his mother, had said, stacking one foil pan atop the other. "You tell Sharon she can just toss these when she's finished. I don't want 'em back, and Lord knows she doesn't need one more thing to worry about." She smothered the pie with plastic wrap. "It's like that poor family's living under a black cloud. Sharon's cancer, Scotty's trouble with the law, now that poor girl, gone, just like that." She'd snapped her fingers after using them to count up the family's sorrows.

When Shelby'd opened the door that day, Lincoln hoped his face didn't betray him. She seemed to have shrunk three inches, blue eyes faded like washed-out denim, gray-purple hollows carved beneath them. He'd never seen her like that.

The family's Christmas decorations were still up, though it was going on mid-January. He'd taken everything down, packed it away, placing stuff with Chloe's name on it at the way bottom of the box. After he'd tucked it in the attic, he'd hung around, watched TV with Shelby because she told him to. She invited him back the next night, then the one after that. It seemed like all that time he'd spent waiting was finally paying off. He should've felt good about it, but this wasn't the real Shelby. More like a one-dimensional, cardboard cut-out.

They'd sat on opposite ends of the couch but the gulf between them shrunk as weeks slipped into months, their knuckles sometimes touching inside a Doritos bag. Soon trees began to bud, and he swapped his flannels for tees. As he stood to leave one night, she'd tugged at the hem of his shirt, pulling him back down. His heart beat so hard, he'd almost pressed his hand to his chest to still the vibration.

"I saw you, but I never really *saw you*, until now," she'd said and kissed him, her lips firm as a promise.

They'd been together ever since. They argued sometimes. What couple didn't? Mainly, she gave him a hard time about still living at home and having no real life plan. Yeah, he'd worked at the same auto body shop since high school, but he had money in the bank and Travis, the owner, helped him add white racing stripes to the F-150's hood. Plus, it wasn't like he was forty, Lincoln shot back, and she lived with her family too. But after Chloe passed and her mom got sick again, Lincoln knew she was there out of obligation rather than choice.

Still, in all their time together, they'd never exchanged words as harsh as the ones they'd hurled at each other in Wyoming. Of course, they'd never kidnapped anyone together before either.

Cal. *Shit!* Just thinking about him, picturing blood and bone, his average hand turned into a Halloween decoration, made Lincoln want to dry-heave. He roamed the store 'til he found the first aid section. He'd seen his father's farmhands suffer bad cuts, serious burns, but this—getting most of a finger chopped off—this was next level.

He'd forgotten to get a cart or even a basket so he had to juggle ibuprofen, peroxide, and cotton balls. He passed a display of BAND-AIDs. This was way beyond that. He needed gauze. Lots of it. No. What he needed was a hospital, a doctor, a hand surgeon. This was insane. The same thought circled again and again, his brain buffering. *It wasn't supposed to go like this. It wasn't supposed to go like this.*

As much as Lincoln wanted to get the hell out of town,

Cal was in bad shape. What happened in that cabin was nothing like what he'd agreed to back in early November.

Lincoln knew Shelby was gutted by the loss of her kid sister, but it was all the unanswered questions—the hows and the whys—that truly haunted her. She'd never believed Chloe had purposely leapt in front of a snowplow because she was depressed over a bad grade on a math final like the school counseling center suggested. She'd rejected the idea that Chloe would go to a bar alone and get trashed the night before a test. Something or someone had brought her out there. Shelby needed to find out what—or who.

She'd nearly given up hope when the tip came in. A student had written to tell her about a guy named Callaway Whitaker who'd been with Chloe that night, gotten her drunk, kept her out 'til she could barely stand, watched as she fell into the path of a snowplow, and did nothing to save her. Then he fled like a coward.

After getting that message, a part of Shelby had come back to life. She started calling, texting Cal, but he never got in touch. Each time he ignored her, it was like he was turning up a dial, tuning her rage to a new, higher frequency.

Lincoln had tried to distract her with positive things—maybe they'd get married, start a new life someplace where memories didn't trail them like sad stray dogs. But she said she couldn't move on until she knew what had happened to Chloe.

"You'd do anything for me, right?" she'd asked Lincoln one crisp November night as they sat around her fire pit, watching the flames crackle and spit, passing a bottle of whiskey back and forth.

Maybe it was the liquor, maybe it was love, but he'd said, "You know I would," without hesitation.

She'd found Cal, she'd said. She'd called his mom, told her they were friends from college. She wanted to send him a Christmas present, she'd lied, she just needed his address.

"The mom sounded snooty at first," Shelby took a long sip, "but by the end of our conversation, she was calling me 'dear.'"

In the glow of the flames, he watched her lips twist into a smirk that made him anxious.

"We're gonna pay Cal a visit," Scotty said. "In Wyoming." He'd been scrolling through his phone. He set it on the arm of the red plastic Adirondack chair and poked at the fire.

Both siblings were eyeing Lincoln. He got the feeling that this wasn't a casual conversation. This was a meeting. Maybe even a sales pitch.

"Wyoming?" He'd frowned.

Scotty cleared his throat. "We just want to talk to him is all."

"And you think this guy who hasn't returned a single call or text is going to agree to sit down and answer all your questions?" Lincoln shifted his gaze from brother to sister and back again. He waited for one of them to crack up, to say they were busting his balls. *Wyoming?* When neither spoke, he said, "You're joking, right? That's a helluva long way to go, and isn't he gonna get spooked and run?"

"We're gonna pick him up." Scotty pushed the heels of his boots into the dirt, tipping the legs of the cheap chair off the ground. Lincoln expected him to topple backward and smack his head on a paver, but Scotty kept his balance. "We'll make him talk."

"I think you've seen too many movies." Lincoln waited.

It had to be the whiskey. He kept expecting them to burst out laughing, but they stayed quiet.

Shelby crossed her arms. "I need to know what happened. I need him to tell us. I want it recorded."

"Recorded?" It got weirder by the second. "What are you gonna do with that other than drive yourself crazy?"

"I want to hear him admit that it was his fault whenever I feel like it. Shit, I may even blackmail him with it."

"Now I know you two have lost it," Lincoln snorted.

"Listen, Linc," Scotty rocked forward, elbows on knees, "you've been here for us. You've been good to Shelby. But you don't know what we've been through. You might think you do, but you don't. You can't."

It was true. Lincoln was an only child. He couldn't imagine what it was like to lose a sibling, then a parent. Still. "You can't just nab a guy and force him to tell you what he remembers from two years ago," he said. "And how do you know this tipster's even telling the truth?"

"If Whitaker wasn't guilty, he'd have talked to us by now."

"We're working on a plan."

Scotty'd been driving to libraries in different counties, he explained, researching rental properties. He'd found a hunting cabin through a site that didn't ask for too much info. He'd driven to Savannah and sent a money order to cover it for a couple weeks. After word spread about Chloe, people from across the county, the whole damn state, really, gave generously to the GoFundMe Chloe's high school swim coach started. But that well had been drained dry by Scotty's reckless spending and their mom's illness and funeral expenses.

"I need this, Lincoln." Shelby reached out and squeezed

his arm. Through his flannel hoodie, he got goosebumps. From love? Fear of losing her? Fear of following her? Didn't matter. If he helped her get answers, maybe she'd be... not herself again, but better? "And we may need to borrow a little cash."

Lincoln should've known with Scotty involved, things would spiral into chaos. Scotty, who'd been stealing cars since his feet could touch the pedals, whose main hobbies were fishing and starting bar fights.

They'd never had a real plan beyond getting a confession out of Cal. And even if they'd come up with one, hacking off his finger wouldn't have been part of it.

"Can I help you?" An older lady with a dandelion puff of gray hair and eyeglasses on a chain offered him a gummy grin.

Startled, Lincoln dropped the bottle of peroxide and bag of cotton balls. How long had he been standing there, eyes glazed over, trying to compare the ingredients in bacitracin versus Neosporin?

The woman stared at him, a frown replacing her smile. Did he look as nervous and messed up as he felt?

He bent to pick up his items. "I'm good, thanks."

Lincoln wasn't good. In fact, his hands shook as he placed the products on the conveyor belt. His stomach cramped. He wanted to blame Scotty's chili. He never cooked the beans long enough. But it was more than that. It was the growing sense of dread creeping up the base of his neck. He didn't want to go back to the cabin. Something—call it an instinct—told him the messes he'd need to clean up were about to get bigger.

25

TUESDAY, DECEMBER 16
CAL

They'd take him somewhere—the hospital, urgent care, shit, even a veterinarian. They had to. They couldn't leave him like this. They wouldn't. They'd put the rest of his finger in a safe place and it could be reattached. That's what would happen. It had to.

It didn't. Instead, they streamed sitcoms in the other room, the overly loud and upbeat theme songs driving Cal out of his mind as he writhed, limbs chained to the bedposts. Rockets of pain shot through his hand and up his arm. His flesh burned and itched like a million fire ants were marching beneath his skin. He'd never experienced anything like this. At the end of the season during his freshman year of high school, he'd dislocated his shoulder. That was a tickle by comparison.

Lincoln, Shelby's boyfriend, was the only one who seemed to care if he lived or died. He'd stayed up with Cal the night Scotty hacked off most of his middle finger. He'd wrapped Cal's mangled hand with towels, eyes averted, muttering, "Keep it elevated" to Cal, and "It wasn't supposed to go like this" to himself.

He slipped Cal a bunch of pills and shots of Wild Turkey to make his shaking stop after Shelby had gone to bed. He came back the next night and sat in the chair, whittling, and rambling after he spread ointment on Cal's half-finger and rewrapped it. He let Cal keep his arm free so he could have a few drinks to take the edge off. After the whiskey mixed with the pills, the pain finally loosened its grip, and he could allow the patter of Lincoln's steady rambling to lull him into a trance.

Cal saw something in Lincoln that didn't exist in the other two: kindness, compassion, sympathy. He'd read stories about people who were taken, held against their will, how they strangely came to love their captors. Did reverse Stockholm Syndrome exist? What if he could get Lincoln to love him? It was possible, and likely his only shot at making it out alive.

And so he listened and nodded when Lincoln talked about wanting to do something big with his life but not knowing what.

"All I can tell you is stay out of commercial real estate," Cal said, the whiskey working its magic, his words slurring as he explained that his dad's business was going down in flames.

"I don't want to follow in my old man's footsteps either." Lincoln sipped his drink.

"What's he do?" Cal asked.

"He's a pig farmer. Brutal industry."

"Jesus," said Cal, recalling how Lincoln's face had turned white as a marshmallow after Scotty cut off his finger. How he'd dry-heaved while wrapping Cal's bloody hand. He couldn't imagine Lincoln slaughtering hogs for a living. "Bet you have a hard time enjoying a BLT."

The thought of a sandwich made Cal's stomach rumble. All he'd eaten for days was chili. Apparently Shelby didn't cook and it was the only thing Scotty knew how to make. Still, it was better than that vegan disaster Brad's mom tried to pass off as chili, all mushrooms and tofu.

Where was Brad? What was that lazy bastard doing right then? Probably icing his knee and whining. By Monday morning when Cal hadn't shown up for work, Brad had to know something was wrong. Cal couldn't afford to skip a shift and lose more money. Did Brad charge Cal's phone, start calling around? Shit, he'd missed his dad's birthday. His mom would organize a search party based on that alone. People were looking for him. He knew they were.

Someone had come knocking late that afternoon. Scotty'd stuffed a pair of tube socks in Cal's mouth before he let Shelby open the door.

From the back room, Cal strained to listen. Was it the cops? No. He recognized the high singsong of teenage girls. He thought of his sister. Emerson had always looked up to him, idolized him. She was probably freaking out not knowing where he was, if he was all right.

"We haven't seen that poor guy," Shelby's voice was warm and sweet again, "but we'll keep him in our prayers."

What an actress. Shit, *he'd* fallen for her performance, her flat tire charade. Because she was pretty. People believed anything if you were attractive enough. He'd gotten by on his good looks his entire life. And his charm.

That charm seemed to be working on Lincoln. He was still chuckling at Cal's BLT joke, or maybe it was the booze.

His laughter faded to a yawn and he glanced toward the door.

"What would happen if Shelby found you in here, you and me shooting the shit?" Cal asked.

"Don't worry 'bout her. She's been taking stuff to help her sleep ever since Chloe... you know..." He stopped, cleared his throat. "It's Scotty—he's the one you gotta keep an eye on, but you already know that." He glanced toward Cal's hand. "Look, I know you've been out of it, and I'm not sure how much you remember from before Scotty..." Lincoln waved his hand in a chopping motion, "but Shelby—she's got a lot of questions and she's not gonna stop until you answer 'em."

"I told her everything the other day." Cal winced. His finger throbbed again. He swore he could feel the part that was missing. How could something that wasn't even there still hurt that much?

"She says it wasn't enough." Lincoln splashed more whiskey into their mugs.

Fuck that. Cal waited, hoping Lincoln would start laughing again. He didn't.

"I mean, you gotta be wondering why you're still here, right?" Lincoln raised his eyebrows. He pulled his knife and block of wood from his pockets and started making little cuts. "She says she needs more details, and it wasn't recorded. She wants it recorded."

"No way. I'm not starring in her fucked-up documentary." Cal shook his head. That ached too. Did he have a concussion? He'd gotten a couple back in high school. "My finger is all they get."

26

WEDNESDAY, DECEMBER 17
CAL

Cal woke to Lincoln's voice, sharp and pleading, lobbying the others to let him go. Every fight traveled through the thin walls.

He heard a thud, then another. He hadn't been out of the small room but he tried to picture what lay beyond it—a table maybe, Lincoln's fist pounding it in frustration. There was the TV, of course, going all day, sitcom theme songs providing the bubbly soundtrack to his nightmarish existence.

"Haven't you done enough," Lincoln growled, "hacking off his goddamn finger? Wrecking his entire hand?"

"He's not going anywhere," Shelby shot back, "not until he tells us what he did to her, 'til he admits he's the reason she's gone."

Then there was silence. So much silence.

Cal had no memory of the drive from the parking lot to this place where he'd been held like a prisoner for who knew how fucking long, but it had to be far from the rest of the world. He hadn't heard a passing car or even a neighbor hollering "Hello!" when Scotty went out to split firewood with the axe that had claimed his finger.

And what had they done with his skis? His Rossignol Soul 7s—they weren't cheap. He'd nearly had to pawn them back in October after he'd lost a grand in a weekend.

"Let him go," Lincoln begged. "It's time to end this. You can't stay here much longer, and I said I'd be home for Christmas."

"Aw, aren't you the sweetest?" Scotty mocked him. "What a mama's boy!"

"I'm not going anywhere until I hear him say the words. Until I have it recorded."

"Shelby, that's—

"That's what? Crazy? No, what's crazy is that my sister is dead because of him," she said. "He needs to suffer. Like she did."

"Anyway, we can't just dump him on the side of the road, not when the whole damn country is searching for this asshole," Scotty added.

The whole country? A surge of hope sent an electric charge through Cal. Someone would find him. This was not how his life would end, chained to a post like an unwanted dog.

"But you're right," Shelby said, her voice louder, closer. "It's time."

THE DOOR OPENED. Cal's mouth was dry, his tongue thick and rubbery as a fat pink eraser. He hoped it was Lincoln bringing him water, breakfast. More chili, anything, whatever. Instead, Scotty carried in two chairs and set them on the area rug facing each other. He moved Cal from the bed to the chair, cinching the chains so the cold metal dug into Cal's wrists and ankles.

Shelby took a seat across from him, phone in hand. "You're gonna walk us through it—Chloe's last night."

Cal's heart galloped. The memory of his last time in that chair flashed behind his eyes like a jump scare in a horror film.

Scotty left the room and returned with the axe, its silver blade gleaming beneath the overhead light. Pain shot through the place where Cal's finger had been.

Scotty swung the axe side to side inches above the ground, a menacing pendulum. Cal closed his eyes and pictured the grandfather clock in his foyer back in Oak Hill. When he looked up, Shelby held out her phone. She nodded and poked the screen with a sharp nail. "Go!" she said.

"Look, I—I told you everything the other day." Cal strained to keep his voice even, respectful. "There's not much more to say."

The axe stopped. Scotty picked it up and hoisted it over his shoulder. "I cut off one finger." He scratched his goatee. "What makes you think I'll stop there?"

Cal had to come up with something, anything, but his thoughts were jumbled. There'd been so many girls, so many drunken nights. Sure, none had ended the way that one had with Chloe, but what did they want from him? It was two fucking years ago.

Lincoln stepped into the room. He kept his head down. "They want to know how you and Chloe met," he said.

Grateful for the lifeline, Cal began. "I—I—I was visiting a friend. We swung by her dorm, picked her up. We went to a couple of parties, a few bars. We both had a lot to drink.

Speaking of—" he could barely swallow "—can I get some water?"

Shelby lowered the phone. "This isn't about you. This is about Chloe. Start over."

Cal's stomach lurched. *What the hell did they want to hear?* He tried to remember the stuff Brad had said about Chloe. "She was smart, funny, beautiful."

"She was our sister, asshole. We know that." Scotty stepped forward.

Cal flinched.

"Start again," Shelby commanded.

Behind her, the axe's blade glimmered. The hairs on Cal's arms prickled. He tried to breathe deeply like Brad's mom had taught them to do before a big game, but he was so far beyond that, he was nearly hyperventilating.

"We—we were having a good time. I mean, she was happy. She said she was going home Saturday. Getting a ride with someone to Atlanta. She was excited for Christmas."

Was any of that true? He'd flipped into autopilot, mouth moving, brain a blur.

"Athens," Scotty corrected. "She was getting a ride to Athens."

Each time Scotty spoke, Cal felt a stab in his phantom finger.

"Why were you grabbing her scarf?" Shelby asked. "Were you trying to strangle her? "Cause she wasn't into you?"

"No, no, of course not."

"Our grandmother made that scarf. Every picture Chloe sent us that fall, she was wearing it." Shelby set the phone in her lap and covered her face with her hand.

Cal heard a sniffle and saw an opening. He needed this

to end without losing any other body parts. He was a good actor too. He'd played Henry Higgins in his elementary school's production of *My Fair Lady*. If he hadn't loved football as much as he did, he might've pursued acting in high school. He could play the role of apologetic asshole, bad boy who learned his lesson, if it meant they'd let him go. So what if she showed the video to anyone? He'd say it was coerced and he'd been out of his mind in pain. They'd lobbed off half his finger, for God's sake!

He waited for Shelby to pull herself together. He looked at Lincoln, slouched against a wall just as he'd been the day Scotty attacked him like a fucking savage.

Shit, he didn't owe these people anything—not after what they'd done to him—but he'd say whatever they needed to hear.

Shelby raised the phone and pushed a button.

"I'm, I'm sorry," Cal tried again with every bit of remorse he could summon. "It was a terrible thing." He lowered his voice. "A horrific accident that never should've happened."

His words made Shelby go rigid. She set down her phone. "It wasn't an accident," she said through clenched teeth. "It was you!"

Scotty sprang forward, axe raised. Cal's heart beat like a kick drum against his ribs. His instincts told him to run but he was tied down. The best he could do was push off with his feet. The chair tipped back. His head smacked the floor. Lincoln lunged and grabbed Scotty's arm before he could drive the blade through Cal's chest.

"No!" Lincoln yelled. "Enough! I'm not watching you hack this guy apart no matter what you think he's done, and I'm sure as shit not cleaning up after you again." He shoved Scotty toward the window.

The part of Cal's skull that slammed the floor was just inches above where Scotty'd clubbed him with the tire iron. How much more could he endure? Maybe this was where it would end for him. He writhed and wriggled on his back, helpless as a tortoise turned on its shell.

"Shelby," Lincoln said, his chest heaving. "Finish this. Now."

Shelby pushed her lips together like she was holding in some choice words, then stood. Looming above Cal, she looked wild, feral, cheeks flushed, hair spilling from her ponytail. He was afraid she was going to kick him again or step on his balls. Lying there, tears rolled down the sides of his face and pooled in his ears.

She raised her phone. "Start over."

Scotty shrugged off Lincoln's hand and stomped out of the room.

Stuttering and stammering, Cal admitted he'd gotten Chloe drunk and convinced her to stay out long after she wanted to go home. They were flirting; he never meant for her to get hurt. He was sorry, so sorry.

"Say it," Shelby grunted.

"Say what?"

"'It's my fault.'"

He could say anything; he didn't have to mean it. What did that cost him? Nothing. He'd done it before—when he told his mom he'd never gamble again, when he told Melinda he was falling for her, when he told Brad he was the closest thing he had to a brother.

His head pounded. His hand throbbed. He couldn't see any other way out of this. Football had made him good at pushing through pain, focusing on one play, then the next. Sometimes you couldn't think about the long game; you just needed to survive the next moment. He was crying real tears now. Exhaustion, fear, and seeing no way out had leveled him.

"It's my fault," he said. "It was all my fault."

Shelby lowered the phone.

"I never meant for her to get hurt." Cal added a hard swallow for dramatic effect. "If I could take it all back, I would. I swear, I would."

"Funny," Shelby sneered. "I bet you'd do the exact same thing. Guys like you never learn—not until someone teaches you."

27

THURSDAY, DECEMBER 18
LINCOLN

Lincoln had assumed once Shelby got what she wanted, she'd set Cal free.

"Not yet," she said. "He should suffer. Like we have."

"That wasn't the plan, Shel!"

"Plans change, babe," she said.

What was the plan? That was the problem. There'd never been a solid plan and without one, how, where, and when did this end?

"He's missing half a finger," Lincoln snorted. "Isn't that enough suffering?"

"I'm missing my whole sister, Linc. So, no, it's not enough."

"You got the recorded confession. C'mon."

"Well, now, maybe I'll blackmail him with it."

"He's got bookies following him and his dad's going bankrupt, so I don't think that's an option."

"You believe everything he tells you, don't you?" Shelby snickered. She hadn't even bothered to look at him. She and Scotty sat at the round wooden table playing gin rummy like it was an ordinary afternoon, TV blaring, fire blazing. Sometimes Scotty forgot to open the flue and it got so smoky, the alarm would shriek. One night he jumped up and beat it with a broomstick until it fell and skittered to the corner where it now sat, silenced.

Lincoln wanted to believe that if Cal's disappearance hadn't become a whole big thing Shelby would've let him go right away. Maybe not driven him to his condo, but left him a mile or two from town, bringing this insanity to an end.

They'd never expected it to make the national news. They hadn't been prepared for that—or anything, really. Scotty and Shelby had come out the first week of December and followed Cal from a distance in the ridiculous SUV with tinted windows Scotty'd bought with some of that GoFundMe money. What they'd do with Cal once they captured him—well, it turned out they'd never thought that far ahead.

Shelby blamed Cal's sister for the story blowing up. Another beautiful, broken girl who'd go to any extreme to find out what happened to her sibling. For Shelby, it should've been like looking in a mirror, but she couldn't see it.

Lincoln found it hard to hate Cal the way his girlfriend did. Yes, he never should've left Chloe, but it sounded like he'd panicked and ran. It wasn't like the guy was pure evil, but he'd never say as much to Shelby.

He tried his best to keep Cal's wound clean, but the finger—what was left of it—looked worse by the day. A green layer crusted over the opening. Pus oozed in the corners. His whole hand was swollen and hot. There was a bad smell, too, though that could've been coming from the bucket that served as Cal's toilet.

"You gotta take him to a hospital," Lincoln pleaded. "He has a fever. Have you seen his hand? It doesn't even look human."

"Why are you so fucking soft, man?" Scotty stopped shuffling cards to stare at him. "For real, Shel? What'd you ever see in this mama's boy?"

Shelby laughed, eyes narrowing. "I'm trying to remember."

"Mama's boy" was a sore spot, something Lincoln's dad called him. The first time that he could recall was when he was five and had bawled for an hour after his dad joked about the fate of the pigs he'd named and loved.

"Dwayne, he can't even listen to me read *Charlotte's Web* without tearing up," Lincoln's mom had scolded. "How'd you think he was gonna handle that?"

After his dad went out back, screen door clapping like applause, Lincoln's mom had cuddled him close, his nose smushed into her hip. He hadn't minded. Her apron always smelled like peaches and cinnamon.

"Don't pay any attention to him, Linc. You've got a big, soft heart," she'd whispered. "The world'll try to harden it. Don't let it."

So maybe he was a mama's boy, but that was still better than being a murderer.

"Call me whatever you want," Lincoln told Scotty and Shelby, "but you two are fucking crazy and I'm leaving Saturday morning with or without you."

28

FRIDAY, DECEMBER 19
CAL

Lincoln came back night after night.

"I'm trying, man. I am," he said. "I want this to end without any more bloodshed."

"That makes two of us." Cal took every opportunity to reinforce the idea that they were a team. If Lincoln couldn't convince them to let him go, how would this end? Cal tried not to think about it, just as he tried not to think about the long-ago night that brought him there.

If only Chloe had listened when he'd said, "Let's go back to your dorm."

"My roommate's asleep." She'd pushed him away. "And I've got an early final."

"You seem like a smart girl. I'm sure you'll ace it." He'd bought her another drink, then another, tugging her toward him with that scarf, reeling her in like a fish.

"Stop!" She'd laughed. "You're stretching it out! Meemaw made this! Where'd Brad go? Let's find him and head back."

How many times had she said it? Who'd heard her? Had

someone been watching them? The thing that stuck like a splinter in Cal's mind was this: Who was the student who'd pointed Shelby and Scotty to him? How did she have those details? Especially the scarf thing. It wasn't Cal's school; he'd just been visiting and had only met people through Brad—and let's be real, Brad was hardly popular. So who ratted him out? If Cal was going to get that info, Lincoln was his best bet.

He came in after Shelby went to bed and spread ointment on what was left of Cal's finger. Sloppy with the gauze, he wrapped it like he was taping up a prizefighter, leaving gaps around the base. Cal thanked him and told him he'd make a good doctor. Lincoln blushed at the compliment, took a seat, and pulled his knife and a hunk of chiseled wood from the pocket of his hoodie. He was drinking more than usual, talking more too.

"You gotta understand, Shelby's not in a good place. Hers and Scotty's mom had cancer. It was gone, in remission, whatever you call it. After Chloe—" he dropped his head and waved his hand, the knife's blade making Cal flinch "—it came back. She didn't last six months. Then Meemaw passed. They've had a real rough time," he offered, a lame-ass apology. "What's that saying, 'Hurt people hurt people?'"

That was sad, yeah, of course, but Cal didn't give a shit. That was no excuse to abduct him and cut off his goddamn finger. He kept quiet a minute, hoping Lincoln would see it as a sign of respect. Then he asked, "So, who was the woman?"

Lincoln scrunched up his face. "Who now?"

"The woman. The one who reached out to Shelby. The one who said I was there the night Chloe..."

Lincoln shrugged. "I don't know. Someone messaged her through her website."

"Got a name?" Cal pressed.

Lincoln puffed out his cheeks like he was thinking hard. Cal waited. There was only one person who knew he was there that night, one person who could guess how that night unfolded. It wasn't a woman.

After a long pause, Lincoln winked and tapped his temple. "You're in luck. Memory's ten times better when I'm drinking."

Cal took a breath and held it.

"I couldn't tell you what she looked like 'cause her profile picture was a little French bulldog, but her name's Shirley Bradley."

Cal knew it. He fucking knew it. The breath he'd been holding leaked out of him. For a second, he forgot about the pain in his hand. This betrayal cut deeper, sharper than a bone sliced clean through. How had he not figured it out sooner?

"Shirley said you got Chloe drunk. You were tugging on her scarf and she was pushing you away but you wouldn't quit it. You let her stumble out to her death. Then you took off."

"That's... that's not what happened." Cal hung his head.

After a few minutes, Lincoln held up the block of wood. "Making another mini garden gnome," he said. "I always tell Shelby, there's nothing you can't learn from watching YouTube."

Brad loved YouTube. Those stupid snowboarding videos. Brad was supposed to be his friend. His oldest fucking friend. Of course Cal remembered the name Shirley Bradley. Max would taunt Brad with it and sometimes Cal would join in. It was so easy to get Brad worked up.

Now Cal felt like screaming in frustration, rage, and the pain that had plagued him every second since he awoke in that awful room.

Lincoln was babbling about woodcarving. Cal needed to focus on him, on making *him* his friend, a friend who wouldn't leave him there to die.

Lincoln's hands moved slowly, carefully, his elbows lifting gently like butterfly wings. Was he giving the gnome a little cap?

"Looks cool," Cal said. "Really." It wasn't. It was pathetic. He couldn't imagine having so few talents that he had to resort to carving fake creatures. Cal gulped the whiskey, hoping a refill might calm the hornet's nest of nerves buzzing in his chest.

"Thanks, man," Lincoln said. "It's just something that relaxes me. I'm not that good."

"Yet," Cal corrected, nudging his near-empty mug across the nightstand. "Keep working at it. Seriously. You got something there."

Lincoln set the knife down and poured a few more inches. "I'll drink to that!"

Cal didn't give a shit about the garden gnome or whittling. He was stalling. He didn't want Lincoln to go. Not that he cared to hear another of his father-son sob stories. Cal had plenty of his own and *his* dad had *his* own—a never-ending cycle of paternal disappointment. It was boring, pedestrian.

Cal wanted to drive a wedge between Lincoln and the others. If he was leaving, Cal needed to go with him. He couldn't think about the possibility of being trapped here with those animals.

"Think you and Shelby'll make it, you know, after this?" he asked.

Lincoln shrugged. "Like I said, she's been through a lot."

"Yeah, man, but the way she talks to you? Scotty too. You don't deserve—"

"It's always been that way. I'm used to it. My dad's kinda the same. He—"

"You shouldn't put up with it. Seriously, you're a smart guy." Again, Cal watched the color rise in Lincoln's cheeks. "They're holding you back. Actually, it's worse than that—they're dragging you down."

Lincoln stayed quiet, focused on the gnome.

"You got talent, man, I can tell. My mom owns this jewelry business and my sister does her marketing and social media. They could help you sell your work. You're good, man. This could be a legit business for you."

"You think?"

"Absolut—"

The door burst open. Lincoln jerked back. The knife sliced straight across the tip of his index finger. Scotty stepped inside the small room and stared from Lincoln to Cal and back again.

"What the fuck are you doin' in here?" He scowled at their mugs. "Playin' tea party?"

"Shit," Lincoln hissed, wiping his bloody finger on his jeans. He set the knife and wood on the nightstand.

"Thought you'd gone to bed," Scotty said. "Then I heard voices. Shelby'd go apeshit if she saw you in here like—"

"What do you want?" Lincoln interrupted.

"We're almost out of firewood. Go get some."

"You get it," Lincoln shot back. "It's cold as shit out

there." Had the whiskey made him bolder or was it what Cal had said about the way Scotty and Shelby treated him?

"I did it last time." Scotty jutted his chin. "You're bailing on us tomorrow. It's the least you can do."

Lincoln looked at the flap of skin hanging off his fingertip. He opened his mouth and closed it again after stealing a glance at Cal's hand. His wound was a paper cut compared to Cal's situation.

"C'mon, get going or I'll tell Shelby you're playing doctor with this asshole."

"Whatever." Lincoln stood.

"And chain him up again!" Scotty hollered over his shoulder.

Lincoln flipped him the bird.

"I'd be careful about doing that, man." Cal held up his bandaged hand.

"Fuck him," Lincoln murmured. "Be right back."

But he hadn't come back; Scotty must've been keeping an eye on him.

29

SATURDAY, DECEMBER 20
LINCOLN

By midweek, Lincoln had started sleeping on the couch. It was comfortable as an ironing board and left his back and neck stiff, but it was better than lying beside Shelby. His girlfriend, the woman he'd hoped would someday be the mother of his kids, felt more like a stranger—a dangerous one—each passing day. She hadn't noticed he'd stopped coming to bed, probably on account of the sleeping pills.

Friday night after gathering the firewood, he'd set his phone's alarm for five a.m. Scotty would be in a Jack Daniels stupor. Shelby typically stayed knocked out until at least seven. He'd leave without seeing either of them, get on the road before first light.

In the kitchen, Lincoln shivered. Waiting for the water to boil, he let steam from the kettle warm his hands, careful to slide it to a back burner before it whistled.

Blowing on his instant coffee, Lincoln's eyes landed on the door to the back bedroom. For a second, he considered taking Cal with him. He looked nothing like the confident guy who thought he was helping Shelby change a flat, all swagger and smiles. He'd lost weight. His teeth appeared too big for his mouth, and the whites of his eyes had a yellowy tint.

Could Lincoln leave him at an ER? People did that with babies they couldn't keep—or was that fire stations? Anyway, Cal wasn't a baby, he was practically a celebrity.

Scotty obsessively scrolled for news, turning his phone to show them the latest headlines. One good thing Cal's sister had done, according to Shelby, was turn the spotlight on the roommate.

Lincoln felt like shit about that too—that random guy dealing with all sorts of nasty accusations because of what *they'd* done. Things were bound to get worse and Lincoln didn't want a front-row seat to any of it. Shelby and Scotty had dug a hole. Instead of trying to climb out of it, they were pulling others down into it.

Leaving with Cal was too big a risk for Lincoln. If Scotty caught him, he'd use that axe and hack them both to pieces, let Shelby feed them to bears.

Lincoln needed to leave. Alone.

He poured the rest of the coffee down the drain. When he turned away from the sink, Shelby stood behind him, arms crossed, startling him.

"You're really going? Leaving me? Deserting us?"

Lincoln nodded.

Her lips puckered, then drooped in a pout. She swept a handful of hair between her fingers and held it out, inspecting it for split ends. How could she be so casual, so cold? Lincoln stepped back and bumped into the oven's handle.

Shelby's small bare feet made sucking sounds as she

crossed the old linoleum floor to the fridge. "Do me a favor?" she said.

He thought back to the November night when they sat beside her fire pit and she'd asked, "You'd do anything for me, right?" and like a lovesick idiot he'd said, "You know I would."

"What now?" he asked. God, he wished she'd stayed asleep.

She let her hair fall back into place and tugged open the freezer. Using a dishtowel to cover her hands, she removed the other half of Cal's finger. It was ghostly white, coated in ice crystals.

"Jesus," Lincoln breathed. He wanted to leave right then, run, and not look back. Shock pinned him in place. He watched in horrified silence as she reached into the cabinet below the sink and retrieved one of the gloves Cal had worn the night they nabbed him in the parking lot. She stuck the frozen nub deep inside.

"Take this to my mother's grave." She'd held it high, with reverence, like she was presenting him with a chalice or a bar of gold. "Plant the finger in the dirt and tell her we'll be home when he's truly sorry." She forced the glove into Lincoln's hand.

"Don't do this, Shel. Please. Let him go. It's not worth it," Lincoln tried to reason with her one last time. "This isn't who you are. Come home with me. Scotty'll follow us. End this now. We'll start over. Just you and me."

"You know I can't, Linc, not yet. We've gotta see this through." Her voice was steady, resigned. Her eyes were fixed on a distant place Lincoln couldn't follow.

"What does that even mean, Shel?"

She shrugged and, on tiptoes, kissed his cheek. "Don't do anything that'll mess things up for us, okay?"

Lincoln nodded. He wanted to say, "Same to you," but the words were lodged in his throat, and he knew she was too far gone to listen anyway.

THE SKY WAS A DEEP, dark navy, no trace of the sun. Even with the truck's heat on full-blast, Lincoln couldn't get warm. He wished he were still on the sofa, but he couldn't stay in that cabin another second.

He'd barely made it a mile before his chest started to constrict and seize. Pain traveled up and down his arms. Was he having a heart attack? He glanced at the passenger's seat. There it was. The glove. The frozen finger inside it—probably thawing out. The sight of it sent firecrackers of anxiety through him.

He pictured Cal chained to the bed, getting sicker, paler, thinner. He didn't want this sin on his soul, and he definitely didn't want to cross state lines with that wretched thing—an abducted man's finger—riding shotgun. What if he got pulled over for something stupid like a busted taillight and next thing he was charged with kidnapping?

He grunted and smacked the steering wheel. *It wasn't supposed to go like this!*

His eyes shifted to the glove. The foul stink of Cal's open wound came back to him, flooding his nostrils. He gagged. No way could he keep that thing beside him. *No!* Shelby had already asked too much of him. *Fuck this!*

Jabbing the button on his left, he lowered the passenger side window, pulled to the shoulder, and flung the glove as far as he could before jamming his foot on the gas pedal and swerving back onto the icy road.

As he put more miles between himself and the cabin, he stared through the F-150's wide windshield, fighting not to lose himself in cloud patterns and the brightening sky, the sun rising ahead of him. For a moment here or a second there, he'd forget where he was, why he was there, speeding away from Wyoming. He still couldn't believe what they'd done. And what *he'd* just done—throwing the finger, as if he could leave the whole mess behind.

And where he tossed it. *Shit.* A snowy field, barely a dozen feet from the side of the road. A road that was only a few miles east of the cabin.

What the hell was he thinking? He'd let his fear of a half-finger lead him to do something stupid, reckless.

The tightness in his chest rushed back. But then something like relief unfurled. Maybe the glove would be found and somehow this would end with Cal still alive. Holding someone against his will was one thing; murder was another.

He kept driving, panic eroding that fleeting sense of calm. If that finger led to Cal, it also led to Scotty and Shelby and maybe him too.

30

MONDAY, DECEMBER 22

LINCOLN

Two bites into a burger Monday night somewhere between Missouri and Tennessee, Lincoln saw the news alert on the giant flat screen suspended above an orange booth. His eyes bounced between words in the captions: Glove. DNA. Bradley Chapman. Critical condition. Car Crash.

Bits of beef got stuck in Lincoln's throat, and he choked as the reporter said it was unclear if Chapman was "fleeing police, internet vigilantes, or simply trying to end his life."

His face burning like he'd dipped it in the grease fryer, Lincoln's eyes darted to the bored workers slouching behind the counter at this no-name restaurant. He felt exposed, certain they'd know he was connected to the unfolding drama two states back. A sickening ache filled his stomach—same one he got when he thought about the pigs, all soft ears and gentle snuffling, awaiting their terrible fate in his family's barn. He dropped the burger directly onto the plastic tray where the last customer's ketchup pooled in the corner.

He'd already figured the glove had been found because Sunday night he'd gotten a single-line text from Shelby:

> You shouldn't have done that.

Instead of the discovery leading to Cal, it had implicated Brad Chapman. This was yet another man's blood on their hands. Shelby wouldn't agree. She'd say it was Cal's sister's fault for mistakenly accusing him. Lincoln knew how Shelby thought. She might even be relieved about the crash. If Brad died, people would assume he'd been on the run, guilty of whatever had happened to Cal. He'd be the one and only suspect, unable to clear his name. What would Shelby and Scotty do with Cal then?

With sweating palms, Lincoln carried the dirty tray to the trash and tossed his dinner. As soon as the news segment ended, he got in his F-150, its blue and white exterior dulled by road salt and slush. He drove, stopping only to refill the gas tank and use the restroom.

The pain in his chest was back. He tried to breathe through it, but that only made it worse. He didn't know how he'd complete the drive but he was sure of one thing: this wasn't going to end well—for any of them.

31

TUESDAY, DECEMBER 23
CAL

During the brutally long days after Lincoln left, Cal's mouth watered at the thought of the whiskey that had helped those endless nights slide into mornings. Shelby and Scotty barely brought him water. They didn't put ointment on his half-finger or change the pus-soaked bandage either. His hand was infected. It had to be; he was burning up, sticking to damp sheets. His arm was swollen. His other fingers had gone numb. He wanted to close his eyes, surrender to sleep, or the dark pull of something stronger.

One thing kept him going. When he got out of there, *if* he got out of there, he was going to kill Brad.

32

TUESDAY, DECEMBER 23
LINCOLN

The "Welcome to Georgia" sign should've been a comfort. The air was warmer, the landscape less sharp, more forgiving. But what was he going back to? Nothing. For the past two years, Shelby'd been his entire world. Their relationship was over. It had to be. He didn't know who she was anymore. He remembered the night she'd pulled him toward her and whispered, "I saw you, but I never really *saw you*, until now." He could say it right back to her, and he wouldn't mean it kindly.

When he approached the turn for the dirt road that led to his family's farm, he switched off the radio but kept driving past the entrance. He wasn't ready to see the twinkling lights he and his dad had strung along the roofline of their small ranch the day before he left for Wyoming. Could he look his parents in the eye and lie about being on a ski vacation with his girlfriend and her brother? His mom would ask a whole mess of questions. She'd want to see pictures, hear about where they stayed, what they ate. He couldn't deal with any of that just yet.

He pulled into a strip mall parking lot and cut the engine. Shelby and Scotty had to be out of the cabin by eleven the next morning. What would they do with Cal? Was he still alive? If they dumped him somewhere, Lincoln didn't trust that they'd be smart enough to cover their tracks. He might not have known what he wanted to do with the rest of his life, but spending it in prison for kidnapping and murder definitely wasn't it.

His stomach gurgled. He'd been too upset to down anything but coffee since he'd seen the news about Cal's roommate. If Shelby and Scotty had released Cal when he'd told them to, Brad Chapman might not have been in that crash.

Maybe Brad's accident was on him too. He'd thrown the glove out the window. How could he have known it would lead to the roommate?

Lincoln smacked the steering wheel. His eyes burned from driving all night. Lightheaded and thirsty, he tugged off his jacket and tossed it on the passenger seat. Stomach acid churned in his gut, creeping into his mouth. He cracked the window and hocked a loogie. Spit dribbled down the glass. Jesus Christ, he couldn't even get that right.

In the glovebox, he kept a block of wood. He'd whittle while he waited for Shelby to fix her hair or makeup before they went to dinner or trivia night at the bar. It passed the time, but mainly it settled his nerves. He reached into the pocket of his jeans for his knife. It wasn't there. He patted the other side. Nothing. His back pockets were empty too. He'd gone days without sleep. He wasn't thinking clearly. The knife had to be in his jacket. He dug deep into the right pocket and came up with crumpled receipts for bandages and ointment. He'd been careful to pay cash. The other pocket held a stack of napkins from a pizza place. No knife.

Running a hand through his greasy hair, he closed his eyes and tilted his head back. *Think! Where is it?* His dad had given him that knife for his fifteenth birthday.

"Make a man out of you yet, son," he'd said.

Hardly a tender moment, but Lincoln had kept the knife on him ever since, thinking of it as a sort of lucky charm.

As he hunted around the floor of the truck, a dizzying, disorienting feeling swept through him, same as when he'd had his wallet lifted at the county fair.

When was the last time he'd had the knife? His brain spun back to Friday afternoon, the kitchen table. Shelby and Scotty played cards while he'd fiddled with the blades working up the courage to tell them he was leaving first thing Saturday. It was probably there.

Another memory swam into focus: later that night, sitting in Cal's room, working on that little garden gnome. Scotty'd burst in and told him to get more firewood. Had he put the knife down or taken it with him?

He could call Shelby and ask her to look for it, but they hadn't spoken since he left. She'd sent that one text, *You shouldn't have done that,* nothing more.

The knife was probably resting on the wooden table right beside the deck of cards.

Probably.

He didn't want to think about the alternative.

33

WEDNESDAY, DECEMBER 24

CAL

Cal heard them fighting. Without Lincoln as their mutual punching bag, Shelby and Scotty were turning on one another.

They needed to be out of the cabin the next morning. A cleaning crew was due at noon to prep it for the next renters.

"Good luck getting the stink out of this room." Cal was talking to himself. Since Lincoln left, he'd been doing that more and more.

Shelby and Scotty mainly ignored him, but they came in together in the late afternoon to check for any blood Lincoln might've missed on the floor or under the bed.

"I won't tell anyone about this—you—my finger," Cal pleaded. He was used to making deals with his mom for more money, bookies for more time, bartenders for one more drink after last call. Now he was negotiating for his life.

For a half-second, Shelby's eyes narrowed like she was considering it.

"He's gonna talk, Shel, you know he is," said Scotty, stroking his ugly goatee. Cal had begun to wonder if it was real or part of a disguise, maybe even a Halloween costume. "People'll be tripping over themselves to get his story. We can't take that chance."

"No, of course, you're right." Shelby shook her head like she was snapping herself out of a momentary lapse of reason. "Maybe we'll dump him in Nebraska. Badlands for a bad man."

They laughed—the first time they'd gotten along in days.

They were going to let him die. The only questions were where and when. Had his family stopped looking for him? Would he ever get out of this dark fucking room? A gripping sense of terror crept over Cal, making him hotter, itchier. This frantic feeling, this constant agitation, was new. He hated it. Was this what other people—anxious, weak ones, like Brad—experienced? He was chained to a bed, unmoving, yet he could barely catch his breath.

Just as he'd done with every football sack, he needed to put the pain and fear aside. *Reset. Focus.* He could still walk out of this. Other than gambling, he'd won at nearly everything his entire life. He refused to lose now. But time was running out. He had to make a play. His mind spun back to his high school football coach delivering the locker room speech he saved for Friday nights. "Half the people on that field are going home winners, the other half losers. Who do you want to be? A winner or a loser? Decide right now!"

Cal decided. He needed to win. He had a final move. His only option, really. The knife tucked inside his bandage.

Lincoln had left it behind when he'd gone to get the firewood the night before he left. Cal had waited forever before reaching for it, making small nicks in the nightstand as he worked it slowly shut with his mangled hand.

The weight of the wooden handle, its coolness inside the

bandage so close to his inflamed skin was a comfort. He'd practiced opening and closing the longest blade with his index and ring fingers. It wasn't easy working around the stump in the middle of his hand but he'd gotten better, faster. Now he needed to use it.

Cal told time by listening to the television beyond his door. When one sitcom episode ended and another's theme song began, he guessed thirty minutes had passed. That was about how long it had been since Shelby slammed her bedroom door after barking at Scotty to clean up the kitchen and put the smoke detector back.

He was still banging around, but for how much longer? Cal couldn't put it off.

"Hey!" he called. "Gotta use the bucket."

Nothing. Had Scotty not heard him? Cal's voice was weak. He was burning up—either from fear or fever. Pulse echoing in his ears, he didn't register Scotty's clunky footsteps until he appeared in the doorway.

"Jesus, man, again?"

"What'd you put in that chili? Laxatives?" Cal's lips twitched. He tried to play it off like a joke, but he was nervous. If he botched this, it was over. He was dead.

"All right, let's go. I got a lot of other shit to do." Scotty released Cal's ankles then his wrists. "Geez, you're a sweaty fuckin' mess." He waved his hand at the dampness under Cal's armpits and the wet ring around the neckline of his T-shirt.

Cal stood and the room spun. He closed his eyes for a second, lurched forward, and slid his pants down with his good hand. He'd lost so much weight, they dropped to the floor. He sat on the bucket, waited for Scotty to turn away, then kicked the toilet paper with his foot. He grunted a few times for effect.

"Hey, can you—?"

"I don't know what kind of arrangement you and Linc had, but I ain't wiping your ass," Scotty said.

"Just need the TP." Cal jerked his head. "Rolled under the bed." He inched off the bucket, letting the stench waft upward. Without Lincoln, the bucket hadn't been emptied in days.

Scotty huffed and made a gagging sound as he bent to retrieve the roll. From a couple feet away, he held it out.

"I can't reach that," Cal said, keeping his voice steady. He'd switched the knife to his good hand while Scotty had his back to him. His fingers trembled, poised to open the longest blade. He'd only have one chance. He had to get it right.

He thought about football again, those Friday night games under the lights. The year they went all the way to states. The announcer's voice booming, "Another flawless performance by the almighty Cal Whitaker!" His dad would imitate it over bacon and eggs on Saturday mornings.

Scotty took a step and tripped on the corner of the area rug. "Here."

His sloppy movements and boozy breath boosted Cal's confidence. Cal reached out his injured hand.

Time froze.

Scotty stumbled closer.

It was enough. Cal tugged him down. In one swift motion, he thrust the knife deep in Scotty's ear. The pop and squish as the blade pierced the skin reminded Cal of carving a Jack-o'-lantern.

Cal's body came alive. He felt wired, electric. He'd done it. Now he had to get up. Move.

Scotty's eyes bugged and rolled, each in its own direction, as a steady stream of blood seeped down his neck. He staggered from side to side, his hand moving to his head, too stunned to scream.

Cal had seconds before the man lunged for him. He shot to his feet, pants below his knees.

Scotty groaned and lurched forward. His foot collided with the plastic bucket. Shit swam in a puddle of piss around Scotty's boots. He took another step and slipped on a soft, wet turd, leaving a brown skidmark on the hardwood before he toppled back and smacked his head on the footboard.

Cal hitched up his pants and darted for the door, expecting Scotty to spring up and stop him. But he was down, clutching the side of his bloody head.

With his good hand, Cal tugged the door open and stepped toward freedom. He hesitated. What if Shelby was there waiting with the axe? He listened. Nothing. The pills must've knocked her out. Cal pulled the door closed. The knob had been switched around to lock from the outside. He flicked the nub from horizontal to vertical, trapping Scotty on the other side.

He stood, panting, trying to get his bearings. The room was dark except for the glare of the TV and the orange glow of the fireplace. It took seconds for his eyes to adjust. The cabin was smaller than he expected. The kitchen and living room were all one space. And where was it exactly? How far from the rest of the world?

He had to get out of there, hurry, yet it was disorienting to be outside the four walls where he'd been held. The sensation left him weak, paralyzed.

Behind him, a thin door was all that separated him from Scotty. It would rattle any second if Scotty regained consciousness and staggered to his feet. Cal hitched up his pants and stepped toward the couch, fighting to concentrate. Across the room was a door. A rectangle of glass at its top, a window to the night sky, a portal to the outside world. He just needed to get there. If he made it out, what next?

Think! Think!

He'd been trapped in bed for more than a week. How did he not have a plan? How had he not figured out what he'd do first if he finally got free?

Who do you want to be? A winner or a loser? Decide right now!

He wanted to be a winner, to run through that door and not look back, but where was Shelby's phone with his recorded confession? He had to delete it. Every fucking take.

He looked around, eyes landing on another door. Her bedroom? She probably had the device in there with her. He was the only idiot who let his phone die and then left it behind. If he'd had it, would his mom, with her tracking app, have located him?

If he didn't find Shelby's phone and destroy it, he'd be looking over his shoulder for the rest of his life, waiting for Shelby to release the recording, his stammering and blubbering out there for all the world to watch. When she did, he'd forever be the guy who got a girl drunk, left her to die, and then pretended it never happened while her family pleaded for answers.

Of course, he'd argue that they forced him to say those things, but that would be an afterthought. A P.S. No one cared about the truth, only the scandal.

As he struggled to consider his next move, a thud boomed behind him.

"Open this fucking door right now!" Scotty shouted. "You're gonna pay for this!"

Cal had already paid—with his finger, with ten days of his life. *This ends here. Now.*

IF HE DIDN'T DO something extreme, Brad, who'd tipped them off, would win. Brad never won. That wasn't how it went.

Cal's eyes darted around the room, landing on the fire where embers shot over the black metal screen and landed on the rug.

Think! Think!

Fire. A fire. What if there was nothing left to show anyone? And no one around to talk about it?

Cal squinted into the flames then took three steps to the table and picked up a newspaper.

His face stared back at him and, beside it, Brad's. A stinging sensation flared where the rest of his finger used to be as he read the headline:

Roommate Remains in Critical Condition After Car Crash.

Now it was his turn to stagger from side to side. *Brad was in a car accident? Critical condition?* He wanted to sink into a chair, read every word of the article, but there wasn't time.

"I'm going to fucking kill you, man!" Scotty's screams grew louder with every threat. "I'm gonna break this door down!"

How much longer would Shelby stay asleep with her brother bellowing like a madman?

Rolling the newspaper into a cone with his good hand, Cal crossed the room in a single stride. He'd never been a Boy Scout. In Oak Hill, that was for losers who couldn't play sports. But getting something to catch fire seemed simple. Putting it out was the hard part.

He held the paper over the flames. Dark smoke rose as it burned. He touched it to the rug. The fringes smoldered and blackened but the fire died out. *Fuck!* It wasn't working. He'd need more than that.

Three Duraflame logs sat off to the left of the fireplace. Frantic, he scanned the small room and found an ignitor on the mantle. He moved fast, putting a log on a wicker chair, another beneath the couch, and the third under the coffee table. Then he lit them. Would it be enough? He couldn't be sure. He surveyed the room again, lurched to the stove, and turned on the gas. Its *tick tick tick* sounded like an urgent *Hurry! Hurry! Hurry!*

Scotty kicked furiously at the door. Cal's hand throbbed. Sweat slicked his forehead and dripped down his back. It was definitely getting warmer but he didn't have time to watch the flames spread. He bolted for the door at the far end of the room. At the last second, he remembered his feet were bare. He stuffed them into heavy boots and twisted the doorknob with his working hand.

Outside, the air was so crisp, so cold, he gulped at it as if he'd been trapped underwater. After he caught his breath, he let out a sound that was half-laugh, half-cry and turned his face up to the falling snow. He took a few steps, shivering as the chill settled in his bones. How had he not grabbed a jacket? The fire and his fever made him forget how frigid it would be. He hadn't thought to grab the car keys either. There in the driveway was the black SUV that had followed him, the one Scotty and Lincoln had been standing behind in the resort lot.

"Fuck!" he hissed into the silent night.

There was no way he could go back now. The wind whipped through his thin, sweat-soaked T-shirt as he turned to glance behind him. Curtains darkened the narrow windows, but he swore he saw a flicker, an orange glow. Was he hallucinating?

His heart banged against his chest as he pictured Scotty, coated in shit, beating the door, like an animal who knew it was cornered. Had he smelled the smoke? The burning Duraflames' waxy toxins lingered in Cal's nostrils. What had he done? He couldn't think about it. He needed to keep moving, pushing forward, but something about the small cabin pinned him in place. It reminded him of the ones he'd built in preschool with Lincoln Logs. With Brad.

Fucking Brad. Cal pictured the headline: *Roommate Remains in Critical Condition After Car Crash.* Whatever had happened to him, he had it coming. This circus of insanity was all his fault. When had Brad reached out to Shelby using that stupid fake name? It had to be early summer. That's when her calls and texts first started coming. Brad had betrayed him and then lived with him for months without saying a word about it. What kind of person did that?

Cal turned to look at the house again.

Was it over? Or would Scotty break down the door? Pry the nails from that board and smash through the window? This time there was no mistaking it. An amber light filled the interior. Cal's heart thundered. He'd had no choice. Either Scotty and Shelby won or he did.

Who do you want to be? Coach's voice echoed inside his skull. *Decide right now.*

He spun back toward the woods. How far was it to a main road? And in which direction? The full moon shone overhead, a ghostly yellow ball sitting dead center in the slate sky. He tried to pick up his pace, but his legs were weak and shaky as he stumbled away from the cabin through a foot of untouched snow. He was wearing Shelby's boots. They pinched his toes, which were already turning numb from the cold. How long before the flames reached the gas stove? Would the whole thing explode? He wanted to be as far away as possible.

The rush of his escape drove him forward. He walked, tripping over gnarled tree roots buried beneath the snow. Every few minutes he stopped to blow on his exposed hand and listen for a car, a dog, any sign that he wasn't completely alone, that he hadn't swapped one awful fate for another. The only sound came from branches snapping under his frozen feet as he wove through the pines. Snow continued to fall. Would it be enough to cover his tracks? His mouth was so dry, he stooped to eat a mound of snow and hoped it wasn't full of deer shit.

Drifting deeper into the woods, the adrenaline wore off and exhaustion set in. How much longer could he keep going, teeth chattering, toes curled, heels blistering, skin stinging? He leaned against a tree to catch his breath. What if he was walking the wrong way? He wanted to take a break, slide to the ground, let the snow cool his burning head. It was too much—this on top of everything he'd endured inside that fucking cabin.

Just as he was about to give in and rest, he heard something. The rumble of a muffler. The faint hiss of tires on wet pavement. He swiveled his head trying to orient to the sound. Somewhere up ahead and to his left? Or was it his imagination, like the way he'd swear his finger was still there, throbbing?

It didn't matter. The possibility that it was real was enough. He dragged his body in that direction.

If he made it to the road, would anyone stop for him? A figure staggering out of the woods like a goddamn lunatic with a bandaged hand and no coat, wearing tiny unlaced boots?

Maybe they'd recognize him from the paper.

Or maybe not. He didn't need a mirror to know he looked like shit. After all those days tied to the bed, he'd lost weight, muscle. And was he even in Wyoming? He had no memory of the time between the resort parking lot and waking up in the cabin. Where would he say he'd been? What was his story? Definitely not the truth. He hadn't thought any of this through. He'd been trying to survive each moment, then the one that followed. But now what?

He listened again. Nothing. He was close to something; he had to be. The woods were thinning out. In the distance he saw an embankment, a slope of white glowing as moonlight reflected off the snow.

Panting, he started up the incline, one frozen, aching foot in front of the other. He slipped and tried to steady himself, touching down with this injured hand, a reflex. Pain shot through his forearm.

"Fuck!" he shouted and ripped off the wet bandage. He could barely look at the stump. Black and purple, yellowish. Hideous. How would he play guitar, tennis—do anything that required two functioning hands? Even something simple like holding a beer in a bar? If he made it out of this, for the rest of his life, people would stare at him.

Shelby, Scotty—they'd done this to him. Whatever happened to them in that cabin, they deserved it. And Brad, too. If he never recovered, wasn't it his own fault?

Cal took another step. His ankle twisted and a clump of snow filled the boot. Screw it. He flung the boots down the hill. They were only holding him back. He could barely feel his feet anyway.

He climbed higher, grunting. Why hadn't he heard another car? Anything other than his own ragged breath. Delirious, he wanted to stop, fall into the soft snow, roll down the hill the way he would've as a child. When he landed in a heap at the bottom, he'd sleep. The cold that had seeped into his bones wouldn't matter.

No. He had to keep going. He thought of football practice. Two-a-days. Wind sprints. High-knees. Guys—the weak ones—doubled over, hurling on the sidelines. Not him. Not Cal Whitaker. When they folded, he went harder. All the times he'd thought he had nothing left, he dug deeper.

He neared the top. The snow shifted. The blanket of white became a crusty wall embedded with gravel and pine needles. As he came over the rise, he saw it, the road like a mirage, wavy and blurred as his eyes teared from the wind. Fresh tire tracks striped the snow.

Stepping into the road, he let out a sound that was more a whimper than a celebratory *whoop!* It echoed through the stillness.

Closing his eyes, he took a breath. He smelled smoke and pictured himself inside the cabin, lighting the logs, turning on the gas. The enormity of what he'd done at the cabin struck him like a thunderbolt.

What had Brad made him do? He opened his eyes, desperate to replace the image.

First Chloe, now her sister and brother.

He heard the sound of gears shifting, an engine revving as it crested a hill.

Could he live with what he'd done?

A flash of light came from beyond a bend. Blinding high-beams growing closer.

He took a step, bare foot landing in a pothole of frozen slush, pitching him into the path of the oncoming vehicle. He went down hard, head smacking the pavement as headlights swept over him.

PART 3

34

WEDNESDAY, DECEMBER 24
JANE

Lynch's number glowed in the dark bedroom, making Jane's breath catch. Racing thoughts took her back to other, life-altering calls she'd received after two a.m. Her father's heart attack. Her mother's fall.

After she'd read Daniel's message, Jane had turned off the ringer. Now the phone vibrated against the nightstand.

If she didn't answer Lynch's call, she wouldn't hear the news he was about to deliver. As awful as it was not knowing what happened to her son, it was still better than knowing he was gone. In this terrible limbo, at least she had hope.

But if she didn't answer, Lynch would call Wade and then he'd be the one to tell her. There was no escape. She picked up the phone. Its cold case sent a shiver through her as she slid a trembling finger to the right and said a wary, "Hello?"

"Mrs. Whitaker?"

Her stomach dropped the way it did whenever she looked down from a great height. She tried to gauge his tone. Was it the same? Different?

It took everything to force out the word, "Yes?"

The bedroom door creaked open. Wade stood, backlit by an overhead hall light, his hair wild.

"What?" he mouthed.

She held up a hand.

Emerson appeared behind her father, rubbing her eyes. "What's going on?"

Lynch was talking but Jane couldn't focus, ears buzzing in anticipation.

"I'm—I'm sorry, can you repeat that?" She jabbed at the speaker button so her husband and daughter could hear and she wouldn't be forced to say whatever he was about to tell her.

"Mrs. Whitaker," Lynch said again. "We've located your son."

JANE, Wade, and Emerson moved silently and separately toward the same goal: getting to the hospital as quickly as possible. Though the man who'd been found on the side of the road hadn't identified himself—or even made a sound—they knew it was Cal because "the body" was missing half a finger.

The body. The words looped through Jane's mind as Wade drove, Em in the front seat, echoing the map app's directions. In the back, Jane dug her nails into her palms and tried to remember to breathe. Since Lynch's call, she'd been panting as if running for her life. Tears slipped down her cheeks. She'd endured the unimaginable. Now she was on the other side of it. Almost. She would see Cal again. She'd begun to doubt she'd ever get that chance. Her beautiful son.

"You'll want to brace yourself, Mrs. Whitaker," Lynch had said.

"Is he...?" She'd been unable to ask what she was thinking: *Are any other body parts missing?* She had to focus on the fact that he was alive. That was all that mattered. Whatever he looked like now, whatever this new version of Cal was, she would be grateful for it.

Wade skidded into the hospital lot. He'd barely put the car in park when Jane flung the door open and raced toward the entrance. After clumsily fighting through the revolving door, she hurried to the information desk.

"My son Cal, Callaway Whitaker, is here. Where—how do I find him?"

A silver-haired man sat stooped over a crossword puzzle. She expected him to look up at her, eyes wide in recognition. *Cal Whitaker's mother!* He'd understand the urgency and rush to tell her the room number. Instead he turned his face toward her slowly, his pencil hovering above an empty square, and asked, "Who now?"

Just as Jane was about to grab him by his flannel collar, Lynch stepped off a nearby elevator.

"I'll take it from here," he said. "Whitakers, follow me." His hooded eyes landed on Emerson. Had he seen her social media posts? Jane blocked it out. She could only focus on her son now.

The Whitakers followed Lynch into the elevator. The lieutenant held the door open for a man carrying an "It's a boy!" balloon. Jane wanted to scream, "Take the next one!" and punch every button until the doors closed, but her hands remained frozen by her sides.

In the unbearable silence, she asked Lynch, "How—how is he? Has there been any..."

"No change." Lynch led them off the elevator. "He's being treated for multiple issues. Best if I leave that to the experts."

They wove through a maze of corridors. The harsh glare of the lights, the random beeps, and the swirl of workers moving purposefully around them made Jane dizzy. All she wanted was to see Cal.

When they turned the corner into his room, the first bed was empty. Jane's heart plunged. Lynch took the lead, pulling back the pale blue curtain like a magician's assistant. Wade said something her brain didn't register.

She was gazing at her son, his eyes closed, sunken in his gray face. Tubes and wires stretched from his exposed hand. The other, his left, was wrapped in white bandages, looking like an enormous Q-tip. Bags of clear liquid hung from skinny metal poles behind his bed. Jane would've walked right past him and not recognized him. Beneath layers of blankets he appeared frail, vulnerable.

She didn't realize she was crying again until she tasted her salty tears.

"Cal!" Jane rushed to him and pressed her lips to his warm forehead. His dark hair was greasy and matted like the fur of a stray dog. He didn't respond. Waves of relief gave way to fear and concern. Her son was alive, but what trauma had he endured? Would he be all right? The same Cal?

"He's on some heavy-duty meds," said a nurse who stood near the window typing into a computer on a wheeled cart.

Jane jumped. She hadn't noticed her.

"To clear the infection," the nurse added.

"Infection?" Jane repeated. "What infection?"

"Your son has a serious infection," the nurse said without looking away from the screen, "and a touch of frostbite."

"A touch of frostbite." Wade scoffed. "Is that like a little bit pregnant? Is there a doctor we can speak to?"

Jane bristled. Was Wade always this rude?

"I'll ask the doctor to stop by."

"Thank you," Jane said, eyeing her husband, who stood at the foot of the bed, frowning. Could he still be angry with their son for moving to Wyoming? The call from the insurance agent came back to her. Cal's death would've solved her husband's financial problems. Was Wade sorry he wouldn't be able to cash in now? She pushed the terrible thought from her mind.

The past eleven days had left her limp, wrung out as a piece of wet laundry. She rested her head on Cal's chest, soothed by the steady knock of his heart, his good strong heart.

"I'll give you some privacy," Lynch said, "but when he wakes up, we want to speak with him right away."

"So you can find the person who did this?" Em asked, her face white as the bed sheets except for that angry pimple raging in the middle of her forehead.

"We want to know what happened, where your brother's been for the past week and a half. If there's been criminal involvement, then, yes, we want those folks brought to justice."

"*If?*" Jane's head jerked up.

"Do you think our son ran away and cut off his own finger?" Wade spat. "What are you saying?"

"Mr. Whitaker, we've confirmed your son had gambling debts he couldn't cover—not a small sum, either. He asked his boss for a month's advance on his pay the day before he disappeared."

Jane felt Wade's accusatory stare. He'd blame her for this

—for not telling him about Cal's high school gambling. As if that would've made a difference.

"Sometimes people get crazy ideas, take drastic steps, if they think it'll make a bad situation go away," Lynch continued. "Typically, it makes things worse."

The room went quiet except for the steady beeping and the occasional hiss of the monitor behind Cal's head. Jane's body stiffened with rage. Could the police honestly think Cal would fake his disappearance? Her son was the victim here. Anyone could see that.

Before she could object, he continued, "What I'm saying is: A lot of time, money, and resources have gone into searching for your son. We want to hear his description of events while the details are fresh in his mind. When he wakes up, give me a call. You've got my number." With a mock hat tip, he turned and left the room.

Jane looked from Wade to Em, then back to Cal. She'd hoped being together—the four of them in one room again—would spark something, a feeling, a nostalgic longing that reconnected them, and they'd go back to what they'd once been: a family.

But Lynch's words, their implication, robbed them of that. His statements hung in the air, pungent as the smell of alcohol mixed with the stench of Cal's wet clothing piled in an open plastic bag, tainting everything.

Would Cal have done something so extreme—caused such worry and alarm—to escape a debt? She thought of Daniel's message: *Your son's quite the daredevil.*

No. Cal wouldn't have put them through that. He'd have asked her for the money like he'd done the last time—when he'd sworn he'd learned his lesson. Her husband had deceived her too, keeping her in the dark about his failing business.

She looked around the room again. They were four people held together by a shared history and DNA, nothing that would restore their family bond or keep them close moving forward.

She studied her son, the rise and fall of his chest, the twitching behind his eyelids. His ears had turned pinkish red, the way they did when he was little and feverish. Whatever he'd endured, she was certain it wasn't self-inflicted. Someone had tortured him.

She leaned forward and whispered, "Who did this to you?"

35

THURSDAY, DECEMBER 25
EMERSON

Cal was alive. Merry Christmas.

As she sat in an uncomfortable chair in his hospital room, Em felt... What was the right word? *Relieved? Surprised? Confused? Doubtful.* All of the above.

She'd been awake, rolling around the lumpy mattress, when she heard her mother's raspy "Hello?" followed by her father charging down the hall. It had to be about Cal, she knew that, but she hadn't expected good news.

Everything had been a shitshow: Max being a dick, Brad's accident, her parents' marriage imploding, the whole Daniel situation. It seemed impossible *not* to believe Cal was dead. For years she'd existed in his shadow. Then she assumed she'd be forced to live with his ghost. To hear he'd been found alive was a shock.

When they'd stepped into his hospital room, Emerson had her phone ready to record. On the drive there, she'd wondered what her first words to her brother should be. The scene had to be perfect. She'd been hemorrhaging followers and picking up legions of haters since Brad's crash.

A video of Cal, their joyous family reunion, would be huge. How would she caption her post? Something about gratitude and miracles but nothing overly sentimental or sappy. It would be picked up by every news station in the country—shared around the world. Everyone loves a happy ending, a feel-good story, perfect for the holidays. And she'd have it first. Exclusive content.

But when she saw Cal, she froze. Were they in the right room? The guy in the bed looked nothing like her brother, more like an extra from *The Walking Dead*. She lowered the phone. Its camera captured only a blur of the bed and floor before it focused on her boots and she stopped the recording. This was too personal.

For the first time since it all began, she thought of her brother as a real person, not a character in a story she'd curated to boost her popularity. To film him without his consent while he slept seemed like an invasion of privacy.

Then she thought of Brad, what she'd said about him, and an ache spread behind her ribs. Dark circles floated at the edges of her vision. The room was too hot. She sank to a chair and held her stomach. Maybe it was the sight of Cal. He was so thin. His hair was a gross, greasy tangle, the kind you see on people who convert their vans into tiny homes and spend the summer following some tired hippie band. And what was that smell? Like garbage mixed with wet dog. It was coming either from her brother or his clothes clumped in a clear plastic bag.

She looked away but was then forced to confront the spectacle of her parents. Their behavior was just as embarrassing and ridiculous in a crisis as it was at home. Her father had shouted, "There he is!" when they entered the room, as if he'd always believed Cal would be found, like he was a misplaced wallet or a set of keys.

And her mother, petting Cal's arm, whispering over and over, "Who did this to you?" like a B-grade actress rehearsing her single line.

For hours they watched him, as if that would do anything. It was hard to look away, impossible to believe it was really Cal.

Doctors, nurses drifted in and out. Her mother grilled them all. What would happen to his hand? Could his finger be reattached? Did they make prosthetic half-fingers? How "real" did they look? What about his cognitive functioning? Would he experience PTSD? How soon could he shower?

No one knew what Cal had gone through so they couldn't say for sure, but doctors were optimistic that with the right meds, he could keep what was left of his finger. In time, physical and occupational therapy would help him use his hand without too much of a deficit, they said.

Em was dozing in a chair that was supposed to recline but didn't when Cal's eyelids fluttered and their mother cried, "Oh, Cal!"

"There he is!" their father said again.

Em looked at her brother and fumbled for the phone in her lap. It still seemed too weird to record this. Cal was barely conscious. His face was as blank as the Word docs where she was supposed to be writing her college essays. He stared as if seeing the three of them for the first time.

He lifted his bandaged hand to study it. "Am I dreaming?" Was he wondering, hoping, that maybe he'd imagined it all?

"No, sweetheart, it's real. We're here," her mother said. "You're safe now."

Cal closed his eyes.

"Where've you been, son?" their father asked.

"Wade, he's been conscious less than a minute!" Jane said at the same time Em whispered, "Dad! He doesn't even know where he is."

Em thought about that cop with the massive unibrow. Did he really think Cal would cut off his own finger? Or did that theory make his job easier? Less investigating, minimal paperwork. He'd said to call him right away, but Em knew her parents would want Cal to have his story straight. Airtight. They might hate each other now, but surely they'd agree on that.

"You tell us when you're ready, honey," her mother said. Did she mean it, or was she merely taking the opposite view? "How are you feeling now?" She brushed Cal's hair off his forehead. "What can we do to make you more comfortable?"

Cal swallowed. "I've been worse, actually." His voice was low and gravelly. Had he been screaming wherever he'd been? Em hadn't spoken to him since the morning he left, back in August. She'd forgotten his habit of adding "actually" to the end of his sentences.

They waited. Would he say more?

"I'm pretty beat. I walked... I don't even know how far." He shifted, adjusting a blanket with his good hand, lips parted in a strange smile. "But I made it, right?"

"Yes, you did!" Jane said in the same high-pitched voice she used with toddlers. She rubbed his arm. "We've been so worried, Cal. You have no idea. We were so afraid—I can't even think about it."

"Where's Brad?" he asked, color returning to his cheeks.

Em watched her parents. Would they tell him the truth —that Brad was a few floors away fighting for his life? That their family, Em in particular, had started something that may have directly or indirectly caused it?

"Did he have something to do with this?" Wade moved from behind the footboard, stepping closer to Cal, who didn't respond.

"You can tell us," Jane said. "You don't have to protect anyone."

"Your mother's right, son," Wade added.

Cal's eyes rolled upward inside his sunken sockets. Was he still all there mentally?

"Did Brad do this?" Jane pressed.

Em sucked in her cheeks. Should she record this? If Cal said "yes," then she'd been right. She'd be absolved, at least partially. Maybe her approach wasn't the best, but Brad had been looking for a new roommate; his DNA was inside the glove. That had to mean something.

Cal looked at Em. Did he know what she'd done to try to find him?

Then her brother shook his head and scratched his nose. "No," he said. "I mean, why would Brad hurt me?"

Em's body caved, Cal's words a gut punch. Jane choked on a sob.

"Why would you think he...? He's my oldest friend. We live together."

Em fought the urge to roll her eyes.

Jane waved a hand and reached for Cal's good one. "Doesn't matter."

"So what happened, son?" Wade asked in a softer tone. "Did it—was it the gambling? Because your grandfather battled that addiction his entire life. I'm afraid it's in the genes."

Em pressed her lips together to stop a bitter laugh from

escaping. Cal could rack up massive debt, making one stupid bet after another, and their parents would blame genetics. So fucking typical.

"Do you want to talk about what happened?" Jane asked.

Em's body went rigid. She was furious that they were treating Cal, who'd scared the shit out of them, like a two-year-old who'd merely wandered off the playground.

"Was it because of the gambling?" Wade tried again.

"Yeah," Cal said softly. "Yes. It was my fault. It was all my fault." Even though he'd just woken up, his words sounded rehearsed, like he'd prepped for this moment. Or maybe Em wasn't used to seeing her brother humbled, accepting blame, taking responsibility.

"I owed some money. I kept thinking I could win it back. I got in deeper. These guys found me and took me some place. I don't know where. They cut—" he lifted his bandaged hand and shuddered "—when I said I didn't have the cash." He scratched his nose again and Jane handed him a tissue. "They must've known people were looking for me so they dumped me in the woods and took off."

"Oh my God, sweetheart." Jane squeezed his good hand, her ropey blue veins rising to the surface.

Wade rubbed his jowls and shook his head. Em prayed he wouldn't launch into a long-winded lecture about history repeating itself.

"Unbelievable," was all he said.

UNBELIEVABLE. That was the perfect word. On the drive to the Airbnb, Em tried to think. There had to be a way to use this, to spin Cal's story to thrust herself back in the spotlight, but she kept coming back to that word, "unbelievable."

Something wasn't right. Well, a lot wasn't right. Her family was a mess. Brad was still in the ICU. Max had gotten into the elevator as she'd gotten out of it. Wasn't Wyoming supposed to be a big-ass state? How did she keep bumping into him? He'd looked straight through her like he had in her bathroom the night he told her to stop posting about Brad. Why hadn't she listened?

Her brother was alive but his tale was vague, lacking emotion. Details made a story come to life. Cal had endured something gruesome. Why did it feel so flat, so "unbelievable?"

Okay, maybe he was so freaked out, he didn't want to relive it. But when had Cal ever not wanted to talk about himself?

"Can we not do this now?" he'd moaned when their father asked him to describe the men who took him. "My head's killing me and my hand..."

She'd seen a nurse change Cal's bandage. As heinous as it was, she couldn't look away. Parts were purply-black like the oil puddles beneath her Jeep.

Most of his middle finger was missing. How often had her brother flipped their parents the bird behind their backs? Was that a coincidence? And he'd scratched his nose. Twice. Cal always did that when he was lying. Em first noticed it when they were kids and Cal would cheat at Go Fish. No wonder he was a shitty gambler.

And the part about being dumped in the woods and walking miles barefoot? Yeah, he had frostbite in a couple of toes, but he found his way out on his own? Not likely. Cal could barely make grilled cheese. Their mother had catered to him his entire life. That said, her brother was smart, calculating. He loved the long game. Em knew what he'd do.

When he felt better, Cal would spin this into a survival story. That would be laughable.

She remembered the time they'd taken a trip to Maine and their hotel didn't get ESPN. Cal had lost his shit. His idea of roughing it was drinking canned beer.

Em wasn't the only one who wanted answers. Someone at the hospital or the police department must've leaked the news of Cal's return to the media. Her phone was blowing up, people begging for info about what had happened to him, how he was. What could she say? It wasn't her story to tell anymore. Besides, nothing made sense and she was done making shit up.

The Airbnb was too quiet. Her parents were resting in separate rooms. They'd all been awake since Lynch's middle-of-the-night call. Em was over-tired but still bursting with chaotic energy.

She needed to clear her head. A forest waited behind the house. Maybe a walk in the woods would help her think or at least slow her whirring brain. She grabbed her AirPods and phone and bundled into her mother's red jacket. It was warmer than her own, plus if there were hunters in the woods, this would help them spot her.

A gauzy fog rose from the snow. It looked like someone had switched on a smoke machine and would've made a cool photo, but she was done posting for a while. She was sick of herself and, apparently, everyone else was too. She'd closed her DMs after some rude and creepy messages. Still, the area was remote and she felt safe walking beneath the soaring evergreens. No one would bother her out here. She shoved in her AirPods and told herself to keep moving forward. Looking back never helped anything, though sometimes it was impossible not to.

Maybe she'd offer one last update. She'd explain that she wasn't a bad person, that she'd never meant for Brad to get hurt. She only wanted her brother back, she'd say, and now here he was. He'd tell his story when or if he chose to. Yes, as soon as she got back to the house where the Wi-Fi was slow but stronger than in the woods, she'd write a final post.

A hawk circled above. The sky was growing dark. Walking had calmed her a bit but her nerves were still jangly.

For so long, Em had dreamt of getting away from her family, seeing the world. Now she wanted to return to the days when she thought Cal was the greatest, she and her mom weren't enemies, and her dad cared more about them than his business.

As the Airbnb came into view, her shoulders heaved and an ache burned inside her stomach. She was homesick for a place that no longer existed.

36

THURSDAY, DECEMBER 25
CAL

"Can you leave the curtain open?" Cal asked the nurse. *What was her name?* He squinted at the whiteboard. *Vera.* He wanted a clear view into the hallway in case anyone came looking for him. No more surprises.

"Expecting someone? A girlfriend?" Vera winked. She was old enough to be his grandmother yet had the bright red hair of Ronald McDonald.

She was just being friendly, but it was getting on Cal's nerves. She'd spent way too much time in his room, fluffing pillows, adjusting blankets, drawing snowflakes and smiley faces below her name on the dry-erase board. Cal was losing patience. Maybe he was having a reaction to all the meds. He felt jittery, anxious, claustrophobic. He wanted to be alone.

When she finished tugging the curtain back enough that he could see into the hall, he asked, "Can you hand me the remote? For the TV?"

"Someone's got a lot of requests!" Vera chuckled. "Good sign. You must be feeling better!" She shuffled across the room, slow as a tortoise, and picked the remote off the radiator. She marveled at the rectangle as if she'd discovered a stack of cash on the windowsill. "Now how'd this get over there?"

"You fucking moved it," he wanted to say but didn't.

"Hoping to see yourself on the news? You're getting lots of coverage—practically a celebrity. Remind me to get your autograph." She winked again. "People were sure you were gone for good. Couple of papers are calling your return a 'Christmas miracle.'"

"Huh." Cal nodded, acknowledging her but not wanting to encourage conversation. He didn't care about any of that. He needed to know about the fire. Had Scotty and Shelby survived or were they "gone for good," to use Vera's words? There was a chance they might've escaped before the cabin went up like a tinderbox. And if that were the case, where were they now? He was staring down two terrible outcomes: either he'd killed them or he'd spend the rest of his life looking over his shoulder.

The police had just left. The whole time they were there, Cal waited for them to bring up the cabin, the fire, to say something that suggested they knew exactly where he'd been, what he'd done. Vera came in handy then, telling them Cal needed his rest and to not upset him.

When the tall cop with the heavy eyebrows asked for a description of his captors, Cal said he'd been blindfolded so he had no idea.

"Can you tell us anything about their voices? Any interesting speech patterns, verbal tics?" the younger cop asked. "Accents?"

Cal could still hear Shelby's southern drawl. *Think you*

could help me? Got a flat. What an idiot he'd been to fall for it.

"No accents. One guy's voice was deep, husky. The other's was kind of nasally. Maybe he had a cold." Cal took a second to commend himself for coming up with that detail. "Nothing unusual that I can remember, but when you think every second could be your last, it's kind of tough to focus."

"You're sweating quite a bit," the young cop said. "You holding up okay?"

"That's his body doing what it needs to do to fight off infection," Vera said. "Are you about done? It's time for his sponge bath."

The thought made Cal want to teleport straight back to the woods, but if it got rid of the cops, he'd endure it.

"I'm really tired, actually, feeling super spacey." He let his head rest against the pillow. His skull was still bruised from the tire iron and his backward fall when Shelby had videotaped him.

"Just a few more questions, okay?" the younger cop— Hanlon, was it?—said. "Bradley Chapman—was he involved?"

Cal thought about Brad. Shirley Bradley. That stupid name. He'd chosen it on purpose, to send Cal a message: *It's me! I waited two years, but now I've decided to blow up your life.*

"Why do people keep asking me that?" Cal frowned. "Where is he?" His parents hadn't answered when he asked that question and he hadn't pushed it.

"Mr. Chapman was in a serious accident."

Cal erased the headline he'd seen at the cabin from his mind and let his face go soft, surprised. It wasn't difficult because at first when Hanlon said "Mr. Chapman" Cal had pictured Brad's dad, grinning and waving while walking that ugly dog. Over the summer, Cal had seen them together in the neighborhood. Each time, he'd been struck by an overwhelming desire to punt that beast over a hedge.

"What happened?" Cal looked at one cop then the other. "Is he all right?"

"No. He isn't." Lynch studied him, waiting for a reaction.

Cal gave him one. "Holy shit." He lifted his head. The rough pillowcase brushed against the bare skin of his neck. Low thread count. He'd ask Vera if they had anything nicer. "Is Brad gonna be okay? Is he here? In this hospital? Can I see him?"

"He's in the ICU," Lynch said, "in critical condition with a serious brain bleed."

"No way, that's..." Cal let his voice trail off and hung his head. He needed to nail the role of concerned friend, but he was distracted. Would these cops reveal that they knew exactly how Brad factored into this whole thing?

"What else can you recall?" Hanlon asked. "You were gone a while. Any idea where they took you? Did they call one another by name? Were they—"

"Okay, that's enough for now." Vera clapped her hands. "It's Christmas. Don't you two have families?"

"Give us another couple minutes—" Lynch glanced at the whiteboard "—Vera. As you said, it's Christmas." He pressed his thumbs into his silver belt buckle and grinned at the nurse before turning back to Cal. "So, by your account, you were abducted, held against your will, had a good chunk of your finger sliced off, and were left to die in the woods. Is that right?"

Cal nodded.

Lynch let out a long "huh."

Cal smelled coffee on his breath and tried not to wince.

"See, now, if I were in your shoes," Lynch pointed his long fingers toward Cal's bandage, "all banged up, good chunk of my finger found by a dog, I'd be shouting out every small detail I could remember. I'd want to see these people caught, punished."

"I do want that, of course," Cal said. "I'm just—I don't know—in shock, I guess. I can't believe I made it back alive, actually." For a second, he considered crying. Would it make them so uncomfortable they'd leave? "I'm trying to remember. It's all kind of a blur. But, hell yeah, I want them punished."

"Then we're gonna need a lot more information. ASAP." Lynch's voice had an edge. Was that a threat?

"If you're afraid, we can talk about protection," Hanlon offered.

"Okay, fellas," Vera said. "Skedaddle. You can come back tomorrow. He'll be more lucid then."

Hanlon dropped his card on the tray where Cal's untouched lunch sat. It was chili. "You remember any details, call us."

"The press is already sniffing around," Lynch added. "Don't grant any interviews. It muddies things. You tip your hand." He looked at Cal's bandage again and smirked. "Poor choice of words. Let me start over. Say too much and you risk tipping them off. Got it?"

"Got it." Cal watched them walk out. He'd expected to feel relief but he couldn't relax, not until he had a better idea of what or who was waiting for him outside the hospital.

He turned on the television, changing channels until he

landed on the story he'd been searching for. His stomach cramped as he stared at the screen.

"Don't look at that," Vera scolded. "Put on a movie—*It's a Wonderful Life*, *Miracle on 34th Street*, even that one with Chevy Chase. Anything but this." She waved a latex glove at the image—a pile of smoking rubble.

Cal wanted to turn the channel, but his hand froze as he took in the destruction, understanding what he'd done. He hadn't had a choice. This was all Brad's fault. *Brad* was the one to blame. This was on *him*.

When the time was right, Cal planned to pay his old friend a visit.

37

FRIDAY, DECEMBER 26
IVY

Ivy's focus shifted in and out like a camera lens, sharpening and blurring again. The doctor's lips, the color of cranberries, moved but Ivy caught only certain words, phrases. "Brain function not where we'd like it to be... hoped he'd wake on his own by now... not responding as we'd..."

"What can we do?" Greg asked, his hand on Ivy's back.

"Let's give it another twenty-four hours. In the meantime, we wait, hope he improves. Some people find prayer to be a comfort if it's something..." The doctor pointed a manicured nail, same color as her lipstick, over her shoulder. "There's a non-denominational chapel on the first floor, across from the gift shop."

"I'm... I'm not leaving him." Other than to wash up in the hall bathroom and brush her teeth, Ivy had kept a vigil beside her son's bed. She was still wearing the same leggings and Life Is Good hoodie she'd thrown on before their flight Monday. If—no, *when*—Brad woke, she wanted hers to be the first face he saw. "I can't leave him."

The doctor's mouth curved up at the corners in a sympathetic smile. "That's understandable."

Her warm brown eyes made Ivy crave chocolate. She hadn't eaten, hadn't slept, done nothing other than stare at her son, sending energy and light into the spaces that needed healing.

Her mother had called the day before to check on Brad and say Merry Christmas. Ivy let it go to voicemail and then felt guilty. She had no desire to talk to her mother or listen as she asked countless questions about Brad's future no one could answer.

These feelings toward her mom weren't new, and Ivy couldn't help but wonder if the universe was punishing her for them.

In October, when she and Jane had planned this trip, Ivy had rejoiced at the idea of going away for the holidays. She'd happily skip the cooking and cleaning that hosting entailed, but mainly, she'd been excited to avoid her mother, who on holidays invariably arrived at the house laden with shopping bags filled with dollar-store junk and clothing she'd picked up at yard sales.

Ivy would tell her repeatedly, "Just bring yourself. None of us needs anything. The boys are just happy to see you."

"Nonsense!" her mother would say. "I'm their grandmother. It's my job to spoil them."

"Then how about small gift cards—?"

"That's no fun," her mother had scoffed.

"Well, neither is a used air fryer or a cardigan missing its buttons," Ivy wanted to shout but instead took a deep breath and gobbled her way through a bag of marshmallows.

Her mother had seen the news. Stories about Brad's accident and Cal's return had spread across the country like an out-of-control wildfire.

Ivy had asked Greg to update her mom. She needed to make other calls. The only good thing that had happened in days was learning that Jean-Claude was safe.

After Florence had phoned from inside the Chapmans' house and they discovered the dog was missing, Ivy had feared the worst. Had the same deranged people who'd broken into her home and spray-painted "Butcher" on her dining room wallpaper taken JC? The thought made her tremble with rage.

She never should've asked Betsy's eighth grader, Miles, to take care of the dog for more than a week. Ivy pictured the pup lost and alone, shivering and afraid, doing his nervous little tap dance. If anything happened to him, this was on her.

No, actually, it was the Whitakers' fault. Emerson had started her crusade against Brad, and Jane did nothing to stop it. This was on them.

In a panic after talking to Florence, Ivy had called Betsy.

"Ivy! How's Brad?" Betsy asked without even a hello.

The word "Unchanged" had barely passed her lips when Betsy interrupted. "Have you seen Jane?" Her voice was breathy, unable to mask her curiosity.

Ivy ignored the question, pressed her fingers to her third eye, and tried to envision her dog safe and calm.

"Listen, Betsy, there's been—" How did she phrase it? Things like this didn't happen in Oak Hill. People didn't break into your home, defile it, and steal your dog. "A family friend stopped by earlier and said she didn't see Jean-Claude. Has Miles—?" Ivy swallowed the sob building in the back of her throat. She would not cry. She couldn't. Even if she had every right to, Betsy would tell the whole town. She could imagine her urgent whisper: "Ivy called. She's an absolute wreck."

"About that…" Betsy sighed. "I know you're dealing with a lot right now so I didn't want to call you, but this dog, well, it's been a terrible inconvenience."

"You have Jean-Claude?" Ivy's limbs went limp with relief.

"Miles left here before eight to give the dog breakfast and take him for a walk but your front door was open, so he called Doug and he went over there." Betsy lowered her voice. "I'm guessing you know about your dining room?"

"Yes," Ivy said weakly, "but you have him? You have Jean-Claude?"

"Yes. Doug and Miles got his leash and his bowls and brought him here."

"Oh thank God. Thank you." Ivy let her heavy head drop into her open palm. "Please tell Miles—"

"Again, Ivy, I know you're in a tough spot right now, but is there anyone else who can take him?"

Ivy's head whipped up. "Sorry, what?"

"He's sweet, don't get me wrong, and Miles adores him, but this is not what we signed up for—keeping him here, I mean. He's upsetting Fiona."

"Fiona?"

"Our cavapoo? You saw her at the cookie exchange, didn't you?"

"Right," Ivy mumbled.

"If you could make some calls, send some texts, I'd love to have him gone by the weekend. My sister's coming with her kids and my nephew is allergic, so I need—look, I'll try too, but I thought you might have someone in mind."

Ivy's face burned. How could anyone—?

"Ivy? Ivy? Did I lose you?" Betsy asked.

"I'll see what we can do."

"Great, and please tell Greg we're thinking of you guys." *Don't say "Thanks, Betsy." Don't say "Thanks, Betsy."*

"Thanks, Betsy," Ivy said and pounded her fist lightly against her forehead.

That had been Tuesday afternoon. Ivy hadn't called or texted anyone. Fear and worry about Brad had left her paralyzed.

The doctor's words, *Let's give it another twenty-four hours,* didn't help.

Ivy was afraid to ask the question "Then what?" aloud. She looked over at Greg, slumped in a chair, frowning even as he dozed. His reddish-brown hair graying at the temples and sideburns. He hadn't shaved and his scruff was nearly white. She felt as if she were watching him age before her eyes, like a time-lapse video, a decade in a matter of days.

An alarm went off on the monitor behind Brad's head. They'd gotten used to the constant beeps and buzzes. Still, Greg startled. He sat up and rubbed his face with his palm.

"I'm gonna get some coffee. Maybe a sandwich." He looked at his watch. It was almost noon. "What do you feel like?"

Ivy wanted to say, "One of everything," but she shook her head. The alarm kept beeping.

"Be back as quick as I can." Greg kissed the top of her head before slipping past the curtain.

Ivy rolled her neck side to side. She felt stiff and ancient. Any moment a nurse would come to stop the alarm. She closed her eyes and rested her face in her hands. She hadn't slept for more than ten or twenty minutes at a time since they'd arrived in Wyoming. When she heard her name, she was certain she'd been dreaming. It was coming from beyond the curtain, the voice familiar.

Disoriented, Ivy stood, readying herself for another doctor to deliver more bad news. Should she run after Greg? She couldn't bear it alone.

"Yes?"

The curtain fluttered and Jane appeared. "Oh, Ivy," she said, reaching to pull her into a hug.

Jane's outstretched arm reminded Ivy of the ugliness at the airport and she stepped back, bumping into the folding chair. Jane's arm dropped to her side. She looked the same as she always did in a periwinkle twinset. She smelled like fabric softener. Ivy inched back again. She hadn't brushed her teeth yet.

"How is…?" Jane glanced toward Brad. An oxygen mask obscured most of his face, tubes snaked out like tentacles. "Any change?"

Ivy shook her head and shrugged. The tears she'd been battling all morning slid down her cheeks.

"I wanted to tell you—" Jane's head tilted back and she breathed deeply through her nose "—how truly sorry I am. Things got so out of control. Wade and I—we weren't thinking clearly. I'm sure you can understand that. You and Greg have always been there for us and we should never have thought—we know Brad would never—and Emerson… what she did… She had no idea how it would escalate like that. You know her, Ivy. Thinking things through has never been her strong suit. Plus, she's a teenager—only focused on herself."

Like mother, like daughter. Ivy stood silent, listening to the wheeze of the machines keeping her son alive. Was Jane really trying to chalk up her daughter's horrific behavior to impulsivity and her age?

"I— I brought you this." Jane held out a Styrofoam cup. "You have no idea how hard it is to find chai latte in the wild west." She smiled and extended her hand.

Ivy didn't accept it. "Cal's back? He's okay?" Her tone was more accusatory than questioning.

"Well, he lost half a finger, Ivy," Jane snorted. "He's hardly okay, but he's alive. And he's strong. He's a fighter. You know Cal. They're keeping him a few extra days. He had frostbite and a nasty infection, possibly a concussion, but he's past the worst of that now. He'll need rehab, of course."

Rehab. While Jane meant rehab for Cal's hand, Ivy thought of Brad's slurred speech during their last few conversations. She felt certain now that whatever her son had taken, he'd gotten it from his roommate.

Ivy folded her arms. "Where *was* Cal?"

The light in Jane's eyes when she spoke about her son faded, and she set the cup of tea on the tray.

"I'm sure you've seen the news. He—he had gambling debts. He should've come to me but he didn't. He was embarrassed, I guess. You know about Wade's dad. It's genetic, the addiction ..." She looked at her boots. When she raised her head, Ivy saw tears in her eyes.

"Speaking of Wade... this..." she made circles with her hands, "everything, it's brought up a lot of stuff for us. Wade's been keeping secrets from me. His business—" she cleared her throat "—is failing. And you were right, I never should've started anything with Daniel. That's just been another..."

Behind Jane, a nurse wordlessly silenced the alarm and hung a new bag. Ivy wanted to ask for a warm blanket for Brad and one for herself. The space got drafty and her son's hands turned so cold in the afternoons, but Jane was touching her arm now, claiming all her attention.

"—we never had what you and Greg do, I knew that, but—"

Where was Greg? Where was her husband to make Jane stop talking, to escort her out?

"I—I think my marriage is over." Jane's shoulders sagged, and she looked at Ivy expectantly, searching her eyes.

A few weeks earlier, this would've been a shocking revelation, one that would've rocked Ivy and sent her straight into caretaker mode. Now she stared, silent. Nothing could penetrate the thick fog of worry for her son.

"Oh, Ivy," Jane pulled a tissue from her pocket and dabbed at her eyes, "I could really use a friend right now. I know this isn't a great time for you, but I was thinking maybe we could take a walk together? Like the old days." She smiled. "The Airbnb isn't nearly as nice as it looked in the photos. Remember I was afraid of that? The woods behind the house are really beautiful, though. You'd love it."

Ivy experienced a sudden sense of vertigo as if she'd stood too quickly. Did Jane think things would return to how they used to be? Ivy gripped the railing at the foot of Brad's bed.

"Brad's going to be fine." Jane touched her arm again. "If Cal could escape and survive whatever he endured, Brad will pull through. You'll see."

Ivy hated blind optimism. She nodded anyway, too weak and tired to disagree.

"I should get back." Jane smiled. "Drink your latte. Get some rest. You look exhausted." She pulled back the curtain and turned around. "And think about meeting me for a walk. Seriously. You were always the one preaching about self-care."

Ivy watched her go and dropped into the chair.

Jane's dismissiveness. The way the conversation always, always flipped back to the Whitakers, to the almighty Cal, made Ivy's stomach churn. This woman who'd threatened to "destroy her family," how did she have the nerve to stand there and ask for forgiveness? Why didn't she tell Jane to go to hell? To never come near her or her son again?

Years of therapy taught Ivy the answer. She'd been raised by a parent who chose things—ridiculous things, other people's junk, really—above her safety, her happiness. She entered friendships with low expectations, willing to accept anything, grateful for crumbs.

Not anymore. Ivy was done with that.

She shuddered. Thinking about Jane's hand on her arm made the blood simmer in her veins. She hadn't experienced the fierce desire to assault someone since she'd overheard a child mocking Brad's lisp on the playground nearly two decades ago. She remembered that afternoon clearly, how her body shook when the boy repeated her son's words, exaggerating his struggle with *th*, *r*, and *l* sounds, tears streaking Brad's pink cheeks.

The boy had laughed and waved his hand, beckoning others to join in. Ivy had started to sweat despite the autumn breeze. How she'd wanted to slam the boy down hard into the wood chips, make him cry the way her son had, step on his hand and hear his bones snap like twigs. Somehow she'd summoned the strength to collect Brad and walk away. She'd managed her rage, contained it.

A wail that had been building for twenty years, maybe all her life, rose from deep in her belly.

She opened her mouth and released it.

38

FRIDAY, DECEMBER 26
LINCOLN

Lincoln hadn't heard from Shelby again—not that he expected her to call and wish him a Merry Christmas, but he'd seen the news. Cal was out. Free. Alive. *How?*

Lincoln and his dad had been watching football Christmas afternoon when Cal's face appeared on the screen and an anchorwoman said, "Missing ski instructor found: Details after the game."

"Holy shit!" Lincoln shouted, waking his dad who'd been napping in the La-Z-Boy.

"What happened?" His father startled back to consciousness. "Tell me these assholes didn't score another touchdown!"

Lincoln couldn't speak, his heart kicking hard and fast. Had Shelby and Scotty taken his advice and let Cal go before things got worse or had Cal escaped? His leg bounced, rattling the empty beer bottles on the coffee table.

"If you gotta pee, son, get up and go," his dad said.

Lincoln stood, legs every bit as jiggly as the canned cranberry sauce his mom placed on the table.

"Any word from Shelby yet?" she asked. "If I don't take this turkey out soon, it'll be dry as a haystack."

Lincoln hadn't told his mother that he'd left Wyoming without Shelby, that they were done, broken up, that the woman he loved had lost her goddamn mind.

"I'll try her again." Lincoln waved his phone and lurched toward his bedroom, a high-pitched whine building between his ears.

Lincoln had already called Shelby twice. He got her voicemail but didn't leave a message. As a last resort, he tried Scotty with the same result.

WHEN SCOTTY GOT BACK, Lincoln planned to rip him a new one. Without telling him, Scotty had stashed Cal's skis in Lincoln's flatbed, beneath the roll-up cover. What the hell was he thinking? If Lincoln had been stopped by cops on his drive from Wyoming to Georgia, and they'd found them, what then? Scotty never thought ahead. Neither did Shelby. That was how they'd ended up in this God-awful mess. Lincoln had hidden Cal's gear in the hayloft in the barn behind his parents' house. He'd make Scotty deal with that as soon as he was back in town.

All through dinner, a fist-sized knot grew in his gut as his mother asked a million questions. Where was his girlfriend? What was wrong? Why hadn't he touched his sweet potatoes? Was Shelby upset because Lincoln hadn't proposed while they were away?

"I've seen at least three engagements on Facebook between last night and this afternoon." His mom drove her fork into a clump of stuffing. "Maybe she was hoping for a ring? Dwayne, just think how gorgeous our grandbabies would be!"

Lincoln could've shut it down by reminding his mom that the holidays brought up a whole mess of sadness for Shelby, but instead he shrugged.

"Take her some pie after dinner," his mother said. "I'll send some for Scotty too."

An ache ballooned in his chest. Whenever he had a problem, he'd tell his mother and she'd help him fix it. Shit, maybe he really was a mama's boy. But this was different. Where could he even begin? "You know that girl you want me to marry? She and her brother abducted the guy who got Chloe drunk and left her for dead. Then Scotty chopped off most of his finger and Shelby refused to let me get him proper medical care. Still want to talk about your grandbabies?"

No, he couldn't drag her into this. This wasn't how-do-you-iron-a-dress-shirt or make a fried egg. This was out of her wheelhouse.

Lincoln placed a foil pie plate on the passenger seat and fired up his F-150. He looped around in circles, slipping down back roads, turning the radio on and off again, checking his phone at stop signs. Through lit windows he saw families, Christmas trees, football on flat screens.

He ended up behind the high school, near the spot where Scotty parked his Chevy Nova back in the day, and tried Shelby again. Nothing. He left a message this time. "Hey. Call me back." He'd almost hung up when he added a quick, "Merry Christmas, Shel." He couldn't help it.

Then he sat waiting, hoping he'd hear from her, skimming every story he could find about Cal Whitaker's miraculous return. There weren't any details about where he'd been, what had happened. But how much longer would that last? Cal was a talker.

He tossed the slices of pie in a dumpster and headed home after he was certain his parents would be asleep. He'd fallen into bed, phone in his hand, only drifting off as the sun started sneaking through the blinds.

THE DOORBELL FRIDAY morning wormed its way into his dream but he woke when he heard his father's booming, "Chief Crawford! To what do we owe the pleasure?"

Lincoln shot out of bed, blood pumping, and pressed his ear to the door.

"Merry Christmas, Dwayne, Doris. Hope Santa treated you right." The chief chuckled then cleared his throat. "Your boy around?"

Lincoln stumbled into the faded jeans he'd left bunched on the floor just hours earlier.

"He's not in any trouble, is he?" his mother asked.

"I'll whoop his ass." His father laughed.

He couldn't hear Crawford's answer over the warning bells clanging in his head and the jangle of his belt buckle. Should he leave the room on his own? Wait for his mother to fetch him? Climb out the fucking window?

"Linc, darlin'?" His mother was using her fake friendly phone voice. Beneath it he heard traces of worry then her gentle knock. "Can you come on out?"

Lincoln stepped into the hall. He tipped his head and his mom kissed it, same as they'd done every morning since he'd grown taller than she was.

"Chief Crawford's here to see you." She bit her bottom lip.

With each step, Lincoln saw the axe, the way the blade caught the light as Scotty raised it overhead before splitting Cal's finger in two. Then he pictured Shelby taking that hideous nub out of the freezer, handing him the glove. He thought he might faint as he turned the corner and saw the chief, a barrel-shaped man with a mustache and ruddy cheeks.

Crawford had been in their home plenty of times. He and Lincoln's dad had gone to high school together. Before he made chief, they'd been on the same bowling team. He was usually friendly, down for sipping Jack Daniels and diet cokes on their back porch, doling out doses of local gossip. But standing in the living room, he looked uncomfortable, like a big man wearing too-tight shoes.

"Chief Crawford." Lincoln held out his hand. His palm was already sweating. Christ, did he need a lawyer?

"Take a walk with me, son," the chief said.

"Whatever you got to say, you can do it here." Maybe it sounded brave, but really Lincoln was afraid to be alone with this man. He wanted his mother close. Hell, even his father would do.

The chief looked out the window to his squad car then met Lincoln's eyes. "Got a call from out west late last night." He inhaled and his chest puffed out a few more inches.

Lincoln's heart ticked like a stopwatch. *He knows. He knows what we've done.*

Even though Cal was alive, they'd done a heap of terrible stuff to him. Now they'd have to pay for it.

"There was a fire…"

Lincoln's ears burned.

"…at a cabin where Shelby and Scotty were staying."

The words didn't make sense. What day was it? Friday.

Shelby and Scotty had to be out of the cabin Wednesday. They were probably halfway back home by now.

"A fire?" he repeated. "When? I've been calling Shelby but..." Lincoln swallowed hard. *So this wasn't about Cal?* "Are—are they all right?"

"Didn't she come home with you?" his mother asked, confused. "What'd you do with my pie?"

Lincoln shook his head. He'd need to tell her something but he was struggling to understand Crawford.

"I'm afraid she and Scotty were still in the cabin when the fire started, sometime Tuesday into Wednesday, inspectors believe."

"Oh my Lord." Doris's hand flew to her mouth.

Lincoln pictured Scotty batting at the smoke detector, its high-pitched shriek coming back to him full-force.

"...would've let us know sooner but it took a while to identify them and then they had to notify the next of kin. Not easy tracking down Scotty and Shelby's dad. Seems Earl went off the grid to skip out on child support. He was always crooked as a dog's hind leg."

"Next of kin?" Lincoln shook his head like he needed to knock the phrase out of it. "What—what are you saying?"

The chief placed a thick pink hand on Lincoln's arm. "I'm sorry, son. I hated to be the one to tell you, but I didn't want you to hear it from someone else. I know Shelby meant the world to you. Scotty had his troubles, sure, but those kids got dealt a bad hand. He'd have pulled himself together if only he'd had the time."

Lincoln couldn't process it, the way Crawford was talking in the past tense. In a daze, he drifted toward the couch, his mom weeping softly, her hand on his shoulder as the words sank in. The chief followed and stood in front of them, looming like a giant redwood, blocking the sun fighting its way through the picture window.

"What—what happened?" Lincoln asked, head buried in his hands.

"Bad combination. Gas stove burner left on, a fire blazing. Everything," he softened his gruff tone, "everyone... burned nearly beyond recognition. A terrible accident—that's the early line of thinking. It's still under investigation."

"You were just there," Lincoln's mom whispered, rubbing his arm. "Those poor kids. That family—under a black cloud, I always said it."

"You were out there?" Chief Crawford frowned. "When'd you get back?"

"Late Tuesday night," his mother answered for him.

"I gotta ask." Crawford jerked his head. "Wyoming?"

Tears stung Lincoln's eyes. Was he crying for Shelby and Scotty or himself?

"What brought you all the way out there, I mean?" The chief adjusted his hat and scratched at his forehead.

Cal. That's what brought them out there. Lincoln could barely think straight and he'd never been a good liar. But Cal was alive and his girlfriend—ex-girlfriend, whatever—and her brother were dead.

It wasn't supposed to go like this.

The reality of it was settling into his skin, his bones. Shelby. His Shelby. Gone. In a fire? Yes, she'd made some awful choices in the past few months but like Crawford said, she'd been through so much.

"The holidays were hard for them on account of losing Chloe and their mom," Lincoln said. "They—we—wanted to get away, see something different. We thought it would be an adventure."

An adventure? Had he really just called it that? What a fucking idiot he was—always had been. How had he not stopped them at any point in their ridiculous plan? Shit, he'd helped finance it.

"What'd you do?" Lines deepened across Crawford's forehead. "Ski? Snowboard?"

Involuntarily, Lincoln's eyes flicked toward the barn, visible through the dining room window. He pictured Cal's skis, poles, buried beneath bales of hay. His heart hammered. "Ski? A little bit, yeah." Had he saved the receipt from the rental shop? They'd gone once, the day before they picked up Cal. The tag was still on his jacket. Would Crawford ask what else they'd done?

"Never been out there myself. Heard it's a beautiful part of the country."

Lincoln nodded, picturing the jagged mountains, their rugged peaks like the spires of a gothic cathedral he'd only seen on TV, low-hanging clouds, elk sitting in frozen fields. All that snow.

But Cal locked in that back room—that was the image of Wyoming he'd never get out of his head.

"Like I said, those kids got dealt a real rough hand," Crawford continued. "Let's just hope they're with their sister and mother now. Let's hope they're all finally at peace."

"Amen," his mother said.

"I should've stayed," Lincoln mumbled.

"What'd you say?" Lincoln's dad asked.

"I should've stayed. I shouldn't have left them."

"Listen, son, no one could've seen this coming," the chief said.

But couldn't they? If they'd known the whole story, if they'd seen Callaway Whitaker's swagger as he'd crossed the parking lot that night when he thought he was helping a gorgeous blonde fix a flat, probably figuring he'd get lucky after he finished, they'd have seen it coming. Anyone who'd watched him thrust his middle finger at Scotty and Shelby with his wrist chained to a chair... Anyone who'd met that arrogant motherfucker could've seen this coming.

So why hadn't Lincoln?

39

SATURDAY, DECEMBER 27
CAL

The gentle hug of the blood pressure cuff woke Cal. Smiling down at him was the young nurse with shiny dark hair and hazel eyes.

Jackpot! He'd get Brad's info out of her no problem.

Cal gave her a slow smile, his voice warm and raspy with sleep. "Morning—" his eyes flicked to the whiteboard "—Penny."

"Hey!" She removed the cuff, her pale pink nails tickling his bicep.

He cleared his throat. "Any update on Brad Chapman's condition?"

"I'm really not supposed to give out that information—privacy rules and all that." Penny looked over her shoulder toward the hall.

Cal raised his eyebrows, making the hopeful, innocent face that had served him well his whole life.

"He's your roommate?" She placed the thermometer under his tongue.

It bought him a second to think. After she removed the stick, he said, "Oldest friend, actually. We met the first day of preschool." Girls loved that. "At least tell me how his family's doing. I bet his mom's probably been there round-the-clock, am I right?"

Penny lowered her voice. "I heard she had some kind of breakdown yesterday afternoon, like, lost it—sobbing, super upset. I mean, not that I blame her. They gave her some sedatives and her husband took her to their hotel but, yeah, she never left her son's bedside." Her nose wrinkled. "Not even to shower. I'm getting all this secondhand so this stays between us, got it?" She pointed at him and he had a sudden flash of Shelby standing over him, filming him. He shivered though the room was stuffy.

"No, right, of course," he said. "I'm just really worried about him, about the whole family, actually."

"Aw," her fingers lingered on the inside of his wrist as she adjusted the pulse monitor, "you're such a good friend. All you've been through and you're still thinking of others." She pressed a hand over her heart.

"I'd love to see him."

Penny hesitated.

He'd told so many lies, what were a few more?

"If he could hear my voice, I keep thinking that might help. It would make me feel better, like I was doing something to help." Cal dipped his chin toward his chest. He needed to nail this last bit. "Maybe that's selfish."

"That's not selfish at all." The nurse smiled, sighed, and then told him exactly where and how to get to Brad.

. . .

IN THE ELEVATOR'S brushed silver interior, Cal glimpsed his warped reflection. He looked ridiculous. He'd put on a second hospital gown and attempted to tie it in the front so his scrawny ass wouldn't stick out as he made his way to the ICU. The nubs of the hospital's thin, skid-proof socks irritated the blisters he'd gotten from Shelby's boots.

Shelby. Her face burst into his mind again, and he flinched. He'd escaped from the cabin three days ago. How long had that blaze burned? Long enough to incinerate any trace of him, he hoped. When he couldn't sleep, he worried that the knife would be pulled from the ashes and link him to the fire. How long would the investigation take? If anyone knew he was there, what he'd done, surely they'd have come sniffing around by now. As far as he was concerned, he was in the clear.

He stepped off the elevator. The ward was quiet, dim, the sun making its slow rise beyond the windows at the far end of the hall.

When he rounded the corner, a nurse at a circular desk did a double-take, eyes widening behind her glasses. Vera was right; he was a celebrity. The woman understood why he'd come and nodded toward a bay, offering a weak, resigned smile. So Brad's prognosis was that grim. Cal was glad he'd gotten there in time. He wanted that closure.

He'd need to stick to the story he'd given his parents and the police, but there was one person who could hear the truth.

Cal pulled back the curtain. He'd timed it just right. The area was empty except for Brad. No doctors. No nurses. No family. Folding chairs flanked the bed. Cal pictured Brad's parents slumped in them, keeping a sad vigil, Mrs. Chapman making futile attempts at yogic breathing.

Cal dragged a chair closer to Brad's ear. Yellowish-purple bruises covered the area of Brad's forehead that wasn't bandaged. He'd never been all that attractive, and now he really looked like shit. The tubes, wires, the mask, his knee wrapped in some contraption.

"Hey, Brad. Oh, sorry, do you go by Shirley now?" Cal waited, half-expecting that might get a reaction. "So, bad news, buddy. Your plan backfired. I might be missing half a finger, but guess what? I'm famous now." He sat back and laughed at the absurdity of how things had turned around.

Two weeks earlier, he was a guy with massive debt and no clue how he'd repay it. One week ago, he'd been tied to a bed, delirious, expecting to die. But now—*now!*—he was a survivor with a story people wanted to hear.

"I've got all sorts of opportunities coming my way. An agent called my mom about a book or maybe a screenplay." Again, Cal waited. He hadn't been out of bed other than to use the bathroom since he got there. The short trip from his floor to the ICU had winded him, but his energy roared back as he stared down the person who'd upended his life.

"Hey, what do you think of this title: *Longshot?* Get it? People were ready to count me out. Big mistake." He shifted, adjusting his twisted double gowns, feeling like a girl in a dress.

"You tried. Your plan showed a lot more hustle than I'm used to seeing from you. I kind of admired it." He let out another low laugh. The space was quiet except for the beeps and blips of the machines. "But, sorry, my man, you didn't win this time either, and, personally, I don't think you're coming back from this. Anything that might've tied me to that Chloe shitshow went up in flames. Once you're gone, this whole thing dies right along with you."

Cal took a breath, inhaling the scent of citrusy floor cleaner mixed with ammonia. The meds made his mouth dry but it felt good to say these things aloud, however softly, like a confession minus asking for forgiveness.

"You thought you knew exactly how things went down with Chloe and me that night. I kept a couple details to myself." Cal licked his lips. "After you went back to your dorm to mope, I kissed her. Here's the crazy part: she pushed me away, told me she liked someone else. Not gonna lie. It stung. 'Who?' I asked. Her answer? 'Brad.'" Cal stopped like the revelation might shock Brad back to consciousness. He remained motionless.

"Can you believe that? Someone choosing you over me? Felt like I'd been sucker-punched. I laughed in her face and pulled her toward me again. She shoved me. Did I push her back? Hell, yeah. Harder than I should have? Absolutely. When have I ever done things halfway?"

The green lines on the monitor spiked and scrunched closer together, pointy as the mountains surrounding the hospital. The beeps came faster.

"With you gone, I can put all of this shit behind me, but, damn, I'd love for you to be here because I'm about to put on one hell of a show." He held his good hand in front of him like he could see his name in lights and was reading off a marquee. "'The Cal Whitaker Story: A Cautionary Tale. How a young man with every advantage got swept up in the dark world of sports betting and nearly lost his life but fought his way back to tell it.' This is my redemption arc. I'm going to be the damaged underdog who reinvents himself by warning others about the dangers of gambling. Everything I did, and I'm still not the villain. Crazy how that works."

The urgent *bip, bip, bip* sped up. Behind Cal, the ward

was slowly coming to life. Carts trundled past. A mix of weary voices were replaced by fresh, chipper ones signaling a shift change. The air smelled of coffee. He'd gotten so caught up in his monologue, he'd lost track of time. The Chapmans could arrive any second. He didn't want to deal with them. In fact, he was mildly offended that they hadn't visited him yet.

Beyond the curtain, the world brightened as the sun threw prisms of light on the scuffed white floor. He needed to get back. His parents and sister would be there later. He'd be discharged, free to head out into his shiny new life. Talk about a comeback.

He stood and took a long look at Brad. This was probably the last time he'd see him. An ache swelled in his chest. Was it remorse, his infection, all the meds, or leftover gas from a weeks' worth of that miserable chili?

He touched the pillows beneath Brad's head. To smother him would be so unoriginal, and what if someone came in? It would be safer to disconnect his tubes or pinch them closed. Cal squeezed two between the fingers of his good hand. The *bip, bip, bip* accelerated. Cal's heart tripped in response. *How long would it take?* He swayed a bit.

"Move. Now. Please." Suddenly, a nurse was beside him, jerking him out of the way.

Cal released his grip and stepped back.

"Oh, it's you!" The nurse's scowl broke into a smile while straightening Brad's wires and poking at the monitor. "You look dizzy, honey. You sure you should be out of bed?"

"Probably not." Cal shrugged, returning her smile. "But I had to check on my pal."

"You fellas have been to hell and back." The nurse shook her head. "Have a seat. I'll call for a wheelchair."

Cal waited until she slipped past the curtain into the hall. He kept a hand on the guardrail and leaned close to his former friend's ear.

"You were right," Cal said. "Did I do some bad things? Yeah. Would I do them again to get where I am now? You bet."

40

SATURDAY, DECEMBER 27

IVY

A black-and-white photograph of a moose on the wall confused Ivy. She blinked and stretched to reach for Greg. His side of the bed was empty, cold. She sat up too quickly, giving herself a head rush. Max wasn't in the hotel room either. It was close to nine a.m. A weird chemical taste coated her tongue. They'd forced her to take something at the hospital after she'd started screaming and kicking the radiator. Her rage had morphed into a bone-deep sadness and she'd started to cry, huge gasping sobs, until suddenly she could no longer breathe. The daughter of the patient in the next bay had started to film her tantrum. Max had intervened.

At another time in her life, she might've been embarrassed by the meltdown. Now she didn't care. Constant worry about Brad, her mother, and Jean-Claude had stripped her bare. A nurse gave her pills and Greg had all but carried her to the rental car, then tucked her into bed.

Despite sleeping soundly for the first time in weeks, her

eyes burned as she reached for her phone on the nightstand. A note rested beside it.

> DIDN'T WANT TO WAKE YOU. MAX + I WENT TO THE HOSPITAL. LEFT YOU THE CAR. COME WHEN YOU'RE READY. — G

He'd drawn a heart at the bottom—same as he'd done since their college days when he'd stop by her apartment and leave a Post-it on her pillow if she wasn't there.

In the bathroom, Ivy sat on the toilet and unlocked her phone. Notifications flooded the screen—voicemails from her mother, texts from Betsy asking if she'd found a new sitter for JC, reporters requesting comments about Brad and a statement on her feelings about Cal's return and Emerson's accusations. Piper had written to see if she'd need a sub for the New Year's Day yoga retreat. In October, they'd chosen "Leaving Behind What No Longer Serves You" as the theme. Compared to what she faced now, her problems back then—finding a job for Max, convincing her mother to get professional help—seemed laughable.

As she scrolled, a message from Jane popped up. She wanted to swipe left, delete it unread, but curiosity won out.

> So glad we had a chance to talk. Your friendship means the world to me. Hope we can take a walk soon!

Heart emojis followed.

Ivy's jaw tensed as she reached for toilet paper. Where did Jane get the nerve? She was crazy if she thought their friendship would go back to the way it had been. And to write something so trite, so clichéd after everything that had happened between them? It was insulting. Did Jane think Ivy had no self-respect? That she'd just forgive and forget all of it?

Ivy's grip tightened around the cell phone. She had no idea what lay ahead for her or her son, but she needed to cut the Whitakers out of their lives like a cancerous growth.

Before she could stop herself, she opened her email and searched for the Airbnb confirmation. She clicked on the address: 25 Elkhorn Court. She remembered Jane making fun of the street name. "We're not in Oak Hill anymore," she'd laughed. The house was less than two miles away. Only three turns.

Ivy would find Jane. It was her turn to say, "Stay away from my family!"

She'd let go of the hatred she felt for the Whitakers. One less burden to carry.

Resting the phone on the toilet tank, Ivy brushed her teeth. Greg had unpacked her suitcase and arranged her things neatly in drawers. She pulled on fresh leggings and a cream-colored turtleneck. As she stretched it over her head, she inhaled. It smelled like home. Would they go back to Oak Hill without Brad—their family of four now reduced to three? Or would they be doomed to stay in Wyoming indefinitely, hoping Brad would turn the corner? Tears slid down her cheeks. She let the soft wool absorb them.

Passing the mirror, Ivy did a double-take. Her pixie cut was overgrown and shaggy, her eyes red-rimmed, a crisscross of lines beneath them. After she told off Jane, her former friend would probably text their neighbors: *Ivy's lost it! She looks like an '80s rocker coming off a bender.* How many times had she been on the receiving end of one of Jane's snarky digs about someone in their town?

Ivy grabbed her coat and the key fob from the table near the door and hurried to the parking lot. The morning sun was a balm on her face. She took a deep breath and let the crisp mountain air fill her lungs. It wasn't as cold as it had been when they'd arrived. The world was still, quiet at this in-between hour, early birds already at the mountain, partiers sleeping off Friday night.

About a mile from the hotel, Ivy reached for her phone to confirm the directions. It wasn't on the passenger seat or in the center console. She patted her pockets. Not there. Had she left it in the bathroom?

For a split second, she debated going back for it. What if Greg called? What if something changed with Brad and she was unreachable? *No.* This would take five minutes. She'd find Jane, say her piece, and leave again. She'd end their decades-long friendship in person, not like a coward hiding behind a screen.

The house was a few turns away. She could picture the directions on her phone: left on Acorn Way, right on Elkhorn Court.

Before she knew it, the rental car was coasting into the first turn, her heart rate accelerating. She'd spent most of her life avoiding confrontation, swallowing disappointment, rationalizing everyone's bad behavior, giving the world a pass. That ended now.

Ivy's breath fogged the windshield. She fumbled to locate the defrost button as the Elkhorn Court street sign came into view. She switched on the blinker though there were no other cars in sight.

On the left, the house appeared as lovely as it had in the photos. Why had Jane complained about it? Just then Ivy saw a flash of red. It looked like Jane was headed out the side door for that walk in the woods. Ivy recognized the jacket, its fur-trimmed hood up. Back in November, Jane had sent Ivy an email with links to a bunch of parkas along with the message:

> *Help me pick! So bored with basic black. You're not afraid to take fashion risks—remember that peek-a-boo shoulder dress you wore to the football banquet? What were you thinking? LOL. Anyway, how about the red? Too much?*

At the time, Ivy had thought, *Why are you such a bitch?* but she'd written back:

> *Peek-a-boo shoulder! LOL! Def. get the red!*

Jane kept a brisk pace as she headed toward the woods. Ivy lowered the window and almost called out to her, a reflex after so many years of friendship.

She closed the window. She'd sneak up on her, catch her off-guard, just as Jane had done to her at the hospital yesterday.

Rolling past the house, Ivy parked in front of a teardown-in-progress at the end of the cul-de-sac. A brick chimney poked up from the ruins. It was Saturday, no workers on site.

Icy bits that would melt as the sun continued its ascent crunched beneath her boots. She'd lost sight of Jane, but that was okay. Ivy needed to work out what she wanted to say. Something short, powerful. She'd tell Jane that her family was responsible for every terrible thing that had happened to Brad. Ivy had been too stunned and exhausted to form real sentences when Jane came to the ICU, but now she was keyed up, moving purposely, the air sharpening her senses.

"You threatened to destroy my family and you did," Ivy would say. "I blame you for all of it. Don't speak to me. Don't text me, and do not talk about us."

Once she opened her mouth, it would all gush out. The purge she craved. In her mind, she rehearsed everything she needed Jane to know. "I don't care about you or Wade or your shitty, failing marriage. Keep your vile children away from mine."

Her thoughts spun, gathering like a storm inside her head while Jane moved deeper into the woods, graceful as a doe, not a care in the world now that her son was safe.

Ivy's muscles ached, stiff and tight after days of sitting in the drafty ICU, hunched in a folding chair. As she hurried forward, her foot caught in a twist of brambles and she fell to her knees.

"Ah!" she cried, snow seeping through her leggings.

Jane must've had her earbuds in. She didn't turn back or seem to hear Ivy's whimper or the sound of branches snapping as she landed in a heap.

Ivy blinked back tears of exhaustion, frustration, humiliation, and took a second to catch her breath.

She'd raised the idea of bringing a civil suit against the Whitakers for starting an insane crusade that led to their son's injuries, but Greg had only said, "Let's focus on Brad for now."

She knew he was right. Their son needed them. But as the days passed and he showed no sign of improvement, she couldn't stem the rising tide of anger that swelled inside her.

One thing that circled through her brain was the fact that she'd almost kept Brad back, not sent him to preschool that September all those years ago. He had a late-August birthday. Plenty of kids needed an extra year. He was so shy. She'd believed the socialization would help him overcome it. If she'd kept him home with her, wouldn't that make it harder when he eventually had to go?

If she'd done it, they might never have met the Whitakers. Their families wouldn't have grown up together, intertwining like dark vines. Maybe they'd have seen one another in the neighborhood or at sporting events but they wouldn't be there now. *She* wouldn't be there now, plodding through the woods to end a twenty-year friendship while her son lay in a hospital bed fighting for his life.

Ivy stood and brushed snow off her leggings with her mittened hands. A large branch lay at her feet. She clutched it to use as a walking stick as she set off again, the weight of it grounding her.

Jane had been right about one thing: the woods were beautiful. Ivy turned her face up toward the endless sky and took a mental snapshot. She wanted to remember this moment. It would signal the end of her life as a quiet people pleaser, a doormat. She would leave behind what no longer served her.

Walking faster, she closed the distance between Jane and herself, heart rate picking up from the physical exertion and the impending altercation. Sweat trickled down her back, pooled in the cups of her bra despite the cool air and the pristine snow underfoot.

As she got closer to Jane, Ivy's feet came to life, moving on their own, light and purposeful as a dancer's.

Wind whistled through the treetops, crows cawing overhead.

Jane seemed to slow. Maybe she was ready to head back.

Cal was due to be released soon. The Whitakers would travel home together. Whatever happened with Wade's business and Jane's flirtations with Daniel, they'd work through it. Their lives would return to the way they'd always been. Ivy was sure of it. But after she confronted Jane, she'd drive to the hospital. If Brad's condition remained unchanged, she and Greg would face a series of brutal decisions.

As the trees thinned, Ivy understood why Jane had stopped. They'd come to a clearing. A pond lay steps away at the edge of the woods. It was mentioned in the Airbnb description, the chance to observe loons and water fowl. She'd forgotten all about it.

Jane pulled something from her pocket. Her phone. She'd probably take a photo of the sun bathing the forest in golden light. Standing just feet behind her, Ivy peered at the image captured on the phone screen. It was stunning. Jane must've been using some kind of filter; everything was heightened, every color sharper—the robin's egg sky, the emerald pines, the coppery-browns and silver of the semi-iced-over pond that reminded Ivy of pennies under glass.

Jane would post the photo and write something about her magical holiday, gratitude for her beautiful family, Cal's return—their very own Christmas miracle. Even in the wilds of Wyoming, the gears of the Whitaker PR machine still churned. *Look at us! We're perfect! We have everything!*

The nerve of her—of the entire family. Even after Cal admitted his gambling had led to his disappearance, the Whitakers hadn't publicly apologized to Brad for what they'd put him through. They'd made no attempt to clear his name.

Ivy gripped the branch tighter, hoping the wood would absorb some of her rage. But as she stepped closer, she found her arm rising on its own as if guided by an unseen force. Years of holding plank and down dogs had made her limbs strong.

She hoisted the sturdy branch easily, as if it were no heavier than a hairbrush. Something inside her had broken loose. She found her knees bending, hips twisting, arms sliding back in a wind-up. As she was about to swing, the camera screen flipped and she saw her own image. Right behind Emerson's.

The girl jumped and spun toward her, surprise, confusion—or was it fear?—in her eyes. "Mrs. Chap—"

Ivy swung. A stinging vibration rang through her hands and up her forearms as the branch collided with the side of Emerson's head. The sound, a terrible, hollow thump like someone knocking on a watermelon to test for ripeness, echoed in Ivy's ears.

As if in slow motion, Emerson stumbled back, eyes rolling upward, AirPods floating then falling like confetti. The phone dropped from her hand onto the slushy bank just before her body shattered the thin sheet of ice.

Ivy watched in stunned disbelief, expecting Em to flail her arms, kick her legs, stand, and then lunge for her. But she lay motionless, sinking deeper as the pond slowly drank her in.

Ivy's breath came in fast, shallow bursts as she repeated the words, "Oh my God! Oh my God!" She turned full circle, certain she could feel eyes on her, guilt already making a home beneath her skin.

What had she done? She'd struck someone! Not just anyone—Emerson, whom she'd held for hours as a newborn so Jane could shower. Emerson, whose hair she'd French-braided while they sat on the beach, Em shoveling sand into a bucket, squealing, "Hurry! Finish! I want to swim!"

Was there time to wade in, pull the girl from the icy water and revive her? Did Ivy even want to? It was largely Emerson's fault that she was there. And if she did manage to drag her out, how could Ivy explain that she'd hit her and then watched her topple, glassy-eyed, into the pond? What would she say had brought her out there when she should've been at the hospital with her son?

She couldn't think, her heart seizing. Covering her mouth, Ivy howled into her mittened hands. They smelled like root beer from the branch.

She stared at the spot where Emerson disappeared, trying to force herself into action. *Get it together, Ivy! Snap out of it, Ivy! Do something, Ivy!*

She wiped her eyes and squared her shoulders. She knew what she needed to do.

Reaching for the branch, she fed it to the still, dark water and looked around once more. Then, she crouched low and collected the phone.

41

SATURDAY, DECEMBER 27
IVY

Ivy fought to make herself drive like a normal person, not like someone behind the wheel of a getaway car. Her eyes kept flicking to the rearview mirror. She was certain she'd see police lights flashing any moment. Instead, all that lay behind her were road, mountains, and sky.

What was she thinking, going there to confront Jane? She should've been at the hospital with her family. What would she tell Greg? She couldn't drag him into this. No. No one could know what she'd done. It had been a sudden, horrible impulse. She'd lost control. Worry, lack of sleep, and outrage had turned Ivy into someone else—a monster. The scene played over and over in her mind and yet it was as if she were watching a stranger. But she'd done it, and there was no going back. She had to move forward. She needed to get to the hospital.

On the passenger seat, Emerson's phone buzzed. The word "Mom" flashed on the screen, and Ivy swerved. A blaring horn jolted her back to the right lane. She couldn't read the message because the screen was locked. What did

Jane want? When Em didn't answer, would her mother begin tracking her? What the hell would Ivy do then?

On autopilot, she drove back to the hotel. Beneath her jacket, Ivy's shirt was stuck to her skin. She'd go to the room, shower, wash away the loamy odor of the pond that lurked inside her nostrils.

The bulky gold room key sat in the cup holder in the middle console. She clutched it and Emerson's phone to her chest, then climbed out of the car.

Legs weak, Ivy staggered across the parking lot. She passed a van with its trunk open. A group of guys stood in a circle on the far side of it, the skunky smell of weed rising above their Angry Birds hats. They were probably the same age as Brad. She hated them. Standing there, carefree, laughing, as one called, "Where the fuck is Nate? Let's go already!" Rap music pumped through tinny speakers.

The bass vibrated in Ivy's chest as Em's phone buzzed in her hand. She stopped. *Sasha*. Ivy froze as if she were holding a bomb. She needed to get rid of the device.

Turning back as if she'd forgotten something in the rental car, Ivy glanced at the boot bags stacked in the van's trunk.

"Here he comes! Finally!" one of the guys yelled.

She needed to move. Side-stepping toward the trunk, she unzipped a bag's side pouch and slid Emerson's phone inside.

Then she hurried, head down, into the hotel, her whole body shaking. In the elevator, she scrunched her eyes shut but could still see Emerson falling, the water parting like an open mouth, swallowing the girl whole. Racing down the hall, she made it to the bathroom seconds before she vomited.

Against the top of the toilet tank, her phone buzzed. If it

were Greg, what would she say to him? Could she tell him what she'd done? Would he help her? No. This couldn't be fixed. Emerson was gone. Greg was the best person she knew. He'd never be complicit. He loved her, yes, but he had limits, and yet how could she live with this, bear this alone?

She wiped her mouth on the shower curtain and knelt to see the caller ID.

"Max," she gasped. "Max—"

"It's me," Greg said. "I can't find my phone so I'm using Max's. But, Ivy—"

"Greg—" Should she tell him she'd lost it? Done an insane, terrible thing? She didn't want to be alone with it. "Greg, I—"

"Ivy." Her husband's voice broke into ragged cries that bounced off the bathroom walls and made her scalp tingle and the hair on her arms rise. She dropped to the floor.

"Greg." Ivy's teeth chattered. This was her punishment. They'd lose Brad because of what she'd done to Emerson.

"Ivy," Greg struggled to move beyond her name, "Ivy..."

"Say it," she cried. "Tell me."

"Brad's awake."

42

SATURDAY, DECEMBER 27

IVY

Ivy raced to the hospital, all thoughts of Emerson erased, Brad her sole focus.

On their brief call, Greg had said their son was awake but agitated.

"Can you blame him?" she'd shouted, not meaning to snap. Brad had been so good-natured, so agreeable his entire life. Just like she had. Where had it gotten them? How much could a person take?

He was perseverating, repeating the same questions, Greg told her. A neurologist had ordered some tests to get a better picture of what they were looking at, but, overall, they were hopeful.

"I'm on my way," Ivy had said, already running to the rental car.

Sailing through stop signs and red lights, she whispered, "Thank you! Thank you! Thank you!" and tried not to think about the smell of the damp earth caked in the treads of her boots.

She didn't care which type of therapies her son needed,

how long it took, how much it cost. She would help him rebuild his life, and it would be better than before.

At the hospital, she dodged the news vans and reporters out front and tore through the lobby to the elevator. When she turned the corner into the ICU, the nurse who'd brought Ivy a dozen cups of tea without her ever requesting them came from behind the desk and embraced her, eyes shining with tears.

Ivy knew then they hadn't expected Brad to live. She collapsed in the woman's arms, relief overshadowed by guilt and shame. She didn't deserve it—this miracle—not after what she'd just done.

The nurse released her. "Go see your boy."

The moment should've been joyous, as euphoric as the day Brad was born and another nurse had placed him in her arms. But while her son had been given a second chance, Emerson was drifting along the bottom of a murky pond—because of her.

"I—I can't believe it," she whispered through tight lips. On her way out of the hotel, she'd stopped at a vending machine and downed two bags of Fritos in the car. Her breath was worse than Jean-Claude's.

The nurse patted Ivy's shoulder, then nudged her forward. She pulled back the curtain. There he was. Her son. She couldn't say his name. A lump clogged her throat. She rushed to him and buried her face softly in his wild, wooly hair.

"I'm so happy to see you." She was crying, her words lost in his tangle of curls. She kissed the part of his forehead that wasn't bruised or bandaged and stepped back to take him in. He looked small and pale, not scared so much as angry. He stared at her, his usually warm eyes dull, hard. Did he recognize her? A chill rippled up her spine. Had he awakened with some superpower that let him know what she'd just done?

"Why am I here?" he asked, an edge she'd never heard before in his voice.

She didn't know how to answer, where to begin. She turned to Greg.

"It's going to take time," he said, more to her than their son.

"We're going to try to get you home as soon as possible, baby." She squeezed his hand. He didn't squeeze back. Had he forgotten?

"Why am I here?" Brad repeated. "What happened? Where's Cal?"

"He keeps asking that," Max said. "Could be the meds."

The curtain fluttered behind Ivy. The nurse who'd hugged her appeared.

"They're going to take him for that scan now."

"When will he be back?" Ivy wasn't ready to let him go. The moment she'd been praying for since Monday night when they'd arrived at the hospital frantic wasn't unfolding the way she'd imagined. Brad wasn't himself; *she* was no longer herself. It was all wrong.

"Should be about an hour," the nurse said.

"Why am I here?" Brad asked as the nurse rearranged wires and moved the IV bag.

Ivy's stomach pitched. Was he better off not remembering any of it?

"We'll be right here when you get back, son," Greg said.

Max held up his hand to high-five his brother. Brad ignored him. Ivy pressed her palms to her eyes as a tech wheeled Brad out of the bay. It would be enough to worry about her son's health, his future. She'd made her life a million times harder. She'd gone to end her relationship with Jane, and in her rage, she'd killed someone. Emerson. She'd have to live with that horrific knowledge, haunted by one question: When would everyone else discover what she'd done?

Sensing her unraveling, Greg wrapped her in his arms. Her body tensed and she wanted to wriggle away from him. She didn't deserve his kindness. She'd done an unforgivable thing—and she was bound to get caught. Her life, her lovely life with her husband, sons, and their sweet Jean-Claude, would be ripped away from her. Everyone would know she was a horrible person. Her mother would die and no one would find her, buried alive in a mess of her own making. Ivy would end up teaching yoga in prison.

"Don't worry," Greg whispered, his moist breath suffocating her, "whatever happens next, we've got this. We'll move through it together. Whatever he needs, we're here for him."

When Greg didn't release her, Ivy nodded, sniffling into his shirt.

"The main thing is he's alive," her husband continued. "In time, he'll be okay. We're all going to be okay."

That wasn't true.

"Hey," he said, his upbeat tone heightening her anxiety, "when's the last time we had a real meal at an actual table?"

"I'm starving." Max stood and led them out of the narrow space.

In a fog, Ivy followed her husband and son to the elevator. Clumps of mud from the pond's newly thawed bank dropped from her boots, leaving a trail. She pinched the bridge of her nose. Every time she blinked, she saw Emerson falling through the ice, her eyes rolling like billiard balls.

Outside the cafeteria, the smell of French fries and fish sticks overpowered Ivy. She clutched her stomach.

"I have to use the bathroom," she said.

"I'll order," Greg offered. "What do you want?"

"I want to go back in time and change everything." She nearly said the words aloud but swallowed them at the last second. She couldn't tell him. Not then. "Anything's fine."

She hurried to the lobby. In front of the elevators, she turned right and left, scanning for the restroom sign. Mid-rotation, Jane appeared.

"Ivy!" She smiled the way she did when they bumped into one another at the farmer's market or post office. "I'm looking for Emerson. Have you seen her?"

Ivy nearly doubled over, bile rising in her throat. "No. Why?"

"She was at your hotel earlier." Jane held up her phone, tracking app open. "Last night, I asked her to apologize to you and Greg. I didn't think she was even listening to me."

"I—we must've missed her," Ivy said. A cold sweat crept from her back to her belly, spreading to her chest and neck. She hated liars, and now she was one. Worse than that—she was a murderer. Her hands trembled. She shoved them deep in her coat pockets.

"Cal's about to be discharged. A bunch of reporters are here—local and national." Jane sighed as if it were a nuisance, though Ivy knew she must've loved every minute of the attention. "It's not like Em to miss a photo op."

Ivy's face froze. What would she normally say? How should she respond? Mouth dry, tongue thick, she managed,

"Can you see where she is now?" She knew exactly where Emerson was.

Jane raised the phone above her head. Ivy had a blinding flash of Em with her own phone raised, standing in front of the pond. Had she taken a selfie? With Ivy behind her? *Shit!* How had she not thought to check? But how could she without Em's passcode?

"I couldn't get service in Cal's room, but—" the screen changed and Jane lowered the device, "—ah, it looks like she's at the resort." She lowered her voice. "Wade is going to go ballistic when he sees these Uber charges. She's probably snapping a thousand selfies. Oh and how funny is this? Remember when I asked your opinion on jackets? She must be wearing the one I bought. I couldn't find it this morning. Does this make me an influencer now?"

Jane laughed while Ivy pictured the parka, its bright red darkening to crimson as it absorbed the pond water. She swayed back, lightheaded. There wasn't enough oxygen in the entire state of Wyoming for her to deep-breathe this panic away.

"Ivy, are you okay? You're so pale." Jane reached out her free hand and rubbed Ivy's shoulder. "Wait, how's Brad? Sorry, I almost forgot to ask."

Of course you did.

"He's awake." The words still seemed untrue, especially because he'd been so unlike himself.

"Oh my God!" Jane squeezed her arm. Ivy flinched. "That's amazing! See! I told you he was going to be fine."

"He's not fine," Ivy said but Jane had removed her hand and was raising the phone again, refreshing the tracker. "He's confused and upset," Ivy added.

People circled them, some staring, others whispering, recognizing them from the news.

Ivy waited for Jane to acknowledge what she'd said about Brad.

"That's it. I'm going to call her." Jane pressed speaker and the ringing of the outgoing call trilled between them.

Would someone answer? Who? What would happen next? Ivy's vision blurred. Her limbs turned limp and loose as if she were slowly disconnecting from reality. Would she pass out in the hospital lobby?

Jane continued to stare at her phone. After everything the Whitakers had done to Brad, Jane couldn't spare a minute to focus on him? No. It was straight back to her family.

Ivy's hatred for her former friend flared. Something twisted inside her. Years of listening to Jane gush about Cal —how smart he was, how athletic, how popular—eroded any good feelings she might have had left, easing her guilt. How many times had Jane texted her photos of Cal while he was at college—in a suit headed to a formal, on a river with the club rowing team—as if she were Cal's grandmother? Ivy had wanted to text back photos of her own sons. *My children matter too!* she'd longed to write. Instead, she'd given the pics a thumbs-up or a *So handsome!*

"Hey, it's Em. Hang up and text me!" Emerson's voice, high and bright, cut through Ivy's thoughts. She struggled to stay upright.

Jane ended the call and tucked a lock of hair behind her ear, exposing one of the silver love knot earrings Wade had given her for their twenty-fifth anniversary. Did that mean they'd made up? "Can you imagine? We get Cal back, now Em's missing?"

"That would be insane!" Ivy's laugh bordered on hysterical. She needed to keep it together, deliver her lines for the part she'd always played: Jane's sidekick. "Remember what you said about her yesterday when you came to apologize? 'She's a teenager—only focused on herself.'"

"You're right." Jane nodded and plucked an imaginary piece of lint from her lavender cardigan. "Well, I should probably get back up there. Can't keep the reporters waiting!"

"Of course not. Go." A surge of sympathy swelled inside Ivy. Jane had no clue what awaited her. The headlines were wrong. The Whitakers weren't heading home with their family restored.

Jane smiled. "I've missed this—us. You always make me feel better. Promise me whatever happens with our kids going forward, we'll never let it get in the way of our friendship."

Ivy didn't know when Jane's world would come crashing down, but it would, and when it did, Ivy would be there for her. She'd caused this. Keeping Jane close would be the best way to stay informed once the investigation began. The Chapmans had been on the outside, the enemies, during the days Cal was missing. That wouldn't happen this time.

Ivy had done a terrible thing but the Whitakers had driven her to it.

She took a moment, as if considering Jane's request that they always remain friends, then she returned the smile. "I promise."

PART 4

43

MONTHS LATER

JANE

Jane spent months expecting Em to walk through the front door, shrug off her backpack, and ask when dinner would be ready. In Jane's fantasy, Em had her phone in her hand, AirPods in her ears. In reality, the phone turned up at the bottom of a lost-and-found barrel beneath a broken security camera near the resort's rental shop weeks before the body was found. Her AirPods, buried in brush beside the pond, were discovered later.

Until the Saturday afternoon in late April when Jane saw Lynch's number flash on her phone screen, she clung to the hope that her daughter was off on an adventure. She'd waited for a postcard, an apology for running off scribbled in Em's loopy half-print, half-cursive. One never arrived. And, really, it was Jane who wanted to apologize. She'd favored her son and gotten bad at hiding it. No wonder her daughter had craved validation from strangers.

Initially, she thought Em's disappearance was a stunt. She could almost hear her justifying it: *Look at all the atten-*

tion Cal got! But as snow melted and tulips pushed their bright heads through the thawed ground, Jane's hope faded. Em hadn't left a trail. The Uber charges Jane had dreaded didn't exist. How had Em gotten to the resort and then back to the pond? How had no one seen her?

When the Whitakers were forced to admit their daughter was really gone, Max came forward. He said Em told him she wanted to skip college, travel, try to make it as an influencer. Sasha and Libby confirmed those plans. Em had made a little money from brands she'd featured in her videos. But her bank account hadn't been touched, and her socials remained dormant. The photo shared the day before she was last seen spoke volumes, police officers and psychologists agreed.

Beneath a ghostly gray shot of the woods behind the Airbnb, Em had written:

Hey. Final post here. Just wanted to say I'm a good person who did a stupid thing. OK, a terrible thing. I wanted to find my brother and somewhere along the way, I made a wrong turn. If I could take back everything I said about Brad, if I could erase the pain I caused him and his family, I would. Believe me or don't. Either way, I'm done.

Cal is back. Thank you to everyone who cared about my brother and our family. I won't say more because it's his story to tell now. I leave you with this: Sometimes it's the people who are right in front of you who are actually the most lost.

"Final post," "I'm done," "I leave you." Though she'd spelled it out and posted it across multiple platforms, initially no one read it as a goodbye. Or maybe they did, but hadn't wanted to say so to the Whitakers, who'd only recently gotten their missing son back.

Early on a Saturday morning in late April, a boy fishing with his father spotted a flash of red at the edge of the pond. A cardinal, he guessed at first. But it was Em's jacket—Jane's, really.

The Whitakers flew to Wyoming to bring their daughter home. United by shared grief, Jane and Wade tried to be gentler, kinder, to make up for the ways they'd failed each other when their son was missing.

Jane reached out to Daniel to apologize for leading the police to his door. She'd expected his forgiveness, his support, in light of all she'd lost.

"I'm sorry for what you've been through, but please don't contact me again," was all he'd written.

She supposed she deserved that. It was Cal's reaction to his sister's death that left Jane reeling. Everyone processed loss differently, but he'd only cancelled two stops on his "Don't Bet On It" tour to attend Emerson's memorial service.

"Keeping busy helps me cope," he'd told his mother, dabbing a knuckle to the corners of his dry eyes before rolling down the driveway in Em's Jeep, top and doors off, gentle breeze ruffling his hair.

Betsy Gallagher organized a meal train for the Whitakers, but it was Ivy who'd been Jane's life raft. Ivy never left her side unless she was taking care of Brad or helping her mother.

"What would I do without you?" Jane asked on their daily walks with Jean-Claude.

"I'm just glad I can be here." Ivy looped her arm through Jane's. "That's what friends are for."

44

IVY

Performing acts of penance. That's how Ivy thought of her days. She shepherded Brad to therapies, found an outpatient treatment center for substance misuse, kept him company while he completed applications to reenroll in college. The light still hadn't returned to his eyes. Ivy wanted her son to trust the world again, yet she felt least qualified for that task.

Her mother reluctantly agreed to professional help. Slowly, they began digging their way out of Ivy's childhood home. Florence stood sentinel, ensuring no new items made their way in.

Ivy made time for Jane. On their walks, they wore their matching necklaces and Ivy subtly ferreted out information about the investigation into Emerson's disappearance.

WHEN EM'S body was recovered, Ivy worried that a skull fracture or whatever damage she'd caused by striking the girl with that branch would be evident. But Jane and Wade declined an autopsy.

"Nothing will bring her back." Jane had sighed, tears traveling down her hollow cheeks.

She's aged a decade in a few months, Ivy thought each time they were together.

Even after the case was closed and Em's death ruled self-inflicted, Ivy stayed by Jane's side—another act of contrition. She'd stopped teaching yoga; the hypocrisy was too much.

"I'm already twisting myself into a pretzel for everyone else," she'd told Piper in her resignation email. She took up running. It was harder on her joints and she hated it, but that felt appropriate.

She quit therapy. What was the point if she couldn't talk about the one thing that consumed her?

Still, Ivy told herself she was making slow, steady progress on all fronts—except when she was alone and anxiety and regret chewed away at her stomach lining. She slept fitfully. If she drifted off, her mind took her to the pond, to Emerson's vacant, rolling eyes, and Greg had to shake her free from the nightmare.

Daily, her husband told her he was in awe of her generosity of spirit, her capacity for forgiveness. Each time he said she was a wonderful role model for their sons, she felt a part of her soul splinter off and die.

She confessed once to Jean-Claude when they were alone in the bathroom. Though his nose twitched and his head tilted a bit as if he understood and absolved her, the admission hadn't cleansed her as she'd hoped.

FOR ALL THE people who needed and depended on her, one didn't: Max. He'd been different since Emerson's body was recovered. He'd stopped eating meals with them. After weeks of avoiding them, he announced he'd found a job and an apartment in Boston and planned to leave as soon as possible. He'd settle in alone. Maybe they could visit later.

With high school graduation season underway, Greg, in his role as guidance counselor, said goodbye to Max at breakfast. Ivy drove their son to the train station, a duffle bag between his feet, JC in the back seat, whimpering for her to lower the window a few more inches.

"I was so happy to have everyone home again." Ivy's lips twisted in an exaggerated pout. "I'm excited for you, but I'm sad for me."

"I know." Max turned to look at her for the first time in weeks. "I know."

Despite the warm June air, a chill rocketed up Ivy's spine.

Max shifted so his back pressed against the door, and pinned his mother in place with his sharp stare.

"The morning Brad woke up, Dad wanted to call you, but he couldn't find his phone. He asked me to track it. Dad's phone was on Elkhorn Court." Max raised his open palms. "You had the rental car. I thought maybe you'd gotten lost on your way to the hospital, but the phone didn't move. It stayed there for a lot longer than it takes to make a U-turn. Later, I found it wedged between the console and the driver's seat."

Ivy listened, an anxious hum thrumming through her. She tried to meet her son's eyes, but she couldn't lift her gaze.

"Later," his voice cracked and he swallowed, "on the news, they showed an aerial view of the area where Em's body was found. The closest street?"

Don't say it! Don't say it! Ivy shook her head.

"Elkhorn Court. I thought, 'That name... why do I know it?' Then I remembered—and other stuff too. Your boots caked in mud, how you weren't answering your phone that morning. It took you so long to show up at the hospital. When you got there, you were acting strange, so unlike yourself. But now I wonder, who are you? Really?"

Ivy had told so many lies, but she couldn't tell another—not to her own son.

"I never meant to hurt her." Ivy closed her eyes and rubbed her forehead. "I'd gone to talk to Jane. I thought it was Jane."

"So what? You were going to kill Mrs. Whitaker?" His voice held all the loathing she deserved.

Ivy's eyes popped open. "No, of course..."

Max only shook his head. How long had he known? How long had he held it in?

"Oh, Max, I'm so..." She reached for his hand and he recoiled. "I—I—I snapped, I just lost it. I never meant to..." His hands curled around the straps of his bag. He was going to leave. She needed to know something, something she was afraid to ask. "Did you... Have you—?"

"I haven't told anyone. I won't. This family's been through enough. That said, I don't want to be anywhere near you."

In the distance, the train's horn blared. Max opened the car door and stepped out.

"Max..." Ivy called. He was already on the platform and didn't look back.

IVY SAT in the lot long after the train left the station, feeling like her insides had been scooped out. Her son was still in this world, but now she wasn't so different from Jane. She'd lost a child too.

45

BRAD

In late March, Brad boxed the last of his things at the condo. While he'd been in rehab, Cal's stuff had been removed. His mother probably did it for him. Either way, Brad was glad to be free of any reminders of his former friend. Cal had tried to visit him once at the facility, but Brad had requested no visitors outside of immediate family.

As he packed kitchen items for donation, the TV provided background noise. He'd barely been paying attention to the evening news when the anchorwoman said something about a cabin fire that had claimed the lives of a brother and sister from Georgia. He dropped a stack of plates and hobbled to the living room in time to hear the rest.

"The blaze, which began early Christmas morning and killed Shelby and Scott Rowland, has officially been ruled accidental by investigators..."

Brad had sold all his furniture so he had no choice but to stand there, reeling, like he'd taken a fist to the face. His thoughts spun, collided, and then slowly shifted into place, forming an awful chain of events. Chloe's family must've been there because of him—because he'd told them about Cal. What had happened from there? All he knew for sure was Cal was missing part of his finger and Chloe's siblings had burned to death. He had a faint memory of his former roommate visiting him in the ICU, but he'd thought it was a terrible hallucination caused by his brain injury and the cocktail of medications pumped into his veins.

Brad stepped away from the TV and backed into the wall, leaning all his weight against it, in a numbed-out state of shock. Had Cal been in that cabin with them the entire time he'd been gone? His gamblers-hacked-off-my-finger-and-left-me-to-die story just more of his usual bullshit? What the hell had happened? For two years, Brad had blamed himself for introducing Chloe to Cal. Now her brother and sister were dead, too. Partly because of him, mostly because of Cal.

Brad's phone sat heavy in his pocket. He could call Lynch and tell him there was nothing accidental about that fire. Where would he begin? How could he explain that Cal had pushed Shelby and Scotty's sister in front of a snowplow two years ago? Then, because Brad sent them a message using a fake name, they tracked Cal down and he set fire to a cabin with them in it and somehow escaped?

No. Lynch would remind Brad he'd suffered a serious head injury. Then he'd tell Hanlon, and the cops would share a good laugh at his expense. Brad knew it sounded ridiculous. Plus, Cal was a star now—bad boy-turned-do-gooder, warning parents and teens about the dangers of gambling with his multi-city "Don't Bet on It" tour. His memoir, *Longshot*, would be released in December to coincide with the one-year anniversary of his return. No one would believe Brad. When had they ever?

In a daze, he finished packing, the thought of Shelby and Scott's deaths a constant, terrible weight that pressed on his chest.

HIS CAR TOTALED, he flew home to Oak Hill in late March in a state of quiet outrage. Cal Whitaker had lobbed another grenade in the middle of his life, and again there was nothing he could do about it. Especially not after Emerson's body had been pulled from the pond at the end of April and the Whitakers were once more the recipients of nationwide sympathy.

Emerson. He didn't know how to feel about her death. In the hours before his accident, he'd hated her. She'd used him to try to make herself famous. Her last post was eerie, yes, but was it a suicide note? The details felt off.

One night in early June when Max was still home, Brad asked his brother, "You ever think it's weird that her phone was in the lost-and-found and her AirPods were beside the pond? Who tosses their phone and keeps their AirPods?"

"Don't you have enough to worry about?" Max had said. "You need to let that go."

Maybe his brother was right. Brad would start over, return to college someplace where the weather was warm and the Whitakers were far behind. He'd gone up against Cal his entire life and lost every round.

Their friendship was long over; now it was time to let the rivalry end too.

46

CAL

He was born for this. Traveling the country and meeting new people soothed his restless spirit and played to his strengths. Students adored him, fathers thanked him, mothers flirted with him.

Whenever someone asked if he was in touch with Brad, Cal gave them a slow, practiced smile and said, "We were close once. I hope to catch up with him again soon."

Cal thought about finishing what he'd started in the ICU, but Brad would be expecting him now—and where was the fun in that? Cal liked the idea of his old pal spending his days looking over his shoulder, ears pricked, always on edge. Cal would strike when he was good and ready.

In many ways, he owed his new life to Brad. And wasn't living well the best revenge?

After presentations in small towns, he'd duck into a bar. Girls—women—chatted him up. If he caught them staring at his stump and they hadn't recognized him, he'd make up a tale. How'd he lose half a finger? He fought off a bull shark in Brazil. Wrestled a bear in Montana. Survived a skydiving accident in New Zealand. They ate it up. What originally seemed like a deficit became a badge of honor.

He'd order a whiskey neat and raise a glass to Lincoln, to the knife that had saved his life. He wished he could've kept it, not for protection but as a talisman—a lucky charm. The last time he'd seen the knife it was deep in Scotty's ear.

CAL COULD'VE FLOWN from stop to stop. Instead, he drove his sister's Jeep, her hair ties still hanging from the rearview mirror.

He didn't want to dwell on her passing. Looking back, searching for answers, hadn't worked out too well for Shelby and Scotty. Cal had an idea of how he could honor his sister. His agent was after him to write a follow-up. Grief was having a moment. A book about losing a sibling, how the roller coaster of social media had derailed her future, felt so fucking timely. It was almost too easy.

He promised his parents he'd never gamble again and intended to keep his word this time. He sought out gamblers anonymous meetings but thought of them more as research, character studies. The details he poached from fellow attendees, these poor schlubs down to their last nickel, made his own sob story that much richer, more realistic. Whenever he felt that itch to place a bet, he told himself there'd be time later when he stepped out of the spotlight.

Still, it was difficult to shake all his old demons. He could be in a remote area like Orchard Lake Village City, Michigan, or a quaint suburb like Dover, Massachusetts, and he'd swear he was being followed. Always a blue F-150 truck with racing stripes. He never caught the plate or got a good look at the driver, but if he were still gambling, he'd bet all his money that it was the same vehicle, lingering a few cars back or lurking in a lot across from his hotel. Each time, he felt a shiver that catapulted him straight back to the woods the night he escaped.

Then he shook it off, told himself it was paranoia left over from another life, shifted Em's Jeep into drive, and moved on.

ACKNOWLEDGMENTS

Thank you to everyone who read this book. Time is precious and I appreciate you choosing to spend your hours with my words.

Thank you to my friends and neighbors who read my work and, despite its dark nature, continue to hang out with me. I'm beyond grateful for your support.

Thank you to my husband and sons who endure my constant pleas to find "the right word" and come up with character names. Thank you to my brother, Chris, who read an early draft and texted me his suspicions in real time.

To all the reviewers, librarians, and booksellers who've recommended my work to readers, I appreciate you more than you could ever know. Thank you to the book clubs who've welcomed me into your homes, both in person and via Zoom. It is an honor to have the opportunity to meet you.

I'm so grateful to the wonderful team at Inkubator Books. Thank you for your enthusiasm for this story and your thoughtful edits.

And to my cat Bubbles, who listens to me read early drafts aloud, I'm sorry and thank you.

If you enjoyed this novel, please consider leaving a rating or review as that increases the book's visibility.

If you'd like to connect or stay in touch, please visit: www.LizAlterman.com

DISCUSSION QUESTIONS

1. The novel explores the complexity and power of friendship, particularly Jane and Ivy's and Cal and Brad's. While these relationships shift over the course of the story, they remain destructive. Have you ever been in a similar "friendship?" If so, how did it impact you?

2. Did you suspect Brad had done something to Cal?

3. Ultimately, who do you think is to blame for what happens to Cal? To Emerson?

4. At one point Cal thinks "People believed anything if you were attractive enough." Is there truth to this statement?

5. Is Emerson a bad person or simply a teen swept up in the allure of social media?

6. How did Ivy's childhood and her mother's hoarding shape her self-esteem and relationships?

7. These characters are complicated and flawed. Which character did you relate to most? Did any of them evoke mixed emotions? Why do you think that was?

8. Jane keeps Cal's high school gambling a secret from Wade, and Ivy states that she couldn't imagine hiding anything so important from her husband. Yet the novel ends with Ivy keeping a devastating secret from Greg. Is hiding something from your partner ever OK? Where do you draw the line?

9. Max knows what Ivy has done yet opts to cover for her. Do you agree with his decision? What lengths would you go to to protect a loved one?

10. In a social media post, Emerson wrote *Sometimes it's the people who are right in front of you who are actually the most lost.* The novel examines the facades we present to the world. Discuss.

11. Lincoln is one of the more compassionate characters in the story. His mother tells him, "You've got a big, soft heart. The world'll try to harden it. Don't let it." How do Lincoln and other characters lose their humanity as the novel unfolds?

12. What do you think will happen next for these characters?

ABOUT THE AUTHOR

Liz Alterman is the author of the domestic suspense novels *The Perfect Neighborhood* and *The House on Cold Creek Lane* as well as memoir *Sad Sacked*, and the young adult thriller *He'll Be Waiting*, a finalist for the Dante Rossetti Young Adult Fiction award. Her work has been published by *The New York Times*, *The Washington Post*, McSweeney's Internet Tendency, and numerous other outlets. She lives in New Jersey with her husband, three sons, and two cats, and spends most days microwaving the same cup of coffee and looking up synonyms. When she isn't writing, she's reading.